THE SOLITAIRE GHOST

BLACKSTON GOLD, BOOK ONE

THE SOLITAIRE GHOST

SYLVIA KELSO

FIVE STAR
A part of Gale, Cengage Learning

GALE
CENGAGE Learning

Detroit • New York • San Francisco • New Haven, Conn • Waterville, Maine • London

GALE
CENGAGE Learning™

LIBRARY OF CONGRESS CATALOGING-IN-PUBLICATION DATA

Kelso, Sylvia.
    The solitaire ghost / Sylvia Kelso. — 1st ed.
      p. cm. — (Blackston gold ; bk. 1)
    ISBN-13: 978-1-4328-2532-4 (hardcover)
    ISBN-10: 1-4328-2532-1 (hardcover)
    1. Gold mines and mining—Fiction. I. Title.
PR9619.4.K456S65 2011
823'.92—dc22   2011007681

First Edition. First Printing: June 2011.
Published in 2011 in conjunction with Tekno Books.

For the yarn-spinners in my family,
particularly my grandfather, father
and my uncle Arthur (Windy)
who passed on some of the stories here.

ACKNOWLEDGMENTS

Thanks to Lois McMaster Bujold, Lillian Stewart Carl, Vreni and Peter Murphy, and Anne Roberts for reading this manuscript in process, and offering useful comments as well as encouragement; to Rosaleen Love for similar reading and also for first remarking on the quartz graves.

I would also like to thank the following people who supplied vital information for the book. Any errors remaining are my mistakes, or deliberate divergences from what they said.

    Narelle Houston, for helping construct the law firm of Lewis and Cotton, and general legal advice.

    Pat Crawley, of Cookstown, County Tyrone, for his great generosity to a stranger, particularly in showing me around the area, and in filling out Jimmy's back story.

    Les Scully, of Industrial Pumps Townsville, for assistance with the layout and details of Ben Morar, and stories about small Australian mines in general.

    The female officer of the Queensland Police who supplied information on police procedure at serious traffic accidents, and whose name I have most reprehensibly lost.

    Senior Constable Peter Shelton of the Queensland Police, who sketched out police procedure for major non-traffic accidents, and who suggested the Superintendent's BBQ.

Acknowledgments

Leith Golding, for IT advice, especially on the ins and outs of CDs.

And Mike Rubenach, for a wealth of data on geology, geologists and gold mines, but most for telling me the yarn that became the center of Chris's story and the trigger for this book.

CHAPTER I

Dorian hurried into the elevator and juggled a trio of lunch bags to reach the button for Lewis and Cotton's eighth-story office. As she hitched her latest barrister's brief up under the other arm, the ghost walked out of the floor.

Afterwards, she remembered that he was tall: when their feet came level, her eyes were opposite his collarbones. Or at least, the collar of his shirt. But he was still hip-deep in the floor when the beard grabbed her eye.

It started at his ears and met above his lips, it fanned over his shoulders and reached halfway down his chest, straight at the ends, curling round his mouth. It belonged in some picture of a Victorian patriarch, but it was dark, the rich bronzed dark of red-cedar wood. A young man's beard, live and thick as a bush.

The hair was probably the same, under the stained and bent-brimmed apology of a hat. Straw, maybe, pale and ropy, flopping down from a high conical peak. Not an Akubra, she realized as it came past her face, not a felt hat at all. Nor was the shirt an ordinary plumber or stockman's working clothes. The sleeves were rolled, but the material was creased like canvas, blue with a broad vertical stripe, and a low round collar like something from a cowboy film.

The braces, too, she remembered afterwards. And the cut of the trousers, nothing like Levis, thick dark stuff whose waistband nearly touched his ribs, clumsy as the boots, hampering as the tools he clutched.

He had the axe and shovel and mattock bundled over one shoulder while his other arm pinned the big metal dish. The hafts were shifting in his hands as he climbed, step by step, in the empty air. He was a pace or so above Dorian's feet when the dish slid under his elbow and fell onto nothing with a silent glittering bounce.

He trapped it against a boot. Stopped. Bent round, groping one-handed while the other tried to control the tools. His hand found the dish, and he straightened while she stood just beside him, dumb as a doorpost, her head almost level with his waist.

He brought the dish up. Then he balanced it on her head as if she was a post, a convenient stairpost set where he could change his hold. As he did it she saw his eyes, somewhere between beard and hat. A young man's eyes, dark as the beard's core, set smooth under thick straight brows. Absent, worried eyes that would never heed a stairpost. That hardly saw the dish.

The weight lifted, his boots moved. And he was gone, silent as a soap-bubble, *ffft.*

Dorian's legs slid her down against the elevator wall. She had time to think how ridiculously high someone had turned the air-conditioning, because she was goosebumps all over, before the doors slid open and she burst into tears.

"In here, nobody'll hit the Legacy this time of day." Still talking, Laura slid into the bar's rearmost banquette. "*I* don't know, Dor, I could kill you, you know. A ghost! An honest-to-God ghost! Walking up steps in the Perp-Insurance elevator! And all you can say is, *I saw him. I can't talk yet . . . Get me a drink.* If it happened to me I'd be over the moon!"

"Maybe, Laura, but Dorian wasn't expecting it—not with an armful of lunch bags and Coke cans, anyway." Anne sank beside them on the maroon plush. "Though," she added thoughtfully, "they did make a lovely crash."

"Well, *I* would've expected it," Laura snorted. "I've wanted to see a ghost since I was a baby, and at work of all places, how come he turned up for Dorian, the ratfink, why couldn't he do it for *me?*"

"He probably will."

"Bulldust, Anne, you're just peacemaking again. He probably comes out once a century on a special day or something, and I have to *miss* it—Jeez, Dor, I really could murder you!"

"Let it alone, Laura. Dorian, are you sure that drink's okay? Scotch on the rocks is a bit much before one o'clock."

"No," Dorian said. She managed to shake her head as well. Their voices wove round her, familiar as their looks: Laura's sharp rural-Victorian accent, Anne's softer North Queensland drawl, Laura's red-gold mane tamed for work in a ponytail, Anne's silk-straight black bob. The tastefully dim heritage bar wobbled, faux paneling and pendant-flower light shades swinging past her eyes. The Scotch wobbled too, deep amber in its glass, shot through with lighter flecks like dark hair with a tint of auburn. Bronzed, cedar-red.

She put the glass down with a snap. "He put that thing right on top of me—" Her voice had started to wobble as well. "I felt it. And he didn't—he never—he thought I was a *post!*"

"You know, that really is weird."

Laura, Dorian thought. Still talking, now I can hear again. Anne's arm still lay on the banquette behind her shoulder, though the hug had eased minutes ago. Perish the thought that a Lewis and Cotton junior partner be seen receiving comfort for arrant hysterics, in a lunchtime bar.

Laura had slid over to help the back-patting. Now she sat straight, staring out over the soft pool of white wine in Anne's untouched glass.

"What's weird?" Anne spoke with the evenness of near irritation. "Laura, honestly—"

"Anne, listen. You can see ghosts, and maybe it's on whatever floor or ground it is in their time, and you can get cold and scared and all that, but you shouldn't be able to, to interact. They're ghosts! You shouldn't—"

"Shouldn't what, for heaven's sake?"

"You shouldn't be able to touch."

There was a pause so deep the lunchtime chatter seemed to echo fathoms over their heads. Dorian felt those eyes again, anxious, unseeing, the weight on her hair. He had put a dish down on top of her, and he was a ghost—

"Laura McFadden, that is more than enough. Keep that New Age chatter for a séance or something—"

"Anne Lee, don't get snarky because you can't figure it out either. I tell you, it's not what happens with ghosts—"

"And Dorian doesn't want to hear it." Anne meant business this time. Dorian had rarely heard her so brusque outside court. "She's had a shake-up already, and this afternoon Moira'll be on her case about the Ben Morar appeal—"

"Never mind the blasted gold-mine, Anne! This is serious."

Laura had lost her ebullience in a breath. Her marmalade-colored eyes went between them with an expression that made Anne pause.

"I don't understand the dish part," Laura said soberly, "but I do know the most important thing about ghosts. And it's not whether they're knee-deep in the floor."

Anne just managed not to roll her eyes. "So what, in your learned opinion, Ms. McFadden, is more important than that?"

Laura pushed her glass away. Then she said to the tabletop, "The most important thing is, they come for a reason. Some people say they're just time-loops, things that—happened—and the place can't forget. But if they aren't time-loops, if they really are, spirits, or whatever you want to call them. . . . Then they come because they did something, or something was done to them. And the karma wasn't balanced. So they can't go away or on or anything. They have to keep coming back."

Anne's fastidiously smooth-bridged nose almost curled. She detested New Age terms worse than forgetful witnesses. "A case of justice—unredressed?"

The irony made Dorian wince. Laura just said flatly, "Yep."

Their eyes met and locked. Justice, Dorian was thinking. And with a fresh touch of hysteria, he sure came to the right place for that—Anne flipped her hair back and with the skill of a thousand lunchtime bouts Laura parried instantly, "That's what we need to know."

"Laura—"

"Anne, will you stop trying to pretend your folks never left milk out for demons or burnt joss sticks for good luck? I'm telling you, this is important. Dorian saw this guy! I don't know if it's the place or the time or the person that matters, but we have to find out why! Because if we don't—"

She stopped. Anne's family was old money in Ibisville, four generations of accountants, lawyers and assorted professionals. She took the allusion to her ancestry as easily as only longtime friends could, the way Laura herself took teasing about her heritage of rock-brained, red-headed Scots engineers. But when Dorian had expected a skeptic's riposte, Anne was suddenly quiet.

So it was Dorian who found herself saying, "If we don't, Laura? If we don't, what?"

For a moment she thought Laura would not reply. Or would dodge as she dodged in countless gossip sessions, when their teasing over her queue of enigmatic boyfriends came too near the bone. But Laura frowned hard and paused. When she answered, it came with more than soberness.

"Because if we don't, he'll come back."

"So if we don't have anything else, let's start at the beginning." Anne had lifted Moira Cotton's favorite sentence and very near her intonation. "Tell us again, Dorian. What did you see?"

Dorian pushed her glass of orange juice across the precarious little square table and stared out past the resident palm at the verandah edge, over the shadowy pier boulders to the dark, breathing presence of the sea. It was tradition that after work on a Friday evening they went to the Sandbar for what Laura called the Unwind Drink. Built literally on the seafront, the Sandbar had a lien on Ibisville's treasured evening sea breeze. It ruffled pleasantly in Dorian's hair, and the lights on the big derricks out along the harbor were brilliant as a Christmas display.

"His clothes were—strange." In retrospect, she remembered more than she had thought. "His hat was very strange. And the tools." The anomaly surfaced. "The hat looked like an old bush guy's, all dented and stained. But the tools were new."

"Beard. Reddish hair. Tall. Old hat, funny clothes, new tools. Anne, what does that sound like to you?"

Laura was as serious as if assembling a brief. Anne answered with the assurance of an expert. After all, Dorian thought, her hobby is local history.

"A new digger. Somebody headed for the goldfields. Maybe someone who worked round here, maybe born here, but not a miner till then."

"Yes," Dorian said, surprised at her own readiness. "I think the dish was tin, and it was bright, shiny new."

"A panning dish," said Laura complacently. "For fossicking in the creeks. He wasn't going to the big mines, then, like at Blackston, he was striking out by himself. Early in the rush, maybe?"

"They opened the field at Blackston in eighteen seventy-two." Anne frowned. "But there were already diggings just over at Crowstock, and out west of Blackston. And the Palmer River, the big rush up north, that started the very next year, in eighteen seventy-three."

"So probably, he was here about eighteen seventy-two, seventy-three? No, that's too simple. Didn't Blackston keep producing almost the rest of the century? He could have come later, been a migrant or something, and thought the fields were still open. Or just wanted to go looking for himself."

"So many did."

In the pause each remembered stories heard all their lives, the flood of humanity that poured to the diggings all over Australia, from Ballarat in Victoria north to Cooktown and west clear to Kalgoorlie. So many desperately eager searchers throwing up jobs and careers, old men and young men, lords and laborers, doctors and ship captains, native-born or in from overseas, Russians, Chinese, Americans, English, Scots, Irish, French, Italians, Greeks. All in a frenzy to reach the field before the gold ran out, not a quarter of them prepared for the facts of a digger's life. The back-breaking labor, the heart-breaking disappointments. The booze, the thieves and killers, the cheating, with or without authority. The bad food and strange diseases. The thirsty distances. The simple heat of the sun.

"One of them's supposed to have pushed a wheelbarrow from here to Blackston." Anne was looking out to sea too, as if she could see the steamers coming, loaded deep with ignorant, eager men.

"And at least one died on the way," Dorian said abruptly as a tourist pamphlet came back to her, one of the little gruesome anecdotes tourist pamphlets love to preserve. "He got drunk at the hotel—the pub—up at the river crossing, and wandered out in the bush next morning. And got sunstroke, probably. They buried him where he died and hung his hat on the tree overhead.

But it was brand new. So somebody came past and took it, and left an old one in its place."

Anne pushed her own glass away with a gesture that said it all. Not merely life lost, but the barest form of memorial. And not from natural causes, but stolen. There's a real case, Dorian thought wryly, of justice unredressed.

"They probably did that in Victoria too." Laura sounded just a little too matter-of-fact. They all knew the other stories, the killings and race riots, so often aimed at Chinese diggers, beaten, attacked or outright lynched. Anne's silence outlined one part of her past she would not want recalled.

"But if he *was* a digger . . . he could have come any time in those thirty years, from anywhere. He could have been anyone. Maybe he never got to the field at all. He mightn't even have a name on a tombstone somewhere—if he had a tombstone! Dor, can't you remember anything else?"

The color of his beard, Dorian wanted to say. Deep and live and rich as cedar wood. The darkness of his eyes. "Nothing that's any use," she said reluctantly.

"How do you know that? Say it, anyhow."

"Well, he looked—worried. As if he didn't see anything here at all. And I don't just mean me. As if everything that mattered was somewhere else. And whatever mattered there—wasn't good."

A group of twenty-year-olds laughed and whooped behind them, beer jugs on the table, boys in beach-shirts and baggy shorts shouting and fooling, girls in tiny chemise tops bouncing on their knees. A birthday party, Dorian decided. Or some special occasion, a new job, an engagement. Or a farewell. Ibisville was a city of transients, from the army base to the University to the big firms whose staff was always getting transfers, passing through. As he must have passed, sometime in the years, with his tools under his arm and that worry in his eyes, heavy as a physical load . . .

"Why me?" she burst out. "Why'd *I* have to see him, what can *I* do for him? I'm just an ordinary person! I grew up without a broken home, I didn't kill my sisters, I went to school and Uni and now I work in a law firm, for God's sake! I was born of poor but honest parents, if it was at the back of South Australia instead of Castlemaine, I've lived here the last eight years, been a partner two years, found a nice unit and I'm paying off a car and going out with Chris, who has to be the legal form of spirit-proof. I don't feel vibes or read auras or channel Indian princesses or—why *me?*"

Anne was still gazing seaward. Laura examined her bracelet, a heavy nine-carat gold chain, a new present from someone. Or a present from a new someone, Dorian's mind side-tracked. She stared from one to the other, wanting an answer, wanting reassurance. This was just a freak event. It happened, maybe it happens over and over, for some strange reason. But it's done now, and it won't happen again.

Laura moved and sighed, uncharacteristically quiet. "I don't know why he came," she said. "And with what we have to go on now—I doubt we ever will."

Anne's eyes moved to Dorian's face. With surprising force she said, "I hope we don't." And tossed back the end of her drink, signaling she was ready to go.

Dorian was halfway home when the holoscreen of her cell phone on the dash lit up like the harbor derricks. Resignedly she pulled over and pressed Answer. She already knew who it was.

"Yes, darling, it's lovely to hear from you too, at this time of night, *such* a surprise! But do you have to page me on Urgent every single time?"

"Aw, c'mon, kid, you know you can't *wait* to talk to me." He was grinning at her out of the tiny screen, with his usual sublime disregard for appearances facing it full on in the harshest light imaginable. From his office work-table, she guessed, or the microscope-bed. The relentless glare brought up every line between his brows and around his mouth, every rioting tangle of dust-brown beard, every grey stipple in the slightly receding hair. It did not bring out the eyes, hazel-green as running mountain water, but she knew they would be narrowed and dancing to match the very visible grin.

"*Sure* you do," she said, thumbing on Save File. "That's why you're stuck up there in Blackston, all set to cover me with apologies and explanations about how Richards is having more kittens over the yield-figures and that cow-head Ralston's got his core-logs in a knot, so the Senior Geologist'll have to save the company single-handed. Again. Yah. When what *I* meant to be covered with was bubble-bath and champagne."

"Ooh, you really know how to hurt a man, ow, ow, ow." He had his hand clapped to a temple to very consciously leave his face free, but some of the feeling in his voice was real. "And it's Friday night and you had a bad week and I'm the biggest mongrel crawling, yeah. I'm sorry, Dorian." With one of his flash-changes, all the impudence was gone. "I'm really sorry, I swear it, I won't send you roses. In fact—" He grabbed something out of phone-range, "I'll do better than roses, see?"

He balanced it on his palm. A dun-gold circle thinner than a beer-coaster, catching back the light in sharp crystalline glints.

"Another drill-core?" She tilted her nose up. "Just another slice of quartz?"

"Not *just* another slice—!" The pained yelp died in a grin. Then his face lit up again, brighter than the screen. "I can't explain like this but it's really totally something else, you're not gonna believe it, I know I've talked about this forever but you'll understand it all this time, and when you see—I just have these last few things to fix . . ."

18

"Yeah, another whole weekend." She sighed, and smiled despite herself. "Okay. It's not just quartz, it's the biggest find since the Welcome nugget. Finish up, and get here next week on flexi time. With drawings where even I can join the dots. But you better bring emeralds, not drill-cores, Keogh, or next time you won't even have Buckley's chance."

"I swear it, kid." He patted enthusiastically at the holo-base. It was their personal farewell. Virtual blown kisses, Chris decreed, were more pointless than in real life. The screen went black on a parting King Kong, "Arrrh!" Dorian sighed, put the phone up, and got back on the road.

Someone was burgling her office at the firm.

Dorian could track it quite clearly, the rumble and click of filing cabinet drawers, the rush of leafed pages, the slap of briefs and hardcopy files on the desk. *Bang!* Her unbalanced nearside drawer that flew in too fast. *Clatter.* The loathed timber penholder her mother had given her when she made articled clerk, that overturned five times a week. *Click.* The hasp of her diary, her own personal diary that should have been in her briefcase. *Rattle, tap, rustle, ripppp,* general debris overturned faster and faster, she would never unravel the mess and the diary was personal but those files were confidential, I have to stop this, I have to get this maniac *out—*

She jerked upright. Or thought she jerked up and half her brain yelped, You can't do this, you're in bed—while the other half recorded a scene that could not be happening either, her twilit office with Ibisville's glow beyond the window, the filing cabinets' silhouette cutting the roof of her apartment block on the saddle under Fortress Hill.

And the candle in its antique holder, like a tin saucer with a handle, on the end of her desk.

It was smoking, the blue and yellow crocus of flame and the

smoke itself blown slightly sideways in a way that said moving air. Naked flame, amid the paper-stacks in her office, in Lewis and Cotton's office. In a building that was air-conditioned, sealed from any breath of wind.

Then the burglar came round the desk-end too.

His shadow flared and swelled grotesquely across the ceiling-rim, a pointed head, a Quasimodo back, a dwarf's thicket of beard. The candle eclipsed. She heard a book or papers hit the desk like a ripe tomato and he began rummaging more wildly beyond. The candle blew back as from a storm gust and she saw his face.

Dark straight brows, a cowlick of dark bronze hair. A thicket of curling red-cedar beard and a mouth set in more than exasperation, echoing the body that spun and spun again in a tumult that had nothing to do with rage. The eyes caught the candle light, darker than the shadows beyond him, growing outright wild now, glancing frantically here and there. He spun one more time and she saw fear become open panic.

Then the candle blew out.

Finally she did sit up. Her mouth was dry, her palms wet, her heart racing, all the classic symptoms of nightmare. She pinched herself, the classic reality test, and her wrist answered, True. You're awake.

In her own bed, in her up-market unit in the new block irreverently nicknamed the Aswan Dam, on the spur of Fortress Hill that overlooked Ibisville center, the unit she had chosen because it faced inland and the office skyscraper was out of sight. The night sounds of Ibisville percolated, car engines passing, revving, changing gear, the rumor of the nightclub quarter, at full throttle for a Saturday night. The bedside lamp was dark. The very solid, twenty-first century bedside lamp that she had switched out—her watch said, three hours ago. The lamp. Not a

naked, guttering candle. She was not in her office. She could
not see the building, let alone inside her office, let alone—

She jerked the quilt aside, threw one glance at the empty
bed-half—damn you, Keogh, where are you when I need you?—
and grabbed for her phone.

"Laura? Laura? Wake up, will you? Hellfire and damnation,"
it was one remnant of her Catholic childhood, her grandfather's
heaviest oath. "Wake *up!*"

The phone let out a noise half-growl, half-yelp. One flash of
Laura with hair everywhere and skin everywhere else and the
screen went black.

"Dorian? What the *hell?*"

"Laura, I don't care if it's midnight or three AM or you're in
bed with Brad Pitt and Johnny Depp together. Get over here.
I've got to—I can't—just get over here, will you? He came back!"

"Okay, okay, but let me get this straight, sheesh, where *do* you
keep your coffee—he didn't come here, did he? He was in the
office . . ."

"He was burgling it. With a candle." Dorian bit down hard
on the wobble and made herself sit down harder on the high
kitchen stool. Somehow the candle was a worse insult to reality
than anything else. "In my office! A naked candle, in with all
that paper, all those files!"

"Burgling?" Laura stood with spoon in one hand and bottle
in the other. "Why on earth would he want to burgle your office? And how . . ."

"I don't know how! I don't know why! He was throwing
things round and he looked half-crazy, but it was my office—
and then the candle blew out."

Inch by inch, Laura set the coffee bottle down. Scraped a
handful of hair back into the clasp. In almost her coax-the-
witness tone, she said, "And you dreamt it. At least—when you

woke up, you were in your bed."

"In my black pajamas, yeah, if Chris didn't make it I can still pretend, can't I? . . . What do you mean, 'at least'?"

Laura looked at the spoon as if it were a firearm and grabbed the bottle again.

"Laura, don't frig around with me, if you know something, say it!"

"I don't know anything and I can't make sense of anything, I'm just free-associating! Slow down, Dor, will you?" The electric kettle hissed. Gratefully, she filled both mugs and brought one across. "Here, get some of this down you. Not Scotch, but it ought to help."

"Help what?"

Laura put her own mug down and ruffled her hair again double-handed. "Dor, you're such a bulldog. Okay. I just thought. If he was in the office . . . maybe you were too."

"What? Laura, are you out of your mind?"

"No, I'm not, it's supposed to happen all the time but it never does to me—any more than ghosts, dammit." She looked briefly envious until Dorian's glare hurried her on. "Astral traveling, your spirit goes out of your body and you think you're somewhere else—"

"And you think *I* did this whacko thing? To get to the office and fight off a burglar? You really imagine I'm so passionately in love with the Anderson-Courtleigh files, or I'd take off in spirit to defend the security of the, the, the bloody Ben Morar appeal!"

Laura flapped her hands in wordless, Of course not. Then she added in her court-riposte voice, "Not for the files, no."

Carefully, Dorian set the mug down, trying not to let her fingers tremble, and drew a good deep breath. Laura, flapping her hands again, got in first.

"You saw him in the elevator and now you've dreamed him

22

or whatever-it-is and he was in your office whether you were there or not! So it's not the firm or the building or the day he's coming for, shut up Dor and let me finish, the next thing is, how'd you know he was a burglar? What did he take?"

In a minute or so, Dorian found her voice again. Getting off the stool, heading for the bathroom and her off-work clothes, she said, surprised it sounded so steady, "Let's find out."

A phone call from a junior partner with suspicions of a break-in at a respected law firm was enough to stir the police, who stirred the security firm. They were waiting when Dorian and Laura parked in the anomalously empty street right outside: a young pair of police from the patrol car, and the familiar gray-haired night-security man. Behind them night-lights shone tranquilly over the Chillagoe marble flooring of the Perpetual-Insurance foyer, and the main door was discreetly ajar.

Dorian's heart did a sequential loop and nosedive. But the security man was nodding at her and holding the keys out, saying, "Looks all right, Miss Wild"—nothing would make him use "Ms."—"when I got here, everything was tight as a drum."

Dorian locked her hands over her arms and rubbed the gooseflesh. Beside her Laura said, sounding admirably composed for someone in a South Park T-shirt and sequined flip-flops, "I suppose we should actually check upstairs."

They all filed into the elevator. Out of the elevator. The security man unlocked Lewis and Cotton's entry. Dorian made like the proverbial homing pigeon down the passage to her own door.

At the last moment she wavered. So it was Laura who reached past to turn her key, push the door open, flick on the light.

The air-conditioning hummed softly. The blinds were closed. The cubicle where her secretary lurked was shut. The filing cabinets were shut. The desktop seemed no worse a maelstrom than on any Friday afternoon, but Dorian knew at a glance that the paperdrifts were all as she had left them. None of the secure files, locked in the cabinets, had been disturbed.

"So you dreamt it, Dor. It still says *something*. If we could only figure what." Laura stared out into the balcony shadows that had already begun to pale with the true dawn. "Something in that office—he wants, he needs, he's tied to something in that office. Whether it's to do with you or not."

"But why did *I* dream him?" Dorian let it fracture in exasperation and fatigue. "Am I supposed to sift through every case in that office—mine *and* Vivian's leftovers, Jesus! Looking for something that just might connect to some fool nineteenth-century digger with a beard and a funny hat—!"

"No, no, of course not." Laura reefed fingers through her hair again. "Oh, God, my brain's shorting out. Lemme go home and sleep on this—Dor? Do you—would you want to come home with me? Just for the rest of the night?"

Because you're a big girl really, Dorian could fill in the rest, and you won't be shaken out of your own bed again. In any case, Chris might still get here to fill it for you. But I'll sacrifice my own company, whoever it was, even if it's still there by now, if company's what you need.

"No. Thanks, Laura." Impulsively, she gave Laura an actual hug. "Thanks really, that's so kind. But . . ." Her eye fell on and became a glower at the cellphone. "Who knows, the Prince of Staybacks might actually get here tomorrow—today, I mean. And you can bet he won't bother to call."

"Okay." Laura returned the hug and kept her own smile up. "Punch him for me if he does, and tell him he should have been here all along. What use is a hulking great Union footballer if he's never around when you need him?"

Maintaining her grumble to the last, she receded through the door. Dorian watched the solid timber panels close and thought,

I know why you offered. Not because you thought I'm shaken up, or I need company, or just someone to moan at till Chris arrives.

It's because we both know, that if the ghost or whatever he is has come back once and whatever it is he wants hasn't happened, it's certain now.

He's going to come again.

CHAPTER II

Mondays shouldn't be this bad, Dorian grumbled, trying to tiptoe in her open office door. Not after a weekend like that, no word from rotten Chris, not a phone call, and me harassed by a bloody *ghost*. . . . She sidled for her desk. I should have called Laura. Got a film. Anything but sit there trepidating with the backlog. She ducked for her chair, but it was too late.

"O-ohh, Dorian?" Mrs. Urquhart leant coyly from the secretary's cubicle, the "Oh," oscillating between a yodel and a coo. "I see you've had a busy weekend." Laura swore "Mrs. Irkitt" had brain-radar, tuned to any junior partner who actually managed sex. "It's just that the senior partners were wanting a word . . ."

"Oh, morning, Gloria," Dorian cooed back. Forty-eight or so, a Cotton cousin's widow, Mrs. Urquhart had worked for the firm since she left school, and never let her current boss forget. "Moira and Dani want me?" Given Mrs. Urquhart's way, no one in the office would ever use a first name, let alone a nickname. "Tell them I'll be round shortly." Unpunctuality was Mrs. Urquhart's second bane. With the concrete-lacquered French roll and those sequined Edna Everage glasses, Dorian thought, if she wasn't driving me crazy twenty-four/seven, I'd call her Possum and we'd both spin out.

She waved airily and turned her back. There was nothing here, she told herself, skirting the desk corner where the candle had stood. It's all one great stupid tangle and that part never happened anyway. You dreamt it. Get the obvious file and move.

The big main office looked out from the floor's seaward corner, over the gap between Fortress Hill and Stanford Crest to a peacock-blue sliver of sea. Palatial new houses on Stanford's skyline radiated white in the early sun. Squinting, Dorian turned toward the corner with its triangle of leather-upholstered couch.

Moira Cotton was wrestling a bale of papers on the low table. As usual her ample figure seemed to cascade over the couchside, she had already creased her pinstripe pantsuit, and her brindled grey hair was losing its clip. But as she smiled and waved and called, "Come in!" Dorian felt herself wallow yet again in that essence of motherliness.

"You wanted to see me, Moira?" She came up to the couches, but did not sit. Behind the further one, Danielle Lewis was still on her feet.

Moira's partner was her perfect antithesis: blue-dark hair to Moira's fairish grey, olive skin to Moira's apple cheeks, tiny to Moira's sprawling height, perfectly groomed, power-dressed, exquisite and exotic as an orchid. And as tough. Lewis and Cotton called Moira the rain-maker, the client-raiser, to her face. They called Dani—the masculine version was the only name she ever used—the Terminator behind her back.

"Hello, Dorian. Yes, we did want to catch up." Dani's voice was the antithesis of her partner's too, low and precise and cool. "You probably guessed, it's the Ben Morar appeal."

"Yes." Dorian came round the couch, sank into the quag of leather, and stretched to lay her folder on the table, where Moira generously swept her own papers aside. "I've been working on this a while. But, um, Mr. Richards is having trouble answering his phone."

Dani sat too, with the trained model's perfect poise and posture, her pearl-pink nails folded atop the creaseless fuchsia-pink skirt. Across the table, Moira looked away as if their eyes had met, and let out a long audible breath.

"Go on," Dani said. "Mr. Richards and his phone?"

"I talk to his secretary and she says she'll have him call me back. But so far . . ." Dorian pushed her shoulders up. "The case transcripts are here. I've repeated several times that Lewis and Cotton are perfectly willing to represent Ben Morar in this appeal, even if it comes to court. But we're hog-tied, if we don't have something to make up a brief!"

She expected a skewering from Dani's steel-grey eyes, so oddly light against her olive skin. But Dani was looking elsewhere.

Moira twisted on the couch and produced one of her enormous gusty breaths. "Oh, George . . ." She twisted again. "You know he's always been like that. Hopeless—how he ever runs a gold mine I can't imagine, the man's a procrastinator to the marrow of his back!"

"I did point that out." Dani's voice was colorless. The timbre and the texture of steel. "At the time."

"I know, I know. But, well . . . he's got himself in such a mess with the station people, nobody can dispute those tests, no wonder old Harvey found against them on the spot, why George never settled out of court I can't *think* . . ."

"But you let him talk you into the appeal," Dani said. "Again."

Moira twisted her hands in a suddenly almost schoolgirl gesture. And Dani sighed minutely and said in her genteel, precise voice, "Moira, I've told you and told you, we can *not* give free briefs to every guy with a nice smile and a good sob story. Whether or not he's wheedled you out of your pants."

"Dani, that's really crude—!"

"Moira, you're just too soft."

"I do *not* give free briefs to every—"

"No, half of them never get your pants off." She tapped one

pearly index nail. It rang like a judge's gavel on the tabletop. "They just tickle your sympathy instead."

"I am *not* a soft touch—!"

"You are. Luckily, I'm not."

It must be true, thought Dorian, paralyzed in her nook as one of the partners' legendary disagreements whistled past her head. All those stories about Moira and her lovers and her cases that a lunatic wouldn't take. And Dani coming behind to stopper the dams and sweep up the bits.

"Dorian, what, precisely, do you have?"

Near-terminal scandal-shock, said the irreverent back of Dorian's brain. Her mouth, luckily cannier, managed, "Ah, um, I have Moira's original notes . . ."

"Yes?"

"Ben Morar became involved in a, a dispute with ah, the Ben Morar Grazing Company, that's the people who own the station, ah, the area round the mine. They sent written complaints about cyanide pollution in the adjacent creek. It waters one of their biggest dams, their cattle were, um, starting to die. Inspectors went in, they did tests, and the cyanide tailings dam, from the gold-processing, had sprung a bad leak. The mining company promised to make repairs. That was, um, two years ago. When nothing happened the grazing company brought an action against the mining company, and it went to court about eight months ago. The mining company was found at fault and had an injunction slapped on them. They decided to appeal—"

"Asking Lewis and Cotton," Dani, glacially calm, "as a favor from a senior partner, on—personal—acquaintance, to prepare the brief."

"Well, Dani, poor George can't afford another court case! Sutton practically drained him with that barrister's bill—"

"Poor George runs one of the state's richest gold-mines. But poor George is a skinflint," Dani still sounded perfectly calm, "who cut corners on the original dam and tried to do it again with the injunction compo. And he's still trying."

Moira sank back, ruffled and moaning like a large, distracted but not combative hen.

"Now poor George is shimmying around wasting our junior partner's time. If he wants a brief, he has to let us make it feasible. We have no new evidence, no more old evidence. And no sign of co-operation in providing any. Dorian, how many times have you tried to get in touch?"

"Last Friday," Dorian kept her voice blank as Dani's, "was the tenth."

"In two months," said Dani passionlessly. "When we're charging her legitimate clients two hundred and fifty dollars an hour."

Moira groaned. "Oh, Dani, I've known him forever. Ever since Blackston, at the old boarding schools. He's not one of these southerners, he's local . . . Oh, I'm so sorry, Dorian—and I'm sure that mine isn't really doing well. I could feel it, Dani, when he talked to me; he was really *badgered,* I've never seen George like that."

Across the table their eyes met and held. Watching another rumor reach absolute if ungrounded confirmation in front of her, Dorian tried not to breathe at all.

Then Moira sighed and went limp and Dani pushed the cascade of papers back across the table and said, "Two phone calls. No more." Dorian was reaching for her folder before Dani's still cool, still precise and genteel voice said, "Thank you, Dorian."

"Anne, I tell you, I nearly died in my tracks. Why on earth would Dani do that?"

"Call Moira in front of you? But you know Moira's incorrigible when it comes to her friends and a free brief—"

"Talk to her like that!"

Anne's brows creased. The lunch bar rattled round them. Across the table, Laura kept quiet. When it came to internal politics, Anne was their expert as well as the longest experienced.

"I think," Anne said slowly, "she did it in front of Moira because she wouldn't say anything to you about the brief—or why it's happened, or what to do about it—behind Moira's back."

"But she still dropped the boom on it."

Anne looked minutely surprised. "She's the Terminator, after all."

The bar reverberated to an influx of articled clerks from Jackson and Griffith, further down the street. Dorian pushed her plate away and said, "It settled one thing for me, anyhow. I'd bet my last Lotto ticket, now, that those other whispers are true."

"Dani and Moira?" Anne half-smiled. "It's an open secret round town. You know the story, Moira's father was the original senior partner and Dani married Lewis's second son. Then he ran away and Moira's father died, and Dani put her hand in Moira's back and said, 'We're not losing this.' And now it's the only law firm with all-female partners' equity in Queensland. In Australia, probably."

"Partners, right." Dorian leant back and let out a Moira-type breath. "Does Moira ever talk back?"

"Oh, yeah," Laura cut in, grinning. "And throws things, sometimes. Haven't you seen the dents in that wall?"

"The wailing wall? Oh, heavens!" It was the wall behind the couches, where Lewis and Cotton had some of their most fraught interviews with clients. Dorian threw up her hands and Laura and Anne both laughed.

As if it had undone some other tension Laura said abruptly, "Now I'll tell you something really weird. Dor had a dream the other night."

31

Sylvia Kelso

Anne put her sandwich down. Laura said, "You tell her, Dor."

Dorian précised, cursing Laura, feeling like a witness herself. Anne's eyes went from one to the other. When Dorian finished, she looked at Laura and said dryly, "You're the paranormal expert. So?"

"So I think it's something in that office, now." Laura frowned. "But there's another seriously weird thing about it all. Whether Dor dreamt or she astral traveled and he really was there," she ignored Dorian's snort, "the thing is, neither of them should have been. That office is eight floors up."

Anne and Dorian chorused, "What?"

"Ghosts go where things were in their time. Like he was walking up stairs in the elevator, like Roman soldiers are supposed to march knee-deep in some cellar in York. But do you think any building in nineteenth-century Ibisville was eight stories high?"

Anne just beat Dorian to her infuriated, "Then what the hell is going on?" and Laura threw her hands up.

"I dunno, I just dunno!"

For once Mrs. Urquhart's post-lunch ambush failed. Safely at her desk, Dorian took the phone and found the number she almost had by heart. Her ears resounded to Dani's cool implacable voice. Then she recalled the look on Moira's face, and slowly put the receiver down.

Dani's the number-cruncher. But Moira's the one who listens, and feels, and flies by the seat of her pants. And Moira said, George was desperate.

Dani said, Two more calls. But Dani didn't say, Start now.

Her hand went out and closed the clients' number book. It stopped as her mind suddenly combusted. Then she reached rapidly back for the phone.

"Laura?" she said. "Yes, I know, you're in court in the hour.

32

Just give me this one minute. Could this—ghost—be connected with Ben Morar, do you think?"

She heard a concussion of breath. Then Laura said rapidly, "Okay, let's go for crazy, that he's a digger's our soundest guess. So if he's something to do with a goldfield, any goldfield, how many cases do you have about goldfields right now? Go through the Ben Morar stuff with a fine-tooth comb, when did it start, who mined there—Jeez, we need Anne for this! Get Jason to turn out the back-files—hey," she was giggling slightly, fraughtly, "it's just another search for precedents, after all. And get back to me, I gotta go!"

Dorian put the phone down. After all, she told herself, it's blindingly obvious if you just go with Laura's view: if this isn't hallucinations or a brainstorm, a ghost has reason to come. And if he *is* a digger, and it's your office, then it might—it must—be about the only mining thing you have on hand.

It mightn't be anything to do with me, personally, at all.

She drew breath as if a mountain had slid off her shoulders and buzzed for Mrs. Urquhart. "Gloria," she said crisply, "ask Jason to come in. And then I need everything we have about the Ben Morar appeal."

"I'm sorry, Dorian." Jason looked as tired and guilty, if not as royally exasperated, as Dorian felt. "That's everything. All I can find that we ever had about Ben Morar, as far as the files go."

"Yes. Thank you, Jason." I believe you, she let the inflection say. You're my clerk and you may be a ditzy club-boy at times but I've never had to doubt your work. "We'll leave it at that, then." You're not the one, she heroically did not add, who's wasted two-thirds of the week and a clerk *and* junior partner's time on a grand goose chase that didn't pay—squat!

Jason left, closing the door delicately, as on an unexploded mine. Dorian stared at it a moment. And now, where on earth do I go?

Call Laura, ask what we do next?

The phone rang. She hissed through her teeth and snatched it up. "Yesss?"

The line buzzed. Then the caller said, "Hell."

"Chris!"

"Are you still mad? I was hoping, if I busted my gut to get here and brought diamonds instead of emeralds, you'd be simmered down by now."

"No, I am simmered down, at least I'm not simmered down but I'm not mad at you. At least, not as much as—what do you mean, 'here'?"

"But you are still mad."

"Not at you. What do you mean, 'here'?"

"Right, right, I give in. Female Perry Mason browbeats witness. Again. I'm in Ibisville, yeah. Out at Luis Torres. And I just wanted to ask, Can I use the key to your flat?"

"Oh, Chris." She felt her jaw relax. "Don't do that little-boy number on me, either. What are you doing at the Uni, for heaven's sake? And yes, you can use the key, you didn't have to—for what?"

"Um." He was grinning now, she could hear it. "Well, I thought, in case the diamonds didn't pay off, I might make some dinner tonight."

"Ah." Involuntarily she leant back in the chair. The phone cord slid out like melted butter and she tried not to let her voice do the same. "I suppose you could do that." Her toes curled in her shoes. Dinner ready when I come home. And Chris cooking it. Ohhh, yes.

Severity was suddenly impossible. She tried for matter-of-fact. "Why are you out at Luis Torres? No, don't tell me. You've been carousing with the guys in Geology again."

"Not . . . exactly." The inflection flickered and steadied. "Tell you what, Precious. You tell me what's made you mad, and I'll tell you what I was doing at Luis Torres. In full Technicolor. Tonight."

"Okay, Gollum." He had called her Precious on the odd jesting and sometimes other occasion, ever since he found her name meant Gift. Suddenly the rest of the afternoon was not merely salvageable but full of promise. "It's a date."

Dorian leant back in her dining room chair and tried not to rub her stomach like a barbarian. Or to simply groan and coil up, like a python with a surfeit of rabbits under its belt.

"What was that exactly?"

"Peruvian stewed lamb, so far as you're concerned. I'll keep my secret ingredients," Chris's smirk spoke his real pleasure, "to myself."

"Peruvian lamb. Right. I'll give you this, Gollum. You're not often moved by the cooking spirit," she drained her wineglass, "but when it happens, it's worth an emerald or so." She reached his plate over. "I think that's my cue to do the washing up."

"You mean, heave the dishes in the washer and slam the door." He followed her round the counter and took the plates firmly out of her hand. "You rinse 'em, if you wanna be macho. I'll stack 'em. That way, they just might come out intact."

"You're such a pedant." Passing the casserole dish brought her round almost against the dishwasher, inside the circle of his arm. Another half-step put her up against his somewhat crumpled, workshirted, agreeably solid chest. "One thing about geologists," she added, as her arm found a firm purchase round his waist, "all that running up and down hills keeps them nice and—fit."

"And one thing about lawyers," the casserole went back on the counter, "they wear so many confounded—clothes." A

35

breath of laughter stirred her hair. Her spine galvanized as beard ends teased the angle of her neck. Both her hands came up to grip a fistful of khaki and she wriggled her shoulders to make him slide off the coat of her suit. "Well," she said into his mouth, "if you hadn't sat me down to dinner before I had time to change—"

"If dinner hadn't been right there you'd have eaten *me*—"

"Mmmn, not a bad idea. How does geologist go as dessert?"

Whatever he said was lost in the laugh. And then the kiss.

"Whoa. Wait just one moment." He was breathing harder than she was, backed up against the dishwasher that was still unlatched. His hands went back to her waist, holding her close. "Before we get past talking . . ." His voice changed. "Precious, what *has* been eating you?"

Dorian blinked. Swallowed, to control the sudden lump in her throat. We've been going out two years this Christmas and you still don't get it, do you? It's not your sense of humor, or your cooking, even what you're like in bed. It's the times when you U-turn like that. When you stop being a career geologist and I think you really mean it when you call me Precious.

Because you remember who I am. Because you put that first.

"Okay." She sounded almost composed, she noticed. "First the dishes. Then coffee. With the come-cleans. Both sides. And then, Keogh . . ."

"Oh, Sir Roger, do not touch me!" He squeaked the line of the old bawdy song in falsetto and mimed trying to climb over the kitchen counter and Dorian burst out laughing and shoved the dirty casserole at his chest.

"So, you wanna tell me now?"

They were on the living room couch, bare feet on the coffee table that Chris decreed made a better footstool, the floor lamp turned down, the windows open on the shadowy rise of Fortress

Hill. Their thighs made a warm touch from hip to knee, but Chris had not put his arm around her. Another thing Dorian liked about him was their common tendency to draw close moments out.

Knowing her weakness, he had spiked the coffee with Kahlua, too. Atop the red wine it made her almost ready to pull him down on the couch. But not, she discovered, quite ready, yet, to plunge baldly into the story of the ghost.

"Um. Well, I said, both sides. And if you don't draw your pictures now, I won't be fit to join dots anyway. So. Out at Luis Torres, in glorious Technicolor. What, exactly, were you doing?"

She felt him gather muscles as well as thoughts. He seemed to solidify beside her, dense and definite as one of his rocks.

Then he said, "You know the stats thing I've been working on?"

Before dinner she would have retorted, How couldn't I know? The thing you've been working on, O mighty Savant, since before we met? Not just *a* statistical model, like every mining company uses. *The* statistical model that's going to save the universe or at any rate revolutionize the mining industry, that you bent my ears about that night you cornered me on the balcony at Lewis and Cotton's Christmas party. And if I hadn't been half-lit, and you hadn't kissed so nicely when you remembered to, that would have been curtains for us.

Now, reading the inflection atop his body language, she said simply, "Yes."

"And I told you . . . if I could get this figured out, I, we could change the whole way we do exploration, we could read the drill-cores entirely differently, we could—well, I know you're not interested in the maths but it would change everything, it'd work with simple percussion drilling, no need for diamond drilling at all, we could find stuff everywhere, not just new fields, places where the old guys couldn't see it because they didn't have our tech—if I could just get the maths sorted out."

She knew already what had happened. And that it would not spoil his revelation if she said now, quite softly, "And you have."

His feet had come off the coffee table already. He put the cup down and said it almost soundlessly into the half-lit space between them.

"And I have."

She was spared trying to find praise without falling into gush. He was talking again, laying out the words before her as if they really were emeralds.

"The last lot of cores. I figured out a new variation. And I ran it. And the results . . . I wanted to make sure, so I brought the slides down to Luis Torres. To get an opinion from Mike. When it comes to microscope work, he's better than anybody in the industry."

He stopped. Dorian waited. He looked round at her, still just barely beginning to smile.

"And he said . . . I was right."

Dorian put both hands on his shoulders. The grin had begun to emerge, in the half-light she could see it flash. "Oh, Chris."

His hands covered hers. He still did not grab her in his usual riotous hug.

"You did it. It works."

"Yeah." Suddenly he did laugh and danced her hands up and down in his. "Yeah, kid, he said, It checks! I haven't just found a gold-mine, I've invented a methodology. In ten years, everybody'll be using it!"

"Oh, that's wonderful!" She did some hand-dancing on her own account. "Chris, that's truly wonderful, after all that time you put in. And it's not just the find, it's the method—"

"I knew you'd get that." His voice changed. Then the intensity was gone, he was grinning at her in good Chris style, effervescent, ebullient. "If you never could join the dots, at least you can see the pix."

"I don't have to join dots," she retorted loftily. "*I* come along and proof the contracts afterwards. This was what you were doing last weekend, wasn't it? The results had just worked out. So you were all lit up . . ."

"Like a Myers Christmas tree, yep." He laughed himself. "But I had to tie the ends off and double-check everything. If it turned out a fluke I'd have shot myself." Dorian clutched theatrically at her heart. "So I'm truly sorry," with equal theatricality, he carried the back of her right hand to his lips, "about the weekend and all. But now . . ."

"But now I may just forgive you, yeah. What's a bubble-bath, against a world-shaking mining revolution?" Then her mind back-tracked. "Wait a minute, did you say you found something? Besides the math?"

He laughed out loud and smothered it. "Ms. Wild," he intoned, "you're a gold-digger, after all. You're no better than the company managers and all the other corporate orcs. Never mind what the maths are, You Found Something! Ore! Yield! Money! Gimme-gimme, quick!"

"Oh, shut up, you scientist! But you did, didn't you? You said you did! That drill-core?"

"You said you did, she squawks! Twenty-two carat bracelets! Choker chains! I can see 'em in your eyes—"

"Chris . . ." She stopped and drew off into the couch corner, eyeing him balefully. "Okay, if your maths are so good, Keogh. Have you figured this one yet?"

He stopped in mid-flight. Eyed her in turn. Threw both hands in the air to mime rejection and despair. "Right, right, not a gold-digger, the kindest, sweetest, nicest," he was sliding along the couch now, miming a desperately exaggerated leer. "Can I get in the bedroom if I take it all back and thoroughly kiss your hands and feet . . ."

"Stop there!" she held him off, on the verge of spluttering herself. "Just give me the précis, Yes or No. Is there a mine or not?"

There was another sharp pause where the foolery died right out of his face. Then he said quite quietly, "I found one, yeah. Right where the old guys worked, going down three hundred meters and more. With their tests, they'd never have picked it up. It's up near the surface, probably two or three square miles of it. Consistent, low-grade ore."

"Oh! Oh . . . wow." In two years she had heard enough about mining to construe the full significance of that. Low-grade ore was useless to the old miners' extraction techniques, but not for modern companies. "A major find. One you could work open-cut?" Less expensive, less dangerous than the deep mines, the preferred modern way, that they had used at Ben Morar before the upper veins ran out.

"Sure, easily—"

He stopped short. A startled expression crossed his face. Then he said, "Uh, I can't tell you where it is. I don't know if— how they'll, we'll work it, I haven't taken this to anyone yet."

"It doesn't matter." Confidentiality was her own second skin. "It's enough to know you found it. And—Mr. Richards should be so pleased." She could safely say that, she thought. Chris knew about the appeal, the whole legal shambles could hardly have bypassed their Senior Geologist, and he must know Lewis and Cotton were taking it, though she had never said and he had never asked. But he had grumbled over Richards's complaints about the yield-figures often enough.

"George? Oh, yeah, George'll wet himself." The grin came and went, absently. "It's a big find, it'll make a hell of a splash. Well, it would—" Again he cut himself off, and this time swerved deliberately back to his own prize. "But *I'm* the one who found it. And not with a pickaxe, either. The Keogh Model." He pretended to puff himself up. "How does that sound?"

"Awful. How about Christopher's Fault?" She knew some geological jargon by now. He let out a bellow of mock-rage and dived for her. And then checked in the middle of the couch.

"Right. That's me in glorious Technicolor. Now. How about you?"

Of a sudden the Kahlua was not working after all. She looked past him, at the rarely used TV, at the speakers of the sound system he had given her last Christmas, matte black against the pale apricot wall. At the James Brown right over Chris's head. It was a painting from his Secret Gardens collection. The Impressionist planes and deep bush colors, smoke-grey, moody greens, granite browns, had held her eye before she ever thought how it would set off her wall.

"What is this, kid? Did you find out Moira and Dani are part-time dykes? Or that Moira had a fling with George, yea-these-many years ago? Laura been channeling Nefertiti at work? They gonna dock your partner's equity? Or," his voice yawed and steadied, "have you had a pregnancy test?"

"No." The last query kicked it out of her. "No, I—sorry. I haven't." She took another breath. "I know Vera never wanted kids and you do, and . . . one day, I think I will. But . . . it wasn't that."

He was frowning now. She could feel his concern, his concentration, settling on her like a weight. Here we go, she thought, and plunged.

"Last Friday—just about lunchtime, in the Perp-Insurance lift—I saw a ghost."

The silence stretched and then collapsed. Chris had made a noise between grunt and hiccup that became his smothered laugh. "Oh, Dorian—date, time, place! You must've been *born* a solicitor!"

His laugh broke free. She felt her spine snap to like an angry cat's.

"You don't believe it?"

It snapped him to as well. But then he flipped along the couch in one quick twist, an arm round her shoulders, the other hand grasping a wrist. "Anybody else, I wouldn't take a word of it. But if you say you saw it, you did."

Dorian felt her very bones relax. She leant back into his arm and for the first time since the doors had closed in the Perpetual Insurance lift, felt safe. Chris isn't Laura, who wants to believe in ghosts, or Anne, who trusts my word because it's me. It's Chris, and he's a solid-state rock-hound. If he says, Okay, at least I'm not going out of my head.

"I'd been round to Ogilvie's chambers, and I was bringing lunches back," she began, and heard the composure, the briefs-reading calm already leveling her voice.

"Laura and Anne and I talked about it," she wound up. "We think, with the hat, and the tools, he was probably a digger headed for the goldfields. Laura says, ghosts appear where things were in their own time. There must have been a house or something, on the Perp-Insurance site, and he lived there, or had to go there, and he was climbing the steps . . ." For a moment she balked. "He dropped his panning dish. And when he picked it up—he balanced it on my head."

Chris had been listening with his intensest concentration. Silent, unblinking, absolutely still. That shot the word out of him. "What!"

"I know, it doesn't make sense, Laura says it shouldn't have happened, you see ghosts but you can't touch them, I don't know how—" Her own voice faltered and his arm was suddenly round her again. "I could take a ghost if I had to, people do see them, I'll accept that, but not this—this—"

"Steady, kid." He was not telling her to forget it or dismiss it as ridiculous. His hand, in one of his rarer gestures, ran lightly over her hair. "Thing is, it happened. If it doesn't make sense yet . . . then there's something we're not reading right. Or something we just don't know."

"Laura said that." But Laura's not a geologist, whose stock-in-trade is unraveling the rock-and-dirt mysteries of the earth. "That's not all, though. He—I don't know if he came back or what—but the second time was worse!"

"I could believe I'd dream about him," she finished her summary, "I could even believe I might, might do this stupid astral traveling thing to the office to dream about him, but if I dreamt it—why was there a *candle* on my desk?"

"Steady, steady." He was patting her hair this time, not only his arm around her but his body arched protectively toward her as well. "Take it easy, kid, it's weird, but there'll be a reason, somewhere. You said you thought he was a digger. Is the Perp building on the old Mining Office site?"

Dorian stopped in mid-word as her own wits caught up. "Oh, Chris, I never thought—!"

"Well, you've had a few other things to think about." He sounded so entirely matter-of-fact she had to repress the urge to rub her eyes. He's already accepted this. Started thinking about it, thinking like a, a scientist or something. Logic. Earth—a half-hysterical bubble of laughter ticked up her throat—analysis.

"*You* were born a geologist." She tried not to hug him too convulsively. "No, I don't know what was on the site. But I, we could find that out. You think he went to the Mining Office?"

"Well, Perp-Insurance is technically downtown. And a new digger'd go there first. To hear the word, see what fields had opened. Get his Miner's Right."

"His what?"

"The permit to develop, to work a claim. Thing is, if he is a ghost and Laura's right, something important happened to him in that building. If it was the Mining Office, one thing could be getting the Right. The other'd be if he found something, something big, and took in the assay results. But the dish hadn't been used."

"Oh. I see. Well, we can find out about the building." The prospect of research, some toehold of fact to gain a purchase, was pure relief. "No, damn it, wait!"

"No." He had got there already. "You said he turned up in the office, and Laura said the office is too high to have been there."

"I don't know that he did turn up in the office, I don't know *what* that was in the office!" Dorian genuinely wanted to tear her hair. "It could have been a dream, yes, but that candle. What was that doing there?"

"Hnnn." It was Chris's, You're-right, let's-think-again noise. "Let the candle go for now. Laura said, something in the office. If not you yourself. And he was a digger, so something about goldfields—"

"We thought of that, and the only case I've got about goldfields is the Ben Morar appeal."

There was a dislocated pause. She knew Chris would not ask her for anything more than he knew himself. He was working out what would not breach her confidentiality.

But in a moment he said, "Tom and Joe—Furlong Mining—found the Christine lode in nineteen-eighty-four. At Ben Morar, I mean. They sold the rights to Ben Morar in eighty-five. The open-cut started in eighty-eight. It ran out about mid-nineties. They turned up Donald South, the deep lode, about ninety-eight. I came there from Broken Hill next year. They—well, mostly me—picked up the deep shoots from Quandong in oh-nine. We've been there the last three years."

Dorian opened her mouth to begin, I don't need the detailed

history, and shut it again. "So," she said flatly. "No mining at all at Ben Morar before *nineteen* eighty-eight."

His eyes pivoted to her, a faint glisten in the lowered light. She said, feeling the afternoon's infuriation return, "And we, Jason and I, went through every word Lewis and Cotton have about Ben Morar. We couldn't find a single thing that seems to tie up with the old fields, or that would tie Ben Morar to this—whatever-he-is. We wasted most of this week on it. Not one thing!"

Chris went to speak and stopped. "No," he said. He actually shook his head as if denying something to himself as well. "Not Ben Morar, then." She had heard him focus on a problem of his own in just that slightly remote, wholly absorbed tone.

He was quiet a moment. Then he said, "The candle. The dish. Neither of them fits the normal, normal, ghost patterns." He said it with hardly a falter. "But they're similar, um, events. Some kind of, call it an intrusion, a fault-line, maybe erosion, could even be detritus," his voice quickened a little. "Something happening to what we call reality that we can't explain."

"Chris, I know we can't explain it but it's happening and I don't want any more! I don't care if it's an intrusion or an erosion of reality—I know you'd love to get the whole theory figured out but we can't do that—!"

"Yet."

He spoke so calmly she stared, the yell frozen in her mouth: I don't care about your analytical scientific brain that wants to pull this apart like a cat with a mouse, I'm not interested in why it's happening. I just want it to stop!

Then her own brain made another panic-stricken bound and she said shakily, "No. If we can't do it on what we have now then we need more data and more data isn't just drilling cores, Chris, more data means that, that, that *thing* coming back—or another dream or whatever that was and you won't be the one who has it, I will—! No! No!"

He pulled her round and held her firmly, wrapped tight against the weight of his stocky compact body with her chin on the hardness of biros or pebbles or whatever was in his shirt pocket, his beard pressed into her cheekbone and her nose full of the smell of light sweat and Surf and whatever else made his scent uniquely Chris. He did not bother with soothing words or even sounds. He simply held on and waited for her to regain control.

When she hiccupped and moved he let her loose. Then he said, "Do you want to use my flat?"

"Huh? Oh." Dorian groped for a Kleenex. She hated weeping only slightly less than losing her composure in court, and it took her a moment to follow his reasoning's newest leap. Then she blew her nose again and put her hand back on his leg, this time giving it a conscious squeeze.

"Chris—thanks." For thinking so fast, for being so practical, for not cooing and calling me honeybunch or even saying, It's not like you to make a production of this. "But really," she had to wipe another sniffle away. "If I can dream or whatever it was here, what'll stop me doing it over on Stanford Crest? And I couldn't . . ." she swallowed. "I couldn't stay there for, for good . . . anyhow."

For a moment his silence re-stated past proposals, negotiations, sometimes outright arguments: you could stay there, if you wanted. Just as you could agree to kids. I've told you often enough, I'd like us to move in together. I'd like to make it permanent.

She had time to run through it all. And time to find the suggestion's other corollary, before he said, too evenly, "No." And she knew he had reached it for himself.

Because moving to Stanford Crest is dealing with the symptom, not the cause. Even if it did work temporarily, it won't affect the problem as a whole.

"Oh, damn it, Chris—"

That time he did say, "Shhh." And, more firmly, "Leave it for now." And then, his hold changing, "You've got work tomorrow, and so have I. Come on, kid. Time for bed."

He pulled her gently up. Then he said with a dry determination at once acknowledging and stemming the fear she had not been able to voice, "This yobbo'll get a treat he didn't expect, if he comes floating through your boudoir tonight."

CHAPTER III

Dorian woke in a bedroom, but not her own.

Memory said, When did I start sleeping in City Hall? It's Wakefield, all that molded plaster I loved as a kid—No, her eyes contradicted. The ceiling's too low, it's not even plaster, it's—

Some material dimpled like brocade, almost my ceiling's cream. But the wall's too close. And it's not deeper cream in reflected street-glow. It's Prussian blue. Dark as ocean in a wavering halo of candlelight.

Dorian sat up with a yelp-cum-shriek and felt Chris convulse against her hip. He reared up with a walrus snort just as the candle-flame whiplashed and the other man spun in his tracks.

She had time to see the second bed with its mosquito-net veils and turned wooden foot, the falling wrack of sheets, a circular wooden stand dangling clothes shapes, the tiny mirror above the washstand, a candle on its marble beside the ewer and dish. A sleep-tumbled bronze cowlick, the beard's thicket rimmed by white. A glimpse of ropy shoulder muscle against an old-fashioned sleeveless under-vest.

Before his eyes flared white as marble and he made his own sound and hurled the thing in his hand straight at her face.

It was a razor. An old-fashioned cutthroat razor that came like a throwing knife with a lightning-gold flash in the candlelight so she threw up both hands and screamed.

And it was gone. He was gone. The room was gone. She was panting and gasping in her own bed with Chris's fingers breaking her armbone and Chris saying hoarsely, "Jesus fucking Christ!"

"He saw us. That wasn't any dream, Dorian. When we moved it shook the candle flame. That's what made him look. He saw us all right. And he threw the razor at us." A short shaky pause. "Poor sod must've been scared shitless too."

"Who wouldn't be?" Two cups of hot Milo and a shot of vodka later, Dorian's hands were still trembling. "In his own house, his own bedroom, he turns around and there's two, two . . . do you think the bed went with us? Like a Tardis or something? Or did he see our whole room, too . . . Oh, God." She fell back on the couch, struggling not to let the laugh out of control. "I didn't even pull up the sheet!"

"No wonder he had a fit." He was trying to half-laugh too, and failing miserably. "Proper young Victorian lad like that . . ."

It trailed off as the crushing truth of that room ricocheted back on them: mosquito netting to replace screens and air-conditioning, the ewer on the washstand for a time without indoor running hot and cold, the clothes on the overgrown umbrella stand. The razor, its long blade flashing like a wing, the bone handle turning in mid-air.

Real as the man, alive and moving in the midst of it, not a dummy in a historical display but another human. Seeing them. Looking back.

"That ceiling. It was pressed tin. I've seen one in Blackston. In the Miner's Cottage museum."

To hell with the Museum, Dorian let her hand-wave say. "Oh, Chris . . . what are we going to do?"

"I don't know."

She sat mute in pure shock. The one weak comfort had been to know it was no hallucination, to share her own fright. But, she realized, I was thinking, he's a scientist, just this much new data will give him answers that escape me.

With an awkward push Chris got off the couch. She stared up, trying not to burst out in questions, or more irrationally, reproach. But he did not look at her.

"I don't know," he repeated. "And," he added to the far wall, "I can't even figure who to check it with."

Stop it, Chris, she wanted to bawl, this isn't some scientific problem that you pass around like party favors! This is my life!

"I'm glad," she tried not to clench her teeth, "that at least you saw it—him—too. So I do have, have, corroborative evidence."

He yanked round on his heel and stared at her. Then he shut his mouth and stood an instant before he spoke.

"You're not listening. *That wasn't a dream,* Dorian."

"You *said* that, Chris. I don't—! Oh."

"Yeah." He flapped his own hand in acknowledgment. "If that wasn't a dream, you didn't dream him in the office either. Or imagine things. That candle was really there."

Dorian felt the hair prickle on her neck. "Then if the candle was real—I must have been, too." Her hair rose in earnest. "And in the elevator . . ."

He met her eyes unsmilingly. "You said it. He put the dish down on top of you."

"Then he was here—I was there—it was all *real.* Oh, God, Chris, *what* are you talking about?"

"I don't know," he repeated. She heard a flaw in his voice too. "But it's not a ghost. So Laura's no use to us. Or even a paranormal expert, if there is such a thing. None of the paranormal stuff will fit."

Dorian gulped as the frail supports of New Age lore buckled under her. "You said, intrusion, erosion?" The geological terms slid through her fingers too, intrusion in what, erosion of what?

"Intrusion, yeah, I think so. Some kind of—incursion?

Overlap, some kind of, of, fold in—in—reality?" He scrubbed at his hair. "Space? But it must be time as well. It has to be. That was the past." It was almost awe. "The real past, the—What the hell would make that happen—how could, *why* could that happen . . . ? I need a quantum physicist."

"A—!" Dorian shut the squawk behind her teeth.

"I dunno who else can handle it. Time, probability, relativity, uncertainty—I'm just a geologist, I don't deal in this woo-woo stuff."

No, Dorian managed not to wail aloud. Woo-woo stuff or not, no other scientist is going to swallow this!

Chris swung round with a decision she recognized, ready to act. Then he saw her face and dropped back on the couch.

"Kid . . . Precious. Look, there's no sense fooling round with this. If we don't know what it is or why it's happening, we don't know how to stop it. And that's what you want, isn't it?"

He put his arms back round her, solid warm bare flesh. He had pulled on his usual sleeping shorts, but nothing else. She pressed against him gratefully. Her conscious mind harangued her with his arguments, We can't fix this ourselves, we can't just ignore it, either we get more data or find somebody else who can. Her memory stubbornly replayed that impossible second in a stranger's bedroom, and warmed-over embarrassment burned her cheeks. He looked right at me. I wasn't even wearing a shirt—

She tunneled her face in Chris's shoulder. But some perverse other self went on remorselessly, And how do you think he felt? Now he knows that could happen any time? That next time he mightn't just be shaving, he could be making love, jerking off, picking his nose.

Next time *we* could be making love . . .

She wrenched herself up. "Okay," she said, too loudly. "Who cares who knows or what they say causes it, so long as they can make it *stop*. Do you know anyone, is there anyone in the Luis Torres physics department?"

Chris's hands relaxed. "Doug," he said. "Doug Poole. Quantum physics guy, lived next door to Vera. Pretty cool with wacko stuff, we'd get down to it on the back veranda after parties sometimes." He looked around again, this time at the outer window, where the sky was starting to pale. "I can get out there this morning . . ."

I really hate these nighttime assaults, Dorian thought. It's losing sleep, atop the shock. She dropped her head back on his shoulder, and felt his grasp change as it had last night.

"Come on, kid." His jaw was slightly out-thrust in a way she did not recognize. "Odds are we won't get another—episode—tonight." Just like a man, or a scientist, she thought blearily, to think something's better if you can throw a fancy word at it. "It's not five o'clock yet. No point hitting LTU before nine at the earliest. And you have to work. Let's *try* to get some sleep."

By eight-thirty he was gone, half a piece of toast still in hand, an abstracted kiss that cut off Dorian's, "But that's yesterday's shirt—!" with a head-shake and the trademark grin. "Don't think it'll worry Doug. If I can just catch him in his burrow before he has a class. . . . Okay, kid. I'll call." The finger of his free hand slid down her jaw, lighter than a caress.

The door banged. Dorian sat a moment in the unit's sudden, almost vacuum quiet. Then she reached for the phone. Stopped, and took her car keys instead.

At the first red light she punched Laura's number and the holoscreen lit instantly. Laura had a mouthful of toast and a handful of hair half twisted up, but she mumbled, "Dor, yeah?" And then snapped alert. "What happened? He came again?"

"He—I—" Oh, heavens, I can't say this on the phone. "There's been a, a development, yes, a—can you come into my office as soon as you arrive?"

Toast vanished. Laura jumped. "A 'development,' hey?" Then excitement became a predatory grin. "Block Mrs. Irkitt for you? Sure."

"So tell me, tell me, quick!" Laura must have dressed with the speed of light, she burst through the office door almost on Dorian's heels. "What happened? What did you see?"

Then she stopped dead, even before Dorian swallowed and managed, "I—we—saw him, yes. And—and—"

She talked fast, stumbling over sentences as the memory revived, the strange room, the furniture, the razor flying in the candlelight. "And the worst was he saw us too! And we were in bed—"

"Oh, Gawd!" Laura's face was a study, consternation smothering the laugh. "Oh migod!" She flopped back against the desk and her brains caught up. "Chris. What did Chris say?"

"Chris says. Chris thinks . . ." Dorian sank miserably in her chair and poured out Chris's words.

Laura shook her head several times and clawed absently at the end of her ponytail. By the end she looked almost as sober as Dorian felt.

"Jeez. It's way out of my line, that's for sure. So what does Chris think we should do?"

"I don't know what he thinks I'm supposed to do, but *he's* gone tearing off to LTU to find a quantum physicist."

"Quantum . . . ?" Laura shook her head as at another punch. "Well, what else can we do?"

"Huh." Laura grimaced. "A physicist could maybe say how it happens in the whatyoumacallit, scientific sense. But that's not why."

"Laura—"

"Don't throw another wobbly with me, Dor. I know it's not a

53

ghost now, but I'm telling you. Quantum physics might say *how* it's happening, but that isn't *why*." Laura's chin set. "Why is something about him and you and—I dunno—Ben Morar, maybe. But it's people, or history, or something. And you won't get those answers from a physicist."

Dorian ripped in her breath. Stared at her friend, and sank back in the chair.

She gazed round her office, the smooth gray wall of filing cabinets, the tastefully neutral vertical blinds, pale mushroom carpet, the two Kevin Rigby prints she had inherited with the room. In one, a huge spray of frangipani painted with almost *trompe l'oeil* realism was climbing out across its painted frame. That, she thought, is how this feels. Everything looks normal, and underneath . . . it could all just turn at right angles to reality and morph into—something completely else.

"So," she said, and heaved in a long breath. "There has to be something about Ben Morar that we've missed. Maybe," her brain began to work, "it was on a road to the diggings or something. And he traveled it. Like the guy with the hat."

Laura nodded. "Anne would know. Or Anne could find out." She stood up. "We can nick out for lunch, she's not in court today. And we can all do some work on the Web."

"After hours, hah."

Laura's snort was perfunctory. Her eyes narrowed. "Dor, didn't Chris mention Blackston?"

"The ceiling, yes. He said he'd seen one in Blackston, in some museum."

"Ri-ight." Laura swung her arms. "We could look for a connection to Blackston as well."

Dorian groaned. "Blackston's a huge place, or at least a huge history, we don't even have a name—!"

"But we've got a face."

"You've seen him," Laura went on, as Dorian stared. "You

both saw him. There are photos of Blackston, I've seen them, whole collections, we could go through—"

"What, on the off chance this guy was going to Blackston, that he got to Blackston, and the double off chance he had his picture taken and the triple off chance it survived—!"

"Well, it's a place to start!"

Dorian's mouth flew open and she snapped it shut. "First," she said dourly, "let's see what Chris finds out."

Chris called just before eleven o'clock. When her cell phone lit up, Dorian had the tenor of his news before he spoke.

"Doug Poole said we were raving lunatics."

"And how's your Friday so far, kid? Up to par?" The rudimentary grin collapsed.

"You haven't seen him yet."

"I can't see him at all. He's on study leave. Away at a conference. In Trieste."

After a minute Dorian said, "Oh."

Chris scrubbed a hand in his beard. "I could call him. But an international call. At a conference. If he isn't still jet-lagged he'll be staggering tired with papers and parties, and . . ."

And it isn't the kind of thing you'd broach, to anyone, any way but face to face.

"In the Department. Is there anybody else?"

"Shirisha Chandra. She's a cosmologist."

"A what?"

"She does Stephen Hawking stuff. Origins of the universe and all that. But."

"But?"

"I don't know her. Never met her before."

Car engines whizzed behind him, dopplering in and out, rush, zoom, roar. Rush.

"I could try her," he said, with no trace of a grin. "But this

55

stuff . . . I'd be twitchy trying it on Doug. I don't mind if she thinks I'm loony. I do want it taken seriously."

"Yes." And if she dismisses it and you, and your real contact's out of touch, we're left with nothing, she thought. "When does Doug get back?"

"Into Oz next weekend. Not due in Ibisville till the end of the month."

"Oh." Dorian quelled an impulse to stamp and curse. A whole fortnight before he's even back in town. And we still don't know if he'll be any help. Her back muscles clenched. I can't even think about going to bed tonight, not knowing what might happen. Where, how I might wake up.

She re-focused on Chris and his expression told her there was worse to come.

"Yeah," he said, as if she had spoken aloud. There was a jagged little pause. Then he said, "Dorian . . . do me a favor. Move into my unit, will you? Tonight."

Her heart made a strange little shiver in her chest. He answered the look on her face.

"I have to get back." He said it almost roughly. "Today's Friday. If I stay down tonight, I can't get these results to George before Monday. And . . ."

And whatever sort of employer he is, your own standards won't let you leave such vital news dangling. Not when you're his senior geologist.

Not even for my sake.

"I don't *want* to go." He sounded outright angry now. "When I think what might happen, I could . . . but I can't pass stuff like this over the phone. I can catch him today and come straight back. Tonight. Tomorrow morning. As fast as I can make it. I know what we figured, it's probably a waste of time—but I'd feel a whole lot better if you weren't in that unit tonight."

Dorian's nape crept. Suddenly it needed no consideration.

"Okay," she said.

His face cleared. The grin flicked. "Did you leave a toothbrush? Well, take a new one." The grin snuffed. "I'll be there as soon as I can. But you know I can't make promises . . ."

"I know that." It had always been an understood, implicit in their relationship. On both sides, work must, at the crunch, come first.

"Anyhow," she said, "we can do stuff down here. Check the Perp-Insurance site. And, I told Laura. She thumbed her nose at your physicist. She says that's just the physical explanation, the real one has to be whatever—people thing—is causing it. So we'll look for people things. Try photos, she said. We haven't got a name, but we do have a face."

"That's a good idea." Chris's own face lit. "A great idea, listen, they have a big archive in the LTU history department, call—oh, dammit. They'll be shut on the weekend."

"We can work on the Web, though. What did you say was the name of that museum? With the ceiling?"

"The Miner's Cottage. You might even drive up. But the photos, if the guy's there you'll pick him. He was shaving, of all things. Soap on his upper lip, he must have some weird style with beard just round the chin. And I've seen those nineteenth-century pictures, all great full-face bramble bushes. He'll stick out like a carpenter's thumb."

"You're babbling." She smiled at him, wanting to do more, reading the depth of his own anxiety in the spate. "There's no surety he went to Blackston, or there's a photo if he did." But she did not want to deny her own hope. "And you're wasting time, Keogh. The sooner you're gone . . ."

"The sooner I'm back." He made a little half-spring. "How high, did you say?"

"Over tall buildings with a single bound." He twitched so the background moved and she recognized the side of his four-wheel drive, the expanse of a parking lot. When he called, she realized, he had already been preparing to leave.

"Your wish is my command." The grin had revived. Now, again, it went out. He said, unsmiling, "Take care."

"You too." She put her fingers up to the lower edge of the screen.

His fingers disappeared behind hers. He took one last look, still unsmiling. Then he nodded. She reached out to press Close. As the holo vanished he had already turned to walk away.

"*Not* a ghost?" Anne's fine-pencilled brows almost collided. "What else can it be?"

"Chris said, maybe a fold in reality." Anne's nose threatened to wrinkle. "But," Dorian added hastily, "he really doesn't know. Probably nobody knows."

"Hmph." Anne contemplated the AusTel building, towering white and inscrutable barely two hundred meters across the creek. A yacht went by between them, furled white sails and hull and sky-blue trim against the murky aquamarine water, its mast sliding surreally past the Dynasty's over-the-water balcony. Laura set down her chopsticks with a snap and said, "We need to find the people. People are behind this somewhere. Physics'll only give us the science."

After another minute, Anne nodded. It would suit her matter-of-fact but devious style, Dorian thought, to bypass all the weird stuff and concentrate on the hopefully more accessible, more natural human cause.

"In that case," Anne said, "we can check the Ben Morar area, for a start. If this is 'people-based,' it must still be connected to Ben Morar, as well as this—other guy."

And with you, her glance at Dorian added silently.

Dorian tried not to glare. "I thought, maybe it's on a road to the diggings or something?"

"That's possible." Anne tactfully ignored her expression. "Where is Ben Morar, exactly? Thirty-five K south-west of Blackston? I don't recall a road there, offhand."

Laura scattered spring rolls and nearly lunged across the table. "Dor, the hat-guy! The guy who died on the road and they hung his hat over his grave! Where was that?"

Startled, Dorian sat up too. "I don't remember for sure, I just thought it was the road from Ibisville. That's the wrong side for Ben Morar—" but Laura was sweeping on.

"Just suppose it *is* him! Suppose they buried him near Ben Morar and now the mine's doing something to upset him, disturb his grave, whatever! Dor, that could be it!"

Dorian gaped at her, aware of Anne coming to attention, willing to forget what Chris had said. *It isn't a ghost.* "Oh, heavens. I wonder . . . ?"

"Where did you find that story, could you turn it up again?"

"I don't remember, some tourist pamphlet. But it was supposed to be the river crossing—"

"Well, there can be other rivers, surely? What if it was the Burdekin? It's the biggest river around."

"I don't know if that runs between Ben Morar and—"

"We can find out," Anne said crisply. "I can check the maps tonight. Dorian, you can't remember where you actually read the story? In town here, in a library, a museum?"

"No, no. I'm sorry." Dorian felt half-dazed with surprise and suddenly desperate hope. *Maybe it really is that simple, a ghost of sorts after all, something to disturb it—him—at Ben Morar, maybe even—*

"Oh, good lord!" She almost overturned her own chair. "There is something happening at Ben Morar, Chris, I can't tell you the details, but Chris worked out his stats thing, you know, the one I told you about, and—listen, swear not to mention this to anyone—it's found something. Something new. It's so new

59

he hasn't even told 'poor George' yet."

"Whee-hoo!" Laura fairly bounced. "That's it, that's gotta be it, it's near Ben Morar and they've upset his grave! We just figure where he is and how to stop it and we're done and dusted!"

Dorian floated through Mrs. Urquhart's ambush and had half-catalogued her clothes for the weekend when the other Ben Morar connection seemed to explode at the back of her head.

Poor George. The appeal. Two phone calls, Dani said. And I haven't made either one. She shoved an unopened file aside and grabbed for her clients' directory and the phone.

"Miss Wild, yes, how are you? Are you after Mr. Richards? I'm so sorry, he's not here. I can have him call you back?"

The words flowed on, Mr. Richards was in Brisbane for a very important meeting, he was expected back any day, perhaps even over the weekend. "The other personnel will be flying up with him, they have a private jet." Ye Gods, who are these people, Dorian's brain inserted, what's poor George *doing?* "I can have him call you as soon as he's free?"

"Yes," said her mouth on automatic, while her mind raced ahead, He isn't there, Chris needn't have gone at all, if they don't know when he's due Chris could come back. Till Sunday night, anyway. Relief bubbled up. She opened her mouth to say, *Is Mr. Keogh there, can you put me through to him?* And shut it with a snap.

The secretary's spiel was winding up. Dorian made appropriate responses while her mind dictated sternly, You have no business contacting Chris through the office, at work, whatever you may know or he may want. Of course he'll know George is away, he'll call you as soon as he has a chance. Or you can call him, on his cell phone.

No, sanity intervened. Not now, when he mightn't even have

arrived. If you can't wait, call him later, when he may have time.

For something other than work, she told herself wryly, and made herself put down the phone.

At four-thirty she stared at her cell phone, perched inertly on the desk-edge, and silently intoned her tenth mantra of, Come on, Chris, get one minute from whatever bird-nest Ralston's built this time, and call. . . . Good intentions snapped. She scooped the phone up and it went off in her hand.

"Kid. Sorry. They've had a funny down the shaft and now Ralston's bitched the yield-figures again. I've still gotta hit the office. God knows what's in there." His beard looked like a genuine bramble-bush, and under the orange hard-hat his hair was trying to stand on end. "I'm sorry. I'm not gonna make it tonight. Maybe," the voice did not falter but his eyebrows dipped, a look she knew, "maybe not this weekend. George's set up some whoop-de-doo with a bunch of bigwigs in Brisbane, and he's bringing them on here. Top security. Tanya won't even say why, but she's got me hog-tied. Whoever nicks off and whatever goes wrong, *I* have to be here. I said, I'll just whip down to Ibisville tonight, and she had a screaming fit. No way, not now. Not even over the weekend."

He shoved the helmet back. In the clearer light he looked more than tired. "So, kid. You get that toothbrush organized?"

"I'll get it." The other unspoken clause of their pact decreed, when your partner's problem is unavoidable, don't complain. "Uh—Tanya told me about George. Being away, I mean. And the bigwigs. She said they've got a private jet."

"Christ. Probably some megacorp like Rio Tinto. Whadda they want with *us?*" Noise swelled in the background, rapidly approaching, yanking his head around. "God gimme patience, what's he done now? Right, Tom, I'm coming, I'm coming, just

61

don't let it explode in your hands—Nah, that was a *joke.*" He pulled his eyes hurriedly back to her. Ralston, she filled in, and another crisis. "Kid—I'll call you. Soon as something happens. Soon as I can."

She nodded, swallowing, putting fingertips to the holo-base. "I'll go over to your unit as soon as the toothbrush's packed."

He nodded too, and the holo vanished on a look of harried relief.

Don't be such a wuss, Dorian told herself, stowing files. What do you want, a life jacket? A ghost-busters' manual? Mrs. Urquhart had made her last pass. Outside came the sound of clerks, partners, secretaries, calling goodbyes and plans, heading home. You're doing the same. Just pick up your gear and Chris's key and head across to Stanford Crest. Think about parking, on that twisty little side road, or dinner, or fighting with his antiquated VCR. You could pick up a movie, maybe. Something nice and long like *The Lord of the Rings.*

No, vetoed her stomach flatly. No ghost voices and Black Riders, thank you. Not tonight.

She reached rather hurriedly for her briefcase and Anne appeared in the door. "Dorian," she said, "are you going home?"

"I was intending . . ."

The slight frown marked Anne's brows. "Is that a good idea?"

Dorian's stoicism collapsed. "Just for a toothbrush, I meant to sleep at Chris's place." With difficulty she stopped herself babbling. "He's stuck up at Ben Morar again but he didn't like me staying home either—"

"Well, would you like to come with me?"

Dorian gaped.

"Sam's away all weekend." Anne might have been discussing her laundry. "One of those All Boys fishing trips down the mouth of the Burdekin. In fact," her brows tipped wryly, "I could use some help. I've got the big Sumner brief to sort out for Monday. And it's a full-time job suppressing Della and Jonathon."

Dorian's thoughts spun madly, joyously. All weekend, out at Baringal Beach, right on the front. She saw the sprawling bungalow in its frame of lawns and hibiscus clumps, Jonathon and Della, four and six and unruly as a monkey cage, ranging the debris of toys and lawbooks and computer manuals and fishing photos in the brightly lit living room. I'd be busy. Needed. Not alone.

"Are you sure? I mean, if something happened . . . I don't know what's likely, but—"

I know what might happen, answered Anne's steady stare. Then an eyebrow rose.

"We-elll," she said judiciously, "if it's worse than Della and the Superglue, I suppose I might back out."

It's working, Dorian thought jubilantly, as she tried simultaneously to stop Della scalping Jonathon, put on another cartoon holo, and cut up the stir-fry for Saturday night. I'm not home, and there's been nothing. Glorious nothing, for a whole thirty-six hours.

She scooped up carrot slivers and mushroom strips and headed Della off from the compost bin. As she turned, Anne came out of her ex-bedroom study, another minute frown on her face.

"So much for roads," she said.

"Eh? Here, Della, take this spoon, at least it's clean. And bang on the tiles, not the corner table—what roads?"

Anne took the garlic bulb. "Old roads, south of Blackston." Carefully, she freed a clove. "In the eighteen-sixties, Bowen Downs, the big station, had a road going west from Port Dennison, that's Bowen. The 'Dalrymple road' to Blackston peeled off that about forty miles out, but it went way north of Blackston before it crossed the Burdekin. Once the field opened, the main road was the one from Ibisville. You could go round by Crowstock, but that branched off west well below the range—Della, on the floor, not in your mouth!"

Dorian snatched and re-adjusted Della's spoon. "And so?"

"So." Anne found the garlic crusher. She sounded as cool as if discussing a flawed defense. "Nothing goes anywhere near thirty-five K south-west of Blackston. Even the modern roads."

Della abandoned the spoon for the cartoon and the couch. Gratefully slicing into a big red capsicum, Dorian managed a punctured, "Oh."

Anne shot her a look. "I can phone people. There's Anthea Trevor. She did a whole MA on goldfield stuff. If anyone knows, Anthea will."

"Yes." Dorian tried not to scoop seeds all over the floor. If it isn't the roads, she thought, what do we try next?

"I have to say," Anne was frowning outright now, "I can't see how it makes sense."

Dorian tried not to sound too desperate. "It has to be something about Ben Morar. Just something we haven't seen." Her heart sank. But what's left except Blackston? A real outside chance?

"The Web doesn't have much detail on Blackston." Anne struck eerily into her thoughts. "I can give you the history archives number, though. Monday, you could try to phone."

"You really think photos are our best chance?" Dorian forgot the capsicum. "An absolute needle in a haystack, a—"

"We have to keep trying," Anne said.

Dorian looked with her at the children, temporarily quiet in the wonders of Disney World, the safety of the big untidy room, and understood.

★ ★ ★ ★ ★

One more night, Dorian thought drowsily, sinking into the hush of wind in the sea-front casuarina leaves and the wave-wash beneath. If there has to be more of this, don't let it happen here. Not tonight. Not where it might wake the kids.

This time it was quick as a sound-byte or a clip from a film. Male voices, furious, unintelligible. A maelstrom of papers in wobbling lamp-light, shelves, tablefuls, some sort of written certificates framed on the walls. Timber walls, slab timber, thick bars of wood with too-wide shadows sinking between, and strange little glass panes in the old-fashioned window, bleary with dust, weaving shadow as the lamps drew in moths. The light flickered over the high-piled desk and the man on his feet behind it, glaring at her. A tall cavernous-cheeked man with raven-black hair slicked back from a ferocious widow's peak and an incongruous black bowtie to match the hair. A thoroughly irate man whose bellow made it the closing phrase of a tirade, an ultimatum. ". . . y'll not do it here!"

Someone was between them. Shoulders, a tall back. He wheeled and the familiar beard lunged past her, revealing dark eyes ablaze and cheekbones bleached almost white. Then she had catapulted up in bed again with her heart banging her ribs and mind crying, Oh, no, did he wake the kids? Before she sank back on the pillow, as if that bellow had been aimed at her.

That was somebody else. A complete stranger. And I heard what he said.

Dourly mixing Wheeties and Coco Pops and cutting off Jonathon's attempt to empty his boiled egg in the cat's dish, Anne said, "Look at it this way. We are getting somewhere."

Dorian plopped Della back on the kitchen stool and applied another finger of toast. She bit back a sour, But where?

"We have a second person. And he sounds really conspicuous. And we can be pretty sure now, that it's something to do with a town. Or a field."

Dorian grabbed for the Vegemite. "What town, though? What field?"

"Well, Chris said, check the Perp-Insurance site."

"I looked. The book said, private homes and lodging houses, right up till nineteen-oh-two."

"Hmm. Well, the hat story might . . . Come on, sweetie. Nicer than the egg, yes. Come on, open up. If we could find that, we could check the story's source. No, don't spit it on the wall. That might give us something else."

"I don't remember where I heard it," Dorian answered wearily, separating the sentences aimed at her and at Jonathon. "Anthea—would she know?"

"Two more spoonfuls, then you can have some ordinary milk. Yes. Anthea might. Or she might recognize the second guy. Widow's peak. Bowtie. Pretty distinctive. You know, I'm sure that should ring a bell."

"And he was angry." Dorian's own stomach curled at the memory. "Furious. So was the, the other guy." My guy, her mind amended and she suppressed it sharply. "He looked the way they keep saying in books. White."

"Angry. Okay, sweetie. Milk, now. Strong emotions. No, in the *glass*, Jonathon. You said he was upset in the office. Maybe that's the connection—no. In the sink, Jonathon, if you don't want it. No, it can't be that. He wasn't upset in the bedroom until he actually saw you. Yes, you can get down now. Wait. Dorian, how did he speak?"

"Huh?" Dorian finally divided her own orders from Jonathon's. "Oh." She let go of Della, who slid headlong for the living-room floor. "The accent, yes. Not Australian. Sort of— sort of—"

"English? Oxbridge?"

"No way. Not English provincial either. At least, not York-shire or anything." She dragged her mind back to that flash of sound, and tried to echo it like a musical note. ". . . y'll not do it here!"

"Brilliant!" Anne actually clapped her hands. "You've got a really good ear, that didn't sound anything like you."

"So how did it sound?"

"Um—not English, no. Probably not Scots. That 'y'—not quite 'ye,' not quite 'you'—and the 'here.' There's a burr on that 'r,' but I just can't place the 'ee.' Maybe—maybe Irish, but I'd never pick which one."

"There's more than one?"

"Of course there are, Cork, Kerry, Galway, Connaught, and that's just the south and west. I don't know if I could pick a Cork from a Dublin, let alone a Belfast. If I ever heard such a thing." She seemed to realize she was babbling and checked herself. "If I get a chance today, I'll phone Anthea. Maybe we can find the hat-source, if nothing else."

But when she came into the living room at lunchtime her brows were bent in a definite frown.

"Trouble with the brief?" enquired Dorian, gratefully abandoning the attempt to read a story to Della without being corrected every second sentence. Anne shook her head.

"I phoned Anthea. Caught her between brunch and this afternoon's barbecue. She's never heard the hat story before."

"Never?" Dorian knew she was staring stupidly. "But you said, she's an expert."

"Yah." Anne massaged the back of her neck. Her silence said for her, Are you sure it was in a tourist pamphlet? Are you sure it was around here? Are you sure you ever heard it at all?

Dorian moistened her lips. "Anne," she said, "I didn't—I didn't imagine it."

"I don't think you did." Anne sighed. "It's too bizarre for that. No, it's just another of those cursed ghosty references that you know exist, but for the life of you, you can't remember where."

Another dead end, Dorian thought, wanting to hiss like a kettle with sheer frustration. Not Ben Morar, not a road, not a grave, not a recognizable accent, not a face—not even a hat!

"I think I'll phone Chris," she said.

Dragged from a fresh but equally confused set of yield-figures, Chris was more exasperated than Dorian. "Damn and blast the man! Or ghost, or whatever he is! Nothing to do with a road, Anne thinks?" He added another profanity.

"Laura said . . . Laura was really excited, she thought it might be the hat-guy, that his grave's somewhere at Ben Morar, and it's being disturbed—" she balked, and plunged. "I wondered if, it was—something to do with your new—the new thing?"

"The new—?" Chris broke off too. Shook his head almost as Laura had. "No. No. Can't be that. Even if—" He shook himself all over this time. "No. We haven't done more than test there. . . . What is it, kid?"

"Oh." Dorian tried not to look woebegone. "It's just, we can't even find a source for the hat story, now. I thought it was a tourist pamphlet, somewhere in Ibisville. But Anne can't find it, and the local expert's never heard of it."

"Ahhh!" Chris's snort conveyed the rest. "The one good thing is, no more bloody episodes," he took a second look and his face changed. "Dorian?"

"You're too clever." Resignedly, she paraphrased the night's event. He listened sharply, then began nodding every second phrase or so.

"They didn't see you, good. And somebody else, that's really good, another clue. Anne can't place the second guy? Damn!

Well, the archives might help. Very quick, though, hey?" She recognized the change of tone. "I wonder if distance's got something to do with it?"

"*No*, Chris, I don't want any more scientific speculation, I've already had Anne on about, Is it something to do with extreme emotion—either side—and it's not." Belatedly, she thought outside her own affairs. "Has George turned up yet?"

Chris snorted like a furious bull. "Not a sign of the bastard! And he's laid the weekend shifts off! Kicking my heels two whole bloody days, going round and round the dog's breakfast Ralston left, stuck in the suits' mess drinking coffee on my Pat Malone!" It was a dry site, like so many mine-camps, Dorian remembered, as she tried not to laugh at the image of him scowling over coffee at an empty room.

"Isn't there even a watchman?"

"Oh, sure, good old 'Tonio. Does me karaoke cabaret!"

Dorian burst out laughing despite herself. "Hey, Keogh, you're in the Dead Marshes and no mistake!"

"I sure am." At last he grinned too, however sheepishly. "Well, I know one thing. If George isn't here by twelve tomorrow I'm whopping the results on his desk and leaving a memo for him and a raspberry for Ralston and lighting out for Ibisville." A distinct gleam in the eye replaced the grin. "Any more midnight visitations, *I'll* deal with them."

"I wish you could." For one halcyon moment she saw Chris bellowing louder than the man in the bowtie, hurling spoons or mugs like Della or Jonathon clear through the other—is it a world? Place, time, fold in reality?

She sighed. He had sobered too. He eyed her sideways, rubbing his chin through the beard. Then he said softly, "One more night. Hang in there, kid."

"Sure. And I can phone the history archive Monday, too."

★ ★ ★ ★ ★

Anne flatly refused to let Dorian leave till Monday morning, calmly telling Sam that she had come out "to help me control the offspring—seeing you weren't here." But to their mutual relief, Dorian woke without another "episode," as she termed it wryly to herself. Then the farewells were over and she was out in the highway stream, watching traffic lights stretch flat as runway markers to the early sun caught in amber on the cone of Fortress Hill, and wondering if "George" had turned up yet. Even if he doesn't, she reassured herself, at midday Chris will pull the plug.

Between updating Laura—"Somebody else! And you heard him talk!"—and incursions from Mrs. Urquhart, Dorian watched the clock. Ten-thirty. Eleven. Eleven-thirty. Just an hour more and Chris'll be on his way. Just half an hour. . . . Paradoxically, her heart sank at the cell phone's cheep.

"Hey, kid." One look told her the personal bad news, though his own expression lightened as he surveyed her. "So you didn't rent out that toothbrush last night?

"Do you mind, Keogh? *You* may be a playboy. *I* have manners. And Jonathon may be the toast of Baringal Beach, but he's far too young for me."

"But last night was okay? Nothing happened?"

She shook her head. And spared him the effort of broaching the unhappier news. "What's going on up there?"

"Ahh." He did not actually roar. It was more of a camel's groan. "George got here this morning. About ten o'clock. Bloody great rented chopper, him and a whole heap of suits. Yanks, I think. Blanket security, haven't even got a name. Now they're barricaded in the manager's office with the air-conditioning. But See-me was George's number one."

"The results?" Her heart lightened. If that's over, maybe he can leave. She remembered her manners. "Was he pleased?"

For a moment Chris did not reply. He was staring past her, his tired if not bristly face set in something near a frown. Then he brought his eyes back to her.

"That was—actually quite weird. I thought he'd be beside himself. And he was pleased at first. Fairly rabbited on, for George. Great idea, wonderful maths, gotta get it in the journals. . . . Then I showed him the actual figures. Told him about the mine."

He stopped. Dorian waited a moment, then prodded, "And?"

"He didn't," Chris said slowly, "go over the moon at all."

"But—!"

"Yeah. Here he is, whingeing about yield-figures, chewing my ear to get the stats model up, squawking like a prima donna the last coupla weeks—I hand him this on a platter, tested, refereed . . . and he sits there like he's found a fly in his pumpkin soup."

"But that doesn't make sense! Why on earth wouldn't he—did he explain at all?"

"No. Didn't say anything. Well, not about that. Tell the truth, the setback thing was just the first thirty seconds or so. Then he got himself together and did the proper tune, wonderful find, great start for the method, have to dig a bonus out of the back pocket, yah, yah, yah." Suddenly his forehead creased. "Without that first half-minute, I'd think it was all serene."

Dorian stared at him, baffled too. "So, what happens now?"

His eyes focused. Then he screwed up his face and she knew what he was going to say.

"I'm really sorry, kid. He wants a presentation. For the suits, soon as I can get it up. The full orchestra, 3-D model, geology and assay results projected on, core logs, topography, development suggestions, estimates, for Chrissake. I'll be up all night and probably tomorrow night as well. Even if I rope in Ralston and Tanya, perish the thought."

He was looking outright miserable. She summoned her own courage and managed a fairly steady smile. "Okay, Wonder Boy." She found her fingertips were on the holo-base. "I'll hold the fort. Phone the archives. Fight off the bogeymen." His expression wavered. "Just get the suit-show over as soon as you can and then, do you think, George would let you off for a night?"

"Well, George'll do it, if I have to take it in lieu of a bonus or whatever carrot he dreams up." His own fingers blotted hers. "Gimme two, three days at the most. With any luck," again his expression wavered and he caught it up, "with any luck, things'll be quiet. I'll get this over by Thursday at the latest. And the minute the suits shove off, I'll be on the road."

"My hero. Sam the Orc-zapper. With a light-pen for sword."

"Stuff that for a joke, if I haveta flatten George I should at least be bloody Boromir!"

His mock outrage made her laugh again. "Oh, you'll have to do better than a presentation for that. A dragon at the very least."

"I could barbecue a coupla suits?" Abruptly they were both laughing, eyes locked, fingers pressed to the holo's base. She said, "Be careful," just as he said, sounding slightly husky, "See you, kid."

CHAPTER IV

Dorian was walking back from lunch when Chris's jigsaw pieces suddenly meshed. Americans. Suits. A hired helicopter. A private jet. A madly important meeting in the state capital, ongoing—negotiations?

Takeover.

Or merger, or whatever the mining industry calls it, she amended, recalling Chris's commentary on firms amalgamating, collapsing, getting bought out or simply bankrupted. And the usual story, a small Australian company eaten by a big overseas corporation, maybe a megacorp with a dozen industries under one umbrella and no in-house sense of their operations, just a phalanx of accountants with their eyes on the bottom line.

Likely they singled out Ben Morar, she thought sourly, staring down the cleft of Leichhardt street to Stanford Crest's bulwark of noon-lit white, because Ben Morar has a rich mine and very little else. Certainly not the financial clout to block a takeover. Most likely George knew, which is what he's been twitchy about.

She stopped short at the pedestrian crossing and stared blindly at the Ibisville Museum, Doric portico columns and austere pediment anomalous against a background of rioting banyan figs.

Does Chris know? Has Chris figured it out?

The lights changed. She started forward. The Perp-Insurance

Sylvia Kelso

building rose beyond the Museum garden, a classic four-square skyscraper, taller, in this perspective, than Stanford Crest itself.

What if he did know? He couldn't stop it, any more than I can, any more than George. Through her mind ran a score of headlines over Australian institutions lost to foreign ownership. Arnotts Biscuits. Vegemite. *Nothing can stop a megacorp, not public outcry, not company fight-backs, not even government intervention, sometimes. Nothing except another megacorp. Sometimes not even that.*

Anyhow, Chris has to know. He's worked in mining all his life, and he's always had his ear to the ground.

Does he really understand what he's doing with that presentation, then? That the whole takeover may depend on the size of the carrot he can dangle in front of them?

She headed for the Perp-Insurance entrance, feeling her own pulse speed up. *Has he thought what might happen to* his *job if they bite?*

He's a good geologist, she told herself dourly, stomping inside and bracing for the elevator. *If they do have a purge and put in their own people, he could walk into a job anywhere. His experience, his reputation—*

His revolutionary new stats model.

The doors hushed shut. For once she forgot the now instilled tension that came every time she pushed the floor-button.

What if the model's what they really want?

No, she told herself, as floor lights flicked by. *This isn't Russia or somewhere, where people get their inventions stolen out from under them, or get killed for them like in some wild-eyed film plot. If they do sack him*—"let him go"—*it'll be their loss. They'll realize that as soon as they see the presentation, they'll bend over backwards to have him stay.*

The eighth floor came up. After the usual unnerving pause,

74

the doors slid back and she stepped out. And stopped half across the foyer.

What if the model really *is* what they want? What if that was George's real carrot? Because the present mine may be rich but the company's tiny, and the new mine wasn't even on his horizon—

Was it?

Laura's clerk Sandy skated past, waving lilac fingernails and an expensive new streak job in brindled red and blonde. Her carol of, "Hi, Dorian!" brought reality back with a jerk.

You are getting entirely paranoid, Dorian scolded, heading for her own office with what felt like unseemly haste. When he went to Brisbane George couldn't have known about the new mine, and he didn't even know the model worked. He might have dropped a few hints, but he wouldn't have had anything more.

And there's no point phoning Chris to tell him what he must already have figured out.

After a moment she pushed aside the waiting file-heap and reached for Anne's stick-on note, with the phone number for the history archive at LTU.

The archive, a recorded message informed her, opened Tuesdays and Fridays, from eleven AM to three PM. She made a sour face and hung up. So now, she told herself, facing the files again, I just have to worry about tonight.

Chris's enclave made two long green-roofed ranges down the top of the Stanford spur. His first-floor unit looked seaward over the ocean-liner-superstructure of the old hospital, to the northern capes. Out on the little balcony, she stood a moment picking out distant island silhouettes: The Palms. Rattlesnake. Hinchinbrook.

We were going there last year, Dorian thought. To walk the

trail, while you're young enough to make it, Chris said, teasing. And I pummeled him with a couch cushion, and we ended up wrestling on the floor . . .

The floor was strewn as usual, film and music and e-book holo sheaths, paper books, journals, Chris's football boots, half a laundry basket of clean or dirty clothes. The TV wore a "Thank God It's Friday" tropical shirt, and the tang of road-dust, spices and citronella from the mosquito repellent—Chris hated screens—hung heavy in the air. She turned brusquely into the tiny kitchen to hunt his latest cache for serving spoons.

When she finally turned back the patchwork quilt Chris's mother had made, Dorian resolutely refused to think about the last time she slept here: the talk, the laughter, the warmth of companionship, the later warmth of making love. It'll be all right, she told herself firmly. In a day or two Ben Morar will sort out, Chris'll be back and we can get serious about this thing.

In the meantime, I'm a big enough girl to deal with a couple of—ghosts.

She woke to a parrot screech, more raucous than a siren and nearly as loud, and almost hit the floor before it made sense. Chris's unit. The neighbor with that bloody bird he's trained to feed on his balcony. And Chris says it shouldn't eat bread anyhow.

The fusillade of screeches said it had brought family and friends. Dorian swore and groped for the bathroom. She was hunting shampoo when the rest sank in.

I never woke all night. He—the ghost—whatever it is—didn't come.

Suddenly buoyant, she yelled at the parrot and hurried to battle Chris's state-of-the-art coffeemaker. Made toast, compiled another list of things to bring back tonight, loaded the car. Headed down through early traffic, bright and rushing in the sun. Hummed her way from the Perp-Insurance car park to the back doorway, charged like St. George into the lift, through Lewis and Cotton's foyer, waving gaily to the receptionist, twisted the key in her door.

He was sitting behind her desk. In her own chair.

The office whited out as from a close lightning strike. There was only the piled familiarity of the desk and the wrong, impossible, blood-stopping image beyond. Beard, cowlick, straight brows lowering, coffee-dark eyes glowering as he jerked his head up. Alive, aware. Seeing, knowing her.

With horizontal wooden slabs behind him, a small-paned window, open on dusty sunlight and a green growing shrub.

Then she reeled into the opposite corridor wall and he came out of the chair so violently it went over and everything was gone.

Except the chair. Which had not fallen at all. Her own chair, upright behind the desk, carefully pulled in, undisturbed.

Somehow she got inside. Made herself shut the door. Fell into the client's chair like some old music hall actress clutching cliché-fashion at her throat. Oh, her brain was saying like a stuck tape. Oh, God, oh, God, oh, God.

In a few minutes she could release the backlog folders, still clamped to her chest. Try to disentangle the laptop, swung with her into the chair. The keys. They're still in the lock. But she was shaking suddenly, teeth nearly chattering, wondering if she would throw up. He was here. Right here in front of me, in broad daylight. In my own office. My own *chair.*

Replay brought up details she never knew were lost. The cowlick, slicked down. The beard's red-dark enriched by a stark white shirt, and a jut that spoke plainer than the brows' line, the eyes' outright glare.

He was angry. This time, he was the angry one.

White shirt, her brain went on, functioning on someone else's initiative. Probably—some idea from a past itself forgotten—starched. Low standing collar . . . no cravat? But not a working man's shirt. Not like he had before. And rolled sleeves. Another detail returned. Rolled halfway up the forearm. Like a man in his own workplace, and that place behind a desk.

Barricaded behind the desk.

The other face flashed past her, cavern-cheeked and furious in the lamplight and she had an infuriating sense of connection just beyond her fingertips. If that one was angry last time and he's angry now . . . Do they work together? They're having an ongoing fight?

No, she qualified her first thought. He wasn't just angry. He was—defiant. As if he was the one in the wrong.

Did the other one forbid something, and he's done it anyway?

This is crazy, she cut herself off. How do I know there's a sequence, let alone cause and effect? They could be two separate moments, days, months, years apart.

But he—my—whatever-he-is—was in that other—episode. They do know each other. We know that much. So if we found Bow-tie, we might find him.

Except the only needle's in the archives haystack, and they're never open to look!

"So *none* of us can get at the stuff."

Anne pushed aside her ham sandwich. Then set her Coke glass down with ominous delicacy.

"Not this week, anyhow," Laura agreed gloomily. "You've got the Sumner thing and I'm up to my ears in Pazzolati's custody screw-up." She stared past Dorian, out the lunch bar's plate-glass window into the rattling street.

Anne tapped her glass with a fingernail, as near exasperation as Anne got. "We do have a connection to somebody else, that's two leads to chase. But there's no point anyone but Dorian looking at photographs."

"Bow-tie," said Dorian. "Would your historian person, Anthea, would she know about him?"

"She might." Anne's frown remained. "I could say we'd seen the picture somewhere."

"Yah, that oughta work." Laura's eyes flicked back to Dorian. "Dor . . . you wanna stay at my place tonight?"

Dorian opened her mouth, and hesitated. "I think," she said at last. "Thanks, Laura . . . but so far, at Chris's place, I've been okay."

She was hardly surprised when Chris did not call that night. She pictured him in the throes of a full-scale geological presentation, which she had seen him wrestle once or twice before. When the parrot roused her, after a moment, she felt unalloyed relief. Nothing again, she thought, groping to open balcony curtains and make out the whalebacks of The Palms, hazy on a distant silk of blue-grey sea. Not here, at least.

Going into the office was not so comfortable. This has to stop, she told herself, clenching her teeth in the corridor, trying not to cringe, hesitate, call for someone else to unlock her door. If it goes on much longer, I'll be seeing minefields everywhere.

And how, said the inconvenient part of her mind that played devil's advocate, do you think he feels?

Tough for him, she muttered, and pushed open her door, restraining the urge to kick it, Rambo fashion, into the wall.

The office was empty. The light was flashing for voice-mail on her phone.

"Hi, Dorian, how's things? I hope you don't mind me calling at work, I just got your machine at home. I'm up here three days for a conference, want to get together tomorrow night— Wednesday night, I mean—for a drink? We haven't caught up face to face, oh, since Adelaide! I'd really love to see you. Oh. It's Jess, of course, I forget there's no holo on these things. Well, you can call me back at—"

Dorian grabbed a pencil and scribbled it down: South Bank, one of the bigger business hotels. And Jess, she thought, heart lifting, it'd be lovely to see Jess again. Talk about Uni, swap scandal about jobs, just get away for a night. Surely, there can't be any problem going somewhere for a drink? Chris will call my cell phone. If he hasn't already called.

The afternoon was enlivened by a call from Anne, between court appearances. "Anthea," she said without preamble. "She doesn't know your Bow-tie person offhand, but she's going to keep an eye out. I said," she hesitated, "I thought he might be connected with Blackston."

With the hope of another quick solution receding, Dorian sighed silently and said, "Okay. We might as well start there as anywhere."

By three o'clock she had almost surrendered hope of hearing from Chris. He did say, Thursday at the latest, she told herself. But her heart leapt when, just before four o'clock, her cell phone lit up.

"Hey, kid." It was a grin, however perfunctory, and he looked tired, but as with released strain. His eyes scanned her alertly enough. "Everything okay?"

"Um—sort of." Suddenly yesterday's encounter hardly seemed worth a fuss. "Good enough, anyhow. What's with you?"

It was a measure of how hard he had worked, she knew, that it took him a moment to marshal his thoughts. Then he said, "Bad news and good news—sort of." A hint of a grin as he threw her words back. "Bad news first. I can't get down tonight. George is determined I have to stick around. Field questions, encourage the suits."

"Oh." She tried to keep her expression up. "How did the presentation go?"

"That? Oh." Things really have been moving fast, she thought, he sounds as if it was a week ago. "I got it done this morning. The 3-D was okay, just had the laptop fall over a couple of times. Trying to simplify the model was . . . but I think they got enough to trust the results."

"And?"

"Well. I guess it'll come out soon enough, and you know this is confidential anyhow." I know you'll respect that, added the inflection, with relief. "The suits are from Pan-Auric. The big gold company, the Montana-based lot. They took over Union-Sud, the French people, a while back. And those two South American companies. The bigwig's a Pacific Vice President, no less. With a whole flipping entourage. Note-takers, gophers, even a bloody bodyguard. And—did you figure they were looking at a takeover?" He read her face. "Thought so. George got me in his office this arvo and gave me the lowdown. At last."

Some animation was coming into his face now, as if he were finally adjusting to the news himself.

"George says he couldn't run the new mine anyway. Not enough resources, not enough funds. At least, he says, this should hold most of the jobs. I think that might have been his funny when I first told him the results. Swings and roundabouts. Still dunno if they'll keep *him* on, sometimes they do the purge thing with little companies."

"And you?" It popped out before she thought.

"Me, yeah. The bigwig didn't follow too much math, but one of his stringers was growing a periscope. They want me too, yes indeed, Precious. A lot of gabbing from George and Pan-Auric both: it boils down to, they know if I stay they're getting the mine and first chop at the model too. George did this number before I started the presentation, reputable geologist, years of

81

experience, had a nose for lodes like a bloodhound even without this revolutionary new methodology . . . bah!"

"Oh, Gollum, you do so love soft-soap!" Dorian laughed aloud. His reaction to flattery was one of her joys with Chris. "So your job's okay." A warmth of more than relief was spreading through her. And maybe, now, she added to herself, George'll get on with his wretched appeal, and I can finish mine.

"Yah, I'm okay, and they're gonna open the mine, yep. Top priority, I gather. Still under wraps, though, they have to clear it with the Pan-Auric CEO. Some guy called Thorpe." Excitement heightened to the first hint of enthusiasm. "Pan-Auric's big enough to make a job of it. Good equipment, good personnel. Specialize in open-cut stuff. Big stuff. It'll make a splash when it does get out. Bet the headlines go clear to *The Australian*'s business page."

"That big?"

"That big." The grin was becoming wolfish. If he disdained personal flattery, Chris had no objection to his cherished projects hitting the news. She managed to make herself grin back at him, answer the excitement that was bubbling up at last. "So you're gonna be the star of the industry, huh? You and Christopher's Fault?"

"Hey, listen, you!" He tried to keep an irate face, failed, brandished a fist. Then the grin eclipsed. "But . . . sorry, kid. Tomorrow, I gotta take the suits on a site tour. George insists."

She could imagine the shrug. The half-rueful, half-hopeful expression, somewhat like a puppy caught outside the yard again, said the rest: So I won't be down before tomorrow night at earliest, and I know how you feel about that.

Dorian elevated her nose carefully, making sure input picked up the shift. "I see. Throw me over for a gold-mine. Again. Well, it just so happens, Mr. Lodehound Keogh, I have a date for tonight already. I might make time for you later. Say, Monday or so." He yowled and clutched his hair and she pretended haughty indifference. He stopped play-acting instantly.

"Did you get at the archives? Has anything else happened?"

She told him about the archive times and he swore briefly. "And, well, something did happen, but not in the night. And it was really quick."

By the time she finished he was looking worried all over again. "Damn George and his guided tour! Dorian, I'm sorry, I can't— well, tomorrow night, I'll do my damnedest, I promise."

"That's okay, Gollum." She summoned a smile. Inspiration struck. "You can comb the archives when you get here. Slave labor will be an almost adequate recompense."

"No emeralds?" He mimed extravagant relief. "You got it. Oh, massa, I your very servile boot-licker, and beside that, I do very good job kiss . . ." He pretended to salaam to the ground, circling his thumbs in excruciating parody of a Oriental sycophant, and willy-nilly Dorian had to laugh. He laughed too. The grin was still there when his image disappeared.

Jess had wanted to avoid the South Bank: "There'll be conference people everywhere." Dorian debated alternatives, and finally, defiantly, chose the Paragon, a somewhat flashily restored old pub a block or two down from the bridge, on the rim of the nightclub quarter. So what if it's old, she thought, he can't chase me everywhere.

Built round an old staircase, the Paragon's ground-floor bar formed a semi-circular ribbon of heavy, polished, original wooden shelf-tables with modern stools, half-lit and crowded under the restored ceiling's extravaganza of rosettes, borders and gilt. Beyond, however, a tiny paved courtyard-cum-restaurant was cool with potted palms and whitewashed iron, and relatively empty on a Wednesday night. Lured by the promise of a good West Australian chardonnay, Jess settled her version of tropical chic happily into the narrow chair.

"You don't look a day older, you know, how on earth do you do that, and in this climate too? I guess it's the looks. I could have killed you at Uni. Black hair and blue eyes and black lashes into the bargain. *Before* the mascara went on." She tilted her glass and surveyed Dorian over it, the same shrewd, blunt presence that had shared lectures and tutorials and the ardors of examinations, indentures and articled clerkdom, the same direct brown eyes under the now fashionably styled shag of russet hair. Before she knew it Dorian was grinning in response, riposting, "And do you remember the night it didn't get on? When you would drink Black Russians before we got dressed?"

They both started laughing. Twenty minutes later they were past memories and job-shop to houses and partners, Dorian sketching Chris's foibles—"you get used to being stood up at a moment's notice for a gold-mine. And he does have a big one lined up this time." She felt a flush of vicarious triumph. "I guess I can tell, it'll be common news pretty soon."

"Pan-Auric, hmm?" Jess twisted her glass. "They were on the diplomatic radar couple of years ago. Dust-up over a Panamanian gold-lease. Lots of local unrest. Settled out of court, as usual. But rumor says it went past the usual free ministers' limousines."

She paused. Catching that slightly indecisive intonation, Dorian prodded, "And?"

"Oh—just their CEO's got a bit of a rep. They reckon Aaron Thorpe can play very rough." She caught Dorian's eye and lifted her shoulders a little. "It's nothing. At least, nothing to worry your Chris."

"No, he'll only deal with the Pacific VP." Dorian suppressed a piece of folklore that said, corporation ethics depend on the CEO. "And I think Chris could handle crooks."

"Know him so well?" Jess looked amused.

"This Christmas," Dorian retorted with dignity, "we'll have been going out two whole years."

"Not bad," Jess agreed judiciously, from the height of a five-year partnership. "Especially for you. In Adelaide you were such a butterfly. A different guy every two weeks."

"Oh, and you were so stable. Who were those three guys you juggled in second-year? When I had to cover for you every weekend?"

Jess laughed. "Oh, Dora! You don't live up to your name. The wildest thing you ever did was think about serial monogamy."

"That was quite enough." Dorian could not contain the grin. "And *don't* call me Dora, I've told you that a thousand times!"

"So you have, and it never did a bit of good." Jess sat back and pushed conspicuously at her glass. "But I don't recall having to nudge you for a shout before. This Chris a Scot, or you started breeding moths in your wallet now?"

"No, I have not!" Dorian feigned outrage as she scooped the glasses up. "And you only just finished that, you know you did."

"And you still bite like a ten-ton mullet." Jess laughed at her, the familiar amusement at getting a rise, and she made for the inside bar, laughing too.

At first she thought the bar had filled up suddenly. And phew, they must have been spilling beer and had in a tribe of construction workers. And blown half the lights, the place is dark as the pits . . .

Her feet froze to the ground. No longer to utilitarian if anomalous vinyl tile, but to rough-laid stone paving beneath a ceiling suddenly dark with smoke and a good three feet lower above a seething, shoving, entirely male horde of drinkers, most bawling at the tops of their lungs.

The barroom had doubled its length and the bar down its left-hand side was wide as a railway bed, its heavy timber corner crowded with glasses, the rest lost in shoving elbows and waving hands. Lamps with smoky glass chimneys dangled overhead, half-lighting wild beards, disreputable hats, peculiar little white brimless caps, murk-colored work shirts and glimpses of stamping, high-laced, filthy boots. The noise was stupefying and the stench a brain-blasting mix of stale booze, tobacco smoke, dirt and sweat. The crowd surged and she recoiled instinctively, snagging her eye on the group nearest the door.

They were squeezed against the opposite wall. A lamp shadowed half the visible faces. But not the one nearest the wall, facing her.

He had a beer mug in one hand. The lamp caught the red glints in his beard, the creases and smudges on the white shirt, rolled above the elbows now. This time he was not looking at her. All his attention was for the men pressing around him, heads together, several talking at once, voices verging on a shout.

". . . charges," she caught, and with greater force ". . . not fit to work a jumper's claim!" Overriding it, "that's the second one," then in a lower voice, "tried to tell him, and Joe got sacked . . ." topped by a suddenly bursting cry of, "tell you, that shaft's not *safe!*"

Not a bar debate. She already understood that. This was more than drunken emphasis, more than the fervor of sport or politics. This was anger, burning up to fury, breaking into open fear.

The crowd heaved, heads and backs momentarily hiding his face. He spoke, though she lost the words. But not the line of brows and mouth that said understanding, sympathy. Determination to do more than hear.

Then a more violent surge of backs sent her leaping out the door, to stumble on courtyard paving stones with a white-painted iron plant stand conveniently under her hand and Jess saying, startled, "Dorian, what's wrong?"

86

Her heart was galloping again, her knees wanted to collapse. All the usual symptoms, she had time to fume. Before she got a better grip on the plant stand and managed, "Nothing, sorry, nothing. I missed the step, that's all. Caught my heel . . ."

And thank God there is a little step, she thought, half-hysterically as she forced herself into the Paragon's bar. Otherwise Jess would ask about it. Thank God for electric twilight and a jukebox and a few people without beards. And please God, let my hand stop shaking before I have to hold another glass.

Not that Jess wouldn't believe me, she thought, lying in bed, watching aircraft landing lights glide red and green across the curtains, but what could she do? Commiserate, and ask the same old questions, and worry? Realize, like me, that it's getting worse, or at any rate, more detailed, there wasn't just sound this time, there was smell. And more people, and . . .

And she couldn't help me, any more than anyone else.

They expected help, she thought, with an abrupt recall of those faces in the bar. That wasn't gossip. They were talking about danger, present, immediate, recounting an abuse, perhaps a crime. And they knew he wasn't an idle listener. Those voices had held more than grievance aired.

They had known he was a partisan. They were sure there was something he could do.

If only, she had thought before she realized, I could have heard what *he* said.

She did not expect word from Chris before midday. Perhaps, she decided, steeling herself, not till mid-afternoon. And just as well, she admitted, finishing client interviews, I can see Kylie Jefferson's face if I stopped halfway through her mother's will for a phone call about ghosts.

It was well past four o'clock when her cell phone lit up. She snatched it off the desk and punched the holoscreen. Took one look, and stopped with the words on her lips.

"What's wrong?"

"Kid . . . Dorian." He did not try to dissemble. Just shoved a hand through his hair and held her eyes. "Look . . . I'm sorry. I'm not going to make it tonight."

"I can see that. What's wrong?"

"Wrong?" He had the oddest look, she thought, with all her own alarm signals going off. Not anger, not shock. Rather as if he had, in the proverbial manner, been hit over the head.

"Did you see—did *you* have a, an episode?"

"What?" It took him a visible half-minute to track. "Oh, the, the ghost. No, not that."

Then it's something at Ben Morar, her brain said, her stomach churning a second behind. "Chris, what is it? Tell me, please."

Her own inflection made him blink. Then, for a moment, his face lightened. He almost reached the grateful, unnerving sketch of a smile.

"I'm sorry, kid. I can't . . . can't tell you yet." But, said the look, even your awareness helps. "I can't," he almost looked surprised. "I can't tell anybody yet. I just have to—mostly, I have to think."

Think? Dorian's brain yelled. You read drill-schemas and topography as fast as book-print, you drive like a rally-competitor and make work decisions at a glance, you don't even scan a menu twice, and you need time to think?

"It's not—well, no, it *is* serious." His face stiffened. "But it's not—something I can hand off to anybody. And it's—"

"Still confidential." Something, she thought, about this damn new mine. Her pulse jumped. Or about the model itself?

Don't say it's turned out wrong?

She opened her mouth and shut it again. No, said two years' acquaintance. If it were wrong, Chris would have known long before. He'd never have let it get this far.

And it won't help putting him through twenty questions to find out. If he wanted to tell you, if he could tell you, he would have. By now.

"Okay," she said to the look on his face. "I'll shut up and let you get on with it. I don't suppose you have any idea . . ."

"Tomorrow morning." He looked definitely bleak now. "By then, I'll have made up my mind. I'll have to make it up . . ." He cut himself off. Visibly traded thought-lines. "I'm sorry, kid, I keep saying that, I know. But it's true. How's things down there?"

She sighed and rolled her eyes. "I had another rotten—episode—right in the middle of meeting Jess. You remember me talking about her? We were down the Paragon. And I couldn't just hear. I could *smell* things as well."

He heard her out, his dour look deepening to a scowl. Once, she thought, he actually bit his lip. When she finished he said almost under his breath, "Blast it." And then, "If this'd just come at some other time . . ."

"Look, don't worry." Suddenly her own conscience kicked in: What are you doing, loading more on him when he's trying to deal with whatever, trouble, calamity, this is? And it must be a calamity, her stomach added, turning over. I've never seen Chris look like that.

"You've got," she refuged in banalities, "enough on your plate. Call me in the morning. Or the afternoon, or whenever. I can wait." She summoned another smile. "I'm used to waiting on gold-mines, after all."

The mild joke went completely wrong. His face twitched as if he had been hit. He went to say something and bit it off. Then in a taut, strange voice he said, "I'll sort it out." His fingers touched the holo-base. "Tomorrow. I'll call you. That's a promise, kid."

She had no time to touch the screen herself. The image had already gone.

Friday seemed more mundane and interminable than ever before. Dorian found herself growing almost irritable with Jason, whose weekend ebullience usually amused her. The hours crawled, ten, eleven, twelve. . . . She asked Jason to bring her lunch, not wanting, if Chris called, to have a conversation such as this promised to be in a lunch bar, or worse, the open street. But despite the food her concentration wobbled. Come on, she thought, staring at the cell phone past another file she had read twice without remembering a word. Come on, Chris, *call.*

One o'clock passed. Two o'clock. Sheer disappointment, then loss of hope, had almost reconciled Dorian to no word that day. When the screen lit up, for a moment all she could do was stare.

"Dorian."

She had never heard, never seen Chris look or sound like that. She very nearly shrank in her chair.

"I'm late. I can't talk now. I'll see you—soon as I'm down." He was almost white. His nostrils seemed to have pinched, and his eyes made her flinch. More than anger, she thought, with a weird recall of the men in the bar. A calamity, yes, a cataclysm, and he's still caught in the aftermath. God, what's *happened* up there?

"Chris . . . ?"

She had not meant it to sound tentative. If not outright timid, she thought, and pulled a breath in hard. "Chris, what in God's name . . . ?"

His eyes focused. She winced. His lips folded tight.

"I should have thought," he said. "I was so wrapped up in the

90

model, and the field, and the hoopla, I never . . . bloody *fool.*"
His nostril rims did go white. "I should have known. Pan-
Auric . . ."

"What is it? What have they done?"

"Done? It's what the bastards are *going* to do. They—shit. I
can't talk about this on the phone." The glare concentrated,
whiter than his face. "Look, I'll be there soon as I can, I've just
got some things to fix. And, Dorian—stay in the office, will you?
I'll find you there. I need professional advice." He read her
expression. "On confidentiality, and defamation laws." His lips
pinched. "And yeah. If you know one, line me up a good
environmental lawyer."

Dorian shut off Save File and sat a moment, the inert phone in
hand. Her breath was short. Her hand, she noticed, had a
tendency to shake. Her mind was running and chattering like a
cageful of frightened hens. What has Pan-Auric planned to do,
and what on earth, with a chill that made her teeth clench, has
Chris already done?

Had the row to end all rows with somebody, her mind
answered, half scared for him and half at him. Done the thing
he always said he'd never do. Blown his stack. Lost his cool and
his temper and had a proper set-to with his employers.

That would mean, logic cut through the emotional fuzz, the
brawl to end brawls with George. Or, she very nearly cringed,
with the Pan-Auric VP himself.

Dorian put a hand to her mouth and bit her knuckles hard.
Then with the speed of fright she started checking in her head
for references. Defamation, employee confidentiality, he said. Il-
legal demands, breach of employee contract? her own caution
added.

And who do I know, here in town, who's a *good* environmental
lawyer?

She checked the clock. Added the distance to Blackston to the distance from Ben Morar. The possible time Chris would need for—whatever he was doing. He drives like the Wild Hunt when he's in such a paddy, but it's past two-thirty now. No way he can be here before four-thirty. More likely, sometime after five.

She bit her lips and called Mrs. Urquhart. "Gloria, would you get some things for me?" She fished out her wallet. "Some biscuits, I think, and some good instant coffee." Otherwise I'll be silly with sugar-debt, when Chris does arrive. "And could you check, is there milk in the tea-room? Yes, I'll be working back. I have to meet," how weird, she thought, to be saying this about Chris, "a client."

Five o'clock crept round. The office wound down through its familiar departure routines and Dorian tried not to feel forsaken as well as tense atop the usual stay-back weariness. I can't be half-asleep when I talk to Chris. He's going to need me. From the way he talked, he's going to need the best help he can get.

At five-fifteen she made her first cup of coffee and opened another reference book. At five-thirty she looked at her cell phone, obdurately silent, and tension mutated to the first stirrings of exasperation. Come on, Chris, did whatever you were doing before you left take another whole hour?

At five-forty-five she picked the cell phone up and punched the short-code for Chris's number. And if he's on the road now, too bad.

The phone buzzed. Probably, she thought snappishly, he's stopped in at LTU to blow off steam with the geology guys. Come on, Chris, pick up.

The buzz stopped. The mechanical voice said, "This number is not answering. Please try again."

Dorian set the phone down hard and glared at it. At a time like this, she wanted to shout, you're not answering your phone?

When you *know* I'll be waiting, and worrying, and . . .

She kicked the chair back and stalked to the window, biting down obscenities. Good Catholic girl, she thought bitterly. I never could swear when I needed it. She hauled the vertical blinds back and glared out at the swelling brown slope of Fortress Hill. Come on, Chris, get here, for heaven's sake. Let's get this over with.

At six o'clock she tried Chris's number again. There was still no reply.

With elaborate care Dorian set the phone down and tried to find irritation, even anger, to damp the curl of something else in her gut. It's six o'clock, and he told me to wait for him. He wouldn't forget that, not for a whole stable of geology guys.

The phone rang. She snatched it up, prayers and curses jostling in her mouth. "Damn it, Chris!"

"Miss Wild? Miss Dorian Wild?"

It was a complete stranger. A man in his thirties, perhaps, dark eyes, short-cropped hair. An indefinable air of authority, and an extra toughness that said, before he spoke again: Someone who's seen a lot, and not much of it good. Security. Police.

Working to keep her voice steady, she said, "Yes?"

"Could you tell me exactly where you are right now?"

"I'm in my office. Lewis and Cotton, eighth floor, the Perpetual Insurance building. That's in . . ."

"Leichhardt Street, yes. I'm Police Sergeant Gifford. We'd like to speak to you. Is the building closed?"

"There's a caretaker. You can ring at the door." Her heart was suddenly jumping under the top of her lungs, she was almost dizzy with bewilderment. And apprehension, chilling to an ice of fear. "Sergeant, what is it? What do you . . ?"

"When we get there, Miss Wild. We won't take very long."

★ ★ ★ ★ ★

They took the longest five minutes in Dorian's life. By the time the knock came she was all but sick with tension, fidgeting round the office from wall to wall. At the sound she hurried to the doorway, fighting not to cry out, Tell me, just tell me, now!

There were two of them, the dark man and a woman, both in uniform. Somehow she managed not to burst out, What's happened, is it Chris or my family, and what is it? Has Chris done something really bad, punched out the Pan-Auric guy or something? Their faces seemed to swim across her vision, and she gripped the edge of the desk.

"Miss Wild," the sergeant said. He seemed to take a breath himself. "We have some bad news."

I know that, she wanted to yell. Just get it over with! Instead she made a sort of noise meaning, Go on. He seemed to understand.

"We found your number in the Most Frequently Dialed local directory."

Dorian's stare brought him up short. He seemed to read it as accusation. His voice hardened a fraction. "In cases like this, we have authority to open phone files. You were the closest person we could find."

Dorian's voice was stuck in her throat. Closest, she could not say, to who? To what?

He looked back into her eyes and braced himself. "I'm very sorry, Miss Wild. There's been a car accident. Your friend, Mr. Keogh, Mr. Christopher Keogh, has been killed."

CHAPTER V

Dorian never recalled the next fortnight except as a series of fragments: discrete splinters of time, carved in her memory like shards of glass.

The police in her office first, the look of anger, shame, pity, on the policewoman's face while the sergeant talked. The pity had been worst. Biting deeper than his voice, though the words carved deepest of all.

A single-car accident, he had said, witnessed by another driver. The car had veered off the road. Clean across the road and over the edge of a bad curve halfway down Blackston range.

Dorian knew the bend. She had driven it with Chris half-a-dozen times. The two memories always interwove, vistas of pale-seeding mountain grass, sparse twisted reddish bloodwood trunks, coastal plain blurred tawny green beyond the pass-heads as the road swept round. A blue chine of hills, serrated like dinosaur scales. Overlaid by the sergeant's words, the witness' emergency call, Traffic Accident Squad alert, ambulance, fire, tow trucks sent. Hours to reach and more hours to retrieve "the—car"—in retrospect she knew he had meant to say "wreckage." Confiscated by the TAS for mechanical examination. Effects retrieved to supply information such as next of kin.

Current explanation, driver error. Most likely, falling asleep.

A cell in her brain had roused at that and wanted to protest, Not today. But it no longer seemed to matter. No doubt she had stared mutely while he talked on. Identification, notification, next of kin, and would she like to call a friend . . . ?

He carefully did not tell her what had happened to Chris himself.

The next shard began on the phone. Laura's arm around her, as she took her private address book and punched in the number she had still not memorized: Chris's parents' house.

And the white stillness in his mother's pleasant, snub-nosed, half-familiar face, the numb look his father wore, the way he put his arm around her as they turned off the phone. The stab clear through shock and everything else that had said, Not for you. Chris is never going to be there like that for you. Ever again.

Her own unit then, Laura finding the bottle she used for Brandy Alexanders, pouring a half glass with some vague traditional belief that brandy was good for shock. Laura glancing sideways, as she sat numbly on the couch, strain in that profile deep as grief itself.

Because I didn't cry, Dorian could voiceover in retrospect. It was all happening two removes away. Crying didn't seem to be an option. What's the use of crying, when you've just lost half your world?

Logic and retrospect could fill the space that must have included a twenty-four-hour medical center, then an all-night pharmacy, where Laura filled a prescription for sleeping pills. Laura and Anne at the unit, arms around her at the kitchen bar. More white time before the airport next day, to meet Chris's parents and his younger sister. Laura and Anne standing with her as the Keoghs emerged into the glare of an Ibisville noon, the coats and sweaters from chilly Toowoomba over their arms. With the family resemblance to Chris in his mother's build, his father's unruly hair, the turn of his sister's head. The same numb, disbelieving, disconnected look on each face.

I did cry then, Dorian would remember. When we all went up to Chris's unit, and I opened the door, and it was still there, the clothes, the books, the football boots, all the pieces of a life. Left behind. Dropped. Like the bits of bomb casing, after the explosive's blown.

Her memory compressed that day too, with its interminable cups of tea and its grisly detail of calls to and from the police, the funeral directors, the church. Unlike Dorian, Chris had been an unrepentant lapsed Presbyterian. The fine print of haggling an unexpected funeral into the city Presbyterian church's schedule was too much. Escaping on his mother's heels from the living room where Chris's father struggled with the pastor's secretary, Dorian blundered into the bedroom, to find his mother, head bowed, standing by the bed. Smoothing and re-smoothing a fold of the patchwork quilt, face striped with tears.

They had both cried then, holding each other, the unhelpful comfort of mutual grief.

It had been better and worse next day, when her own mother flew in from Adelaide. That shard remained, her mother surfacing from the airport crowd, the suddenly alien tilt of her dark head, the unfamiliarly formal southern dress and matching coat, then the too familiar hug and the timbre of her voice saying, "Oh, baby, I'm so sorry." Melting her willy-nilly into another flow of tears.

And that jarring encounter with the Keoghs, the first meeting of partners' families, wary maneuvering that should have come at a differently stressful, happier time. The logistics that seemed to close in like a choking fog, food, beds, transport, notice of the funeral to the *Ibisville Courier,* calls to uncounted acquaintances, family, friends. Anne or Laura's image surfacing here and there, grateful moments of her own lost reality.

The next shards always came in a cluster, sharp and distinct as still-open cuts. Chris's funeral.

She had a clear snapshot of people entering the church, with its small freestanding spire and plain hexagonal building dwarfed by the close loom of Fortress Hill. The fluid patchwork of shadow around figures in tropical formal dress of long shorts and knee-high socks, or full-length trousers and short-sleeved shirts. The respectfully lowered heads, the squared black shine of the hearse in their midst. The expectant hush in the church, with its flutter of fans and undertoned voices, as she sat in the front row with her mother on one side and the Keoghs on the other, and tried to look steady-eyed at the cluster of red zinnias and white carnations on the coffin lid. Not to think so clearly, That's all I have left of Chris.

The service she almost lost. It was not her own ceremony, and it was worse than strange to hear some unknown clergyman fumble through what passed for a eulogy on someone he had never known. She recalled an earnest face, sandy hair, the practiced soberness of his voice. The resistant tension in Chris's father, who had wanted to fly Chris south, have the service "in his hometown, with people he knew." Then the other shard would replay, Chris's mother staring out to The Palms and saying, "Down there, it's all people we know. This is where he worked. Where he lived. His—Dorian, his friends, they're all up here." The inflection adding, with its extra twinge of grief: Dead or alive, this is where he belongs.

Far clearer were the moments at the end, after some of Chris's football mates bore the coffin out. And she had to face the well-wishers, as the hearse drove away.

Some were her friends, some Chris's, some more than friends. She retained a clear image of Vera, dabbing at her nose, her light fawn hair disordered by the breeze, managing a muffled, "So sorry," and a hug that said, Forget the tensions of the past. We've both lost him now. A succession of football cronies, weirdly formal in work or funeral clothes, a couple of Luis Torres geologists. Then Dani Lewis with Moira at her elbow, Moira sniffling, Dani exquisitely composed in a slate-gray suit, but with kindness flickering through the conventional words. Less unexpected, Jason and Sandy. And to her astonishment, Mrs. Urquhart as well.

Then a tall man in dress trousers but a blue shirt and tie that recalled graziers, long-limbed and rangy with grey-blonde hair and bones that belonged in a Marlborough ad, clutching both her hands and saying earnestly, "Miss Wild, Chris was a good man—and a very, very fine geologist. We, I, the company are very sad at this, this unexpected . . . He'll be missed. He'll be very badly missed."

He had tailed off while she stared up at him, wondering if he knew he looked like an Australian Gary Cooper consoling some cowboy's widow. Blessedly, the battle to suppress fresh tears stopped her saying baldly, Who are you? But her face must have spoken. He gave a sort of shuffle and ducked his head. "Sorry . . . I'm George Richards. Ben Morar. We, ah, the company felt, should send a suitable representative . . ."

He tailed off again, giving her a lost but subconsciously hopeful stare. Light burst on her. George. Moira's poor George. Bloody George Richards, forever whining about his yield-figures, trolling his company on the market for the biggest shark. Bringing in Pan-Auric. Putting Chris over the edge—the double meaning raised hysteria in her throat—with whatever they planned to do.

Whining to Moira to sort out his appeal, leaning on a woman the way his face has taught him to expect will work, the way he expects, right now, to lean on me. To find him words and make sense of his mumblings, and get him out of this tiny little trouble. Again.

Clearest of all she recalled gritting her teeth. Giving him a

blank, but with savage determination not a hostile, stare, mouth-
ing something suitable, and holding his eye, until she wondered
there was not blood on her lip where her teeth had set, when he
finally turned away.

After that came the "refreshments." In retrospect Dorian wished
furiously she had over-ridden the older generation and called it,
as she had a rebellious sense Chris would have wanted, a wake.
Catered by parish volunteers in the adjacent church hall, it was
another endless span of people pooling about her, moving
thankfully off to nurse cups of tea and dive back into the pond
of the everyday. While her mother and the Keoghs orbited
vaguely, and Chris's friends made valiant attempts not to leave
them alone.

Until the other stranger loomed at her, a fresh-faced youth
with a sun-bleached forelock and a scatter of peeling sunburn
on his cheeks, a short-sleeved shirt balancing between business
smart and "George's" grazier-in-town clothes, his expression
somewhere between hope and a kicked puppy's uncertainty.
"Miss, um, Wild? I, ah—I just wanted to say . . ."

She tried to summon politeness, if not her best shadow smile,
but her eyes must have demanded, Who are *you?* Because his
sentence wavered and the sunburn became a flush.

"I, ah, my name's Ralston. Tom Ralston. I, ah, worked with
Chris. At Ben Morar, you know?"

Her face must have said, Yes. He straightened and brought it
out in a sort of gabble. "He was really, really good at what he
did, you know. They're really gonna miss him up there. I dunno
why they—why he—" the flush deepened painfully. "Well,
anyhow . . . he did a lot for me. He—uh—" his eyes dropped as
he read that she already knew what Chris had done for him. "I
cocked up a lot when I first started, and he never blew his

fuses . . . I—just—I would have wanted to say, Thanks, you know."

She did know. He grabbed her hand and gave it a pump and backed away, as she finally fled into the kitchen to blow her nose and wipe off tears.

In the next shard the guests had ebbed away. Caterers were tidying up. Amid the tide-wrack of paper plates, dirty cups and emptied sandwich plates, Anne, Laura, the Keoghs and Dorian's mother clustered, the final link to a world that Dorian felt swimming away as well, leaving her stranded on a distant planet, quite alone.

She heard Anne and Laura arranging cars and destinations, and found a touch of gratitude. My friends. Where would I be, how could I have faced this, without them?

Anne slanted her a look, then began to talk of driving the Keoghs to Chris's unit. "You might like to rest?" It's one-thirty PM, Dorian realized. The aftermath of a funeral always takes so long.

She had an overwhelming need then to be alone, just to curl up on a mat like a sick dog and clutch at her grief. She tried to paste on an expression of attention and concern, but after one look her mother began in a smooth, familiar voice, "Anne, I might come with you, if there's room. Dorian, wouldn't you like to change?"

She had kept her face still against an almost frantic gratitude to them both. They know me well enough to know what I need now, and it isn't comfort, at least, not that sort of comfort. I just need a minute or two, a breathing space. Change clothes would do, yes.

She had said something about, Yes, back to my unit for a moment. Then she was walking in clear winter sunlight for the car.

With a sense of taking refuge she parked, hurried up the underground steps, along the corridor to her door. Turned the key, and stepped through. Into a room that was not her own.

She knew the ambiance though, instantly. The same low, dimpled cream ceiling and close-pressing Prussian blue walls, now with an ox-blood fascia rim, the old-fashioned furniture, dresser-cupboard, fussy corner table. Not the bedroom. The house's lounge—parlor, something amended—maybe its only communal room. The trappings of low-price gentility crowded the central table, with its starched white cloth, the little vase of flowers, the straight-backed, thin-legged chairs.

The cloth was littered with debris. Used cups and saucers, some old-fashioned willow pattern. Dirty plates. A sprinkling of glasses, crumbs and food scraps, but no cutlery. Not an ordinary meal. Something special, numbers of people, too many for the room to seat. Food droppings and boot marks, mud or gravel pats, her weirdly detailed vision told her, strewed the floor's matte-polished planks.

Not a party in the usual sense. Because it was broad day. And the host? Last guest? The room's only occupant was sitting across the table. Head in hands, elbows on the cloth, settled amid the domestic flotsam. Wholly, terribly still.

He was wearing another white shirt, and a waistcoat as well: dull dark satin over his shoulders, dark wool, maybe a minimal stripe, down his chest. Some kind of band round each upper sleeve. A gleam of cuff-link, silver or pewter, against a cedar-dark wing of beard. The matching coat hung on a chair. Good clothes, best clothes, she had time to think, more than a Sunday go-to-chapel suit. Before he lifted his head.

When thought came, it said, He looks like I feel. And then, in the beating stillness: I didn't know, if men cried, they got red noses too.

Then her muscles tensed instinctively as memory snapped,

He'll jump up, he'll throw something, watch out. But something held her there, immobile. An eerie curiosity, a fascination deeper than simple fear.

He did not jump up. Or throw anything. He just looked at her, with those eyes as red as her own, as if her presence had been expected. As if she were the last, predictable straw on a load that had long since broken any reaction's back.

The way I feel, she thought. As if the whole damn world could end, right here in front of me, and I just—wouldn't—care.

The moment stretched out, and out, and out. She wondered if time would ever move again.

Then, at last, those eyes focused. Now he was seeing her. Really seeing her. Taking in her own red nose and eyes, perhaps, a face she thought must look equally stripped. Working out what they meant.

Something changed, not in the face, but in the mind behind it. Understanding. More than understanding. For a moment, palpable as a touch and clear as writing, she knew he had not merely deciphered her grief but shared it. From his own abyss, raised a ghost of fellow sympathy.

She felt tears prick and almost pulled away. Now, she thought, it will break, the way it always does. But she still stood, held in mid-stride, her good black shoe planted over the first boards inside the doorway, feeling through her own dark suit the other room's different, baking heat. Watching him watching her.

Until, just perceptibly, the eyes widened. He drew a sip of breath. She saw him reach the decision, before his hand began to move.

His right hand, rising to his forehead, slower than a wind-drift, touching, falling. Reaching his chest. Moving, with the same deliberate, breath-held slowness, to his right shoulder. To his left.

He had crossed himself.

He thinks *I'm* a ghost. Or a demon or—God knows what he thinks. The momentary outrage snuffed. What *could* he think, with no idea of quantum physics, or any other explanation? No wonder he goes crazy when this happens. I would too.

But this time he had chosen, intended his response.

He was still staring, with what she thought must be the mate of her own painful intensity. Does he want me to answer? To do the same thing? Or is it . . .

Is it a test, to see if I disappear?

She was intensely aware of every detail, the starched cloth, the used cups, the harsh light through the window with its little frilled curtain rims. Like everything else, obsessively clean. As integral to this encounter as the man, sitting there in the dark formal waistcoat, the pristine shirt. Everything about him immaculate except the reddened eyes, the ravaged face. And that fixed, that not quite desperate but suddenly, desperately resolved stare.

He drew in his breath. He was looking straight in her eyes, he was going to speak to her, she had no doubt at all, and whatever the message she was frantically urgent to receive it. It would have some crucial significance for them both. His lips pursed to begin a word.

And he was gone.

Her own reaction was pure instinct. She rammed a heel in her careful beige carpet and cursed.

"Hellfire and blast!"

Come back, she wanted to bawl at him. Talk to me! Tell me what you wanted to say—tell me what you feel. It might be some help!

At least, to me.

Or tell me what happened to you—who you lost. Is it

something to do with why we keep—colliding—like this?

With why the collisions are coming faster? Getting longer. More detailed.

Her lungs seemed to congeal.

Is the fold in reality, or whatever it is, getting closer?

One day—is one of us going to come right through?

She stood staring at the James Brown on the living room wall, silent, accomplished, obdurately twenty-first century. Not dark, reddened eyes above a snowy shirt. . . . She whipped off her jacket and ran into the bedroom, a small furious part of her mind crying, I'll never wear this suit again, while the rest nailed her fiercely back into worse but different reality. I've already got more here than I can handle. Let me alone! Don't come back!

He didn't, thought coalesced, as the next shard opened out of a night's blank. He didn't come back. And this is . . . the second morning after—the funeral.

With the Keoghs gone. Mum gone. I'm here with an empty unit—two empty units—and the busyness over. The present closing in.

And with it, the inner bruise of grief.

Chris is gone. Gone for good. I'll never see, touch, hear him again. Somehow, the thought of that voice silenced, lost, was almost the worst of all. Not simply the nicknames and jokes and laughter, but the timbre, the turn of idiom and flex of language that was Chris, deeper than touch or vision, Chris and nobody else . . .

She shut her thoughts off and got deliberately out of bed. Showered. Told herself she would give the black suit to Lifeline that very morning. Lectured herself, I'm lucky. I don't have to work today. While the rest of her mind retorted with equal bleakness, But you have to go on. Whether you want to or not. Find something to fill the hole Chris left. There's the rest of a life to deal with. To get used to it.

To find out you'll never get used to it.

Enough, she told it. I'm still here. And if I'm here, I suppose I have to eat.

As she pulled the fridge door back the thought came unbidden. Who did—he—lose? That disturbing moment of personal connection returned. She had never doubted it was a funeral, a close loss, bad as her own. What's he doing now, her mind persisted, in that other reality?

And then with ghoul's amusement, At least I didn't have to clean up my own funeral meats.

A southerly wind skirled into the balcony. She leant over the uncustomarily washed dishes, while the brilliant air urged, Go out. It's winter in Ibisville, the best time to gallivant.

Go somewhere like a tourist, with Chris . . . without Chris?

You could, her conscientious half replied, do what the Keoghs asked: clear out Chris's flat.

"You'll know what it all is, far better than us," his mother had said, an arm round Dorian, blinking away tears. "Never mind the will. If there's anything you want, you take it, now. And Dorian, for one thing," the tears had begun to run, "I'd like—I want you to have the quilt."

So they had leant together a moment and cried again for what the quilt had stood for. For what they had both lost.

No, Dorian thought, with no doubt at all. Not yet. I can't bear to do that yet.

No files sat on the dining table. Her laptop was closed and dark in the corner. Today, I don't even have a backlog to attack.

Faintly, another thought impinged. She pushed it away. It came back.

If I don't want to—do Chris's things—I could at least—think about—this other thing.

Because Chris is gone, she told herself flatly. He's not going to help anymore. Not look through the archives, not dig up quantum physicists, not come up with odd-ball scientific angles and make you curse and complain and . . . from here on in, whatever happens, you have to deal with it by yourself.

And more will happen. You already know that.

If I looked at the archives I might, just might, find a photograph.

A funeral notice? A name?

Except, her wits finally cut in, it's Friday. The archive's closed. Again.

She stood a long moment gazing at the James Brown, seeing bush colors out over the Blackston range front. Then she squared her shoulders and picked up the phone.

"Jeanelle?" she said, when the Lewis and Cotton receptionist answered. "This is Dorian. Would you tell the partners? For today, I think—I need—to come back to work."

Next Tuesday the Traffic Accident Squad telephoned her.

"Ms. Wild? This is Sergeant Gifford. Traffic Accidents. We handled Mr. Keogh's incident, if you recall." The subtext said that very often, those he dealt with had not. "As his next of kin representative, you can legally receive the TAS report. There'll be a hard-copy, but I can e-mail it to you in advance. Or," the official voice thawed a fraction, "you can receive it in person. In case you have any further questions to ask."

Dorian held the phone in her hand and looked out the vertical blinds into another pure winter sky. Steadying her voice before she said, "Thank you. I'd prefer to have it—in person. Just in case."

The report came on official paper with a Queensland Government badge and imposing headings, mostly shucked by Dorian's unimpressed memory. Time of notification, exact site of accident, proceedings of officers on site. File numbers of archived photographs. Description of vehicle. Description—her mind jumped that part—of proceedings to free the deceased. Paramedics', and later fully qualified medical report.

The part she would remember perfectly was the Vehicle Inspections report.

Dorian read that twice. Before she lifted her eyes to Gifford, seated correctly upright in the client's chair, and said, "But . . ."

He looked as sealed-in—as cauterized, she annotated dourly—as ever. He did sound a little gentler as he said, "Yes, Ms. Wild?"

"It says here . . . vehicle defect. It says," she had to swallow, to beat back images of what the words actually meant, "steering fault."

He inclined his head a millimeter. "Yes, Ms. Wild. Our mechanics are very careful." The subtext added, though not belligerently, They have to be. "A nut was lost from the steering apparatus. As the report says, we consider it must have been left loose, and gradually worked its way up until an extra stress—or just routine movements—pulled it off."

Dorian shut her eyes a second. And opened them as he said, quite gently, "So it wasn't driver error, after all."

He thinks, someone said back behind reality, I should be grateful for that.

"But," she said, sitting up straighter, tears forgotten now. "But."

"Lack of maintenance, yes."

Dorian waited a moment to collect herself. Then she said, "No."

He stared.

"Chris might drive too fast, or make a mistake . . . especially that day. But he wouldn't have gone to sleep. And he would *never* have let the maintenance lapse. He had a good mechanic—I take my car to him. And Chris was a geologist. That car was his livelihood. It had to go over bush roads and off roads, and—he was *fussy* about that car. He'd have checked."

There was a very long pause, while he stared at her with his opaque police eyes. Then he said, flatly now, "Mr. Keogh's employer has said that he left—very upset."

You can't have it both ways, she wanted to retort. Either he let the maintenance lapse or he made a driving mistake. She did say, as politely as possible, "That wouldn't affect the maintenance."

A tiny line came between his brows. "The company says— Mr. Keogh had been asked to terminate."

Dorian felt her mouth open as if he had hit her in the wind. It was a good thirty seconds before she could say, "You mean— he'd been sacked?"

"Do you have any evidence otherwise?"

Pure police now, coming back at her like a hammer on a faulted rock.

"But—"

Her head reeled as the memories re-ran. That last phone call. Chris said, What they're going to do, he said, Get me a lawyer—I thought he was going to fight the project, he thought Ben Morar or Pan-Auric might try to silence him, I never *dreamed* he would walk right out—

Let alone get sacked. Chris? Never! Especially not then, the model, he said they were mad to keep it, George praised him to the skies . . .

But after the blow-up they must have had?

Her pulse hammered. Suddenly she heard Ralston at the funeral, a sentence fragment that had seemed mere irrelevance. *I dunno why they—why he—*

I don't know why they sacked him?

I don't know why he left?

Her fingers made dents in the crisp government paper. She

gritted her teeth. Something must have happened, he must have left for good, but one half-sentence isn't proof, even if it wasn't totally ambiguous. No. I can't say, one way or the other, if he jumped, or if they pushed.

But I bet it was George who told you he was sacked. Coming on to me at the funeral about how sad they were, how he'd be missed . . . Gifford's face swam behind a momentary red mist. The bloody hypocrite!

Gifford was watching her in earnest this time. When she met his eyes again, he said, very deliberately, "Ms. Wild, do you want to pursue this?"

His stare added, Is there something concrete that you know? Or are you just partisan, denying anything could be Chris's fault?

Her own professional reflexes cut in. I have no evidence against a steering fault but my own knowledge of Chris. And all too certain knowledge that he *might* have made a driving error, that day, and done the final damage himself. And I know he was upset—upset! But I don't definitely, fully, know why.

Yet.

The surge of heat, anger, rage boiled up like magma but without its lack of control. All the grief and loss compacting into fury that was not merely a phase of bereavement but determination. An impulse with a target. A purpose, a point.

She heard herself say coolly, "No, Sergeant. I don't have enough evidence to pursue it. But I will say, for your or any other record, that faulty maintenance on that vehicle was very unlikely indeed. Chris's mechanic will corroborate that."

Letting her own eyes add: I'll let this pass for now. But don't consider the case closed.

He gave her another of those piercing police stares. Then he inclined his head, a nice blend of courtesy, respect, and acknowledgment of an unfinished bout from another duelist, and showed himself out.

Dorian sat where he left her, hands clenched on the desk, teeth clenched in her mouth, jaw clenched above her throat. The office wavered round her, but not this time through tears. This time it was as if she swam through water tinged with blood.

Just as her vision began to clear a phone rang. A moment later Mrs. Urquhart rounded her partition, asking with her hushed version of sympathy, "Ohhh, Dorian? The, ah, police just called. They're asking," with lower if greater intensity, "if you'd take delivery. Of, ah, Mr. Keogh's effects."

They must mean, Dorian realized, the things from Chris's car.

An hour ago, the mere thought would have brought her back to dissolution. But when she looked up, Mrs. Urquhart very nearly recoiled, though she thought she had sounded almost normal, if a little cool, as she answered, "Yes. Tell them I'll pick them up tonight. Get me the address."

Amassed, they came to one anonymous cardboard carton. A pair of work boots, Chris's car anorak, a couple of old shirts, two pairs of revolting socks. Sunscreen tubes, a water bottle, Chris's bush hat. The usual contents of a glovebox and steering well, road maps, a torch, loose change, his sunglasses' case. His cell phone, scratched and dented in a way she refused to think about.

And Chris's briefcase, capacious and ubiquitous, with its battered brown leather and its old-fashioned buckled straps. Jammed to the limit with papers and disks that it had somehow brought almost undamaged through the wreck.

Dorian unloaded it all on her dining table. Yesterday night, she thought in wonder, I'd already be in tears. But tears had burnt away. She surveyed the mass with more than a lawyer's eye. Lawyers, she thought, don't assemble briefs with this sort of cool, implacable, almost terrifying determination. This personal, deep-kindled intent, like a burning glass. This kind of rage.

The briefcase held maps too, maps whose layout she recognized at once. Geological maps, with drill-sites marked, topographical features, nothing the layperson would expect, like town names and roads. A couple were very new. Others went back to some tattered specimens with "Donald South—'01" written in Chris's distinctive pointed hand. The newest ones had only dates: 5/12, 6/12, then, 23/7/12. Very fresh and clean, with drill-sites and topographical details in color as well.

She stood staring, thinking, This must be the presentation map. This is what he showed Pan-Auric. This is the picture of the new mine.

And I can't read the thing.

There were hard-copies of other findings underneath: Donald South, Quandong, records from earlier work at Ben Morar. They had been jammed into a folder as if they mattered less than old Christmas cards. Not by the accident, she realized. Chris did this himself.

The hard-copy of the new mine presentation was not there.

Behind the papers were ranks and more ranks of CDs. Dorian leafed through the holders: Quandong Assay Reports, '02–'12. Survey reports of unfamiliar sites. CD after CD of "Core-logs, Ben Morar." A solitary CD labeled, "CK—Personnel Files," that made her lip twitch on the edge of tears. Trust Chris, she thought, to pack every core-log for the last fifteen years and shove his personal stuff on a single disk.

But none of the labels said, "New Mine Survey Reports," or, "New Mine Drill Reports," far less, "New Mine Presentation."

Dorian set the last pile aside and stared over the glistening heaps. He put this together in a hurry, she thought. More than a hurry, in that state he was in when he called me. Not just agitation, extreme stress. He grabbed whatever mattered in that office and he packed the lot. Whether they kicked or he jumped, he was getting out of there. For good.

So damn it, Chris, where'd you put the new mine reports? And the stats model itself?

A slow curl of ice crept upward under her breastbone. If they're not here . . . why aren't they here? Chris would never have forgotten those.

Did he put them in—and somebody take them out?

No, her wits said after a while. Not the police. They'd never do that, if they did know what they were.

Somebody at the accident site?

No, sense discarded in a minute or two. The guy who—saw it—wasn't involved. He stayed there, though, till somebody came. Nobody could have got at the—wreck—before the police arrived.

She felt her breath hiss through her teeth. Did he stash the things up at Ben Morar, for some crazy reason? Wilder thoughts catapulted through her head, Did he leave under duress, did somebody take them from him, wilder thought, at gunpoint or something, and *make* him leave?

She thought again of Chris, the sum of Chris that she had known, and her breath went out on a wild little laugh. If anyone tried that there would have been blood from here to Ben Morar, and they'd have had to shoot him at the last.

Besides . . . if anyone tried to rob him, he would have told me, on the phone.

Wouldn't he?

She turned half-blindly and picked up the briefcase, shoving her hand deep into the back compartment, and a hard thin edge impacted her fingertips.

A separate pocket in the back lining held a single CD. As Dorian held it up letters glittered in the lamplight, Chris's pointed printing, a single word.

"Palantir."

"Seeing-stone." Anne for once burst out laughing. "The smartass! It's for seeing stone!"

"What?" Laura asked blankly, and Dorian stared at her laptop while Anne, still smiling, answered, "It's in *The Lord of the Rings*. The Palantir, the crystal ball. Seeing stone. He meant it for the stats model. Seeing-stone."

"At least," she amended, turning back to the screen, "it did for Chris."

"I can read the title," Dorian agreed, trying to pry open her teeth. "It's the model, sure enough. It's got Chris's name and the intellectual property claiming clause. I can open it. As for what it does . . . when it comes to all these formulae, I don't understand a thing."

"But the results are there, aren't they?"

"In the other file. Well. The presentation's there. The stats analysis results. The 3-D model, and the PowerPoint slides. Geology, topography, estimates. Time and cost for development, estimated first-year yield."

"So we've got it all, haven't we? We know . . ."

Laura's voice trailed away. Dorian could feel the stare on her profile, surprised, wary, sliding toward nervous as she kept staring at the screen. As she said, trying to hold the monotone. "Every damn thing. Except *I can't tell where it* IS!"

"Steady." Anne came to her shoulder as Laura recoiled. "Surely it says . . ."

"It says in geological terms. X km south of the so-and-so fault, Y km away from the such-and-such plate, Z km up from whatever-it-is of so-and-so schist—or quartz or granite or some other geological gobbledygook." Even to herself the words sounded weird in her tamped-down, almost muted voice. "So far as I'm concerned, it might as well be double-Dutch."

There was a daunted pause.

"Well," said Laura at last, "Ben Morar—George—somebody has to know."

Dorian did not have to swing round. Anne's look must have said for her, Are you crazy? Ask *them* where it is?

"If not them, then the geology guys. At LTU. They could read this stuff!"

After a moment Anne said, "Yes. I suppose they could."

There was another too long pause. When she still did not look round, Anne said, "What are you thinking, Dorian?"

Trust Anne, was what she had thought, to pick up the under-text. She turned about from the computer and said, "I'm thinking . . . the—Palantir CD—was stashed. And the hard-copy of the presentation isn't here."

She could not go on, for all the rage. It was Anne whose eyes narrowed. Anne who said presently, "You think Ben Morar—or Pan-Auric—had something to do with that."

Dorian met her eyes. "Maybe. I do know . . . George lied to the police."

Laura's mouth slid open. "You think they did something. Made some sort of claim. Some sort of threat—"

"I don't know," Dorian said. "Yet."

For some reason, she remembered, Laura shivered. Then, recovering, conceded, "So, we don't tell anybody else. In case they have spies everywhere," the joke did not quite come off, "even at LTU. After all, we don't *have* to know where the field is right now."

"Not yet," Dorian said evenly, and Laura shivered again.

"I wish," Anne was frowning harder, "Chris had told you what they planned. He meant to make accusations, apparently, and bring some sort of environmental suit. But if we can't read the model, and can't find the site, and can't ask for help . . ."

Dorian bit words behind her teeth: *He would have told me.* And, *He meant to do it himself.* They were both far too obvious.

"The first thing I'm going to do," she said, "is find out what happened that day. If they sacked him—or if he pulled the pin."

Anne's eyes turned thoughtfully. After a moment she said, "And just how will you do that, short of phoning Ben Morar direct?"

Dorian grinned at her. She rarely grinned. It was that, she supposed, which almost made Anne jump. "Moira," she said, "*she* can ask 'poor George.' About Chris, *and* the appeal."

Anne did jump then. It was Laura who said, "God, Dor, you're getting ruthless," in a tone that held as much shock as respect.

They clattered out on their way to work. Dorian walked back into her living room, eyeing the recalcitrantly enigmatic data she could not read, feeling the rage rise like heat turned up in a furnace, only growing at the check. Things don't match, not what George let me think and what he told the police, not the accident report, not this presentation lost. Something's there to find, and I will find it. I'll find out what happened to you, Chris. Whatever I have to do.

It was almost expected, when she looked up past the table to a wall no longer there.

He had a knife in one hand and a half-peeled potato in the other. It must be the kitchen, she thought, before the reek of frying mutton and the wave of raw onion atop it choked the gasp in her throat. The heat they rode on was a mere after-thought, a wood stove's blast on a tropical summer day, though the slash of gold light behind him could have been morning or afternoon. She had one glimpse of old-fashioned cooking imple-ments, hollowed wooden chopping board, a hand-held egg-beater hung from a shelf. A voice called somewhere beyond the room's far side. He called in reply, too brief and blurred to decipher. Before he swung about and they stood face to face.

With just my table between us, she realized, and her lungs emptied. Air, smells, light undifferentiated. His kitchen and my living room telescoped.

This time his sleeves were rolled shoulder high, and the shirt collar gaped. The cowlick hung limp. He had been rubbing an eyebrow and something was caught in it, perhaps flour. And there was a long apron tied incongruously round that narrow male waist.

He had frozen too. Mutely, they stared, while the cooking mutton sizzled and spat and somebody outside banged what sounded like an axe lustily into wood.

As her eyes adjusted to the murky light she realized his grief had also aged: there was a look of chronic tiredness under the distraction, but this time he was composed. Already reacting to her presence. Eyes focusing, then moving, as hers had. Taking in her surroundings, she realized, making what he could of them, before he looked back to her.

Then with the faintest, ironic twist of a mouth corner, he half-lifted the knife.

A salute, she understood, even as her own nerves twitched to duck.

She took a sharp little breath that stabbed her ribs like a real blade, and lifted a hand back.

I'd never have done that, she remembered thinking, a week ago. But now—who cares?

His eyes went wide. She saw him swallow, and his lips parted. Then he put the potato down behind him without looking where. The knife went after it. He visibly braced himself.

She looked at the width of table between them. Her heart was suddenly jumping as fast as the pulse she could see in the hollow of his throat. Deliberately, she took the first sideways step.

His chest rose to an equally sharp breath. He took his own step. Forward, toward the realities' verge.

Something banged fiercely on the wall behind him. A young male voice bawled, "Jesus Mary'n Joseph, man, what're ye doin' in there! The stew's caught fire!"

When her knees stopped quaking, Dorian thought, I can't believe I did that. "Jesus, Mary and Joseph"—she could hear the brogue in it, heavy as bog-peat—what was I thinking of? If I'd kept going—if *he'd* kept going—if the, the episode had lasted. If we'd actually touched . . .

Her tongue dried. Ice crawled down her back. Would we have exploded or something? Would the whole universe have blown up?

You touched before, memory reminded her. He put that dish, that rotten dish, right on your head. Not by intent, instinct retorted, as her breathing sped up. Not when we could both see, when we knew each other. Not when we intended it.

She whirled away from the wall. Back to business, you absolute idiot, and try not to do anything that stupid again. Call Moira, get this next part on the road.

She snatched the cell phone up. Only in her hand did the different heft and shape and texture tell her she had taken Chris's instead of her own.

For an instant sheer reflex made her want to fling it like a toad. Then conflicting reflex broke through: It's Chris's. It's something left of him.

So let's see if it still works. She tried to sound airy, but the other reflex had already clenched her hand. She bit her lip and punched On.

The phone beeped at her with instant machine agitation. She

had time to think, It's not broken. It's still live. Then the holo-screen was flashing, over and over, Message not sent. Message not sent.

Message to whom? About what? With an eerie sense of turn-ing time back, of séances, of a dead man's hand in hers, she punched, *Replay*.

The screen filled with motion against one solid shape. With an exquisite pang she recognized Chris's cheekbone and a beard-corner. And beyond, a flying grey-green blur of trees and bush.

"Dorian," he said.

Her spine crept. Without knowing she sat down on the near-est chair and braced the phone on the table, eyes glued to its screen.

"Precious." The pause had set her teeth on edge. So did the note. Icily calm, as she had never heard Chris before. As she knew, beyond doubt, he had responded to professional crises in the mine.

"The cell phone's jamming for some reason. I'm saving this now. I'll send it soon as the phone clears. Make sure you keep it, will you?"

The extremity of emotion in the last call he had made her was gone. He sounded remote, but not at all relaxed. Strung like a fighter-pilot going into battle, distant. Inhumanly cool.

"Because I'll need this as a record, later on."

The blurry trees swooped and swept up again. The whole picture jerked and there was a distant rattle and bang. A creek, she deciphered. Chris braking, changing gear.

"I've left Ben Morar. Told them to stick their job. Cleared my office. Or tried to. Pan-Auric . . ." the cool tone burred for an instant. "Pan-Auric are turning out bigger shits than I thought. Reinschildt's goon—the bodyguard, big bastard with an Army fuzz and a redneck U.S. accent—did a standover job. Said the presentation was Pan-Auric property. I told him to suck himself. He pulled a gun on me."

The landscape ducked and lifted once more, then swirled sideways as if a plane had banked. Dorian cringed and tried not to shut her eyes. It's a miracle, she thought, you got as far as the range.

"So," Chris said, too evenly, "I gave him the hard-copy. He said he wanted the disks as well. I said, 'What disks?' He said, 'The disk copy of this. And the disk for that pretty maths thing you did it with.' I said, 'That's my intellectual property.' He grinned at me and patted the gun and said, 'This is mine.' "

Dorian's fist clenched. She felt the burn of fury behind her own eyes.

In a moment Chris's voice resumed, with a lethal little drawl. "So I threw a couple of disks at him and said, 'Fuck you, you sod.' And looked at the laptop. And he said, 'Sure, boy.' And he put that under his arm and said, 'Now turn out that case of yours.' "

The laptop, Dorian nearly cried aloud. I should have realized, I should have remembered it isn't here. When you've never gone anywhere without it since I've known you . . .

"This goon," Chris enunciated every word, "made me unpack my briefcase. Then he went through my papers and my professional records. He even wanted to take the disk of the bloody computer game. Palantir. *The Lord of the Rings* thing, you know?" Dorian felt her eyes pop. "I told him he should try to play it, any time he thought he'd built up an IQ." Her eyes squeezed shut instead. Oh, Chris! Why didn't you just hire a sword and train for matador? "He threw it on the floor and said, 'Another pansy Brit game, huh?' Then he walked off. So I packed that with the rest and got the hell out of there."

The car's engine revved, the picture wobbled again. Dorian winced at the too familiar sound of Chris's racing change. Palantir, she thought dizzily, he thinks someone could be eavesdropping, he's started to talk in code.

"When I get down," Chris said, "I'll tell you the full story. And you can see the whole thing. Christopher's Fault. The Solitaire Two presentation. I'll show you in the seeing-stone."

Dorian's stomach curdled. God help us, if anybody in Pan-Auric's a Tolkien fan.

"Then I'll call the TV news and that guy you know on the *Ibisville Courier,* and the chairman of the Green Party in Ibisville, and I'll tell Queensland—Australia—what Pan-Auric's planned for this mine. Make sure you turn up that environmental lawyer. And start getting together a suit for menace or harassment or whatever you want to call it as well."

The landscape vanished. So did Chris's beard. Half a hand nearly blotted the holoscreen. Chris's voice said, "Take care, kid."

Then the holo disappeared.

Dorian sat staring with the phone in her hand. Her jaw had clenched solid but her belly muscles were shaking and her eyes were torn between rage and tears. That was Chris, her mind said. That was Chris, leaving me a message. A coded message, and a witness record. So they'd know there *was* a record, if they were listening. Or—no, the phone wasn't sending. In case they got hold of it. . . . Her mind jumped what that meant. But so they'd know other people had been told. And that the model, and the presentation—that's what it has to be, whatever he means by Solitaire Two—were safe somewhere. He got them away after all. The tears rose and trembled in a mix of loss and vicious joy. So they'd know they hadn't beaten him, and they'd know what else he was going to do.

That call wasn't just anger. Or even a simple record. That was a declaration of war.

CHAPTER VI

"So will you call Gifford?" Anne said.

They were in Laura's office. Anne and Laura were both too quiet and a little wide-eyed, and Dorian thought they shared the weakness in her knees.

I was going to call him, she thought, yes. Call straight away, play the message, hector him: Now, who do you believe? And then I thought again. And nearly dropped the phone like a ticking bomb.

Because it's the only evidence. That George lied, that Chris wasn't sacked. That Pan-Auric wanted that presentation at any cost, and they were prepared to steal the model as well.

And maybe, they were actually prepared to get rid of—anyone trying to blow the whistle on whatever they're doing.

Then I thought, Have they checked the laptop yet?

And told myself, of course they have, they probably did that the minute the goon brought it in. And there probably was a copy, Chris wouldn't have all his eggs on one disk. He might wipe his office computer. He wouldn't wipe the laptop as well.

So maybe, till now, they thought they'd got it all.

What will they do, the minute they find they haven't?

"Did you make copies?" Laura asked.

Dorian nodded. Of course I did, I nearly broke an ankle getting to the spare room for CDs. Copy the model, copy the presentation, download the message, not take it off because Gifford or somebody has to see it in situ, but not risk a single copy either. Once Pan-Auric get the alert they won't sit up and put out their wrists to be slapped.

They'll come after it, her brain clicked again, as frantically as it had while the laptop booted with excruciating slowness and her hands trembled on the Palantir disk. They won't waste time arguing or claiming innocence or even taking it to court. They'll come after it, like they did with Chris.

"I put one in the bank," she answered Laura, trying not to glance at the door. "And one in the L&C safe. And I thought, I might put one in, um, each of our files." Not all the eggs in one basket. I'm taking care, Chris.

Laura nodded immediately. Anne followed. Then, "Gifford?" she prodded. "It's new evidence. It could change their findings. Materially."

Laura pulled a face and pre-empted Dorian. "Tell Gifford and he'll go straight back to Ben Morar. Brace Pan-Auric. Or at least, brace George. Hey, we have this message says your geologist wasn't sacked. He walked. What'll George say?"

Anne stared. Dourly, Laura stared back.

"First thing—*only* thing George can do is lie again. Gifford already doubted Dor on the car maintenance. If we don't have anything but a tug of words. . . . They'll toss it, they don't have time for wild goose chases, any more than us."

After a moment Anne produced her own minimal grimace.

"It is still only hearsay against hearsay. With the weight of—belief—on Ben Morar's side. And Dorian's an interested witness."

Dorian did not need her to finish: and we're still withholding evidence, when every reflex says we should pass it on.

Every reflex, another reflex retorted, except the one that says, Pan-Auric isn't playing by the rules. So if we do, we'll lose.

"We have to wait," Laura insisted. "At least till we get

something from Moira—Dor, are you going to tell *her* about this?"

"No," Dorian said at last. "Not yet. Moira'd be upset. And odds-on she'd say something to George, and then—I'll just ask her," she heard the steel come into her voice, "as senior partner, and the case initiator, and because we only have one phone call left, on Dani's terms—to contact George. About the appeal. And I'll tell her we've heard . . . that Chris was sacked."

Both the others' eyes narrowed. Laura nodded, hers beginning to glitter. "It'll be . . . useful . . . to see what George says."

Anne eyed Dorian meditatively. Then she said, "Will you mention the takeover?"

"No." This time Dorian had no need to consider. "That was confidential. I shouldn't technically have known at all." Laura rolled her eyes. "Besides, it'll be instructive, to see what George says about *that.*"

Laura growled. Anne's fingers slid on the desk. And stopped.

"If you shake George's tree," she said, "you know, you're shaking Pan-Auric's too."

Dorian said, "I know."

Again, mysteriously, she felt Laura nearly flinch. But Anne's frown deepened and her fingers went flat.

"It's George," Dorian said. "Whether Pan-Auric told him what to say or not, he knows where *he* told the story. So he'll have to think the cops passed it on. Legitimately or otherwise."

"If that's the only place he told it," Anne said.

Laura sat up, beginning to glare. "That's defamation, if he spread that about Chris—!"

"We have no proof it is." Anne was still watching Dorian. "Except the message."

"*Somebody* else must know! The people at Ben Morar, the, what's his name, the other geologist—!"

"Maybe." Anne had not looked away from Dorian.

"Maybe no one else does know," Dorian said. "But I bet George hasn't spread it, either. I bet he only did it as a last resort, with the cops. He'd know it's too risky to put around in general. In case Chris did tell someone else."

Anne looked unconvinced.

"It's George," Dorian said. "Whether he's in with P-A or making his own decisions, he won't tell them about it coming home to roost. Not George. Not 'yeeettt.' "

She whined the last word, parodying procrastination, with the savagery of her own feelings burning through. Not George, she thought, he won't own up or pass it on until he has to. He'll sit there and hope it goes away, until it blows up in his face.

Anne's face answered, Too many unknowns. Too many variables. We should let this alone. Dorian felt the anger heat in her again. I'm going to do it, hung on her tongue. Whatever the cost. Or the risk. For Chris's sake.

Anne eyed her for a minute. Then she said, "Let's see what George says."

You'll push this, Dorian ciphered from the tone, whatever I do. So we'll risk your guess on his procrastination. But whatever the result, after this gambit, we'll be thinking again.

Moira's busy, Dorian told herself, as Wednesday dragged to its end. You can't expect her to drop everything else to pick up your ball. Even if you handed it on with all sorts of dulcet excuses about possible conflict of interest, and you don't think you can handle this case after Chris. And careful use of your own feelings, not that it needed much, with poor Moira already almost in her own tears. Just be patient. Remember, Pan-Auric doesn't have that message. Nothing more will happen, until your own pawn moves.

It was almost eleven o'clock Thursday when the phone pinged and Mrs. Urquhart said with her usual breath-holding deference, "Ohhh, Dorian, I have Ms. Cotton on the line, she'd like a word with you."

Dorian ground down her usual impulse to retort, Ohhh, Mrs. Urquhart, would you just tell her I'm drunk on the office floor? "Put Moira through, please," she said.

"Oh, hello, Dorian." Moira sounded her usual slightly flustered self. "The Ben Morar thing, I've just phoned them. They say George isn't available."

Dorian stared blankly at the rogue frangipani in the Rigby print. He has to be! her mind shouted. He knows you, you're his lawyer, his senior lawyer, he'd talk to you. He can't have gone anywhere, with Pan-Auric in the throes of a takeover. He has to be there!

"I—ah—I'm sorry, Moira. Did Tanya—did his secretary say where—when . . . ?"

"Tanya?" Moira sounded more flustered. "This was a man. An American. I did ask when George would be in again. I even asked where he was." A hint of distress at such rudeness. "He just kept saying, I'm sorry. Mr. Richards is not available right now."

"And he wouldn't give you an estimated time, a schedule?"

"It's ridiculous, yes. He's the manager, they have to know where he is and what he's doing! And why on earth he'd hire an American . . . !"

He didn't, Dorian thought with abrupt, icy certainty. Pan-Auric did. Maybe they've gone ahead with the takeover, maybe they've already purged the office staff. Maybe they've purged George as well.

Or got rid of him, too.

You are being absolutely insane, she told herself, clenching her hand on the never-used blotter. This is Australia in twenty-twelve, not some back-of-beyond U.S. mining town in the nineteenth century. People don't do things like that! There isn't any need!

No, her memory answered implacably. There wasn't any need to pull a gun and try to rob Chris either. But they did.

"Dorian, I'm sorry, are you there? I said, I didn't ask him about the rumor, either. That your, ah, that they sacked Mr. Keogh. . . . After all, it's none of his affair."

Dorian yanked her wits together. "No," she said hurriedly. "No, thank you, Moira, I can't imagine what some—American— would know about that and I'd prefer he didn't, naturally. I just don't understand about Ge—Mr. Richards, I mean."

This time Moira's sigh was crisp enough to call a snort. "Nor do I," Moira said. "George knows who I am, he might have, ah, stalled around with you, but with me?" It was not umbrage, but there was an edge to her voice. "Whatever he's playing at, we've done as Dani said. That's the second phone call. I really think we have no option but to wash our hands of the thing."

Dorian hesitated. "We're officially abandoning the Ben Morar appeal?"

"Unless George . . . no. Whether or not George gets back to us." There was no mistaking the note of finality. "Archive the notes, Dorian. Yes. We're finished with it."

"Drat it!" Laura said.

They were in Dorian's office, Mrs. Urquhart politely banished, carving twenty minutes off their respective schedules. Laura sprawled on the desk-edge, ravaging a twelve-inch Subway special, while Anne, upright and very near irate, occupied the client's chair.

"If Moira's spat the dummy, we've no legitimate reason to poke around Ben Morar at all."

"No," Dorian said.

Anne gave her one sideways glance. Dorian met it solidly.

Don't ask me to stop, she let her eyes respond. Don't ask how I'll do it, if you're worried about legality, but don't ask me to stop.

Anne looked down. Then she said, "Have you thought what will happen, if we do get other proof?"

"We take it to the cops," Laura said with her mouth full. "Like we said. TAS to start with, because if there's doubt it was an accident, they'll pass it to, what is it, Coronial Investigations."

"Proof that Chris wasn't sacked," Anne said, watching Dorian again, "still isn't proof that he was killed."

"Well, we'll get that too!"

When Anne did not reply, Laura put her lunch down hard. "If we can get the cops asking questions, they'll turn something up. From P-A, if they can't get anything from George. And then the truth'll come out, one way or another. Isn't that what we want?"

When Anne still did not answer she swung round on the desk. "There'll be records. We can find employee testimony." Anne looked at her and she stopped in mid-sentence.

Then she said, "They wouldn't fudge records. Not once we get to an actual case."

"All they need," Anne said levelly, "is a letter officially sacking Chris. But even if we have other proof, they can do damage control. And if there was something fishy about the—accident—they will. They'll bring a counter-suit for defamation. And hire a lawyer."

"But if it comes to a case! To a murder charge—!"

Despite herself Dorian flinched. Anne's voice simply grew more steely.

"They can afford a mega-level corporate lawyer, and a high-power barrister. They probably have their own in-house people. They could hire a Queen's Counsel. Then what do we do?"

None of them had to say it aloud: In law as on the battlefield, God goes with the big battalions. We don't have the funds to match them. Not against a megacorp and an international-level lawyer.

For an instant Laura looked very young and almost frail and Dorian felt a new shoot of fury, that anyone could make Laura look like that. Truth *should* win, she shouted silently. Justice *should* prevail! Laura *should* be right, we should be able to beat Pan-Auric and make George eat his lie, if we do nothing else.

And we all know reality's not like that.

She felt her teeth grit again. The words seemed to come without conscious thought.

"I don't care if they hire the whole Supreme Court, or if they do get off on a murder charge. I'll find out what happened up there."

Anne looked at her sharply. Her voice was sharp too.

"And then?"

"And then . . . go public. Spread it through every paper. Make it clear that Chris wasn't sacked, and whatever happened, *it wasn't his fault.* Even if they never get a conviction, I want the mud off him."

"At whatever cost?"

"They can only sue me broke—"

She stopped. Anne's look said, Is that all they might do?

What if they send that goon after me?

Her spine chilled but she set her teeth. "If they try anything else I can hire a security firm. Put in surveillance cameras . . ."

What if they don't stop at me?

I could keep Laura and Anne out of a court case. I could take the risk for myself. But what if P-A does send that goon, and before the case breaks?

What if they find those disks in Anne and Laura's files?

"You shouldn't get involved," she said. "I can do this. I will

129

do it." She found she had actually bared her teeth. She pulled a civilized expression back on her face. "But not you. We really don't know how far Pan-Auric will go . . ."

Laura was staring. Then she straightened with a growl.

"Dor, you're my *friend*. I'm not gonna sit on the sidelines just in case some Yank mega-rat tries to squash us all—not to mention Chris!" Her eyes glittered. This time it was tears. "You know what you're thinking, what that message is saying, those bastards mightn't just have bailed him up and tried to steal his model, they might have . . . ! I'm not letting *anybody* get away with that!"

"Okay, okay." Her throat choked with a warmth that was part panic, part relief. "But . . ."

She could not finish, That's easy for you to say. Like me, you're single, up here away from your family. Not like Anne.

She looked at Anne, who was watching her again. The usual cool reticent gaze, but this time with a certain flint above the steel.

"Most times," she said, "I'd agree. I'd think about the kids. And Sam. But Pan-Auric hasn't just been ruthless, and unscrupulous. They've shown a complete disregard for the law. Whoever, whatever they are: this is not acceptable."

Dorian knew better than to argue. But her throat shut tighter still.

"A case," she managed, "of justice unredressed?"

Anne nodded very slightly, acknowledging the quote from that first afternoon at the Legacy. "Justice," she said. "Yes."

The silence extended as if to emphasize something. A declaration. A vow. Then Anne looked at her watch and came out of her chair.

"We need to meet again, to figure the next thing—Dorian, you will do that, won't you?" The look was almost an appeal. She knows, Dorian realized, how angry I am. How reckless, the

130

other voice warned, you might be.

"I'll call you tonight." She stood up too. Hand on the doorknob, Anne looked back.

"I'll be waiting." Her eyes finished the silent conversation: I believe you won't do anything really stupid. But make me sure.

The door closed and Laura headed for the bin with her lunch remnants. "We need the mine site first, Dor, don't you know anyone in LTU geology? Or can't you get them to swear confidentiality, if you're that worried about leaks? And then solid testimony from Ben Morar. Can we find out what they did with George's secretary? And what *is* P-A going to do? It must be hell on a high wind to—"

"I know some names at LTU, that's all." Dorian swept up the Coke bottles and turned for her own trip to the bin. "As for Ben Morar—"

There Laura's truncated sentence hit her. As she spun round she heard the gulp.

A tiny sound, the barest click in Laura's throat. As she stood frozen halfway to the desk. And he took his second step past the door.

Walked through it, Dorian's brain said in the hiatus. The way I must with his.

He had a white shirt again, sleeves rolled, tucked into the heavy dark trousers with their high old-fashioned waist. The cowlick was disarranged. The beard came close to bristling. His eyes had fixed hard on Laura but he swung them suddenly as he had before when the first shock passed, and saw Dorian.

She saw the recognition. Felt the adrenalin pound in her own pulse. Her mouth opened, she never had time to think, This time *I'll* speak, this time I will get it in before . . .

He shook his head violently. Looked shocked solid. Then, carefully, deliberately, put a finger to his lips.

Her heart did a double loop. He doesn't just know me, he's

thinking, he must have remembered it broke before when he tried to talk.

With the held breath stifling her, she nodded and touched her own mouth.

His eyes followed her hand. Fixed an instant. She had time to notice, in this good light, the full line of his own lower lip, ambushed in its thicket of beard and so at odds with the set of the mouth, before his head swung away.

Scanning the office, she realized. Trying to see as much as he can, to make the most of however many seconds he—we—have, before whatever it is breaks.

Laura had solidified in place. Dorian saw her profile, concrete-still. The movement as she swallowed, when his stare must have encountered hers.

He swung, that look coming back to Dorian.

The contact went through her like a lick of flame. More than recognition. Acknowledgment. Familiarity. That moment across my table. He's remembering too. Her breath went short as if she were facing a real alien. A genuine ghost.

Can we speak? Can we touch? This time, what might we do?

Her heart sped up. Her lips trembled to move.

His eyes flicked. Then he did move, fast as a bird or striking snake, darting at the desktop, both hands spread in one flashing sweep.

And was gone.

When Laura stopped hyperventilating in the client's chair, she got out in a half-whisper, "God."

Dorian did not have to say, I know what you feel.

"I think my eyes blew out. And I don't have a bone left in my legs."

"It takes you that way," Dorian agreed. But though her own knees had hardly stopped shaking some reflex already had her scanning the desk, demanding, What did he see? What did he . . .

"He took my pen-holder!"

Laura bounced almost as high as the chair-back. "Dor! What-inhell?"

"He took my pen-holder!" Dorian heard her own voice scale up. She flung back and swept both arms at the desk. "Look at it! It's gone!"

She heard Laura suck in a breath and stop. The heaps of files, letters, precedents, stared back at them, paper inches thick. With the bare space that had been her heavy wooden pen-holder shouting in the midst, a fence with its gatepost torn away.

"Dor," Laura said after a minute. "Dor—my hair's standing up."

Dorian hugged her arms about her, as she had in this office once before.

"How did he—*why* did he—"

Dorian wrenched her own brain back to life. Just don't think for the moment that something from your office is off in some other, other reality, that somewhere somebody has his hands full of wood and metal and plastic, concrete, tangible, like nothing he, they has ever touched. Don't ask what they'll do, back in nineteenth-century—wherever it is—with a handful of fine-point BICs.

Her mind convulsed in half-hysterical laughter, then in forced respect. "The rat," she heard herself croak. "He's ahead of us all. He's not having kittens and he's not trying to communicate anymore. He wanted something from here, and when the chance came he grabbed it. With both hands." The bubble of hysteria nearly burst. "If he told anyone about what's happening, and they never saw me—us. Or never believed it. Well, now they have to. Because now he's got something—r-real."

There was a long, ringing pause. Then Laura whispered, "God. It'd be like—handling bits of a UFO."

Dorian fell down in her own chair, feeling as if she had run up ten flights of stairs. But presently Laura stirred. Undid her hands, still clenched in front of her, and said, with a very queer inflection. "Dor—he came back."

Dorian bit down hard on, You're telling *me?*

Laura eyed her. Then she shook her head sharply. "Dor, what'll you do now?"

"You mean, apart from read the back file on the Kotzakis maintenance—again?" Dorian gave up on flippancy. "I don't want to try the geology department yet. I don't want to stir Pan-Auric till I know what really happened that day. Why Chris flipped out. What they plan to do."

"Dor," Laura almost snapped, *"he came back!"*

"Laura, what does that matter! You asked what I'd do?"

"If he came back he's still involved in this! It's not just Chris and Ben Morar!" She leant forward with sudden fierce urgency. "And it's still getting more intense or whatever you want to call it. Longer. More complicated. Closer. Whatever else this is about, it's something really, really important to do with him."

"Damn it, Laura, we tried to trace him and just got a bunch of dead ends—"

"The archives," Laura said flatly. "Forget Ben Morar. Drop Pan-Auric. They'll keep. It'll be safer if they keep. Go to the archives and look for *him.*"

Dorian stared, pinned by Laura's intensity, feeling her own pulse re-accelerate. The hair prickled, again, on the back of her neck.

"I don't know what it is," Laura said, nearly under her breath, "but it's there, Dor. And whatever it is, it has to be the key."

Dorian moistened her lips. Her own voice had dropped, she found, when she said, "Okay. We start from the other end. Tomorrow, I'll go out to LTU."

★ ★ ★ ★ ★

The sprawling LTU campus lay almost in the foothills of Mount Stewart, a mixture of imported palms and sprinkler-fed lawns and unreconstructed native trees swamped in tangled grass. It took Dorian two phone calls and a return to the gatehouse before she unraveled the labyrinth of internal roads onto what the map labeled Western Campus, and unearthed another utilitarian grey concrete double-storied block, half-obscured from the road-edge. Staring from the car-park through a vertical maze of metal posts that upheld a Disabled Access walk, Dorian decided that, sign or no sign, it matched the position on the map labeled "History."

It took five minutes swearing and hunting directions to locate the entrance, clamber up a broad stairway beside photographs of World War II bombers and American servicemen, and in a nest of corridors find a door with a polished wooden sign reading "North Queensland Photographic Collection." She drew a breath from the aroma of wood, dusty carpet and old paper that recalled the Lewis and Cotton archives, and knocked.

"Photographs of Blackston? Yes, we have plenty of those." The archivist was a short, solid woman with an efficient if underplayed manner. "You're welcome to look. Through here."

"Here" was a cell-like room with a single table-desk below shelf after shelf of fat, mysteriously labeled ring-binders. Dorian set down her laptop, trying to hearten herself with the sight of another researcher in the room behind her, while the archivist gave her an index tour.

"These are local Blackston collections. These are North Queensland collections, by topic. Mining, for instance. Grazing. Quite of a lot of those have Blackston photos as well. You don't have anything more specific in mind?"

"Ah, not at this point, no." Dorian tried not to blurt, I have a very specific face in mind, and I can tell you what he eats, where he lives, what he wears. "I'll start with the local collections," she said.

Two hours later she let a ring-binder slap shut and tried not to feel as if time had gone swirling through her fingers, like water down oblivion's drain. It's so fragile, she found herself thinking. The fabric of the past, its preservation is so haphazard, so slapdash, so . . . What do they mean when they say, History? How does it count, to chain half-a-dozen names in a connected narrative, when all these others have just slipped away?

It was the untitled photographs that haunted her. People in best clothes at the doors of their houses, a family, a man holding a toddler, so clearly an important day. But what, and for whom? People lining hotel verandas, or outside a shop, staff mustered for the occasion, or passersby frozen while the photographer waited for his plate to expose. The careful portraits commemorating somebody's wedding, christening, debut, the snapshots remembering somebody's mine, somebody's claim. Or just the faces, an anonymous moment their only memorial. "Early Shift, East Liontown." "Gold Escort, Einasleigh." "Onlooker Viewing the Rainbow Mine." Unidentified street, unknown mine, unnamed building, two men outside with dog . . .

He could be here, she thought with incipient despair. He could be in any of these photographs, with the loungers along the Miners' Arcade, propping a post by the Excelsior hotel, among the mine-shift in their curious brimless caps—her heart had jumped when she recognized them—candles by their boots, squatted against some anonymous slab wall. And if I did find the face, what use would it be, without a name?

Stop it, she told herself fiercely. You know he arrived somewhere because you saw his house, and he has close friends or a wife or family, because at least one died, and I don't think he's a miner, not in that white shirt. So you might find him in the town photographs. And you may as well start with Blackston because it was the biggest northern field, with a better chance of supporting somebody who dressed like that. It isn't hopeless, at all.

But, she decreed, rubbing her eyes, it's more than enough for today.

She gathered the laptop, thanked the archivist, and headed out. As she unlocked the car her cell phone went off.

"Dorian?" It was Anne, sounding unusually crisp. "Where are you? At LTU? Come into the office as soon as you can. I'll be free at one. Anthea just called me. She's found Bow-tie."

"Dionysius T. O'Rourke," Anthea said in her slightly ABC-announcer voice. "Familiarly known as Dinny O'Rourke. The T's for Timothy, we think. Born in eighteen twenty-two at Dingle in County Kerry. Studied at Kilfenora Seminary, eighteen forty to eighteen forty-five, then decided to be a journalist instead of a priest. Went to London, probably married an actress, had a son and three daughters, got himself in a lot of hot water trying to bring an action for adultery against Lord Palmerston, of all people. Who was nearly eighty at the time. Anyhow, your guy made London too hot to hold him, and emigrated. He was in Brisbane in eighteen sixty-six, as editor of a Roman Catholic paper. In eighteen seventy-three he reached Blackston, and hired on as editor for the *North Queensland Miner*. Then he bought a half-share. By eighteen seventy-five he owned it all." She looked up at Dorian. "The bowtie was his trademark. He was Blackston's leading newspaperman, but he and the paper were known all over Australia. They did an article on him in the *Sydney Bulletin* in eighteen eighty-four."

Dorian felt her breath go out on a long, grateful sigh. The room full of papers, the framed certificates on its wall, the angry Irish voice shouting in the candlelight. *North Queensland Miner*, she repeated, savoring it like food or water. At last, something concrete. A name, a place, a time.

Anthea passed her a photocopy. "There you are. I was fossicking through this stuff on northern newspapers when I found the drawing." She frowned. "Was that what you saw? I'm surprised you didn't have the name."

"I don't remember where I saw it," Dorian said in a hurry. Her invention spurred, she added, "I thought it was actually a photograph."

"Bound to be plenty of those," Anthea said genially. She was a round grey-brown woman in her early fifties, wearing the usual sandals and sundress of a part-time academic in Ibisville. The only thing distinguishing her from a Sunday market shopper was the papers and folders sticking above her cloth carry-bag. "Anne said you'd been out at the LTU archives. You'll probably turn Dinny O'Rourke up there, no trouble." Her lips quirked. "He was, ah, highly visible.

"Opinions on everything," she expanded, as Dorian looked a question. "And a regular slangmaster, in and out of libel suits. Taken as a radical in his time. At least, he claimed to support 'the working man,' and he trained quite a few Labor journalists. Of course, he was also a hard White Australia supporter, and a sectarian—raised Cain about 'Orangemen'—and some of his comments about the indigenes . . ." She rolled her eyes. "But they were all that way, back then." She smiled a little. "If you dry up the archives, you can always go to Blackston. Dig in the *NQ Miner* files."

"The *NQ Miner*—!"

"It's still going, yes." Anthea's brows rose a little. "They have a big flash building in the middle of Landers Street. That's the 'new' main street. You can't miss it. Left-hand side, halfway down the ridge."

"He has to work there." Laura was practically jumping down the phone. "That's why the white shirt, he's a reporter, that's why the guys talked to him in the pub. And he turned up a scandal, something about mine safety and what's-his-name—O'Rourke—wouldn't let him blow it open cos he was on the owners' side!"

"Nice idea," Anne's voice said acidly down the conference line, "except O'Rourke *wasn't* on the owners' side. Catholic, and radical. He hated landlords and Protestants and practically everybody with money in Blackston. And he fairly trumpeted it."

"Jeez, Anne, do you have to torpedo everything? Why were they fighting, then?"

"I don't know. We don't have enough to tell yet."

"Then Dor can go back to the archives! Now she knows what she's looking for—"

"No," Dorian said. The plan had formed as they spoke across her. Now it came out solid as if settled for days. "We've got a place now, a real place at last. I'm going to Blackston. I'll look in the *NQ Miner* files. For photos, and something about a mine blow-up, for starters. And while I'm there—"

There was a sudden pause. Anne broke it, sounding a little too cool.

"While you're there?"

"I'll look for Tanya," Dorian said. "And try to get in touch with Tom thingummy. Ralston. See if I can meet him somewhere out of Pan-Auric's hair. And ask if *he* thinks Chris was sacked."

CHAPTER VII

I can't just phone Ralston at work, Dorian thought, closing the new folder optimistically labeled "*North Queensland Miner Files.*" Or call on him out there. He probably has a flat in Blackston, but the address? Not in the phone book, if he rents. He must have a cell phone, but the number?

Chris's phone. Of course. It'll be on Chris's phone.

Logic said she should have left the phone at the bank with the CD, but something else, something more primitive and arbitrary, had refused. Chris's phone, it said. Something he handled, something he used every day. I want it here, with me.

She dug the phone from its cache in her highest cupboard, and sat down at the dining table. Still charged, she thought, flicking On. "Tom" was the third tag in the Numbers file. At the top of the list, her own cell phone number stared back at her. The name-tag said cryptically "P-D."

Dorian, she decoded. Precious-Dorian. You rat-fink, Chris.

Her eyes filled and she put the phone down as it washed back over her like a poison gas. He's gone and he'll never make any more silly jokes like that, never use this phone, never call me and make excuses about missing another weekend. I'll never hear his voice again.

In a while she found a handkerchief and blew her nose. Then she copied Ralston's number. Then she switched Chris's phone off and held it a moment against her cheek. She shut her eyes, hearing that last message, seeing the scrub flash by outside, picturing his face beside her, as close as the phone. This was with him. This was with him then, and I'll never be . . .

Anger's good, she thought at last. Being angry's a very good thing, because this can't happen so often. And that's a very good thing too.

Gently, she laid the phone down and reached for her own. Checked the time, just before five PM. Punched the number. The phone crackled and hummed. Suddenly the holoscreen popped and Ralston looked out at her in a yellow hard hat and a startled expression. Dun-gold dust blotched even the sunburn on his nose.

"Uh?" he said.

Dorian said, "Tom? We met at Chris's funeral. Dorian Wild. Do you remember? Sometime soon, I'd like a couple of words with you."

Dorian had been to Blackston five or six times, and from the first she had thought it was like going into another country. First the almost straight secondary road from Ibisville to the range foot, running through dry-tropic lowland trees and heavy grass, with a sense of claustrophobia on the almost completely flat plain between distant banks of hills. Then the climb up the range. And suddenly upland distances, grass going fine and short, trees thinning to scarcity under what always seemed a brilliant light and an enormous open sky. Then the high-level bridge over the Burdekin's half-mile of rock-islanded channel, and finally the sense of anticipation as the road, flushed pink now from local granite, dipped through the last creeks, and the five little hills above Blackston rose on the sky's fawn-silver edge. Then a leisurely traverse past old wooden houses to the town center, with its heritage buildings newly painted and bedizened with nineteenth century ornament, like a flock of flamingos amid the prosaic modern substitutes.

This time she looked at the pure light and naked slopes and thought, There'd have been smog. The smelters, the stampers, the houses, the pubs, cooking fires, candles, lamps. . . . And dust. And stench. No sealed streets, no sewers, pit-latrines and horse manure from one end to the other. No trees, they cut all those down. But crowded, the diggers, the mine-workers, the engineers and assayists, the builders, the grocers and plumbers and butchers and blacksmiths, the families, the officials, the owners, the managers, the toffs. The gamblers, the speculators, the big names and money, the power.

The newspaper people, she added this time, recording it all.

And the mines. She had seen the photos now, the eastern horizon starred with its pyramid sequence of poppet-heads, the high brick mill-chimneys, the biggest hill razed of trees, windrowed with mullock heaps, wrapped in smoke and flying dust. And all of it alive, the wheels of the poppet-head winches turning, the lift engines clattering, ore hoppers rumbling to and fro, the wagons passing with timber for fuel or building, stampers thundering, people yelling, blasts going off. The faces in the photos flowed past again, colored and moving now, superimposed on the bland spaces, the broad deserted streets. They called it The World. The second biggest city in Queensland.

And it's all shrunk to this.

After a few splutters Ralston had been happy enough to meet. "I can get into town next Monday. I have some stuff to do." He had hesitated then, and she saw by his eyes that he was wondering why she had called, if grief and nostalgia could be motive enough.

"I don't want to prejudice your position at Ben Morar," she had said quickly. "I'd just like to ask a few questions. Get somebody else's take on—on why Chris—left." And the wobble in her voice must have been eloquent enough, for he said in a hurry, "Sure, sure, we can meet, what about the park? I can get in by one o'clock or so."

"That would be fine."

She knew the central park, a couple of blocks from the street Dinny O'Rourke had persisted in calling Miner Street. The park was named Lister, after another early notable who had suddenly acquired a face. She had seen a photo of the park too, when the gracious big trees and manicured lawns and bitumen paths had been nothing but saplings and bare earth. Parking on the side-street whose huge gutters still carried storm run-off fierce enough to drown in, she thought, Pretty smart, Ralston, not to suggest some café or hotel, where people who know you could more easily see you with some strange woman, and maybe, later, P-A could put two and two together. But then, Chris said you were cack-handed about geology. Not politics.

She found a table and unloaded her lunch. It was all so normal, so everyday, school-children running through, tourist parties, the growl of a ride-on mower in the sun. She shivered and thought abruptly, How come the other one hasn't turned up yet?

Oh, that'd be all I need, she scolded herself, a nice tête a tête and him running off with the salad rolls and frightening Ralston out of his skull. Don't jinx yourself, right? Sufficient unto the day. She looked out in the street and saw a dust-rimed four-wheel drive with a logo on the door pull up.

"I really miss him, you know?" Ralston tried to stop himself fidgeting. It was, Dorian sensed, more than chronic unease round a strange woman. "And not just because he, um, sorted out my problems." He took another mouthful, chewed, and sat still. "I can hear him yelling now. 'All right, Tom, just put it down before it blows up on you—no, no, that was a *joke*'—!"

Dorian winced at her own shard of memory. Ralston twitched his eyes away and said, half-muffled, "He didn't mean it, you

143

know? He—"

He stopped altogether and swung face on to her at last, making their eyes meet. "I, um, I should tell you. They've, um. Made me Senior Geologist."

Dorian thanked heaven for recent practice in keeping a straight face. *God help Ben Morar, you couldn't track a lode with nuggets in your skull!* Another quote from an irate Chris. She managed to swallow her own mouthful and respond almost politely, "I'm sure you'll do a good job."

"Well, I'll *try*, but I'm not Chris, you know?" He did not preen himself at all, at which she felt relief. "I think, they just promoted me because I'm there and I know the mine, and—well, I was pretty relieved they kept me on when they've been a bit ruthless, you know?"

Dorian bit her tongue on, I *didn't* know, tell me everything! She dropped her eyes to hide what felt like a veritable hunter's glare and managed an encouraging but neutral, "Hmm?"

"Not the miners, I mean, but the office people. They've replaced Tanya, she was Mr. Richards's secretary, you know, she's been there since she had a job. She was pretty sick about it. I saw her at the White Horse the other night." He broke off with another flush.

"It's a small town," Dorian said. "Pan-Auric would hardly expect you to ignore people you know just because they've—gone elsewhere." He looked absurdly relieved. "I daresay Mr. Richards will miss her, though."

"Oh, no, George, um, Mr. Richards—he's on leave. They've put in another guy, a transitional manager they call him, one of the Pan-Auric people. He seems okay."

But he's not. Dorian read that wavering intonation with an ear attuned from dubious witnesses. Though you don't want to say so, when you're newly promoted yourself and hardly adequate to the job, and you know it. And you've stepped into a dead man's shoes.

Not the time to start probing why the transitional manager's questionable, let alone follow the ramifications of George being sent off. Whether it's temporary or permanent.

But I could ask where he is.

"Oh, Mr. Richards is on leave? I suppose he's gone away. The Gold Coast or something."

"I don't really know." Ralston came belatedly to an awareness of leaking gossip, if not company information. "I, um, you wanted to ask something about Chris?"

"Yes." She had to stop there, waiting out the little spring of tears. But however genuine, she could not have found a better gambit. Ralston's look changed to anxiety, outright concern, he put down the hamburger and nearly reached out to her. She gave her head a little shake, the brave bereaved partner mastering grief.

"I just wondered," she said, "what you, ah, thought—happened that day."

His eyes slid to her and away again. They were a non-descript grey-green and they could not have said clearer that he had heard the sacking story too.

"Was Chris—did Chris seem upset to you?"

"Upset? God, yes." The slightest hint of respect, implication that he was an expert, was enough to tip the scales. "I've never seen Chris like that. He was *ropeable*. Not yelling. He'd do that for anything little, shout and forget. But the big things . . . the time we had the shaft cave and we thought the whole conveyor-belt had bought it, he was like a calculator, you know? Call the incident team, warn the stockpile, check the seismometer. Fast as hell, and never shouted once."

Remembering that voice on the phone, Dorian thought, I've heard.

"But that day." Ralston put the hamburger down again. "Well,

I suppose, if you just had the brawl of your life with your own manager, and then the visiting bigwig as well—"

"He had a fight with the Pan-Auric VP?"

He must have taken her tone for shock and the abbreviation to mean Very Important Person, rather than the more tell-tale Vice President. "Oh, yeah, they got into it in the office, hammer and tongs, George before lunch and the VP afterwards." The flush surfaced again. "Tanya said she could hear them clear to the utility room."

"But he didn't tell you—you didn't see him afterwards?"

The flush vanished. But his eyes held steady, as the look changed from remembrance and shared concern to something more like wretchedness.

"He went into his office. He was in a hurry. I didn't want to—intrude. I—I wish I had seen him, you know?"

To have exchanged last words, she thought. To let you, now, lighten the feeling of guilt.

"So you've no idea what they fought about?"

He shook his head.

Dorian took a breath. She tried to keep it cool, if not casual.

"The police told me. Ben Morar—I presume Mr. Richards—said—he was sacked."

His hands twitched. His eyes flew up. Then he shook his head. "All George—Mr. Richards would say, was, very unfortunate, Mr. Keogh is going, no comment. Even to us."

And you won't say any more. Not to put your own job in jeopardy.

Behind them a sprinkler began putt-putting as it hurled its circle of water over the smooth-clipped grass. A pair of flies homed in on Ralston's hamburger. Dorian looked away to the Boer War memorial bandstand, lavish white-painted ironwork under a dome-ended green roof.

"Did Chris tell you anything," she aimed to sound neutral,

"anything at all . . . about why—what made him do it?"

He took off his bush-hat and pushed a hand into the instant flop of forelock. His eyes went to the sprinkler and back to her. "There was something," he said at last. "I didn't understand it, but . . ."

Dorian held her breath.

"The day before, you know? After the, the presentation, that went like clockwork, he got me in to help and it was all fine, he was really relieved. He didn't say much, but I could tell. Then they did the site tour, and . . ."

He paused, forehead corrugating. Above the hat-line his skin was baby white.

"He came back, and he was . . . I mean, we'd just sold a new mine to this whopping big company, and George had been pouring butter all over him and the P-A VP calling him 'son' every second word, and . . . It was like, all of a sudden, he wasn't listening. I had to take him the yield-figures that afternoon, and he just went, Okay, fine. Like he didn't see them either. Let alone," for a moment with a painfully adult irony, "me."

He was thinking, Dorian annotated silently. He'd just heard whatever changed everything, and he'd been hit a body blow. He told me, I have to think.

"So you never knew . . . ?"

He brought his eyes back to her. "Miss Wild . . . Dorian. I don't *know*. But next morning, he was in the office with us, me and Tanya and the PR guy, Tony. P-A wanted a press release and Chris had to check the stuff. And he was telling them the mine-figures, man, that thing is *huge!* It may be low-grade but when they get in there with an open-cut they'll make the Kalgoorlie yields look sick. Chris was right in the middle of it, we were all excited, even Tony, and he doesn't know schist from—um—crap. And all of a sudden . . ."

The sentence trailed away. He stared along the street, its

wooden houses flanking wide gravel verges across the saddle of bitumen, all beginning to dance in the late morning haze.

"All of a sudden Chris stopped. Then he said, 'I don't know why I'm doing this.' And he put the maps and stuff down and said, 'Tanya, I want to see George immediately.' And he walked out. Tony said, 'Wait, whoa, I need more stuff,' and Chris kept walking, just kept on walking, with Tony carrying on and me and Tanya gawping, like he didn't give a damn. Like he didn't know any of us. Like none of it was *real.*"

Dorian felt her own nape prick. What did he see? What changed, in that one minute? What took the frangipani out of its frame, so reality suddenly didn't cohere anymore?

She brought herself back to the present. "And he never told you what he meant?"

Mutely, he shook his head.

She swallowed, and launched the critical question. "Or what the plans were? For the mine?"

He looked startled. "Well, I saw the yield-estimates, and the presentation proposals, of course, I suppose they'll put in an open-cut, that's what they do, you know."

"But nothing in detail." She tried not to sound accusing, when he ran down and sat looking sheepish as he realized how little he did know. She nodded, letting her body language add, I didn't expect more. When he relaxed again, she added, "And not where it actually is?"

He looked startled, then embarrassed. "Um, ah, Dorian, I—ah—Chris always said, That was, ah, company information, you know? And I, ah, I—"

"No, you can't tell me, naturally." She was determined not to curse aloud. "I just wanted to be sure somebody did know besides Chris. If, if all his information was destroyed in the—the crash."

It sounded thoroughly inane, but he looked away sharply and

a dull red stained his cheeks. "No." He sounded constricted. "No, it isn't lost."

And there is no way, she gritted her teeth, that I'd ask you to read the map for me, even if you would. Your loyalty to Chris was never very high, and it may not be to Pan-Auric either, but you're shrewd enough not to keep this interrogation quiet.

She nodded in turn, trying to look relieved and loyally zealous, and tossed the final question like a barrister's Parthian shot, a devastating after-thought launched over a shoulder when the witness had already relaxed as the interrogator turned away.

"I suppose you can use the stats model too?"

"Chris's model?" It went up at the end before he could stop it. "Oh, no, the company couldn't use that, not without his permission! Or him being there. Anyhow, I don't have a clue how it works. Listen, Tom, he used to say, you get me in enough hot water with the god-forsaken core logs. Get the same figures three times running and I'll give you a look-see."

"Oh." She tried to sound more surprised.

He pulled a rueful face. "I'd come in and he'd be working on it, chortling like a kettle or tearing out his hair. But I never got to see it, even. He had that thing locked up tighter than a Westpac vault. He used to make jokes about securing his old-age pension—because you can't patent maths models, you know—and he had a fingerprint password on the laptop, of all things. We used to kid hell out of him and say he was so smart, one day he'd cut himself, and the thing'd never recognize *him.*"

He stared suddenly away across the park, as if he, too, felt the approach of tears. Dorian was thankful she could seem silenced. Her brain seemed to have blown out to explosion point.

A fingerprint password. So the goon took it for nothing. So they probably tried to get in and God knows what they did then, cursed the goon up hill and down dale, took an axe to it?

Brought in an IT person and told them some story about losing the password. Or just told them—her throat contracted bitterly—the truth. The guy who had the fingerprint's dead, and they need the information. There must be ways round a password. Even a fingerprint password. There's nothing locked up that someone hasn't figured how to unlock.

If they did that, they could make copies. Claim it as their own. And I only have the CD and the phone recording to say otherwise.

Thank God I did make copies. At least, if I have to fight them, there's some evidence.

But I still need to know what P-A did plan. Most of all, I have to find where the cursed thing *is*.

She gathered herself as if to close a client interview. "Thank you, Tom. I'm very grateful you could find time to talk to me, and just, tell me a bit more about Chris. About . . ." she did not have to counterfeit the fracturing sentence, or the effort to blink back tears. Through their swim she watched him scramble to his feet, his expression a mixture of compunction and relief, and navigated through their brief, awkward farewells.

Find George, she told herself, as Ralston's vehicle started. He's the only one who might know the big picture. But her thoughts ran uncontrollably backward, demanding, What did Chris see? What happened in those few minutes in that office? *I don't know why I'm doing this.* What changed, that he could be showing off the mine one minute and the next headed for a monumental brawl with both his bosses, and then pull the pin as well?

He said, Get an environmental lawyer. He said, What they're going to do. But an open-cut mine, that's nothing unusual, even a big one, and with gold they'd use cyanide refinement. It's dangerous, yes, for pollution, but that can be managed better than it is at Ben Morar. And none of it's anything Chris hadn't seen before.

She stared across the street as Ralston had, trying to reconstruct the past from hearsay, from motives lost now beyond the grasp of history. All that emerged was the ornate woodwork under the nearest house's veranda eaves, painted to white lace, lovingly restored.

Why did he leave the CD unprotected? If he had a fingerprint password on the laptop, why didn't he cover the CD?

He wouldn't have known . . . her eyes filmed and she shook her head as if to clear them. He wouldn't have known I'd have to open it for him.

Did he maybe not have time?

Her spine crept as she heard that message again. Did the goon come in before he finished? Everything that mattered on that one CD, absolutely unprotected, and him bluffing the goon to get it out, oh, lord, Chris, playing matador isn't the word.

Insanely risky, yes, but he did it. So now I have it, and I have the rest to do for him. So let's get under way.

George, her brain looped back as she gathered things up. He's "on leave." He has to have a home address. Maybe here in town, even. I can get it from Moira. Or the L & C records. Or while I'm here, just check the phone book. Keep an eye out for, or very carefully, ask after Tanya. She would know.

In the meantime, I'm here to chase the other mystery. So next stop is the *NQ Miner,* and the archives around eighteen eighty-four.

As Anthea had said, the *North Queensland Miner* office was halfway down the slope of Landers Street, well below its intersection with the original mine-track, which had run to the end of the nearest, biggest hill. Black's Tower Hill, Dorian remembered. Blacktower Hill, now. A reservoir perched halfway up, but with the mines gone the rest had reverted to rock and native grass, tawny-silver or burnt amber in the sunlight, slurring the marks of the past like its altered name.

The *Miner*'s building had not reverted to anything. Gazing up at its gilded, pillared, carven stone facade, Dorian had to repress a gulp. This can't have been a newspaper office, surely, even a leading newspaper office? Heavens, it's fancier than the Stock Exchange.

She started across the relatively narrow, almost untrafficked street. None of this would be here, she thought, stepping up on the sidewalk. No bitumen, probably no sidewalks, just horse manure and dirt. And dust. Maybe street lamps. If this was a main street they probably had it lit at night. Gas, or something. Her knowledge of nineteenth-century progress was blurred, though she had seen corrugated iron and street lamps in some of the photographs. Would they be here by eighteen eighty-four?

Climbing the three stone steps to the narrow modern glass door, bracing herself to coax entry to the archives, she thought, I'll find out. It may take a day or two, but I'll find out. She reached for the door. It split from top to bottom and swung out in her face.

Dorian went flying onto her backside with a winding thump. Her shoulders slammed up against something hard as iron but rough as untrimmed wood. Light flooded down over her shoulder, though where she sat was dark.

Oh God, she thought. Oh, God.

The entry had become a pair of wooden doors with long glass panels down each side. The stone building front had slid backward into unpainted horizontal planks, with a veranda reaching out to wooden steps. Each tread showed dark as cliff-falls in the melodramatic light, shadows deepened by a glow behind the doors.

Doors that somebody, with a back to her, was loudly locking shut.

She heard the grate of jambs. A padlock snap. Still gasping

but in sudden panic she yanked her feet up and pressed against her support as the figure turned abruptly and came down the stair.

Beyond the veranda overhang the light exaggerated every salient of his face, deepening the eye-sockets to pools of night, sheening the beard's dark with tiny red glints, stressing the bosses of cheekbone, the set, in tiredness or preoccupation, of the mouth. The white shirt was smeared with darkness too, collar open, sleeves rolled. He went past within feet of her. Hauling his coat on, pulling open the gate, turning onto the street. A late-night worker, fatigued beyond thought of anything but the way to bed.

The gate clicked. Almost at her elbow. The other side of the gatepost, she realized. She heard his boots, a slightly slow but even stride, receding to her left. Scuffing rather than clapping, as boots would on plank or bitumen. Moving on naked dust.

Retreating, steadily, leaving her alone.

She took one half-sobbing breath and the foreignness rolled in on her, dust and dung and the multitudinous reek of lamp, candle, fire-spew, the choking, almost metallic flavor of the mines, some pungent chemical waft fighting horse-smell and rampant human sweat. Something equally acrid breathed behind her as wind flickered the light.

The night-chill struck with it, stabbing through jeans and light jacket like a stockman's spur and with a strangled yelp she found herself on her feet. Her backside hurt. She grabbed the gatepost and her hands jarred on untrimmed wood and her heart seemed to come right out her mouth.

I'm touching it. I'm here and I'm touching things and it hasn't gone away.

She clawed at the gate. It was hip high, of small narrow planks. She shook it, wildly trying to find the hasp, then realized the fence was just a pair of rails. She ducked under the top one

153

and was on the sidewalk. Under the lamppost, staring round the street itself.

The closest buildings were dark, a long indistinct rank of old-fashioned mostly peaked roofs, skylines holding, here and there, the silhouetted end of a sign. There was no moon. Only the gas lamps shone, to left and right, making their own murky dusk. Smog, said some part of her brain that was still recording, just like you thought, all the dust and smoke.

And it's dark—but it isn't quiet.

Men were singing somewhere downhill, a tuneless thoroughly alcoholic chorus punctuated by the slam of wood under china or glass. Light glared onto the street. A bar, she thought instantly, it's a bar and it's late. The opposite buildings were shut too, though here and there a half-glow crept round their backs. It's late and everybody's going to bed. Except the drunks.

And whatever on earth's going on down there. She swung right round as the drinkers' chorus ended in a discordant range of final notes, and the more distant sound drilled through. High, nasal, unintelligible, more singing, and underneath it, a shrill cicada clicking and a drone like subterranean pipes.

Didgeridoo. I can hear a didgeridoo. Not in some tourist display. That's a didgeridoo, being played for real. In a corroboree.

And it's not going away. It's still here. I'm still here and I've moved and touched things and seen him and nothing broke. I'm still here . . .

Without thinking she started to run.

Up the street, away from bar and corroboree both, the way he had gone, her brain ratcheting in a panic whose only clear thought was, Find *him* again, I've got to catch up with him, and more crazily, He's the only person I know.

In the dusk ahead something moved. The voices warned her before they cleared the street corner, slurred and half-coherent but vehement in argument and complaint. The smell preceded them. Well-abused alcohol, unwashed clothes. Dirt and sweat and smoke.

She stopped in her tracks. Run, hide, instinct howled, duck off the sidewalk, into one of those verandas, anywhere, just get into the dark. She twitched sideways and the chatter stopped.

"An' who's that, then?" It came drunkenly if half-affably, a deep burry voice with a definite Irish slant. "Wanderin' up here on 'is Pat Malone this time o' night?"

Somebody shoved one of the figures, which reeled. Another voice broke in, "What, settlin' to close out Dinny O'Rourke and peg the whole street f' y'self?"

A bellow of mirth. Acid comments, then a definite forward surge. "Come out, then," the first voice urged her. "Come out like a decent man, and let's see you under that lamp."

Dorian's feet went back in pure fright. Run, run, terror urged her and the shreds of sanity shouted, No, no. Not now, they'll chase you. You can't. You can't.

The next lamp was behind her, its light a broadening tide. In a last hope she retreated right to the post, so the light might fall from above, to distort rather than reveal. Don't talk, she warned herself fiercely. With jeans on, they might take you for a boy. But if you talk . . .

What would half-a-dozen drunken nineteenth-century miners do to a woman out on the streets at night? A woman dressed in what they think of as men's clothes?

Her back came up against the post. Her pursuers converged.

She had a blurred sense of hair, far too much hair, tangles outrunning the brim of motley hats. Some brims turned right up in front, giving a clearer view of beards plainly beyond mortal control. When they spoke she saw their mouths move, and caught another faceful of alcoholic breath. The light brought up more thick trousers and the heavy, filthy boots, a vaguer impression of vests, checked shirts. There were things in their hands, but she was past thinking what.

They drew a half-circle about her, hulking like the twenty-first century nightmare of a redneck pack, though above the alcohol the voices as yet held little more than curiosity. And wariness. The man who had spoken first leaned forward to stare at her, and frowned, by his voice.

"T'ain't the newspaper johnny. Nor Jimmy, neither. Though t'is round his time to leave." He leant closer. "A lad, hey?" Involuntarily she pulled her head back. "Too tall for the *Miner* boys."

"If Mrs. Callum'd let 'em out. This time o' night." His neighbor closed in on the words. "New chum, are y'? Just off the train?" Before Dorian could react he reached for her jacket front.

Instinct and reason shrieked together, He mustn't feel the fabric! and, He mustn't get too close! Dorian hurled herself round the lamppost and ran.

The bellow behind her was half drunken amusement and half hunting reflex roused. She ran madly down the street center with some cell of brain insisting, It's clearer out here, you won't have such a chance to trip. The remaining shreds of intelligence howled, Get up a side-street, they'll drive you right into the corroboree. Everything else screamed silently, Oh, make it finish, get me *out* of here . . . !

The roars rang against buildings and all but drowned the thump of feet. Somewhere doors banged, she had a sense of increased light, candles, kindled lamps, other cries crossing the hunters' shouts. From in front came a louder shout and beside her appeared a cross street's gap. Dorian all but fell round the corner and against a wooden fence.

The side street was entirely dark. The buildings were further apart, smaller, houses, her over-tired mind said, houses inside yards, this is a fence, here's a gate. If I could get inside . . .

Uproar burst behind her. Someone shouted a "View Halloo." Someone else shouted about "kangaroo dogs" and right beside her a real dog exploded in a fusillade of barks. Dorian choked a sob and ran.

She found another cross street within two hundred yards. By then she was completely winded, stumbling and sobbing for breath as well as from fright, driven on by a bow-wave of frenziedly vocal dogs. Oh, God, she cried silently, why doesn't it break? Why can't I get *out?*

Another corner came up. Beyond planning, she turned that one as well.

She was marooned in a wide pale space of dust and dusky starlight, rimmed by the shadow of fences and gates. As her wind gave out entirely she brought up, wheezing, hands on her knees. Only after a good minute did she realize the other change.

There were no freshly roused dogs.

Behind her, in the cross street, the canine uproar had begun to subside. All round her houses and yards lay quietly indistinct. Ahead, perhaps two hundred yards away, was the street end, marked by blurry but unmistakable artificial light, but where she stood it was all quite dark.

And the human pack had subsided as well.

She straightened up and worked to recover the rest of her breath. Her heart was still racing, her mouth dry, her eyes on the verge of all but uncontrollable tears. As the immediate panic subsided the rest came back, rising, peaking, crescendoing so she almost wept aloud.

It's happened again. The fold's got closer or whatever it does. And this time I can't get back. I've fallen right through.

I can't get back.

She very nearly sat down in the roadway and gave up al-together. But as her knees bent, a night bird swept across the street. A moment's flash of motion, a dark, unnerving silhouette and then, rising over the uphill roofs, a resonant, melancholy, Ho-Hoke.

A mopoke. She stood swaying, heart thumping, torn between tears and hysterical mirth, and under it an equally ridiculous leap of almost joyous relief. *It's a mopoke. A big bush owl. A local one. Chris told me, when we heard it along the river one night. Back in Ibisville.*

The tears trickled then, but her breathing steadied, and her feet seemed to steady too. *Oh, Chris. I've lost you now twice over. I'm stuck in some—some—other country—and I mightn't ever get out.*

Ice seemed to fill her mouth. She jerked her head aside and began to walk.

Still there were no dogs. The lighted street drew closer and some reason revived. *I've boxed the block. That must be Landers Street again. Maybe the drunks will be gone and I can—*

She stopped walking and again the enormity fell on her. *Maybe I can what?*

Dorian put her fingers in her mouth and bit them as hard as she could. Tears dripped and her head still seemed to be floating on panic like an overdose of oxygen, but thoughts struggled through.

Landers Street. Where the NQ Miner office is. In this world as well as mine. Where I might find the only, only person in this world who won't, at the very kindest, take me for a raving lunatic.

No matter if it's night and he's gone home to bed. He works there. He has to come back.

She crept back down Landers Street, keeping to the shadows wherever she could, trying to walk the open spaces as if she was a man, and a man who belonged. The bar-chorus had given up, but the corroboree was still going, and the street was perilous with little groups of tardy drinkers meandering home. It seemed a decade before she could slip past the last streetlight and through the rails of the *Miner*'s fence.

On the veranda, she thought. In the shadow, and just wait. And pray that if he doesn't come to work till morning, at least the paper will be a daily, and tomorrow another working day.

She launched across the few feet of vacant dirt. Lifted her foot onto the lowest wooden step.

It creaked and altered texture under her weight. Then the next stair leapt out in high relief as daylight blasted over her shoulder like a stage light going on, she lifted her head and stared into the shine of a single glass door with *"North Queensland Miner"* blazoned across it in ornate twentieth-century type, set in a facade of solid if ornamented stone.

"I don't care *what's* in the files! I'm not staying here another day—another hour!"

The voices at the phone-end rose in warning and she bit down hard on her own lip and crushed herself lower on the bench. A park bench, out in blessedly open air and sunlight, though that was turning toward the mellower light of afternoon. Safe isolation to conduct a panicky phone conversation and get what she had thought would be unqualified support.

"Dorian. Dorian, are you there?"

It was Anne, anxiety as well as shock coming through despite her usual control. Dorian swallowed hard. Blew her nose and managed a half-muffled, "I'm here."

"Is there anywhere—a brand-new hotel or a café or something—where you can get a drink? Or just some good strong hot sweet tea?"

Shock, her mind commented wryly. Remedies for shock. I seem to have done nothing but weather shocks since this began.

"I'd say, come home now, but I think you're still far too upset to drive?"

Dorian swallowed again. The urge to huddle was all but irresistible, the compulsion to shut her eyes and open them over and over, to be sure it was all still there. Twenty-first century Blackston, dozing in the Friday afternoon sunlight, modernly sanitized, empty of dust, stink, darkness.

Life.

She crushed that thought like an intrusive ant.

"I'll be all right." Her voice still wobbled like a well-pickled drunk—she cut that simile off still more brutally. "I just had to tell somebody . . . get it out."

They broke into a mutual chatter of commiseration and concern. "Should one of us come and get you?" Laura broke through. "I can get off in the next hour. If you wanted to wait—"

"No!" With an effort she controlled her voice. No, her thoughts ran, all but chittering with fear. It's three-thirty now, time must have slid in there somehow, Laura couldn't get here before five at the earliest and by then it'll be evening. By the time we leave it'll be getting toward dark.

And I know, the way animals know the presence of a predator, I mustn't be in this place at night.

"No," she sliced fiercely into the fresh outbreak of concern. "I can drive. I have to drive. I can't stay here. I can't . . . Anything could set it off again. Anything! Just walking down Landers Street." Her whole back shuddered as if a ghost had breathed on her neck. "I'll go to the service station, out on the highway. Get some tea. Have some, some, something to eat. Then I'll start."

Anxiety and instruction poured down the phone. She listened with half an ear, Drive carefully, get more tea at the first wayside stop, don't dare try to drive fast down the range. Ring us at the Burdekin, the next high-level bridge, the fork for the Haughton river road. "I wish to God you'd let us come and get you," Laura was saying, "I'm sure you shouldn't do this alone."

I have to, Dorian thought. Chris is gone, and you're not here. You never really will be here, when it comes to the crunch. I have to do this alone. I don't have any other choice.

She shut her eyes as a wave of desolation washed over her, more hurtful than the fear. Oh, Chris. Why do I have to deal with this whole madness by myself?

She looked out across the sun-gilded lawns and saw instead the parlor in that other house, the funeral debris. The look of understanding, faint but unmistakable however transient, on that face.

Wherever he is, he lost someone, and he has to deal with all this too. If not, not like what just happened to me. But he'd know. Even if he couldn't help, he'd know.

She straightened her neck a little and altered her grip on the phone. "I'm all right," she said, sniffing tears into the back of her nose. "I can do it. I'll take it quietly, I'll call you every half hour. But I don't care about the *Miner* files or anything else in this place. I have to get out of it. Now."

Chapter VIII

"There's some weird kind of synch going on. I mean, look at it. After the first time, in the elevator: your office, his office, then yours. Your bedroom, his. Your kitchens. At the pub. After . . . funerals. Then at the *Miner*, he's leaving, you're coming in." Laura's frown crimped deeper. "It's a pattern, it has to be. If we could just get the clue . . ."

"I don't want any more clues." Dorian took another solid swig of brandy and leant back hard into her own couch. "I don't want anything more to do with it."

Laura opened her mouth and shut it again. In Dorian's other dining chair, Anne's brows came down too. But she left Laura to make the obvious riposte.

"Dor," quite gently, "you didn't want anything to do with it any time. But it—whatever it is—wants something to do with you."

"Laura—!"

"Shh." Anne was beside Dorian, taking the glass, sliding an arm onto the couch back. "Just leave it for the minute, Laura, all right? Dorian's had too much for one day. Let it be."

"Too much, yes." Dorian felt herself start shivering again, as if the hours and miles between had disappeared. As if she were still in that street facing a doorway that had metamorphosed from glass and stone to wood and back to stone. "I don't care what it's about or why it's happening, I don't want to know who he is or what the hell he wants with me—!"

"Or about Chris?"

The quiet was like a slash.

Laura had said it coolly enough. She still looked cool, but there was a set to her jaw.

"I thought you meant to find out what really happened? Clear Chris? Blow the whistle on whatever P-A plans to do?"

"I will do that! I can clear Chris somehow, I'll find Tanya, I'll get to George. If I have to I'll brace the blasted transitional manager. That doesn't mean dealing with this, this . . . ghost!"

Laura's chin jerked. Even Anne twitched.

Dorian glared at them, seeing the words in Laura's face: You already know he's not a ghost, and whatever's happening with him and you and time and space, it can't be separated from the Ben Morar tangle. They're part of the one thing.

Dorian put her head in her hands. Then Anne's arm did come round her shoulders and Anne was saying flatly, "That is *it* for tonight. Dorian's wiped out and tomorrow's the weekend, and she's coming home with me."

Dorian was abjectly grateful that this time Baringal Beach seemed entirely invasion-proof. With her usual bland steeliness Anne refused to talk about anything but Lewis and Cotton cases and domestic trivia. Dorian cooked, or watched TV football with Sam, or ran after Della and Jonathon, she walked or swam with the family, then fell into bed and slept.

And on Sunday night she dreamed.

She was in Chris's unit. The power was off, or the lights had failed, because it was twilight-dim, but she knew it was Chris's unit, as she knew the chaos on the floor. We tidied this, some mega-commentator complained as she began sifting hurriedly through the nearest pile. We tidied it before the funeral. But now Chris needed something in here, urgently, desperately. She did not know exactly what, but he was due any moment, and she had to have it ready when he came.

She scurried from pile to pile, papers, clothes, e-books, dusty football boots. Whatever it was did not surface anywhere. With haste nearing panic she tossed things right and left, any moment he'll be here.

Then he was there. Standing by the outer doorway, tall and silent, indistinct in the gloom. She wheeled round beginning to cry in dream-speech, I can't find it, it isn't here . . .

He was not stockily compact and half a head over her. He stood head and shoulders taller, rangy as a hunting dog, and his workshirt was white instead of khaki.

And red lights flecked the deeper darkness of his beard.

She had jerked upright and hurled the bedclothes off. Her heart thundered, her palms were wet. There was wetness too, on her cheeks. Damn you, she bawled silently into the empty quiet of Anne's spare room. You've got into my office, my unit, my life—now you're pushing into my *dreams!* Go away, go away! I don't want anything to do with you!

Driving into town Monday, after the furore of dispatching Sam to work and the children to daycare, Anne said, too casually, "Now what do you have in mind?" And Dorian, glowering as billboards passed above blurry grass, ant-hills, scrubby grey-green eucalypts, bit down the impulse to pour it all out as usual.

If I do that Anne will go round the same arguments. He keeps coming back, you can't ignore him, it's all part of the same thing.

The highway tilted for a steep overpass. Fortress Hill's skyline slid down the windscreen and up again, obdurately the same from any angle.

Well, damned if it has to be the same thing, Dorian fumed. I'm not letting it.

Hoping not to sound sullen, she managed, "Find an address

for George, I think."

"Check the L&C records?"

"Maybe."

She could feel Anne's glance. She knew that to Anne her tone had telegraphed unmistakably: I'll do what I think I have to do, about Chris. But don't get after me about this crazy ghost connection or fold in reality or whatever it is, because right now I won't have anything to do with it.

The traffic halted. She stared at the approaching flank of Fortress Hill, austerely umber grass marbled with eucalypt-green trees, granite temporarily gilded by the morning sun.

The traffic moved forward again. As Anne put the car in gear she said, too carefully neutral, "Good enough."

Dorian stood holding her door key and taking long breaths as if to go out on a stage or start a deep ocean dive. I hate this. I should be able to walk into my own flat without feeling I need a bomb squad to escort me.

She bit her lip hard and jabbed the key into the lock.

And it was just her own unit, the week's debris undisturbed on the dining table, Chris's briefcase propped against a wall, the Friday breakfast dishes beside the sink. The air smelt slightly fusty from two days' closure, and the James Brown oversaw the living room, its smooth grey rocks and angled planes of green-grey foliage as reticent, as cryptic as the side of the Blackston range.

After a minute she let her breath go and started inside. She could feel tension subsiding as if she really had walked a patch of mines. Okay. Tomorrow, I do it then. Check the L&C records. Start going after George.

"George?" Anne reminded her, as they set out for the courts on Tuesday afternoon. And Dorian answered truthfully but irritably, "No home address at L&C. It's Ben Morar or nothing."

"Not a good idea to ask Moira," Anne observed ruefully. "Not without a story of some sort."

"I suppose I could try the phone book." Dorian urged her brain to work. "If I knew which town. I don't know how to trace Tanya either. I don't even know her surname. I couldn't have asked Ralston, and Chris . . . Chris never said."

She looked away sharply into the sunshine, blinking back another unexpected film of tears. She sensed Anne making a business of changing her briefcase grip, adjusting suit lapels. In a moment, instinct said, she'll suggest some other project. The geology department, the archives.

"Anyhow," Dorian tightened her grip on her own briefcase, "there's another thing I should do. The Keoghs asked me to— turn out Chris's flat. It's—almost a month—and I haven't been near it." A month, her own thoughts said in a kind of wincing shock, a time at once immeasurably short and longer than centuries. "Who knows," she made herself sound hopeful, "I might even find an address for George. Heaven knows," the memory of that domestic chaos slid before her and she shut the dream-picture out of it, "I'm bound to find everything else."

They turned the corner to the court entrance. A sudden wind-gust flapped their skirts and feathered Anne's cheek with straight silken black hair. Her expression told Dorian she shared the memory, and with it amusement, affectionate, nostalgic, that for an instant blunted grief. For a moment Chris was all that mattered. She returned Anne's brief, rueful smile.

Tomorrow night, Dorian promised herself, unlocking her front door. Then, if Chris doesn't—didn't—have George's address, the phone book. If I have to ring every Richards on the list. She shoved the door wide with vigor if not enthusiasm and stepped through onto the wrong floor.

Bare, dusty wood. Marked with boot-tracks that said, lapsed housekeeping, as plainly as the slightly dulled furniture, the untidy dresser-top. The dirty plates, again, on the central table. And a man's voice, sharp, distinct, not English but not Dinny O'Rourke's accent, saying with throttled ferocity, "If they'll not do it, then we move now an' to hell with 'em!"

Then the listeners' faces spun him half to his feet and he froze, one hand flying to a hip, the other braced on the tabletop.

He was older than the others, lean and wiry with five o'clock shadow on a clean-shaven, hard-lined face. Dirty cream trousers, a collarless dun-brown shirt, small strange pouches, not tool-holders, on his belt. A threat in the whip of that hand that froze Dorian's breath.

The man across the table had frozen too, solidified in his chair. Black eyes, short black curls, a villainously dirty navy shirt, like a prototype T-shirt, the sleeves ripped out. Skin that never grew up in Australian sun, emphasizing a flamboyant dark moustache. Sheer stupefaction blanking a probably good-humored, even impudent stare.

The third man sat, this time, at the table head. He had pushed his plate aside for a pile of papers that had entangled a teapot and a half-sliced loaf, and he had been ready, at the very least, to fling words at the older man. Now his anomalously coiled posture promised far more than that.

Dorian's mouth dried. She heard a fly buzz against a window pane. The steady roar that underlaid it, like a distant city's voice. The creak of a chair. Clear and weirdly recognizable from period TV dramas, the jink of harness and creak of wheels, the soft thump of hooves as a horse and some sort of vehicle passed outside.

In an alarmingly expert furtive movement, the older man pivoted his eyes. The man at the table-head made one fierce gesture and the other froze, hand still in mid-reach.

The third man met her eyes.

The electric shock went down her spine. Then the fear changed. Recognition, memory, became glimpsed potential. Acknowledged, luring to them both.

Dorian's pulse raced. Do I . . . if I move . . . what will happen if I do?

The second stretched. Her heart thumped. And then that faint, ironic half-smile she had seen in his kitchen shifted a corner of his mouth.

He raised a hand. This time it was an acknowledgment. A greeting, to one already known.

Before he reached for the table-edge and started to rise himself. As a host would, accepting, welcoming, an unexpected but known guest.

And in one eternal millisecond Dorian made her choice. She yanked the key from the lock and stepped back and let the closing door speak for her, deliberate as a slap in the face.

I won't do it, she bawled at the silent wood. Her heart thundered, her legs quaked as if she had quarreled ferociously with someone in the flesh. I don't care if you'd have welcomed me, if I've insulted you or upset you or—whatever I did. I won't have you in my world, and I won't go into yours!

"Dor, that proves it! You can't try to sort out Ben Morar and ignore this! He's still coming back!"

"He might come but I don't have to go!"

"That won't help! *You* fell through last time for who knows how long. But the time before that two of us saw him, and this time three of them saw you!" Laura very nearly tore her hair. "It won't stop just because you say so and where the hell's it going to end?"

"So it's better I go looking for stuff at the *NQ Miner,* or his picture in the archives, and fall through and never get back?"

Dorian glared. Laura glared. Anne struck in swiftly, "You could go to the physicist and try to find out. What might be happening. What might happen—"

"Ah, bah, if he *could* explain what happens he can't tell us why! That's nothing to do with physics! And physics won't sort it out!"

"I am not going to the archives and I am not going to Blackston!" Dorian's nerve and temper gave way at once. "I'm not doing any more of this!"

"*Dor*-ian—!"

"Both of you stop!"

They wheeled in pure shock. Before they could recover Anne snapped out the rest.

"Laura's probably right but there's no sense pushing it like this. Dorian's probably over-reacting but anybody would after what she's been through. And yelling at each other just makes it easier for Pan-Auric to get off scot-free. Now will you both take a good deep breath and *think?*"

There was another age of reverberating hush. Then Laura gave an explosive sigh and yanked the clasp right out of her hair, ran her hands through the tangle, turned round twice and sat down in her office chair, thump.

"Goddamn it," she said. "Lee, I *hate* it when you're right."

The residual tension shattered. Dorian sank down into the client's chair. Anne let out her own sigh and leant both hands on the nearest filing cabinet.

"All right," Laura said. She drew in another huge breath. "I'm sorry, Dor. I shouldn't be—pushing you like that. It just feels so—urgent. So—important. Like this is the key to everything, and if I don't make you listen it's all going to smash."

Dorian rotated her shoulders and tried to rub away the band of tension that seemed to have become a fixture across her neck. "I'm sorry too," she said dismally. "It drives me crazy, that I'm being such a wuss. I know it's all tied together and eventually I—we . . . will have to deal with it. But how do I know what'll set *it* off again? Ben Morar's in Blackston—well, near Blackston—and *he's* in Blackston—When it happened before, at least the, the damn episodes ended properly. But when I tried in Blackston I fell right through!"

The silence rang like a hypersonic drill. And how do you know, it demanded, that next time, I'll ever come back?

She shuddered involuntarily. As if in response Laura twitched in her chair. "Dor, I know it's . . ." She stopped. "All right. I'll try not to shout at you. But . . ."

"But," Anne said in her softest most neutral voice, the one reserved for thoroughly hysterical clients, "the 'episodes' are still happening. That one was another escalation. And it happened here."

Dorian dropped her hands and stared at the wall. Instead of her Rigby print, Laura's office had a small Peter Lawson original, a farmscape on the Tablelands. The trademark near-Impressionist landscape, lush green cleared land, white dots of farmstead, swam under big cottony clouds, richly shadowed in lucent after-rain light. For a yearning moment she wished she could simply step into that simpler, distant world, where the biggest problem was the milk price and the highest hope next season's Wet.

Which is stupid, she berated herself, because those things were just as bad for them as megacorps and criminals are for us. And they lost people too, and it wasn't half as pretty as it looks. Any more than those really were the good old days, back where he is, in that further past.

I've been there, and I know.

"Okay," she said. She straightened her shoulders. "I'll do what I have to. I'll go on trying to clear Chris. If more episodes happen—then they happen. If clearing Chris takes me back to the archives—I'll go. If it means Blackston . . ." She set her teeth. "If that happens, I'll go, I suppose. But for now—only if it's to do with Chris."

She was aware of Anne staring, all but outright glaring at Laura. And Laura's mute protest, resistance, before she sat back. "Right," she said. "You're the one doing this. And Chris does come first. I just hope," with a wry note that was pure Laura, "this other thing follows your rules."

Dorian went in her own office door, taking more deep breaths, telling herself, It doesn't have to happen, and if it does you can turn around and walk straight out. As she passed, Mrs. Urquhart leant from her cubicle.

"Ohh, Dorian? You've had a call from Jackson and Griffith. Mr. Farrell asked if you'd ring back. Something about a will."

Will, Dorian's brain said blankly. Farrell? Oh. Mike Farrell, Jackson and Griffith succession lawyer. Drinks margaritas at Christmas parties, and sings. Terribly. "Thank you, Gloria," her mouth responded. "As soon as I sort my appointments out."

"Hello, Dorian, how are you? How have things been?" In professional mode Mike Farrell was as soft-spoken as he was unobtrusive, but the courtesy held a personal note. "So sad, losing your partner like that."

He came to the funeral, Dorian remembered, staring at his face in the holoscreen. One of the many who filed past, shook hands, kissed cheeks, murmured or muttered something. She pulled herself together and made bearing-up noises. He nodded, with what felt like genuine sympathy. Then he gave a little *tsk* to clear his throat and said, "Actually, it's about Chris I'm calling you."

Dorian's world tilted like a suddenly grounded ship. She heard herself say, "Chris?"

"He made a will, last year, after Karen nagged at him. You

know Karen. She handled his unit's conveyancing, but of course she didn't stop at that. It's quite straightforward, but I do need to, ah . . ."

The world tilted back the other way. Dorian gripped the underside of the desk. Her mouth produced a listening, "Mmm?"

Mike Farrell gave her his courteous, professional half-smile. "Chiefly . . . Chris named you his executor."

"We had the, um, certificate arrive this week. Signed by the paramedics at the, um, site, and the doctor on, ah, arrival." Mike Farrell shifted a little in his chair. Dorian knew he meant Chris's death certificate. Signed by the ambulance crew at the crash and the doctor who examined Chris's—

Body. She made herself think the word, staring grimly at a corner of the highly polished wooden desk, aware of the elegantly underlit office around her, the legal routine's patina masking bloody reality. Chris's body. Chris's death. Cleared by the certificate. Officialized.

When all it really says is that he's legally—dead. And what he died of. Nothing about how that happened or why. A death certificate can be issued if there's a bullet hole smack in the person's forehead. It doesn't have to say anything else.

"So," Mike Farrell went on, after another too careful pause, "we, ah, contacted you."

Because with the death cleared, lawyers can take the next step. Notify the executor, begin to implement the will.

The continued pause said he was waiting for her to respond. Gauging the state of her emotions, perhaps preparing professional aid for a distressed client, as she would herself. The thought made her meet his eyes, very grave under the smoothly barbered hair. She said, "Yes."

He looked minutely relieved so she guessed her composure

seemed intact. "I don't know if, ah, Chris discussed this with you at all?" When she shook her head, he passed a long envelope across the desk.

Dorian slid it open, not having to read the carefully underlined headings, client's name, document name, law firm's identification. The familiar phrasing stared up at her, Last Will and Testament, Christopher Brian Keogh, Ibisville in the State of Queensland, Bachelor, the form revocation of other wills, then the Executor clause. "I appoint Dorian Evelyn Wild Executor and Trustee of this my Will . . . hereinafter referred to as the Trustee."

He expected me to be here. He couldn't have expected this, but if ever it happened, he relied on me to sort it out. However nominal it seemed then. And not just because I'm a lawyer. She knew that as if he had said it in her ear.

She looked to the actual legacies.

Knowing Chris, she expected the disposal to be brief, and it was. Any current superannuation or life insurance to "my sister Bronwen Harris." A handful of stocks and shares to "my mother Elizabeth Anne Keogh and my father Brian Matthew Keogh." Then "the rest and residue of my estate, to Dorian Evelyn Wild."

When she finished, it was the first subclause that still stood before her eyes.

"All my intellectual property, including the mathematical model known as 'Christopher Keogh's Core-Log Statistical Analysis,' to be published or disseminated as the Trustee sees fit, to Dorian Evelyn Wild."

"The unit's, ah, more than half paid off," Mike Farrell was saying. "You could assume the mortgage yourself, or sell and pass it on. Or rent, and retain ownership. I assume," he smiled slightly, "you'll take over Probate?" As a lawyer herself, he meant, not needing Jackson and Griffith to do the rest: apply to the Supreme Court Registrar, advertise in the *Ibisville Courier*.

With Probate granted, begin distributing legacies.

Dispel Chris's legal reality, she thought, as she would his physical remainders, going through the flat. Books, papers, journals, to sell or to keep. Clothes to sell or give or simply throw away, because those she could not re-use.

Unlike the patchwork quilt.

Unlike the model, the other side of her mind jabbed her fiercely, pay attention and don't get maudlin here. *That's* what's important, damn it. Chris left it to you, up front and legally. In every sense, he's made you his heir.

Dorian folded the will and put it away. "Thank you, Mike." She made herself sound calm. "I'll take the copy now, if I may. And yes, I think I can see to Probate." They went through the details of transferring files, exchanging clients. Dorian took up her briefcase, working not to tuck it in both arms against her, and made for the door.

Inheritor, she thought, emerging into the almost garish sunlight. Heir. To more than the unit. More than the model. More than the other legacies. She gripped the briefcase to her with a fierce sense of cherishing, of protectiveness.

I'll sort it out. All of it, Chris.

"Chris did what? Made you executor, yeah, that's only sensible. But he left you the model? Really left it to you? The Palantir!"

Laura spun in her usual fashion when animated on a cell phone and Dorian caught a whirl of balcony, distant river, Mount Stewart's skyline, crisp hyacinth in late afternoon. A shoe and trouser-leg, not jeans but indubitably male.

Then they all disappeared. " 'Scuse me a moment," Laura was saying. "Call from a friend." A bang heralded closing balcony doors. Laura collapsed in a lounge chair and stared into the holoscreen like an eaglehawk finally sighting prey.

"So you can legally protect it! Whatever P-A does!"

Dorian nodded, momentarily tongue-tied. But Laura needed no boost now.

"So what'll you do, will you publish it, put it out for the industry—you could call a press conference! Announce the mine!" A gleeful skirl. "Really shake P-A's tree!"

"Laura, wait—"

"And now you can legally ask the LTU geology guys about the mine site! And," she nearly squeaked like a schoolgirl, "officially put the squeeze on George!"

"What on earth, how would I—"

"Oh, Dor, be imaginative, you're executor as well as beneficiary, you can prod Ben Morar to be sure it's clear and without claim. You can ask to see Chris's contract, even. If they won't let you at George you can go out there and look his address up in *their* records—and if that doesn't work you can front Moira instead!"

"Laura, that's—I'm not even sure it's legal!" But her own lips had turned up, her own reflexes stirring. Chase, they said, quickened with vengefulness. Hunt. Pursue.

"Do it anyhow!" Laura's teeth showed. "It's the best lead yet. If you really want to know what happened to Chris?"

"I do."

She thought it sounded normal. But she saw again that odd flicker of nerves or apprehension in Laura's face.

Then Laura was up and spinning again. "Call Anne, see what she suggests. Tomorrow we can make proper plans. Gotta go now. I have," for a moment the grin went thoroughly wicked, "company."

"I saw that," Dorian answered dryly, and let the holoscreen flicker away.

She put her phone up and stared at the James Brown, her brain finally reaching functional legal mode on her own affairs. The only uncertain part of that will's the model clause. Intellectual property. What do I know about bequeathing intellectual property?

Firstly, that Laura's right. Chris wasn't self-employed. And when you work for companies, they usually have some say. So, how did his contract with Ben Morar cover stuff he developed working for them?

She got up and went to Chris's briefcase, still propped against the living room wall. The remembered disk emerged from what felt like thickets of core-logs. "CK—Personnel Files." She booted her laptop and slid it in. Another thicket of file-names confronted her. She tried the directory headed "BM."

"Contract," said the first file. "Contract," said the second, and the third. With a pungent mental comment on Chris's filing system she clicked the first.

Terms of Employment between Christopher Brian Keogh and Ben Morar Mining Company, 21ˢᵗ March, 1999.

Dorian paused. If this is the original, there must have been changes, or why wouldn't this one do? She started scanning down the page.

There was no mention of intellectual property. When did he start developing it? she wondered. The model—the Palantir— Christopher's Fault? Shreds of data revived from an Intellectual Property seminar. "The two most important things about bequeathing Intellectual Property," said the specialist's gruff but incisive voice, "are proof of ownership and correct titling."

Dorian felt her mouth curl. So five gets you ten, these others are modified contracts making quite clear what the model was and whose it was. She heard Ralston saying, He had that thing locked up like a Westpac Vault.

The second contract was dated fifteenth September 2008. She found the new clause at once. "Regarding the mathematical model titled 'Christopher Keogh's Statistical Core-Log Analysis

Model,' Ben Morar Mining Company shall have full rights to any finds made by use of this model. The model shall remain the exclusive intellectual property of Christopher Brian Keogh."

So by 2008 he had enough on the page to guess what it might be worth. What it might do. And back when it was just pie in the sky, I bet George was more than happy to claim the hypothetical results and let the model go.

The contract dated twenty-third December 2011 had an addendum. "In the event of my death or any other termination of this contract, all rights in the model titled . . . revert to the beneficiary for intellectual property named in my will, Dorian Evelyn Wild."

She felt her eyes fill yet again. He didn't just take care for himself. And whether or not Karen put him up to it—I can check the date of that will—he went on taking care. Closing all the loopholes. Looking after his baby.

Putting his trust in me.

Then new-learnt paranoia cut in and she sprang up like the proverbial scalded cat. This was just sitting on my lounge floor! I never even opened the CD. And if Ben Morar knew—if Pan-Auric knew—! I can't get it in the bank tonight but I have to make copies, now!

"You could go to Ben Morar, yes." They were in Anne's office. Dorian had met her at the building door, CD copies in the briefcase clutched under her arm, trying not to shoot glances round the early morning street like some paranoid industrial spy. "At least, if you wanted to verify Chris's contract, you'd more likely phone them, but we could cook up some story." As Lewis and Cotton's equivalent of a succession lawyer, Anne was used to queries on wills. "Dorian, just calm down. You're here. The CDs are in the safe. You can take the extra to the bank at ten. Jackson and Griffith have the will's master copy. You can get them to keep a duplicate, if you're that worried?"

Dorian managed to move her hands more than a foot from her briefcase and sit back in her chair. "Sorry. Sorry." Her pulse still tended to accelerate, her breathing to speed. "It's just . . . will or no will, P-A's goon only had to take Chris's briefcase, and we wouldn't have a leg to stand on. And it's been sitting on my living room floor—!"

"Well, it isn't now." Anne sounded deliberately soothing. "Anyhow, they still don't know you have the model. Let alone Chris's message. And if they did, what could they do?"

Dorian looked round the office, so completely ordinary, so absolutely usual, so apparently proof against everyday illegalities. So like her own, where the abnormal entered so easily. "Well . . . sue me, I suppose. Contest ownership? No. Probably I'm just being paranoid."

"You have cause." Anne's dry smile emerged. "But P-A don't know your name, let alone your address."

Dorian gathered up her briefcase. "Of course they don't." She headed out, trying to banish the stubborn memory that kept springing up among the everyday. Chris's voice over the cell phone, too light, too cool, talking about a hold-up at gunpoint. Saying, *Pan-Auric are turning out bigger shits than I thought.*

At her unit door she thought, This time. Tonight. Chris's flat. I can't stall anymore. I have to face the familiar, stabbingly familiar personal debris, the things that will repeat at me, one after another, Chris. Chris bought me, Chris read, watched, laughed at, talked about me, wore me or used me when we . . .

She cut that off with new-learnt brusqueness and shoved the key hard into the lock.

I should have been warier. I should have waited, was her first, futile thought.

He stood in the middle of her living room. His living room. Parlor, her still objective part amended. Before she took in the overthrown table, the chairs flung down with backs or legs smashed, the spray of broken crockery over the boards. Strewn food, crumpled heap of cloth, a still-wet splash that might have been tea. The other china shards, and the swept-bare dresser top just above. Sheets of loose paper spread like leaves. The dresser cupboard, a jagged star punched into its delicate glass front.

His shirt had a shoulder seam ripped, buttons missing at the throat. The cowlick stood on end, the beard bristled like a cornered beast, a match for the glare. But not for the swollen lip, or the scraped, bruised sense of his whole expression. As if he had run face on against some unforeseen brutality. Or the actual bruise, already showing dark through the contusion's red, that was going to blacken his right eye.

He had jerked round as the door moved and his fists clenched to match the glare. Their eyes clinched and held with the violence, the immediacy, of a crisis surprised.

Then he let his breath out, a shaky little jerk. The fists relaxed, if they did not undo. The expression changed, from rage and defiance to a flash of recognition. To a welling bitterness.

He thrust out his chin. His eyes said, clearer than speech, So, here you find me. Bruised, probably bashed, certainly humiliated. Unable to defend my house. To stop whatever happened here.

Walk out again, then. Walk out now.

The silence stretched between them, drilling like a scream. Dorian felt her mouth half-open, and shut. That stare blasted her, bitterly defiant. I don't need anyone to see this. Especially you. You are not a demon visitation, you are a person. Someone I would have welcomed here. And you rejected it. Go.

Dorian's lungs were empty. Her legs wobbled. From pure

instinct she shut her eyes.

Light beat against her eyelids. White, unchanging. Motionless. Repeating, to the time of her heartbeats: He hasn't vanished. You have another chance.

She opened her eyes. The usual outrage, the usual questions drummed somewhere at the back of her consciousness: What happened, Who did this, Why? Remote as the usual useless banalities: Are you hurt? Are you all right?

There was a peculiar emptiness under her lungs. You shouldn't do this, something distant warned her, and something else, wildly reckless, retorted, Too bad.

Moving very slowly, she set her briefcase down.

When she straightened up he was still staring. But now she could see his eye-whites. The defiance had become simple shock.

Dorian unbuttoned her jacket and slid it off. Let it slip down over the briefcase. Met and held his eyes, and began rolling up her sleeves.

The rising bruise suddenly stood out like a thundercloud. His hands made one quick involuntary motion, to beckon or ward off she could not tell. Still holding his eyes, she said as softly as she could, "I'm sorry." And stepped forward over the threshold edge.

Her foot came down on carpet. The briefcase sat against her own door's jamb. Her out-stretched hands, her rolled sleeves, were still offering a message already out of date.

Slowly, Dorian pulled her mouth shut. Her hands back. Yet again her heart raced, her legs went weak, but this time there was a cruel inner wrench. As if she had been in rapport with a friend, joined in mutual reliance, and that bond had shattered too. Torn apart, painful as an overstrained muscle. Lost.

Uncounted time later she reached drearily down for her coat, gathered up the briefcase, and pulled the door to. Took one step forward and stopped.

The James Brown stared out across her living room, but the stereo speakers were on their faces beneath it with cords pulled out and her CD collection sprayed beside them like thrown cards. Half the books were off her corner shelf. The backlog on her living room table marked a whirlwind's wake, spilling in turn onto the floor. Through her bedroom door showed a prospect of tumbled clothes, open cupboards, up-turned drawers.

And Chris's briefcase was no longer there.

CHAPTER IX

The air went red as it had in the office after Gifford left. Then Dorian was at the unit phone, her fingers punching triple zero, her voice telling the Emergency operator, "Police." And more loudly, a few clicks and moments later, "There's been a break-in at my flat."

"Burglars do operate in the daytime, Ms. Wild, yes. Especially where they know the tenants are at work. Preferably in the afternoons. But you said, Break-in. And the windows are okay. The door's intact."

The young constable was warmer than Gifford, but Dorian could feel him cooling by the minute toward that ingrained police wariness. "I don't know how they got in," she said, and heard the snap sharpen in her own inflection. "Aren't there ways to do that? Pick locks? Skeleton keys? But you can see someone was here."

She just suppressed the exclamation mark. He nodded. His partner, an older woman, stood by the dining table, listening. Eyes tracking everywhere.

"But you said, nothing's gone."

"Not my valuables, no, my jewelry, the TV—I don't keep cash here. But my partner's briefcase—!"

"Yes, Ms. Wild." She tried not to snarl, Must you name me every time? Is it politeness or do you just have to remind yourselves who I am? "But we did find that, in the parking lot."

"Empty!" The snap got in despite her efforts. "All his work records, all his—all the other things—gone!"

"They probably grabbed the briefcase as a last resort. Maybe they were disturbed. They'd take off with that, to look through later. And when they found only records . . ."

No stranger to the juvenile courts, Dorian could complete the rest with bitter readiness. Finding nothing they valued, the thieves would toss the lot in the nearest trash. All Chris's maps and core-logs. All the ephemera of his working life.

Just the damnedest good luck the personal records weren't still in there. And the model too.

Then connections snapped together and she bit her tongue to stop the physical jerk.

Now, her mind spun desperately, now do I say, Those records might have been what they wanted? Do I blurt out: I've good cause to think this wasn't just petty theft?

Do I say, contact Sergeant Gifford in the TAS?

She had a vertiginous sense of crossroads rushing at her, far too momentous decisions to be made on the moment's spur, and a more vertiginous certainty: If I want this to go legal, I speak now. Else I don't speak at all.

And what will happen if I do?

At panic speed her memory replayed Laura's forecast if they actually had passed Chris's message to the police. Straight off to Ben Morar, and questions asked. What little element of surprise we do have lost, and maybe overwhelming forces roused for the counter-attack.

Has anything changed?

Except, reason cut in with icy rapidity, that we've lost the surprise. Because, she realized with shock, the counter-attack's already been made.

Can you prove it? The lawyer in her retorted. And what happens if you make the allegation without proof?

They were both looking at her, the policewoman blank-faced, the young constable with barely dawning surprise. Not suspicion, yet.

And before she thought, the decision had been made.

"I daresay," keep playing the part, outraged householder meeting random vandalism, all too common and the cops can hardly ever riposte. "I daresay it's lucky I have this much." Snarl just a little, if you turn furtive now they really might look at the holes in this, why the briefcase went but not the jewelry, how they got in at all.

"Very well." She made herself shrug, biting the rage down. "I've reported the crime. You'll let me know if anything comes of it."

"Of course, Ms. Wild." He at least was relieved to be let off the hook. He turned with the barest pause of decency for the door. Dorian kept her eyes pointed carefully after him, though every hair on her skin seemed to follow his partner's pause. The final look around. Then, with the usual enigmatic police nod, her movement in his wake.

Dorian stood and watched them go. As carefully, she kept her eyes from the fallen speakers, the papers and books. The briefcase, leaning empty-bellied against the wall.

I've done it. I'm a lawyer. And I've just tossed the legal option for dealing with this. Right out the door.

But how much of this was in the reach of law?

Her teeth clenched. The red slid back across her vision and thoughts burnt through it like a promise of vendetta: No, not a matter for law, you bastards. But justice is another thing.

It did not surprise Dorian that Anne and Laura arrived within ten minutes of her call, any more than that they instantly set to picking up, sorting out, stowing away, along with her. It only half-surprised her that they did it with no outcries, no questions, and more anomalously, no wrathful comment about delinquents and vandalism.

It does surprise me, she thought in a moment's hiatus, that they aren't scared. Because if they don't react as if this was a normal break-in, they have to have guessed what it might be. And that ought to scare anyone.

Only when the living room and bedroom had reached a semblance of order did Anne step back, run her eye across retrieved books and righted speakers, and turn again to Dorian.

Automatically Dorian set down the folder in her hand. In the bedroom, Laura laid her armful of clothes on the bed, and came out, her own look repeating, Conference time.

Anne said, "Did you check Chris's flat?"

"I didn't get there yet, there wasn't time—" Dorian re-aligned the question to present concerns. "You think . . . ?"

"I think," Anne said coolly, "that we check there before we think anything." She picked up her bag. "I called Sam. He's taken the kids home. I've got another hour or so."

Chris's door was shut. Apparently intact. Dorian could not keep herself from almost tiptoeing up, as if a mine could erupt under her feet. Or from reaching out, to give the door one timid preliminary push.

The lock was firm. But then, she thought, so was mine. She turned the key, pushed again, and stood back with an abrupt double twinge of apprehension. It isn't just Chris's flat, I'm not just going to remember him. The other thing, the—episode— that could happen too.

But the door opened on modern walls and carpet, the familiar furniture, the achingly familiar view out long windows to the sea.

And the chaos strewn from wall to wall. Even as half her mind cried piercingly, It's all just the same, the other half

185

snapped, This isn't the dream. You tidied this up. After the funeral.

She turned to Anne beside her and said, "Yes."

Laura craned between them. Began, "It doesn't look any different," and stopped.

"No."

Dorian did not have to go on. Anne stepped forward, gingerly, lawyer's reflex to avoid disturbing evidence. More like a cat in wet grass, Laura went after her.

In mid–living room they both stopped. Anne's eyes moved, Laura herself revolved, scanning the mess of fallen journals, e-books, things from walls and shelves, the disordered couch-cushions, the table pulled out of place.

The intact glass doors to the balcony.

Anne's shoulders lifted almost imperceptibly. And set. She turned, shepherding them both before her. "The Sandbar," she said.

"Anne, of all the loony—why the Sandbar? Why not Chris's place? Or Dorian's? Or mine, if it comes to that?"

Anne took up her usual white wine and gave Laura a thoroughly unusual steely look. The evening wind fanned hair across her cheek and the chancy light on the Sandbar's open frontage hid all expression but the set of her mouth and jaw. "Because any of those could be bugged," she said.

Laura yelped. Dorian felt an electric charge of shock and fear and all too affirming comprehension: Because after seeing Chris's place she thinks neither was an ordinary burglary. That means it has to be P-A. So if they have the tech to get in like that, they could have bugs as well.

She said, "The Sandbar's the one place—the one bar, even—where people can't get close enough to overhear."

Anne nodded. Feeling Laura deflate beside her, Dorian was

conscious of an ironic, half-reluctant relief.

"So you think it really was P-A. After the contract. Or the model. Or both."

Anne pushed the glass to and fro. Dorian's own wits began to mesh.

"If it was the contract, it could be just—damage control. To be sure—make sure—theirs is the only copy. So," her mind leapfrogged, "they must—might—be going to change theirs. Falsify it. Claim the model's their own."

Anne stared at her, unblinking. Far too still.

"But if they wanted the model . . ." Dorian's breath went. "If they wanted the model, then they know there *is* another copy. Not in their hands."

"*Now* they know." Anne clicked the glass-foot on the table in her trademark irritation point. "*How* do they know? And what else?"

It took a moment to work through. Then Dorian jerked her own glass so hard Coke leapt in a fan over the tabletop.

"Oh, God! They know about *me!*"

"They've connected me and Chris," she heard herself babble, while the Coke ran black-dark as old blood across silvery metal and dripped down on the planking floor. "George told them my name, or they checked the contract at Ben Morar, and they've found my address—maybe they asked Ralston, no, he didn't know . . . or—or—they have a contact at Jackson and Griffith—they know about the will!"

Laura exclaimed something. Dorian did not hear. The Coke was still dripping. Anne ignored it. Beside her, Dorian's peripheral vision said Laura had a hand to her mouth, but her inner vision was the only thing quite real.

If they know about the will, the next thing they'll come after is me.

She wanted to curl up, slink away from the table and the

open bar-front, run fast as her legs would carry her for—

For what?

My unit? My office? The police?

A plane out of here?

Anne's place? Laura's place?

Chris?

There isn't any refuge, cruel reason cut it into her. Not in my unit any more than my office, they know about those already. The police couldn't do much but bodyguard me, temporarily, if we could make them believe this at all. P-A's a megacorp: there's no safe place anywhere else. Least of all with Anne or Laura, who might get hurt—killed, her ratcheting mind threw up in a last honesty—along with me.

And Chris . . .

She felt her eyes fill and jerked her head away. He couldn't save me, any more than Anne or Laura. He couldn't even save himself.

Anne put the wineglass by, leant across, and closed a hand on Dorian's. A firm but not hard clasp, asserting more than reality. The touch of reassurance, loyalty. Support.

"We can assume what they know," she said. "What we need to ask before we go any further is, How much more do they know? And how?"

The sea-wind blew on Dorian's face, chilling the tears. She gulped, staring out into the dark of ocean, while evidence and deduction formed and joined, and slowly mapped disaster's shape.

"If they turned over my unit," she heard herself recapitulate shakily, "they know who I am. That means—they saw the will."

"Or," Anne returned levelly, "the contract itself."

"But if they checked that—!" She gulped. "If they checked that now, they *are* doing something with it."

"Then the next question is: Why now?"

"Uh." Dorian's wits clawed for traction. "Uh—it has to be the will! Oh, lord, Jackson and Griffith!"

Anne sounded more deliberate than before. "Suppose, maybe, that they didn't smash the laptop? And they've just got it unlocked?"

"The laptop! I'd forgotten . . . no. Wait. Even if the contract *was* on the laptop, that wouldn't give them my address." She clenched fingers in her hair. "And knowing I had a claim wouldn't tell them I had a copy."

"Even the will," Anne cut in evenly, "wouldn't tell them that."

"No. No. It's got to be something more. All of a sudden, they've got all the pieces. Who I am, where I live. The claim. The copy. They've *had* to search my flat . . ."

Laura was uncharacteristically still. Anne said, "Whatever message that sent you."

Dorian stared. Anne leant forward and set fingers down sequentially on the table. "They could have made it look like an ordinary break-in. They didn't. They didn't care if you figured someone was looking for something."

"And," she added, too coolly, "they did the same at Chris's flat."

Dorian gulped. Anne held her eyes, that look steelily expectant. But it was Laura who grunted as if punched in the back.

"They *wanted* you to know—they *know* you know who they are!"

Dorian found she had jerked back in her chair. The half-empty glass turned right over. "Oh," she heard herself whisper, as a fresh surge of Coke blackened the tabletop. "Oh, *God* . . ."

If they know we know, that break-in's not just covering tracks. Or careful lawlessness. It's a gauntlet. It's a challenge. It's saying, Come and get us, girlie. We know you've fingered us. See how much we care.

88888888888888888888888888888888888888888888888888888 stop.

Pan-Auric are turning out bigger shits than I thought.

Dorian wet her lips. Sound seemed to come back as if she had turned on a CD: wind, wave-wash, people laughing at the table behind. I don't, she tried to say, I don't, I can't take it in yet. I'm too scared even to wonder what we should do.

Anne shoved her glass aside. "What matters first," she said sharply, "is, How?"

Somebody should count to ten, Dorian thought. I've just been challenged—personally challenged—by a megacorp. I need a breather, before I can get up.

"How good," Anne said, "is Jackson and Griffith's confidentiality?"

Laura finally moved. Dorian jumped. "You'd know as well as us," Laura said. She shrugged. "They have to be as good as ours."

"Which means," Anne said into the falling pause, "anybody in the office could reach the confidential files. If they had the right story, or the right need."

"Yes, but—!"

Anne turned her hand over. "A friend of a friend. Internal stuff. Somebody asked someone something. Or let them in. Or someone gossiped. It wouldn't take much—"

"No." Dorian's wits came half off the floor. "That will was made, what, eight months ago. Nobody in typing or the paralegals would remember now. Or be interested. And if anyone asked a solicitor—Mike Farrell wouldn't just smell a rat, he'd lay out baits!"

Anne returned another of those steely stares. Dorian gulped. "You think, *our* office? Jason? Sandy? Heavens, Mrs. Irkitt? No! It couldn't be!"

"It mightn't have been intentional." Anne was frowning now outright. "Out with friends, trading shop, they throw in their

190

penny's worth, Oh, I remember typing that. They mightn't even know."

Laura put a hand to her mouth. "Oh," she said. "Oh, Jesus God."

Anne and Dorian both whipped round. Laura did not heed. She was staring past them, and in the flickering light she looked the color of turned cream.

For a second her eyes shut as if to lock out reality. Then she wrung both hands together and flung them out across the table to grab Dorian's.

"Oh, Dor. Oh, *God*, Dor! I know how it happened. I did it! It was me!"

"Troy," Laura said. She sniffled into her third tissue and stared through Anne's windscreen at the night-lit Esplanade, and said the name in a tone that made it the ultimate obscenity. "Troy . . . *Sorenson.*"

Who? Dorian started, and shut her mouth at Anne's glare.

Laura mopped a fresh fall of tears. Dorian waited, feeling as if she had been hit, repeatedly, over the head. She shot a glance out into the next empty parking space. Anne's right, no way we could let Laura fall apart in public, but let's just hope, if P-A *has* fingered Anne as well as me, and they do have bugs, they haven't got to tagging her car.

Paranoia, a vagrant thought answered wryly. When they get round to it, nobody does it better than lawyers.

Laura sniffed and struggled to sit up. And looked round, the effort visible, to Dorian in the back seat. "Do you remember, Dor? You phoned me. At home. The evening you knew about— Chris's will."

Dorian nodded. Then her mouth went dry. "You had someone there."

"I had *Troy* there." She squeezed the tissue as if it were a throat. "If I'd had a grain of sense . . . If I'd just been more paranoid!" A half-laugh nearer a sob. Then she blew her nose again, visibly steeling herself. One of her "boyfriends," Dorian thought suddenly. Another one we've never met.

"Troy . . . he's a Yank. Forty. Maybe more. That clean-cut—American WASP look. Going grey. Crop-cut hair. I—don't mind older guys. Or guys with a bit of—edge. I kind of liked the hair, on the fashion, I figured. If I'd just *thought*—!"

Audibly, she ground her teeth.

"I met him, the week before this whole thing blew up. Last night—I just *assumed* he was clean."

Anne and Dorian waited. Questions, now, would be more hindrance than help.

"He told me," Laura said, too clearly, "he was with an international company, up in Cairns. Some kind of building consortium. Security."

Dorian's neck crisped. She heard Anne breathe in, and Laura said it for her, bitterly distinct.

"A Yank, yeah, up here in NQ, in security. Any odds he *wouldn't* know Chris's P-A goon?"

Anne said, cutting each word like glass, " 'Army fuzz.' "

Dorian stared. But Laura repeated savagely, "Army fuzz," and hurled the wad of used tissues into the windscreen. "Chris said that, yes. About the goon's hair. And I never thought!"

"But—but—" Dorian's bludgeoned wits floundered to catch up. "Army haircuts, yes, security, yes, Yanks, okay, but that they're in the same area doesn't mean they know each other. U.S. security people are common as ants—"

"Get a grip, Dor! I bet you the P-A goon's forty at least if he's a VP's bodyguard, and I bet you he's ex-Army, and I won't even touch the odds they knew each other way back, maybe in the same unit—I bet he's a bloody personal *friend!*"

"But, Laura, where's your proof, your—"

"The proof's in what happened, Dor! If P-A did have the laptop, they don't have the will. If they did have the will, they still wouldn't know about your model copy. Our own clerks don't know that. But P-A had some source that covered it all. You called me yesterday. He was there. Tonight you come home, the place is turned over and the briefcase gone! How much clearer can it get?"

Dorian spluttered. Laura said flatly, "He could have heard through those balcony doors, if he was listening. Probably he didn't mean to. But I said something he understood. Something he'd heard about. From his mate. He'd listen then. He was down here. On the spot. And he could get in a flat, no trouble. He's security too."

Dorian's brain seemed to wobble in her head. "But what— how—"

"Come *on*, Dor! He called Goonboy at Ben Morar. Or wherever he is now! Hey, Okie, this is Troy, remember that Brit guy you talked about? I got some news, I'm down in Ibisville. And good ole boys stick together. Whatcha bet Goonboy said, Do me a favor, get her address, turn the flat out—"

"My address—! But how—"

Laura put her head in her hands and groaned. "My bag was on the table. I left him in there. I was having a shower, before we went out. Can anybody be such a fool and live—!"

Still three steps behind, Dorian protested, "But Chris's flat! How did he—!"

Laura blew her nose again. Coldly now, she said, "He turned my bag out. It had my organizer." She all but literally tore her hair. "And my cell phone! He only had to check the latest incoming . . . then query the address. Else he just tapped my organizer. With a flash-chip he could copy the whole contents. That wouldn't take five minutes. . . . And I did my make-up too."

"Odds on," she added, flatter still, "Goonboy put two and three together himself. The phone call would tie you to Chris. He probably told—Troy—to look at your place. For an address, a key." Her voice went suddenly tired. "Maybe Troy nicked Chris's own keys from the briefcase before he tossed it away."

Dorian wanted to double up and flatten as if to meet a bomb-blast, both hands clamped over her head. "No! No, it's too much! Too many assumptions, too fast, too, too . . ."

"You want to back Jackson and Griffith, then? If the leak was there—or at our place—why didn't Goonboy get it long before? Why's it happen just right now?"

"Wait—wait—!"

"We don't need to." Laura's voice sank. "The sequence is there. The logic's there." She bent over again and banged both hands against her forehead. "Oh, I am such a *fool!*"

Anne said, cooler than poured ice-water, "Do you remember what you said?"

Both Dorian and Laura jerked their heads up. After a moment, with the tiniest hint of impatience, Anne added, "On the phone."

Trust Anne, Dorian thought half-hysterically. Never mind blame, let alone sympathy. Cut to the consequences, and don't bother spelling them out. Track essentials back to where the slide began.

Laura's jaw had sagged too. Then she pressed both hands to her temples and paused.

"Dor called . . . just after we came in."

"Where were you?"

"In the living room—"

"Both of you?"

"Yes." Laura's face said she recognized the technique. Lead the witness to recollect small details, be sure you get the nearest

194

to complete recall. Anne nodded. "And you took it on your cell?"

"I had it right there. Dor said, I've had this weird thing happen. Mike Farrell called. They've cleared the death certificate. Jackson and Griffith have started to action Chris's will. He made me his executor. And he's left the model to me."

"And you said?"

"I said, Really, truly, or somesuch, and went out on the balcony—"

"What somesuch?" Anne shot it out as if shutting a trap. "Exactly what did you say?"

A car passed, filling their own with headlight glow. The wind outside hushed through the parking bay's big banyan fig.

Laura's fingers twisted in her hair. "I said . . . something about, Made you executor? Only sense . . . And . . . really left you the model? Hey, that's fantastic, that means—"

"You said all that in the living room?"

"No, I went out—"

"Before or after?"

Laura checked. Then her head went down and she groaned.

"I said most of the What-it-means outside. But inside . . . I remember now. I didn't just say, The model. I said, The Palantir."

The silence plummeted till Dorian felt the bottom must fall out of the car. She was half-aware of Anne's rigidity in the driver's seat. Of Laura's profile, chalky in the tenuous light. Of the peculiar inability to get her breath. This must be what it's like, in the seconds after a terrorist blast.

Then Anne said, "Let's do some reconstruction here."

The silence popped. Laura wheeled about to Dorian. Visibly bit back words. Grabbed another tissue and said, "Go on," in a voice Dorian had never heard from her.

Anne said, "If, for the moment, we accept Laura's theory for the leak." Though she sounded absolutely non-committal, Laura winced. "On the phone, 'model' would mean nothing to this Troy. Unless he already knew about Chris. And Ben Morar. And the connection with 'Palantir.' "

Laura sucked in a breath and stopped.

"One consolation," Anne went on in her precise courtroom voice, "at least you weren't set up."

Laura's hand flew to her mouth. Dorian gasped.

"To know early enough that Sorenson needed to chat up Laura, they'd have to know so much about Dorian that Laura's input would be superfluous. They could just bug or tail Dorian herself. But to know they needed that, they would also have to know about the will."

Laura's mouth fell open. Anne nodded.

"Like you said. Before yesterday, that could only mean a leak at Jackson and Griffith, and a much earlier break-in. Even so— how would they know they *needed* to check Chris's will?"

"So console yourself." Dorian could hear the faint, wry smile as Anne touched Laura's shoulder. "You're only one kind of fool."

Laura's shoulders relaxed for a moment, and re-tensed. Dorian tried to get her breath. Anne was already going on.

"But the phone call reaction does mean that—Goonboy—not only remembers Chris. He remembers the word Palantir. He might even figure Chris diddled him with the briefcase. And he knows—now—what the Palantir actually was."

Let me out, Dorian thought. I want to open the door and get out and walk away. From the car, from this chain reaction of disasters, this ever-widening X-ray of calamities.

But her brain went on working with the impetus of sheer adrenaline, If Goonboy talked to his friend, damn him: *yeah, this guy at the mine back-chatted me, I fixed him, though, haw, haw, haw, I rigged his car and terminated him.* The darkness swam with rage and grief and the thoughts kept running forward, as if she had a bug on that crewcut head: *But the sonuvabitch got his precious Palantir thing away after all, now this dame's got the legal claim AND the copy, I gotta get it back before she wakes up and the shit really hits the fan, if the boss—*

The thought-chain whiplashed. Dorian nearly shouted, "Did he tell the VP?"

"About sabotaging the car?" She raced the words out before Anne and Laura could interrupt. "He might tell about pulling the gun, he might turn in the laptop. But unless he had orders, would Goonboy say he wrecked the car?"

As both of them gaped Dorian ran with her thoughts like a fire in long grass.

"Say he didn't tell and he fixed the car on his own account, but now they've heard about the will and turned up the contract, and he knows he's in big shit. He's—killed a guy—and done away with stuff they need and P-A's going to drop him from ten thousand feet—so he's got his mate to eliminate the copies. He's trying to keep it all under wraps. . . . Just the way it happened in the war with Iraq, secret forces and prisoner abuse and God knows what, if he *was* in the Army maybe he was even there. He's just—taken the law into his own hands." Her own hands slapped the seat-top. "So maybe we only have Goonboy to worry about!"

"Only!" Laura started laughing half hysterically. "Only a pair of ex-Army Yank security goons with guns and bugs and God knows what and no control at all!"

"Wait, wait, Dorian's got a point!" Anne sat up with a jerk. "Lethal car sabotage is extreme, even for a megacorp. Goonboy *could* be working on his own, and have boasted to his mate—oh, damn, damn, damn! There's still too many variables!"

"*What* variables, Anne?"

Anne rounded on Laura. "What if he *is* working for P-A?

What if thingummy's changed jobs and is working for them too? Or is it half and half, and Goonboy wrecked the car on his own and then came clean to P-A when the will turned up? Or earlier? What if—we can't do a thing until we know more!"

"Well, well, what else do we need to know?"

Anne snorted and ticked off on her fingers. "From the old balance sheet: Where the mine is, precisely what P-A planned to make Chris go off the rails, if he was sacked or walked. From the new one: Did P-A order the accident, what actually happened to the laptop, what was or wasn't on it, and does it matter? And did or didn't P-A order the break-ins? That enough?"

More than enough, Dorian thought. Bad enough to be hunted by a pair of goons on a private search-and-destroy mission. But if the goons aren't wild cards . . . if, behind them, looms the juggernaut of a megacorp not merely aware but implicated, an accomplice, a giver of orders from the very start . . .

"Wait." She felt her back jerk. "Goonboy wouldn't just come and take stuff from Chris without orders. He—the VP—" Chris's words came back "—Reinschildt had to send him. That means . . ."

"That means P-A at least instigated the sequence. Whether they were responsible for all of it," Anne sounded icier than ever, "is another matter."

Laura grunted. Sat a moment lowering. Then grunted again. "Okay, we have to have more data. How?"

"Oh, God, not now." Dorian's nerve and endurance failed together. "All those what-ifs make my head hurt. I'm tired, I'm hungry, I'm scared, I don't want to—what are we going to do *now?*"

Anne gave her one swift look. Then she turned and switched the ignition on.

"For now," she said, over the engine's cough, "we're going to a motel. All of us. In the morning we're going to work." She glanced quickly up the Esplanade and pulled out. Beside her Laura demanded, "And then what? Jeez, Anne—"

"Then we tell Dani," Anne said. "Everything."

Chapter X

Dorian had seen Dani's office often enough to ignore the furnishings. Today the desktop's lake of polished silky oak glistened ominously, the oatmeal-leather corner suite squatted like an ambush site, and in the big Anneke Silver multimedia collage the watercolor suggestions of a eucalypt grove, barred white and lemon framed in slabs of violet, were blank as unknown bush. The sort of leather amulet at the bottom, brown as curling bark, looked like some lost explorer's relict.

Lost. Unknown bush. She had not expected to sleep last night, but now it came back sharp and clear as a photo-flash. Chris: I dreamed about Chris.

Really Chris, this time. I saw him standing by his four-wheel drive, both of them intact. Talking on his cell phone. Stance, gestures, sharp and decisive, settling a problem, I'd know the cadences in his voice. Sun dappled on his hair and his khaki workshirt, absorbing him into the shadows, losing him amid the white trunks and leather-brown bark-patterns in a clump of eucalypts.

Brief and acutely, her throat ached. She shut her eyes a moment. Then she opened them hurriedly as Dani came in, immaculate as her desk in a suit too muted to call yellow and too creamy to call beige, nodded them to the sofas, and sat herself, hands folded neatly as compasses in her lap.

As her eyes swept them Laura and Dorian involuntarily leant back. Dani looked at Anne.

"We have a problem," Anne said, "that centers on Ben Morar. We think it may overflow on Lewis and Cotton as well."

The debate on what and how to tell Dani had raged over security, the danger to their jobs, to the firm, the risk of mentioning the ghost. Of not mentioning the ghost. When the shouting finally ebbed, Anne had said evenly, "If we don't tell her, and the fallout reaches the firm, I'd leave before she fired me. We owe it to L&C. As for what we say . . . I'll do the talking. Leave that to me."

Now as Dani's eyes swung like gunsights Anne folded her own hands and began to summarize.

"As you know, Dorian's partner Chris was Ben Morar's senior geologist. He developed a statistical analysis model, to change the way they read drill-cores, when they're prospecting. He found a whole new mine somewhere. As you may also know, Ben Morar's been taken over by an international megacorp. Pan-Auric. They're planning to develop the find. But Chris didn't like their plans. He had a major disagreement with George Richards and a Pan-Auric vice president, and he resigned. Left for Ibisville, made an appointment with Dorian. Told her to find him a good environmental lawyer."

She stopped. Though not a finger moved, Dani's eyes seemed to have frozen from the pupil out.

"But as you also know," Anne said, "Chris never arrived."

Dorian realized how well Anne knew her audience when, in another five seconds, Dani's nostrils flared minutely. Then she said, "That wasn't an accident?"

Anne inclined her head. The leap of reasoning did not seem to leave her surprised.

"We have no proof." This was one of the gambits Dorian had resisted most strongly. Anne had merely shrugged and said, "With Dani, never overpush your case." Now she went on steadily, "The TAS ruled it driver error or bad maintenance.

But Dorian knew Chris. Bad maintenance is out of character. And driver error, on a road he drove at least once a week?"

In another second Dani said, "You said, he turned in his job?"

"We have a call. Left on his cellphone. Delivered when Dorian used it—afterwards. The police said, Mr. Richards claimed he was sacked. Chris said, he resigned."

There was a pause so long Dorian had to fight not to chew a fingernail. Then Dani's stare pivoted. She said to Dorian, "You didn't pass that to the police?"

Dorian squashed a twitch stillborn. "I had no substantiating evidence," she said. "I told TAS the bad maintenance ruling was—unlikely. They were reluctant to proceed on that alone. If I'd taken the call to them, they would have checked with Ben Morar. All Ben Morar, or Pan-Auric, had to do was produce a termination letter and contradict me."

Stop there, Anne's gimlet look warned. Dorian halted gratefully, more than aware that Dani could deduce the rest as rapidly as she spoke: Child's play then for the opposition to label Chris a liar and Dorian biased, and slough it all.

Dani's pause went another ten seconds. Then she looked back to Anne and said, "And?"

"In the call, Chris said that a representative of Pan-Auric took the hard copy of his mine presentation, and what this person thought was disk copies of the presentation and the model. Took them by force. The hard-copy wasn't in his briefcase. Dorian found the disk-copy hidden in the back, under a misleading name."

Dani nodded, evidently reading Anne's inflection and expecting more.

"The day before yesterday, Jackson and Griffith notified Dorian that Chris had made her his executor. And left her the model. When she went home last night, someone had got into her flat. The place was turned over, and Chris's briefcase gone. The police found it, empty, in the parking lot."

Dani's eyes whipped and Dorian found herself spurting, "They didn't get the original disk, I'd taken that and copied it and put copies elsewhere. And they didn't get the contract, that says Ben Morar gets the finds but the model stays Chris's property—"

The grey eyes went blizzard cold. "*Where* are the copies?" Dani said.

"Dorian made the obvious choice," Anne slid in. "The bank has one set, but there are others in her office files, in mine and Laura's files, and one in the Lewis and Cotton safe." She held Dani's stare, and Dorian, her own heart going too fast, thought, She knew Dani'd pick up Lewis and Cotton involvement first and faster than anything, and we've gone to the brink of unforgiveness by keeping it quiet this long. Only full disclosure is going to keep Dani even objective now.

Dani's gaze pivoted again. Dorian said hurriedly, "I didn't know they'd get down to burglary. I didn't know they knew who I was, let alone where I lived. I wouldn't—"

Ever knowingly have involved L&C, she never had time to finish. Anne cut her off. "This is where we go from facts to allegations. And suspicions," she said.

At the pause Dorian's hair pricked. Then Dani swung head and body as well as eyes toward Anne and said, "Yes?" and Dorian felt Laura brace herself.

"We deduce," Anne said, "an information leak. It looks eighty percent sure that someone at Pan-Auric learnt the contents of the will by overhearing a phone call between Laura and Dorian."

Dani's eyes swung again. Laura, abnormally stiff, said, "I was going out with a—an American. Security. He was in my flat when Dorian called. We think he knew—the person who took the stuff from Chris. And that person had talked, so he understood the call."

Dani's lips set all but imperceptibly, but like Laura, Dorian had to try not to cringe. Another Moira, Dani must be thinking, another lawyer who lets feelings override her brains. Another whole generation blundering for her to pick up the bits.

Laura's neck stiffened for all-too-clear protests and exculpations and again Anne cut smoothly as a scalpel between.

"We think the two consulted, and this one broke into Dorian's flat looking for copies of the model or contract or both. We're ninety percent sure because he tried Chris's flat as well."

She stopped again. Dani had solidified as she sat. It was no longer flesh and blood on the sofa, Dorian thought, it was calculating, computer-fast living steel.

But it still sounded like Dani, if a little colder and more precise than usual, when she said, "What do you want from me?"

Anne took a tiny breath. It was all Dorian had to guess that she was relieved.

"We don't have evidence to support any police action," she said. "There were no signs of actual break-in at Dorian's flat, and almost certainly there'll be no fingerprints. We have nothing more to give TAS about the crash, let alone justify a homicide investigation. We only know that Chris lost his property by force, and the perpetrator worked for Pan-Auric. And he was the Vice President's bodyguard."

Dani's brows contracted. Dorian could see her summing all that, possible company knowledge, company involvement, perhaps at the highest levels, and extracting the corollaries.

Anne nodded faintly and went on. "We don't have evidence yet, either, for a civil or environmental pre-emptive suit. We don't know what they planned, or even where the mine is."

Dani tapped one fingernail on the other hand. Anne said, "The burglary has exacerbated all this. We think we need to pre-empt any more—lawlessness. Firstly, to alert Lewis and Cotton that they may—inadvertently—become involved. Secondly, to figure out what really happened. Thirdly, to protect Dorian."

Dani's eyes turned. Anne said, "The bodyguard pulled a gun on Chris."

She let Dani assemble the rest: And Chris is dead. This person, or his associate, has already been in Dorian's flat. He didn't get what he wants. But he knows he has to, urgently.

Two shell-painted fingernails moved. Then Dani said precisely, "Lewis and Cotton are a legal firm. We do not support any type of vigilante action. Nor will we be involved in any—ineffectual court cases." We won't frank any sort of private revenge, Dorian translated. And you were right not to tackle TAS yet. Be grateful for your own sakes, because we might have disowned you if you lost badly and noisily enough. "On the other hand, we categorically deny that any business, however large, is above the law." Dorian saw Anne give a tiny sigh at her own verdict's reprise. "Lewis and Cotton will not accept such behavior. If it threatens our staff we will respond."

Dorian felt her breath go short. It isn't just lip service. She means what she says.

Dani turned, and Dorian did her best to withstand the chill of those grey eyes.

"You need more data," Dani said. "Leave the corroborative evidence and the copies where they are. As executor, you can legitimately enquire into the circumstances of—Chris—leaving Ben Morar. With intellectual property, don't you have to ensure the title's clear?" She glanced at Anne, who nodded almost as gratefully as Dorian. "You could call or visit Ben Morar. But—do you already have some plans?"

Only to chicken out, a part of Dorian's mind yelled, and keep chickening, while in a sudden internal stillness the rest ordered, Now. Choose. It's no longer a private thing, a vendetta in spite of the law. But it isn't safe, either. And nobody can decide but you.

Final commitment. Double jeopardy. Because if you go after Pan-Auric, you have to go to Blackston. And that means putting yourself in range of this other thing as well.

Dani was waiting. Anne and Laura were waiting too. Something else waited, she had the strangest sense, a presence, nothing so strong as an awareness, merely a persistence of presence, looking back over its shoulder from very far away.

Then the images rolled past her, Chris's shelves turned out, his briefcase stripped, her books tossed headlong, her clothes across the floor. The unbroken windows, the securely locked doors. Power and money's arrogance, blind to all but its own ends, oblivious of what damage it caused, what chaos it left behind.

A glass dresser front shattered, a chair broken on trampled boards.

The rage burned up like flame atop an uncapped oil well, an oriflamme, a banner the wind could only spread. No, damn you, she said silently. You're not getting away with it. Not here, not there. Not with either of them.

"I meant," she sounded a little too loud, "to contact George— Mr. Richards. He's on leave. Or suspended, or something. But he must know the big plan. Where the mine is, and exactly what made Chris walk. I thought, if I had an interview, I might confront him with the phone call. Ask *why* he told the police Chris was sacked."

Dani's stare had sharpened like the point of a knife.

"I know it could be—risky. But it's better than trying Ben Morar direct."

Dani's eyes were unblinking as a computer's Ready light. If Pan-Auric really will use murder, Dorian could follow the thought-train, better to encounter George outside Ben Morar, because a junior law partner's body could just disappear, out in that bush. More completely than the drunkard who was buried under his hat.

The steel-stare flickered. Dani said, "As executor, you're the logical choice. I'll give you compassionate leave. See—George. Get what you can out of him. Be aware he'll alert Pan-Auric the minute you're out of sight. I'll give you his address. His family are old Blackston. They still have a house up there. Once you've seen George, come back. Unfortunately, I don't think we can spare three partners at once. So stay alert. Keep contact with Lewis and Cotton. Report what you've done. Detail what you plan." The stare had chilled again. If we have data, and something does happen, it said, we can make your opponents rue it, however little that helps you.

God, Dorian thought, nodding fervently, I wouldn't want to be them if something does.

"Lewis and Cotton," Dani said, "would prefer to avoid publicity. But we will support any brief on this that will stand up in court."

Dorian felt Anne's twitch, saw Laura's elbow jump. No trumpets, no communiqués. But they too had identified another declaration of war.

Thank you, she wanted to babble. I'm sorry we sprang this on you, I'm sorry you have to be involved, sorry it ever started—but Dani was already rising to her feet.

"What you need is your own bodyguard." She sounded dispassionate as ever. "But since that news might spread in unsafe channels, probably better not. Before you go, write up a statement covering all this. Do it yourself, and put hard-copies in our safe and the bank." She started forward. "And keep me current."

For Dani, according to firm-lore, this was a full-scale alert.

They all rose as she headed for her desk. Anne said, carefully diffident, "Should we advise Moira?" and Dani's eyes swung back to her, solid ice.

Too flatly, she said, "No."

Halfway down the corridor Laura broke out in something not quite a laugh. "Jeez!" she said shakily. "She *could* give points to Arnold Schwarzenegger. . . . *No.* Just like that! And did you see her face?"

"She's right," Anne spoke so brusquely it underlined the parallel. Dani listened to Anne, Dorian thought, probably hired Anne, because she saw they're two of a kind. If Anne hadn't brought her this, she might not have listened at all.

"She'll tell Moira," Anne was saying, "what she needs when she needs. If we just fill her in wholesale, the first thing Moira'll do once she stops squawking is get a horrible case of conscience. And then she's as likely to go and warn 'poor George' just cos she feels so bad. At us for bullying him, at herself for thinking ill of him, who knows? Dani's been there before."

"Yeah." Laura drew a careful breath. "She's just so—fast. You'd expect a few more questions, a few swear-words, a couple of—ohmigods or something."

Anne looked at her curiously. "Haven't you seen Dani in full terminator mode?"

"I guess not. I thought, so, but . . ."

"She doesn't fool around. Especially if L&C, or L&C people, are involved." Anne's brows flicked. Is she too wondering, Dorian thought, how far, if it came to protecting Lewis and Cotton, Dani would actually go?

Then Laura balked in mid-step. "Anne, we didn't tell her about the ghost."

"So?"

"So what if something happens? Something . . . he is involved in this, I know he is!"

Dorian could hear Anne suppress both sigh and curse. She herself grabbed Laura's arm and pushed her on. "Never mind the dratted ghost." Dorian had reluctantly mentioned the latest episode the night before. Now, with Dani's momentum behind her, it seemed almost easy to set it aside. "Come on." She hauled Laura toward her own office. "Come and draw off Mrs. Irkitt while I get this statement done. Anne, can you get that address? And figure how I'm supposed to keep in contact, and with who? Then I need both of you to help me figure how I'm going to crack George."

Because, she realized, this isn't just going to be an interview. It's going to be an interrogation. Dani expects, and I fully intend, to break the so-and-so. Get the truth.

Finishing her statement took Dorian half Friday. The other half went on postponing or passing on her current caseload, amid efforts to keep Mrs. Urquhart unaware. "No, the leave's indefinite," Dorian was saying around four o'clock, as she fell back on her e-mail for the fourteenth time. "That means, I don't know when I'll be back. But yes, Laura will pass work on." The last three times the Inbox had been empty. This time there was a post.

"Dear Ms. Wild," said the formal opening, "I remembered your questions about Dinny O'Rourke the other day, when I was out in the NQ Photo Archives. If you haven't seen it yet, you might be interested in this attachment. Best wishes, Anthea Trevor."

Dorian ran her eyes past the name and her fingers flicked Open automatically. As the image came up she felt the blood leave her face.

It was the *NQ Miner* office. The old *NQ Miner* office. Slab walls, wooden veranda steps, two-rail fence. She could almost feel the impact of that gatepost on her back. But this time it was broad daylight, and here too the staff was out, posing before their workplace in the street. Dinny O'Rourke, trademark bowtie very visible, one foot elegantly propped inside the fence. Outside, two younger men faced him like bookends, solidly built, the stiffness of prolonged poses making their puffed chests and lunged legs slightly ridiculous; though not so much as the two boys aping maturity between them, one with a shoulder pulled up to his ear. The *Miner*'s boys, said a cell of memory from that darkened street.

And beyond them, two other men, one slight and fair in white trousers and pullover, standing formally, hands linked, offering a smile. English, newcomer, printed on him even to Dorian's untutored eye.

The second had one hand propped on a fence-post and the other on a hip. The posture announced, Australian. Getting photographed. Unimpressed. He wore high-waisted, dark, heavy trousers and a white shirt, sleeves rolled, collar lost behind the beard that cascaded over his chest. A beard that reached his mouth but not above his lips. High cheekbones and forehead, dark, deep-set eyes, unsmiling. Through the camera, across time, she felt the living weight of that stare.

"Ohhh, Dorian, the Trang Quai file, I'm sure this should be dealt with—"

Blood snapped back to Dorian's veins. "Just pass it to Anne, Gloria . . ."

Her lungs managed to start breathing. She felt her hand shake. His eyes held her, unsmiling, unblinking, as he had looked at the photographer. Not a challenge so much as a stonewall: Preserve my face if you choose. It will tell you nothing about me.

But it's him. Whatever his name is, he was there, then, at that moment. In the street, on the staff of the *NQ Miner*. In—her eyes slid to the photographed caption—eighteen eighty-four.

She managed to make her fingers move. The image folded into electronic space and Dorian sat back, determinedly not shaking, thinking, Why did Anthea have to turn this up *now?*

Mrs. Urquhart produced another distraction. Dorian met it automatically. Gradually, under the ongoing babble, her mind rallied.

It's just a coincidence. Corroboration, yes, but nothing more. It's not some sort of—omen. In an hour you're going home to pack and Laura's spending the night with you. And tomorrow you're going to Blackston. Putting a Forward on Anthea's message and clicking Anne's e-address, she thought dourly, I don't care if the whole *NQ Miner* staff's waiting on the highway. I'm going. And that's that.

And you have to go alone, Dorian harangued herself, as the Burdekin high-level bridge receded. Like Dani said, they can't spare three partners at once. And there's no point waiting till Monday, if George isn't at work, and who knows what could happen over the weekend? After all, the office might shut, but the mine runs twenty-four/seven. Chris told you that, long ago.

And if there isn't—now—anybody to play bodyguard, you have your cell phone. L&C knows where you are.

The road assumed its pink granite tinge. She pulled brusquely round a cattle transport, the last ridge topped and the skyline formed into Blackston's hills. As her stomach squirmed she told herself fiercely, Forget the other stuff. Focus on George.

The address was on Blackston's northern side, among the bigger old houses: mansions, Dorian sometimes thought, sprawling, single-story Queenslanders on huge allotments, trademark festoons of wood or iron fretwork along their verandas, ventilators like oversize iron chess queens crowning their roofs. Sometimes the cluster of nineteenth-century out-buildings, stables and kitchen and servants' quarters, had been preserved. And nowadays, big trees shaded clipped green lawns.

Dorian checked numbers, her mind chattering, I know it's Saturday and mid-morning and he could be anywhere, but if you can't risk a preliminary phone call, you have to take that chance. . . . The house was big, single-storey, corrugated iron roof. A rampart of orange Japanese honeysuckle draped artistically along the front veranda rails, the side was shaded by a heavy old mango tree.

And a four-wheel drive sedan stood in the open garage, its back thick with familiar yellow dust.

She drove steadily past and prepared to circle the block. As she swung into the side-street among suddenly decrepit houses, the bitumen vanished. The signpost said O'Rourke Lane.

Dorian gritted her teeth. Any more little "coincidences" and I'll . . . then a laugh snagged in her throat. I bet Dinny O'Rourke wasn't happy either, when his share of fame came down to this.

Nothing reacted to the sound of her parking, to the click of the front gate. The veranda had a full-height latticed door, a convention, since the flanking rails were waist high. Dorian settled her briefcase firmly under an arm and rapped.

Across the veranda the inner door stared back at her, announcing the conventional old Queenslander plan: encircling verandas, passage bisecting the inner block, formal rooms front to left and right. Then bedrooms, dining room and kitchen, or in the oldest houses, a kitchen entirely detached. The veranda boards were silvered grey with age. The inner walls were tongue and groove timber, painted a matte dusty green. Heritage colors, they called it nowadays, though this paint was anything but fresh. Long squatter's chairs dotted the veranda, cane tables, potted plants. Too loudly, she knocked again.

This time voices rattled somewhere out of sight. Female voices. The slightly distracted coo and drawl of well-bred but elderly Queensland women who have given the illusion of femininity, if not helplessness, most of their lives.

"If that's Elsie, tell her I'm coming after lunch."—"Yes, dear."—"Even with the pageant, she can surely run admissions until then."—"I'm sure she can ..." A step sounded, grey hair showed wraith-like in the passageway. "Elsie, did you want Connie right now—oh."

She stopped halfway to the outer door, a woman George's age or older: nondescript print housedress, perhaps permanently waved hair. The kindly, enquiring, weather-lined face of inland women, who fight the sun tooth and nail but take human decency on trust. "We don't—" her eye measured Dorian's suit and she visibly discarded, Avon lady. "Did you want someone, dear?"

"Good morning." Carefully, Dorian smiled. "I'm from Lewis and Cotton, the solicitors. I wanted a word with Mr. Richards. Some enquiries about Ben Morar, if he was available."

"Oh, the mine! Lewis and Cotton?" Her brow furrowed, but the reflexes of a lifetime, to receive graciously, to smooth business with hospitality, had already unlatched the door. "If you'll wait a moment. I'm sure he hasn't gone out." In a younger woman her turn would have been brisk. "Connie! Connie, it's a lady from the solicitors, wanting George!"

Incomprehensibly, the house replied. Its representative cocked her head and nodded, pleased. "Yes, he's down the back yard, the chooks have scratched out their netting again. Connie'll tell him. Have you come all the way from Ibisville, dear?"

"The road's very good nowadays." Dorian's smile felt as if it would crack. Small talk, that too was obligatory, the old bush rules would still apply. Nobody leaves a visitor-cum-guest standing at the door. In a moment she'll offer me a cup of tea. Lord, is she George's sister, or—with shock she realized she had never asked—his wife?

"I'm so sorry, dear, I'm Beryl, George's sister. Well, Connie is too. The children are all down south, we've kept the house going and we used to look after him, but now," the wave of a sun-spotted hand amplified, Now we're old enough to need looking after ourselves. "Connie helps down the Folk Museum, you know, so interesting, but I don't have the head for it. I do work with the church, not the old St. Paul's, of course, that's a theatre now . . ."

Stop it, Dorian wanted to yelp. Stop sealing me in this coffer-dam of gentle, old-fashioned, small-town gentility, this comfort-able, upper-middle-class feminine life. Museum volunteer, church helper, all of it worlds away from dust and ore and yield-figures, everything that makes the money on which this bubble rests, floating like a maidenhair fern, elegant and fragile atop the mud.

But it's what they must always have done, the mine-owners' and managers' wives, sipping their tea in Shelley china and talk-ing church bazaars, while round them the field roared and the mines belched smog and the violence and money and reality of the place raged like a walled-out stream. Used, but never ac-cepted. Politely ignored.

And I'm not here to meet some family scion still nobly sup-porting his aged sisters and his ancestral house. I'm here after George: the Ben Morar manager and ex-CEO. The man who brought in Pan-Auric. The man who shilly-shallied and lost his company and lied about Chris.

More feet sounded in the passage, heavier and relatively fast. George strode onto the veranda, wearing aged khaki trousers and a shirt much the worse for contact with dirt and, by the rents, chicken-wire. "Did you say Lewis and Cotton, Beryl, who did they—oh."

He knew instantly. The expression went awry from the classic mold of the face. Dorian seized the instant to step forward, offering her hand, saying, "We have met before, Mr. Richards. Dorian Wild."

"Miss Wild . . . of course. Of course. Ah . . ."

"I'm here with a couple of questions. Just routine. Some things from Ben Morar that we're tidying up." Don't give him time to rally, instinct warned her, don't let him make this social, he'll run for the women's shelter shamelessly, and you'll never have the heart to crack him in front of those gentle elderly faces, with their cup and saucer in your hand and their homemade biscuits in your mouth. "It'll just take a minute."

"Ah. Ah, er, of course." She had mixed his signals too, she thought. She'd made it clear she wanted business only, and he wouldn't refuse in front of Beryl and risk a catechism afterward. But he can't do the tea thing either, now.

He was nodding, trying to look poised, as if the decision was still his. Is that how women did it in those days? She moved a half-step forward and he gave way, ushering automatically. "Yes, of course, sorry, I'm not exactly tidy . . . the office is down here."

Along the left side-veranda, into the damp of frequent sprinkling and the dense shade of the mango tree, to a back, auxiliary room, perhaps a bedroom once. A window air-conditioner stood incongruously in the outer wall. The tongue and groove timber had been painted, general-duty cream. Inside was the usual modern paraphernalia of computer, papers, desk. Bookshelves, her eyes swept as rapidly as she could, mining books, A4 report folders, the miscellany of a working business, not a library. The only seat was the desk's work-chair, but George hurried through the far door and fetched an ancient straight-backed chair for her.

Dining-table set, Dorian thought. A heart-shaped back, elegantly spindly, with what had been a hand-embroidered cover on the upholstery. She sat down and tried not to seem afraid it would disintegrate under her.

"Miss Wild . . . ah." George was patently still short of an opening. "I—ah—" transparently, he abandoned further condolences about Chris. And he was not yet up to a bald, What do you want? She glanced swiftly round again, catching photographs this time. George with a boy and two girls and a woman, elegantly dark and groomed; then the boy in graduation mortar-board, then a wedding picture, very likely one of the girls. "Those are your children?" She pretended polite interest. "Do they still live in Blackston? And you and your wife? You all live here?"

George's shoulders twitched. "Peter—my son works in Sydney. The girls are married, down the Gold Coast, Cairns . . ."

"And Mrs. Richards?"

"My first wife," he said flatly, "lives in Maroochydore. Now, Miss Wild, you said something about Ben Morar?"

First wife. So there's another one somewhere. Two sets of alimony and settlements, maybe, and more children, too. But he was not going to take any more diversions. She made a business of opening her briefcase and extracting a copy of Chris's will.

"Ben Morar, yes. Just this week, I heard from Jackson and Griffith. They handled Chris's—my partner, Chris's will. He made me his executor."

He sat half back in the chair, his mouth making a small involuntary O.

"And he left his model—his statistical analysis model—to me."

His eyes went wide, also perhaps involuntarily. Vengefully, Dorian held his look. Yes, you lied to the police about him, you've probably let P-A have their heads over the model and the contract and maybe the accident, and hoped to duck it all. Now your chickens are coming home to roost.

"So as executor, as well as heir, I have to check the intellectual property inheritance. Find out what arrangements covered the model in his contract. With Ben Morar, that is."

Don't tell him you've already seen the contract, had been Anne and Laura's final tactical decision. Give him the chance to hang himself first.

"The—the contract, yes." His looks made it seem theatrical when he simply shoved a hand through his hair. "The model . . . I'm not sure, offhand, I can recall precisely what the details of the agreement were."

Dorian raised her brows. You can't? You were CEO, this was your Senior Geologist, the model was written into a triply re-negotiated contract, you just sold a major mine on the strength of its results?

"I don't have work stuff here . . ."

Dorian let her eyes flick round the shelves. Then what on earth is all this?

"Not personnel details, those are classified, they're out in the mine office. You should go to Ben Morar—"

"If it's just the details, that won't be necessary." Oh, you are a smart buck-passer, she thought, as well as a champion procrastinator. She fished quickly in her briefcase. "I have a copy of the contract—all three contracts—here."

He visibly controlled a gulp. Managed an approximation of surprised relief. "That's very efficient of you, Miss Wild."

"Well, Mr. Richards, I feel this is a very important invention. I wanted to check the agreement with the person who originally negotiated for Ben Morar. And the CEO. And I didn't know if we'd have access to the records, you being on leave." She sounded as guileless and hoped she looked more limpid than he did. Because he was staring across the desk with conclusions just melding into reaction. And it's not, her stomach said, just shock anymore.

"May I ask how you got these, Miss Wild?"

"Why, yes, Mr. Richards. The contract was among Chris's personnel records that he took with him when he left Ben Morar. It was passed to me with his other personal effects."

She almost felt him flinch. Then he held a hand across the desk.

"You're welcome to keep that copy, if you'd like." She concentrated on staying guileless. Let him know I haven't been silly enough to bring the original back in his reach.

"Ah, thank you, yes." He was paging through it, too fast to be reading, this is just another spar for wind, she thought savagely, he has to know every syllable of the thing, especially after he's just sold that mine. And he knows quite well what it said, or why's he look like he's bitten a lemon now?

"Miss Wild . . ." He put the papers down and re-combed his hair. "This all seems to be in order, as, as I recall we negotiated it."

"And it was signed?"

She held his eyes, thinking of his sister Beryl, consciously being sweet and innocent, and letting the repetition say it for her: I want that nailed down, yes.

"Ah . . . it was—it is signed, yes." He ruffled over the last page, with the light-pen facsimiles of his and Chris's signatures. "But, ah . . ."

Dorian waited.

"Er—you know, the company's been sold."

"Yes?"

This time she let the question show. What difference does a sale make to a contract sealed and signed?

"And uh—I don't know what, ah, the, ah, the buyers would want to do about—"

Dorian frowned. "Surely, Mr. Richards, they're quite clear on the law. The contract signed here makes the model Chris's exclusive property. The final version, also signed, makes it

equally clear, that in case of termination of—of the—contract—"
don't, she cursed herself, wobble now—"the model goes to
Chris's designated heir."

"Ah, ah, yes, but . . ."

"But?"

Don't ask if another version was negotiated, she cut herself
off. He'll grab the chance and say he doesn't know and send
you to Ben Morar again. Because he can't be sure if P-A's
already fiddled the contract, and he doesn't dare either betray
that or make concessions they might refute. All he can do is
stall.

"Ah, Miss Wild, I think the best thing is for you to go out to
Ben Morar and enquire at the office, ah, check with the personnel officer . . ."

"Mr. Richards, I'm not an expert in industrial law. But to the
best of my knowledge, a signed contract is binding on all the
signatories. Isn't that right?"

"Ah—uh—"

"And all parts of the contract are valid?"

"Yes, ah, but . . ."

"And Chris's contract has been—terminated. So it can't be
changed by a later form of the company. It's already—closed."

She stared into his eyes, the faded blue epitome of cowboy
integrity, and thought, Come on, you bastard. Put up or shut
up. Yes or no?

But the hint of tears she could not suppress had evidently
shown him a pretext for more sidestepping. "Miss Wild, I don't
know if this is the best thing for you at the moment—"

A red fog slid across the room and was gone. All right, Dorian
thought, and gritted her teeth.

"I'm quite well, Mr. Richards. But why should I go to Ben
Morar? This is a copy of the contract. You've ratified it. Will
whatever they have out there say any different?"

For a split second his pupils dilated. Then his eyes went hard. "Miss Wild, are you implying some sort of discrepancy? Some mismanagement, some—"

"I wasn't implying anything, Mr. Richards." *Oh, you are a weasel.* "I merely wondered why another copy would be different."

He drew himself up. "It's usual to verify *both* sides, Miss Wild, in this sort of case. After all," he touched the papers, "while you can vouch for this as coming direct from Chris's records, and doubtless from the solicitor's office, I have no guarantee . . ."

Delicately, he left the rest unsaid. *No guarantee that Chris didn't falsify that clause, and then simply present it to the solicitor as a fait accompli.*

And if the office copy differs, he can swear he didn't remember after all. Don't lose your temper, Dorian cursed. *The damn man's a mining CEO as well as a natural weasel. Of course he won't crack like a rotten egg at the first tap.*

"That's certainly true, Mr. Richards. I'll check this with the Ben Morar office, then." She saw the telltale loosening of eye-corners, the minute signal of relief. "And I can tell them you've verified this one, if there *is* a discrepancy."

His carefully suppressed glare riposted, *You bitch.*

Yeah, she thought. *You can't say, My word doesn't count. And you can't renege on what you just said. So if they have fiddled the one out there, the onus for proof will be on you. Let's see how P-A likes that.*

"Ah . . . I would certainly want the copies compared." He was really sparring for wind this time. "And I'm sure there'll be no problem." He handed the papers back, then made the prelude to a rising motion. "Will that be all, Miss Wild?"

Handing the hot potato onto P-A, she thought furiously. *Ducking out on the problem like you've done with all the oth-*

ers. Hoping the backlash won't come back on you.

Well, I'm not done yet.

"Actually, there was one other thing. When the TAS people brought me the final report on Chris's accident, they said their mechanic put it down to poor maintenance." After so many repetitions, she could bring it out almost without a quaver. "They also said, they were told Chris had been sacked."

She used the unvarnished idiom, and true to character, he winced. Then winced again, one hand raised theatrically. "Miss Wild, really!"

Not "asked to terminate" or any other pretty phrase, she thought, and no, no polite feminine female would come so near speaking ill of the dead, or whatever it is. And you shan't hide behind that either, damn you.

"Yes, it's very upsetting, Mr. Richards. To me as well. But I think it ought to be resolved. Do you know if this is the truth?"

The hand came down in a hurry. "I, ah, I—Miss Wild, is this necessary? After all—"

After all, Chris is gone, and you're his de facto widow, and surely, he was hinting with that so-useful politeness, it would be less painful to you to leave this in decent ambiguity?

She held his eye and let flint come into her own. "I'd feel much happier, Mr. Richards, if—one way or the other—I did know."

He hesitated so long she realized she was holding her breath. She tried to let it out imperceptibly, while he stared at the backs of his hands. And finally, with that beautifully managed simulacrum of decent employer forced to deliver unpleasant news, produced a short, reluctant nod.

"I hoped no one need ever know about this, Miss Wild. But if you must . . ."

"He was sacked?"

She probably said it too sharply. It was grief and rage, but vengefulness too. And she saw the flicker of revenge, near to pleasure, in his own eyes before he nodded again.

"I'd prefer you kept that to yourself, Miss Wild. Chris—Chris was a good man and a very good geologist, and we worked together for years. One unfortunate incident . . . just too much to overlook . . ."

She sat back and let her chair creak as it would. "Oh, I can believe there was an incident, Mr. Richards." She worked very hard to keep her voice noncommittal. "But there's something very strange here." His eyes lifted, he looked a little taken aback, but nothing else, yet. "You see, after he left Ben Morar, driving to Blackston, Chris dictated a message to me. On his cell phone." He looked startled now. "And when I got that, with his other things—the message was still there."

His back had gone straight. He knows there's an ambush, somewhere. Dorian took her phone out of her briefcase, set it on the desk, and pressed *Play*.

Don't take the actual phone, Anne had said. He won't know one from the other. But take the message on a phone, so he sees it in situ. So he thinks it's real.

The rattle and hum of engine and bush road filled the little office. And over it, the rhythms of Chris's voice.

"Told them to stick their job," made George frown, but he manufactured a look of bewilderment. Dorian could hear him readying disclaimers, Chris was upset, talking to his partner, protecting his ego, he couldn't admit the truth. . . . But then Chris said, "Reinschildt's goon," and she saw the jerk George could not conceal.

"Standover job," said the holo-image, with all the icy fury she recalled. "Pulled a gun on me."

Across the desk George had pushed back in his chair. The expression now was wholly unmanufactured. More than righteous shock.

"Took my disks," said the holo-image. "I gave him the hard-copy." Dorian narrowed her eyes and shut out her own feelings, watching like a cat at a mouse-hole. "Disk of the bloody computer game," Chris's image said. "Palantir."

George's eyes had dilated, but that was all. "When I get down," the image said, "I'll tell you the full story. Christopher's Fault. The Solitaire Two presentation." George's hand jumped on the desk so Dorian's heart jumped with it, shouting, Yes!

The bush and the beard blotted. Chris's voice said, "Take care." And the recording shut off.

The echoes seemed to die, slowly, in the office's hush. George had pulled his eyes away at the last. Had swung the chair a little, half-lifted a hand and let it fall.

"It wasn't," he said into the desktop, "supposed to be like that."

Dorian waited. Her every fiber itched to demand, What's Solitaire Two? Instinct honed by eight years of witness interviews countermanded, Don't risk a dry-up. Let him make his own start.

"I didn't know about that. Reinschildt—Reinschildt must have sent Brodie—I never knew! I would never have . . ."

Sanctioned such a thing. The sentence broke off with a little pushing gesture clearer than words.

"I never imagined . . ."

He yanked his eyes up and glared across the desk at her. "Damn it, you have to understand. Reinschildt, Reinschildt's a Pan-Auric Vice President, in his own area he's god. And Chris." Suddenly he slammed his hand on the desktop. "Chris was a good man, a good worker, a good geologist, he—what in God's name got into him?"

"Got . . . ?" Dorian let body language say the rest. Attention, spurious sympathy: let his knee-jerk responses to a woman make him think me a confessional, anything. Just don't let him stop.

"The mine—the find—it was his! His work, his model—I'd given him the credit, they'd have kept him on, they were falling over themselves to keep him, damn it, he did the plans himself, he made the estimates, he was *happy* about it! Then he comes ranting and raving like a rabid greenie—as if Pan-Auric's plans were totally different!"

What plans, Dorian did not have to prod. Her attention, her silence, were question enough.

"In heaven's name! A dam on the Burdekin tributary, we'd have paid the station and put it in ourselves, Pan-Auric could do that with a tenth of their Pacific budget and have change! We'd need that much water for the leaching mats, yes, what's so horrific about that, they use leaching all over the U.S.! As for trucking the cyanide up, they do that too, what if New South Wales passed laws against it, this is Queensland—with the proper precautions it's no worse than, than what we're doing now!"

He seemed to remember the tailings dam problem and his eyes swerved and in panic Dorian made a wordless encouraging noise. Perhaps it worked. In another moment he was off again, flushing now as his own memories revived.

"But no, it'll degrade the environment, the risk is unacceptable, we're going to rape a quarter of the state. As for the mine!"

He spluttered, waving his hands, so she could picture him confronting Chris.

"An open-cut, of course it'd be an open-cut, that's Pan-Auric's specialty. He proposed it himself! And Reinschildt said, a Big Pit, big as Kalgoorlie, the showpiece of Queensland, what in hell's wrong with that? We'd pay compensation, naturally, save what we can—but he comes raving about commercial rape and historical destruction and we can't just wreck all this forever for a, *a couple of gold bangles and some yuppie's ankle chain!*"

The end went up within brushing distance of a squeak. She could picture the scene in that office as if she had been there. Chris lost it completely. He didn't just change his views, he argued and protested and when that didn't work he must have raged. Whatever tipped the scales turned him in an eyelash-fall from a dedicated company geologist to a—a—"rabid greenie" doesn't cover it. God, she wanted to yell. What *happened*, Chris? *I don't know why I'm doing this.* What was it? Doing what?

George was still staring, on outrage's ebb. In a moment he'll remember who I am and any illusion of sympathy'll get scrapped. She jerked in a breath and tried for a concerned expression, adding confusion in her voice. "Yes, that's—that's very odd—"

"Not like him at all, no." George took it for what he wanted and gestured with the remnants of anger, bafflement. Regret. "And with Reinschildt he was worse. I thought the man'd have apoplexy!" Suddenly his own face colored. "But I never expected—I never thought—"

That Reinschildt would think to take—steal—a rebel geologist's own property. At the point of a gun.

"I don't understand." Dorian made a weapon of truth. "Why would Chris do that? You say the plans were nothing unusual." I know what the plans were—are?—now. But it's still not the key. None of this sounds odd, any more than what Ralston said.

So if it wasn't what they planned, was it where?

"If this was only a version of Chris's proposal, then was the problem something else? Was it the actual site?"

George's breath had gone in for a full-scale oration. It stopped in his mouth.

"Miss Wild, the mine site is classified company information." Now there was awareness of real authority in his glower. "I'm not at liberty to . . . In any case . . ."

He stopped again. His eyes dropped. And something in the

angle of his head, his shoulders, shut the words in Dorian's own throat.

George pushed a pen across the desk. Pushed it back. Dorian let silence speak for her, urging wordlessly, Go on.

"We have to have the mine." He said it softly, hurriedly, to the desktop. "Ben Morar, the lode's finishing. Chris—even Chris couldn't find what isn't there. The yield-figures, I couldn't—" He cut that off. "I encouraged him to prospect, I hoped that damn model would—I *needed* this find, I *needed* Pan-Auric—" His head came up and Dorian suddenly remembered Moira's words. *He looked so* badgered. *Not like George at all.*

"Miss Wild . . ." abruptly the glance was past badgered, it was desperate. "You have to understand. Beryl—Beryl's husband never made much. Connie never married at all. There's Susannah as well. Eileen. The alimony . . . I had to keep the company going. I have to keep this house. The shareholders . . ." He stopped suddenly and put his head in his hands.

Very, very slowly, Dorian let her breath out. Tried not to move her leg, on the verge of cramp. Does a priest, some cell of her mind wondered, learn the tact, the tactics of listening, among the skills of a confessional?

On a breath she said, "The shareholders?"

For a moment she thought he would not reply. Then his shoulders rose and fell.

"They're local." His voice sounded suddenly dead. "Not just the family. Johnson and Fairweather, the stores. Harris, the solicitor. Half the station people . . . some of them put everything into Ben Morar. Superannuation. Investment money. I couldn't—I can't . . ."

A hen cackled outside. The old house creaked, and from somewhere inside came a fragment of Connie or Beryl's voice.

You can't tell them, Dorian thought. You can't bring yourself to look them in the eye and say, This mine is failing. You've

wasted your investment, and your best move is to get out. So
you used a weak man's bravery and kept going, making stupid
economies, stalling the appeal, not fixing the dam. Hoping, God
rot you, that Chris's long-shot would pay off. I bet you did
know something when you went to Brisbane to meet Pan-Auric.
Or you spun them an inflated story about the model. And when
the mine came through, I bet it seemed like your own private
miracle.

I ought to melt for you, oughtn't I? A family man, the support of his aging relatives, the hope of his local acquaintances,
the savior of his town. Just when you thought it would be all
right, the whole thing was going to be knocked out of your
poor, kind, well-meaning hands. Who could blame you, whatever
you did?

Even now, when Pan-Auric owns the mine. And Chris is dead.

Rage seared back through her like a wash of acid. She gritted
her teeth and managed, with every resolve she had, to sound, if
not gentle, near polite.

"Well, Mr. Richards, if you can't tell me the mine site, or
what other factor might have made Chris—change his mind—
and I still need to check his contract at Ben Morar—"

She took her phone off the desk. Folded the contract. The
rustle brought George's head up. As his eyes followed her hands
she thought, One last try.

"Can you at least tell me—does Pan-Auric mean to go
ahead?"

For a moment she thought he would answer. Then his stare
narrowed. He sat a little straighter, visibly re-assuming the
persona of mine manager, local pillar of the community, family
support.

"I'm sorry, Miss Wild." And he's not going to admit that
they've shelved him, either. That in fact, he doesn't know what
they plan. "I think that's classified information too."

He followed her out, talking about the share market, the risk of advance information, and more delicately, that people with property in the mine's way would raise their compensation price. Ghoul, she thought. Hyena. You've sold them out. The people who invested their money with you, whoever these people are on the damn site itself, you've sold them all out, and now you're trying to make sure your thieving megacorp doesn't have to pay even what justice would demand.

The rage boiled up so she had to clench her teeth and walk mutely round the veranda, as if he had convinced her, and she were in full, silenced retreat.

CHAPTER XI

Dorian sat in O'Rourke Lane with red fogged vision and fingers shaky on the steering wheel. That man. That—dingo. Now, as memory replayed the encounter willy-nilly, she could tally their opposing balance sheets.

I told him I have copies of the model and contract. That I rightly own the model. That I know about Goonboy. That he lied about the sacking. I showed him practically my whole hand.

In return I have a better idea what P-A planned, but not if it's going ahead. I only *think* he didn't know about Goonboy bailing up Chris. I *think* he didn't recognize "Palantir." But I never got to dig about the Solitaire thing, the only one that did get a reaction. I still don't know where the site is. And he never admitted that he lied about sacking Chris.

What's more, I can't go back and ask why he said it, or who told him to.

Eventually she unlocked her hands from the wheel. The red faded. So, she asked herself bleakly, I've had my try at George. What now?

Report, said instinct and caution. Consult. And not just over a cell phone. Write it out, burn a CD, mail it to Lewis and Cotton. Record the phone conversations too.

That means, Hole up, replied commonsense. Find a motel, resign yourself to staying more than one day. Apart from anything else, if we do decide you're going to Ben Morar, you'll have to wait till Monday for the office to open. However that raises the risk of—something else.

As the sweat of anger cooled, her spine chilled. Resolutely, she shut out the thoughts. I said I'd go to Blackston for Chris if I had to, and I do. And I have to go to Ben Morar, and if I have to stay up here—alone—for two nights—I will.

I can fill the time easily enough. Phone, do the report. Check around town for Tanya. Do some research. Kalgoorlie. Ralston said it. Big Pit like Kalgoorlie, George said. She could hear the capitals. If I can't figure yet where this one is, at least I could fill out P-A's plans.

She drove down George's street, found the crossroad to the park and the town center, and at the park's lower corner, her eye caught the facade of what had been the Park Street Hotel.

It's a motel now. It still looks a hotel, though, two story, upstairs verandas, white and green paint, pillars and iron filigree, lovingly restored. Garden. Expensive. Old. Dangerous? Like the Paragon bar, a weak spot for an eruption of the past?

But the more expensive, the better chance of Net facilities. And the better the security.

She hit the brake and flicked her indicator to turn before the entrance went past.

The discreetly concealed rear parking lot was busy and full. Something on in town, Dorian thought. They may not have a room at all. Beyond the antique etched-glass door, down a paneled passage, past heavy, well-restored sideboards, a mirrored hall-stand, she found reception in the old hotel hall.

The girl behind the counter reached, "Can I help you?" before the phone at her elbow rang. She snatched it up, pressing it carefully among gel-spikes of red-tipped hair, and conducted a three-minute Yes-No, Sorry, Thank-You conversation before she turned to Dorian.

"Sorry, miss. Were you wanting a room?" At Dorian's nod her carmine lips pursed. "Some people have the luck. That was the Jenkinsons out at Bindaloo. Their caretaker hit a 'roo going home, he's in hospital. They've got cattle on agistment, now they'll be checking waterpoints themselves over the weekend. You could have their room. Upstairs, twin, hundred dollars a night?" She reached for the heavy, leather-bound register. "If you just sign here?"

"Is there something on in town?" Dorian asked, pushing it back, and got a look of patent disbelief.

"Amateur Races, started yesterday." Is there someone in the world, added the inflection, who didn't know? "And the Historical Society's doing their pageant. Blackston One Forty. Back to the Gold Rush, all that stuff. Re-enactments in the Stock Exchange. People dressing up in the street. Here's your key. Number twenty. Could you park in the numbered lot?" The phone rang again and she wheeled on it.

So what if it's a historical pageant, Dorian lectured herself, negotiating the old timber steps, creaking along the veranda. It's nothing to do with you. Anyone could scale this veranda, paranoia warned. She was grateful for the very modern security grating over the door's glass panel, the Yale lock beneath, the chain inside. And the door itself was old, solid inch-thick planks.

A corner room, twenty's further side had a tastefully grated window looking diagonally on the park. Despite the overcrowding twin beds, there had been a valiant effort to merge amenities like a counter, electric jug and TV among the old bedroom furniture, wardrobe, bureau. Washstand, with a decorative basin and ewer atop. Washstand, as there had been in that other Blackston room . . .

Don't jinx yourself, she thought fiercely, checking the phone jack behind the bureau. So it's an old hotel and it looks like his room, and they're—resurrecting the past outside. It doesn't have to invite "episodes." Pay attention here and now. Ben Morar. George. Report.

"Stay there," Dani said the minute she finished. "Phone the mine office today. If they're shut, wait till Monday, yes. Try to locate the secretary."

"I should have nailed him to the wall." Dorian felt herself begin to fume again. "He made me feel sorry—despise him. And I let him off. I should have said, *Why* were the cops told Chris was sacked? *Who* told them? And made him answer it."

There was a millisecond pause. Then Dani said, "If you did that he would still have stalled. But he'd have panicked as well. No telling what Pan-Auric might do then." Her inflection changed, signaling closure. "Keep me current." Before the phone clicked off, she added evenly, "Take care."

Calling Anne and Laura, a longer summary, exclamations and chagrin to match her own, took another half hour, but the final verdict was the same. "No," Anne said, at last, "you don't really have anything firm yet. I think you have to go to Ben Morar, after all."

"Should one of us come up?" Laura broke in. "Dor, I really don't like you going out there all alone. And if George does push the panic button, they'll have a day and more to plan."

"What can they do?" Anne sounded overly crisp. "If you go to Ben Morar, you go in broad daylight. You tell the motel you're going, you tell the mine you represent Lewis and Cotton, the minute you're through the door. The best they can do is refuse to show you the contract. And that plays right into our hands."

"Yeah." But Laura's tone spoke volumes more. What about this pageant, a deliberate evocation of the past in a place where that past nearly claimed Dorian last time?

Deliberately, Dorian shut that off. "I've plenty to do here," she said. "I'll write the report and copy it," she glanced at her watch, "then e-mail it to you." Twelve-fifteen, said the watch face, by the time I finish the post office will be shut. "Maybe, this afternoon," while it's light, "I can ask around town for Tanya. *Somebody* must know who she is."

By one-fifteen the CD was burnt, she had e-mailed copies to Laura, Anne, and Dani's special firm address. Her stomach rumbled. Lunch, up town, she thought. Two birds with one stone.

Ten minutes later she had her laptop and briefcase stowed in the hotel safe. In a moment of impulse, she changed her suit for a white blouse and a fawn cotton version of the new tiered calf-length peasant skirts, found her straw hat, and decided to avoid parking problems. I can walk three blocks, even here.

The minor streets were as she remembered: broad, empty, lined with wooden houses and scattered trees. The park corner where she had met Ralston went by. Then her road opened abruptly on double, triple-storied building fronts, and her stomach gave a sudden frenzied squirm.

Landers Street. This is Landers Street. And I ran round that corner back there, with the dogs just behind. . . . The vivid noon sunlight, the glare of white paint and corrugated iron and greenery behind her, the canyon of bitumen ahead swam as if water had washed across her view. No, she thought, clutching at a wall beside her. Not here, not now. No!

Her vision steadied. Landers Street was its modern self, sunlit, bitumen, narrow sidewalks, medley of low squared modern concrete and glass and lofty, ornate nineteenth-century wood and iron. Cars passing, people everywhere. Far busier than last time, she realized. Then she absorbed the number of cameras, the mix of jeans, stockman's hats and boots among the tourist unisex uniforms of loose shirt and shorts, and her eyes lifted to the banner spanning the street's upper end.

"Blackston One Forty," it proclaimed in ornate script. "The Gold Rush Comes Again!"

And the world's here again too, she thought, dodging a video-bearing family audibly American, side-stepping a pair of Japanese honeymooners getting photographed on the pillared porch of the old National bank. She threaded a gaggle of young graziers, less flamboyant hats than the stockmen, shirts like George's funeral gear, then caught a Lancashire glottal stop from the scarlet-faced woman offering a map to a blue Queensland Police shirt and hat. And, good heavens . . .

The past has come as well.

The skirts caught her eye first. Sweet-pea pink, misty blue, voluminous, sweeping the sidewalk with the lowest flounce. Then the hats, huge-brimmed, tilted insouciantly, just not quite Melbourne Cup spectacular. As slightly out of fashion as the parasols, frivolously small, long-handled, pale cream or white, held at the correct, photo-preserved tilt. Shading the long, lace-trimmed sleeves, the full-color, animated, consciously smiling young or middle-aged faces. Cleaving their way up-street through a delighted clatter of camera-buttons and a bow-wave of spectators, stopping traffic as oblivious tourists backed off the sidewalk for a better shot.

Well, the receptionist warned me, Dorian thought. "People dressing up in the street." And here they are. Modeling the upper-class women, the managers' and owners' wives, just the way I thought of them, such a short time ago. With a few self-conscious male heads among them, straw boaters, white trousers, sideburns, cutaway coats. A full-length beard, cedar-dark and curling, over a sleeve-rolled white shirt.

Dorian's hand clamped on an iron lamppost base. Landers Street spun like a kaleidoscope.

He was at the rear of the group. No, he was hanging onto the rear of the group, treading on the heels of the group, starting to crowd them like an antelope with lions at its back. The vertical sun lit him mercilessly, the disordered cowlick, dark-smeared shirt-front, crumpled sleeves. Sweat on forehead and cheek-bones, his head swinging to and fro, and the panic, almost tangible, that had started to whiten his frantically darting eyes.

For a blind-struck instant, all Dorian could think was, No. No. Then the rest hit like a blow in CPR.

I didn't fall through. He has. The pageant, the damn re-enactment did break the reality fold or whatever it is. And this time it's taken him.

And he's as terrified as I was. Of course he's terrified, it's broad daylight and it's always happened in my flat or my office, he's probably never been outside like this before.

And for how long?

Her feet were moving. She had no idea how. She was simply going forward to the pageant-players while sun and chatter and bright, meaningless smiles slid round her like details on a tapestry, the first costumed women's faces went past, the men's faces were altering too, self-consciousness become irritation, surprise. Somebody was flapping at the rear, a couple of middle-aged tourists had cut him off the herd, gushing over his costume, his beard, "Oh, my, you grew it specially, that was so brave!"—"By the storefront here, could we just get one photograph . . . ?" His eyes had glazed, he was coiling like a bayed stag, in a minute he would explode, shout, knock one of them down . . .

"There you are!" Dorian's voice rang like a gong in her ears. "I've been looking for you everywhere!"

His head whipped round. His eyes went white. But the rest of that expression said his knees would be melting worse than her own, his heart shaking him in near-blind relief.

She shouldered past the two tourists with some form of, Excuse me. Produced a bright, happy-friend smile. Dimly felt them, admitting the priority of acquaintance, beginning to withdraw, to release their catch.

He had stopped. The pageant-players moved on. The crowd folded round them and she was right beside him, looking up, as she had known she would have to, into his face.

"I'm so sorry I couldn't find you before." She was prattling, she could hear herself, and it did not matter, nothing mattered except sounding normal. Shifting attention, asserting reality. Making time for him to reclaim composure, and her to get them out of here.

If he doesn't just disappear.

He was right beside her, hot sun and proximity making the contact intimate as touch. He smelt of something acrid and mechanical. Surmise said, the press: printer's ink. And wood-smoke. And sweat, and something that was probably, a child-hood memory claimed in just-not hysterical identification, Sunlight soap. He was staring down at her, that stonewall expression still half-cracked by panic, shock. Relief.

He's totally lost, the way I was. Only for him, someone's here. There was time for a flash of gratitude before the next thought hit.

And I have to get him out before he does come undone.

If he doesn't vanish . . . but I don't have time to think about that. Any more than about the movement of her hand, reaching out, finding his arm.

The contact went through her like the proverbial electric shock. Her fingers jerked, his muscles leapt and in the hiatus where time went nano-fast she had room to think, We've done it. We've touched.

He was breathing hard, eyes white, muscles petrified under her hand. Shock. Comprehension. Our bodies have confirmed this is reality. Hand to hand. Skin to skin. Flesh and blood.

And he must expect it to break any minute too.

Without conscious plan or knowledge her hand moved as a nineteenth-century lady's would to claim an escort, into the crook of his arm. Maybe, she thought, she had said, "Shall we go?" Or perhaps the movement itself said that, a motion of his own world, one he would, even now, understand.

Because as blindly, as automatically, he half-turned beside her. His elbow lifted and came out a little to support her hand.

And they were moving up the street, just another couple, another diversion for the pageant-parade, costumes rather makeshift, but passable. . . . Someone actually took a picture. A digital camera, Dorian thanked God as her heartbeat steadied. If it'd been a flash, who knows what he'd have done?

An intersection appeared. Dorian's heart leapt, she closed her fingers and muttered, "This way." Beside her, he made some sound. Deep in his chest, a deep voice, something unintelligible that her brain said could have been, "Aye."

The sun hammered the cross-street, glaring in Dorian's eyes, beating on her shoulders and head. And he doesn't have a hat at all, and it's how far to the motel?

She missed a step. Her mind went broadside too. When did I decide on that?

He had checked in turn. He, said her scrabbling wits. Him. Reality. Here beside me, walking. Talking. Sort of. Not disappearing. Solid flesh-and-blood.

He was staring round now and the panicked look had reappeared. Her own brain translated what he must be seeing, the impossible mix of past and present in Landers Street, repeated here, in this street he must have known in his own world, just this moment lost or altered crazily, in the broad light of day.

And we've touched, we've walked, it must be five minutes now.

Her stomach twisted wildly. She ducked her head and tugged at his arm and as if he had shared the thought and the denied corollary, he moved.

One cross street, two. At the green verge of Lister Park his head came up. He made an incredulous, wondering sound in his throat. Then two cars and a four-wheel drive roared past them and he yelled aloud and nearly pulled her off her feet.

Stumbling sidelong, fingers wrenched almost open, Dorian managed, "Wait, stop, wait!" She yanked with both hands and he shied once more and stopped, shivering. She could feel it through his upper arm. Sweating, too, of course he never imagined anything like a motor vehicle, I'm lucky he didn't go clean berserk.

"Carriage," she babbled the first equivalent into her head. History revived. "Horseless carriages, like the train—no, not the train—" His head had swung, he gave her a scathingly incredulous stare, they had trains by the eighteen eighties, blast it. But getting Henry Ford, the car industry and the internal combustion engine in a hundred words was too much. "Oh, damn it, I'll explain later. Just come on—"

He balked. When he set his feet it was like pulling on a railway sleeper. Solid, heavy, bolted down. He stared her full in the face and said his first intelligible word. "Where?"

His eyes were darker than his hair, deep brown, not black but darker than coffee, than water stained by peat. Slitted into the sun. Impenetrable as his stare into that camera. Not fractured any longer. Battered by that look, Dorian tried to translate twenty-first to nineteenth-century terms and failed.

"The motel—the hotel." Suddenly it seemed a blessed sanctuary. "My room, we can talk . . ."

She stopped short. He had reared his head back so the stare became outright rebuke.

"Ye've a room? In a *hotel?*" His eye tracked downward. He visibly shuddered and yanked his stare up again and she thought a faint red tinge showed above the beard. "That—dress," he winced a little, "is better than the wee thing y' had last time. But . . ." The "time" came out broadened to "taime" and the "but" as a glottal-stopped "boot." And now it was a definite flush. "I canna—I couldna—"

The "I" was "ai," the "canna" sounded more like "carn." Struggling for verbal translation, Dorian took another minute to make the historical transit as well.

He presumes I'm a decent woman. And no decent woman in his time would have a room in a hotel, let alone offer to admit a man. He's embarrassed. He's scandalized. He's—

Shocked and dislocated and disoriented and I'm damned *if I'll have him criticizing my clothes and my customs before he even knows where he is.*

"Well, I do have a room," she snapped. "And in this, in my, where we are, women do that! It's perfectly ordinary! Now come on—damn it, I won't stand arguing in the street!"

"Dinna *swear!*"

"I'm not swearing, all I said was, Damn! God, all this and I have to cop a wowser too!"

"A decent girl doesna—" It came out "daecent," and the trailing edge on the verb was almost another glottal stop. But there was nothing unintelligible about the look on his face.

He doesn't know "wowser" but he gets what it means. And I can feel he's said that same thing before, over and over, to someone else. Some other girl. But he knows now how far outside his rights as well as his world he is, to have said it to me.

"I'm sorry." She took a deep breath and tried to master her own kneejerks. "I shouldn't have said that, either. I'm—I'm—" *Not going to plead like all those little fifties women, that I'm* "upset." "This, this isn't something I'm used to. . . . Look, let's just get to the motel—hotel, right? We can go on from there."

Go on where, her brain said, traveling forward linearly as a train. Here? There? Where?

He's still here. It must be ten minutes now, and he hasn't disappeared. We're standing arguing like a pair of idiots on the corner of Lister Park, me and somebody from the nineteenth century. And he's still here.

Again she saw the realization, the knowledge, the impossible, terrifying corollary flash across his face. And knew what it must mean to him, before he jerked his chin down and took a hurried step forward and muttered, again, "Aye."

But at the bitumen verge he balked once more, staring, prodding with a boot-toe, then turning with more than personal panic this time, demanding, "Whatever *is* this?"

"Bitumen. Road surface," she glossed hurriedly. "We use it for the, the cars." Another couple were roaring up. He shied, but this time not so badly, and his eyes went back to the road almost at once. She could see curiosity beginning to surface now. The curiosity, the wonder, of someone from a time almost close enough to deal with this world. To comprehend it, not as magic, but as an undreamt-of extension of his own.

And I don't have time for Road-surfaces 101 either. "Come on," she urged, looking for a break in traffic. "I'll explain. We can check it on the Net."

"The *what?*" said that deep voice behind her. But this time he came.

Dorian was thankful for a back stairway, and to reach the veranda with just another half-check, a stare, and a silent shaken breath. He remembers this place too, she thought. And dismissed it, pushing her key into the lock.

Getting him inside brought another jib. But then he visibly recalled her comments, and pushed over the threshold, though as he stalled short of the bed-ends and she went past to set her bag by the TV, she saw the tips of his ears were red.

And we can't both stand like a pair of stones in the middle of a motel room, waiting to . . . Her eye found the electric kettle. On a surge of relief she said, "Would you like a cup of tea?"

He made a sound between a gasp and a snort. Then he said, with more than irony, "What I'd *like*'d be a long drop o' whisky." It came out "whiskey" with an "i" nearer short "u" and a sigh that said it was barest truth. "But I'd no' look to find that here."

With an inflection that consciously added, Observe, I'm not criticizing this time.

"No—well." On her part she tried for something approaching conciliation, if not ease. "If you want, we can go down later. To the bar, the, the Ladies' Lounge, anyhow." He'll think I meant the main bar, where the men still go in outback pubs. And heaven forbid I should scandalize him again. At least, superfluously.

She filled the kettle. Plugged it in. Increasingly conscious of the hush behind her, upturned cups, threw in teabags, opened the little refrigerator—

"What in God's good name is *that?*"

"It's a—oh, heavens." She leant on the bench and found she had driven both hands through her hair. "Look, that and this and, and, all the other stuff you see, they're just part of—here. I can't—I can't explain it all just now. Not when I don't even know if—"

If you'll be here to explain it to.

Their eyes met and they both jerked their heads away. He made a sharp little motion with both hands, that had hung awkwardly at his sides, and half-turned to the window. Stood staring at it, out it, while the kettle came to the boil, and she poured the water. Made the tea.

"Do you take sugar?" I can't believe I said that. As if we were just having afternoon tea. . . . But his head came round. From the look on his face, the irony had not been lost. But he shook

241

his head. Said, "No milk," and came two steps closer to take the cup.

Dorian drew a deep breath. But he had already set his tea down on the bench end and confronted her, four-square now, those eyes weighing on her face.

"I crossed m'self," he said, "an' ye didna disappear. An' ye're no banshee. I've touched ye now. Ye're flesh an' blood." It came out nearer "blud." The dark stare sharpened like a railway spike. "It's time to ask then, before I take bite or sup wi' ye. Who are ye? *What* are ye? An' what d'ye want—*have* ye wanted—wi' me?"

The dialect jungle finally parted. Dorian stood staring up at him, feeling her jaw go slack.

Not a devil, you think, because you made the sign of the cross and I didn't disappear. Nor a banshee. The original sense came back. Bhan sidhe: not a wailing ghost, but a fairy woman, part of the inhuman host. But if I'm neither devil nor cruel Fair Folk, I may be something else. And you won't eat or drink with me, the old taboo on creatures of the otherworld, before you know.

She wetted her lips. Swallowed. Then she said, putting word on word like bricks. "I'm just an—ordinary person. A—human being, I suppose. And I don't—I never wanted—any of this. What I have to do with you—why this keeps happening—I don't have any idea."

He pulled his head back, tilted his nose, and stared. She held his eyes, letting that speak for her. Truth is truth, and I can't do any better than that.

The stare eased. He sighed from the bottom of his chest, pulled up his shoulders, and let them slump. Then he said, "Aye."

It came out in a long-drawn cadence, wordless, eloquent. Acceptance. Resignation. A social tic that had become reflex, part of himself.

"There are—we have—some of my friends have some—theories—about it. But—we don't really *know.*"

He looked back to her, frowning now. But the resignation had changed. He reached out for the teacup. Took a long swallow. Did a double-take. Then with a wry, more than ironic half-smile, set it back on the bench. Whatever my mind fears, that look said, the rest's already judged you human as me.

"An' what do these 'friends' say?"

"Uh." Dorian grabbed her own cup. "Most of it's very—complicated. Like the, the—" she waved at the refrigerator. "But we keep coming back to—it must have something to do with you."

"Wi' *me?*"

"With you." And now she was possessed with urgency, as if Laura had leapt to her elbow and started shouting, Ask him, find out who he is and what he is and everything else that matters, quick, any moment he could disappear! "So now you know I'm not a banshee and I know you're not a—who *are* you?"

He had half-pulled back again. But their eyes held, as they had held in the street, in her office, in his parlor, across that funeral tablecloth. Then, again, he made a little gesture of acquiescence. A man's gesture, she thought, in a world where courtesy demanded that women have precedence.

Before he drew himself up and said with that ready irony, "M'name's Ji—Seamus—Keenighan. M'mates call me Jimmy the News." A mouth-corner twisted. "The rest call me Jimmy the Mick."

Dorian drew breath, plunged back in a time that had been only legend to her. Resurrecting the shibboleths her grandparents had shadowed out, that had never impinged on her own life.

She said, "You're Catholic."

"Aye."

He had his chin up. She stood, staring, while the realities meshed: another time, a different world. A place, even in Australia, where your religion is the first thing that categorizes you. Not your age, your gender, your color, your political opinions, but your creed.

She said, "So am I."

It was more instinct than policy, but she knew it had worked. The chin came down a fraction. He took the cup again.

She said, "And you work for the *North Queensland Miner.*"

"For Dinny O'Rourke, aye."

He said it without a charge, of either loyalty or enmity, she thought. "But—you're Scotch?"

"I am not! And I'd be a Scot, no' a glass o' whuskey, if I was!"

"But you say, Aye?"

"I'm fro' Dungannon. County Tyrone!" He pronounced it "T'rone." "D'ye know nothin' about Erin at all?"

"Not much." Dorian was still too busy decoding pronunciation, and sense atop it, to take offence. "Isn't that in the north?"

"T'is the back-end o' Ulster, if that's what ye mean." His bristles were still half-up. "An' should that matter, at all?"

"I don't know. I don't know what matters." Dorian turned her hands out, feeling the insurmountable wall loom again. "I don't know if it's who you are or where you came from or where you work or—I don't know!"

His look went sharp. He moved to step forward, and stopped. He sees I'm distressed, she thought, with an odd little catch below the breastbone, and he'd do something about it. But he knows it's not his place.

He swept a hand around him. "Did none o' ye—these 'friends'—wi' all this—stuff. Do none o' ye have any idea? Not even how I—how we do this, this—"

This interception, she completed it. This bizarre crossing of realities that's gone on this time, now, how long?

"Chris said it might be a fold in reality." She yanked her mind back to the lesser hurt. "Some kind of quantum thing— I'm sorry, that's a, a sort of physics, that, that deals with probabilities. He was going to talk to a physicist—"

"An' who's Chris?"

"He's—he was—a friend—"

Partner. Lover. Her voice had said it all. His face translated. She ought to have blushed, she thought, but defiance kept her chin up and her eyes meeting his.

The stare changed. He said softly, "The wee man, the first time I saw ye . . ." Then he blushed himself, from ears to upper lip, flagrant, blazing red.

In bed with me, Dorian extrapolated, and averted her eyes and tried not to blush either on her own account or in sympathy, before wits cut in.

"That wasn't the first time I saw you."

His chin jerked up, this time in sheer surprise. She said, "Before that—I thought you were burgling my office, at work. And before that. You put your, your panning dish down on my head."

"I did what?"

"I thought you were a ghost. It was cold as ice and you were walking up steps in the middle of the Perp-Insurance elevator. You dropped the dish and picked it up, and rebalanced it on top of my *head.*"

He looked as if he had seen a ghost himself. His eyes were slightly crossed, his mouth hung at half-cock. And that damn lower lip is so vulnerable, above the first soft bristles of beard . . .

Dorian yanked her eyes up. He blinked and made a waving motion. "I'm no'—I *remember.* I was just in Ibisville. Dropped the dish, on the steps o' Ma Lang's boarding-house . . ." His hand made the cross as if involuntarily. "Ye were *there?*"

"I thought I was. I saw you, anyhow. We thought—Chris thought—you were maybe going to the Mines Department, or somesuch. To get your Miner's Right."

"An' much use that ever was. Twelve months chasin' mirages behind Crowstock, till I caught m' wits again. An' went to Blackston and talked Dinny into a new compositor, back where I belonged. But the other time. The 'office' . . ."

He stopped. "Aye." It came slowly. Amazement, and a bizarre relief. "I'd written a piece. At home. An' I went to the front room—the *parlor*—" The emphasis made it somebody else's term—"for m' notes. But it—changed."

Into my office, she thought. Different table, different chairs, different papers everywhere.

"I thought I was dreamin'—or crazy or—" With a jerk of the beard he cut it off. Of course. He wouldn't confess to fear. "So what else does Chris think?"

Her face must have spoken for her. This time the stare seemed to rivet her to the floor.

He came a step closer. Then he said, almost without expression, "He's dead."

Words stuck in Dorian's throat. She could only turn her face away, and curse silently at the tears.

"That was who . . ." He had not moved again. It was only the tone, the sudden softening of that queerly accented voice from harshness to thickened velvet, that brought him near. Near as he had been the day of the funeral—the funerals, she knew suddenly—watching her across the tablecloth.

And she could finish his sentence, beyond doubt.

That was who *you* lost.

Close as a touch, as shared experience, as kinship. Knowledge, understanding, shared.

Dorian swallowed. And managed, with very little shake, if to the window, "Who was it—with you?"

Cars passed, a Dopplered rush, people chattered downstairs. She heard crows cry, somewhere in the park, almost louder than his reply.

"Bridget."

The timbre said he was not looking at her. He had turned away, keeping the boundaries of both their griefs, staring at the other wall, the floor.

"M' eldest sister." Another, almost endless pause. "When I took on at the *Miner*. Send the girls out, I told Ma, I've wages now, I can look after 'em . . ." It shook suddenly, ragged as an unstayed bridge-pier. "Ah, I thought I could . . . An' there was naught back there for 'em, wi' Pa dead, an' both our jobs on the *Banner* gone. An' her an' the girls back out by Rock, hoein' in the tatie patch, save us, wi' that fat-necked sod of a brother bletherin' about charity. Could I have shifted Ma I'd've taken 'em all, I *knew* it had to be better here. But Bridgie was the only one."

Carefully as if moving crystal, Dorian turned. He was staring down at the countertop, into his half-emptied cup.

"Bridgie had the nerve for it. An' the cheek, she'd make a whole shift laugh. A tongue in her head and a spark in her eye, every day was . . ." Light on water, the gesture said. Gaiety. A dance. "Small wonder Patsy Burke was a case for her, first time they'd a crack." It came out somewhere between "creak" and "crake" and Dorian discarded thoughts of cocaine sales. Sometime, I have to get him to translate. But not now.

He had come to a stop. She whispered, prompting as she had not done with George, this time to ease rather than interrogate.

"Was it . . . childbirth?"

From an eye-corner she saw his head whip round. Astonishment and more at her having leapt four steps from attraction to courtship to marriage and on to those times' all too frequent result.

Then the rigidity eased away. To the countertop he said, "Aye. They did wed. But t'was cholera took her off."

Dorian felt herself breathe, "Oh." Remembering other history lessons, not about the high rate of childbirth deaths, for mother or child, but about disease on the fields. Bad hygiene, worse medicine, and the graveyards filled with anonymous dead.

"Patsy," he said, still not to her, "I think it's nigh broke Patsy's heart."

And yours as well, she thought, feeling that verb-tense like a jab in the solar plexus. For you, as for him, it's still only yesterday.

"I'm so sorry." It's so banal, she cursed, and yet, what else is there, without formality or fulsomeness, that I can say? If I was family, I could hug you, at least we could touch.

And if I did that now, you'd run like the proverbial scalded cat.

"Aye," he said again. That long falling cadence, not so much announcing closure as admitting grief had worn the mourner out. Then, again, she felt his attention shift.

As quietly as she, he said, "What happened to Chris?"

She felt her eyes fill. She felt but did not see him move swiftly around her, the cup taken from her hand, something nudging the back of her knees: the seat of the counter chair. Inviting her to sit while he slid down across from her, perched incongruously upright on the end of the nearer bed. The eyes fixed on her face, the silence saying, without importunity, When you're ready, then. You need to tell it, too.

"Chris." She took a deep breath. "He was a geologist." She glanced up, did they have geologists then? But his eyes answered, Yes. "He worked at a mine. Outside Blackston. He invented a, a new way of reading drill-cores. When they're prospecting."

"He did *what?*" He had jerked forward as he sat. It was not shock, it was comprehension. And more than that. "He had a way to read assays? To pick the way a reef runs? With a, a drill?"

"Aye. I mean, Yes. The assays, but not from the actual ore. From the drill-holes they make before they mine."

"Jeeezus." He said it more like "Jaezus," but the length made it reverence. "They can do that before they dig?"

And we don't have time for Mining 101 either, damn it, there's so much he doesn't know, so much he'd love to know. "They do that nowadays, yes. Chris, Chris had this, this mathematical model, he analyzed the drill-cores differently. Statistical analysis . . ."

He waved the detail aside. That dark stare was almost drilling through her. "An' it worked?"

"It worked. He found a mine. A big mine. Two or three square miles. Low-grade ore, but they can refine that, nowadays. They could have got it out, with an open-cut."

"A who?" He was nearly springing off the bed. "No, no, sort it after." He's already adjusting, she realized, bypassing stuff he knows we can recap. "So they did it?"

"Well, the company—the manager went looking for a takeover. A bigger company, that could carry the cost." He was nodding impatiently, mine mergers, she realized, are as everyday to him as they were to Chris. "And they bought it. The mine. They would have kept Chris, they wanted the model too."

His eyes narrowed. In a moment he said, "What went wrong?"

"I don't *know!*" She heard her voice rise and pulled it down. "Chris was happy, he called me, he said it'd be big enough news for *The Australian.* . . . Then all of a sudden he changed his mind. Tried to stop the mine. Had a huge row with the manager. And the takeover Vice President." She heard him whistle through his teeth. "Quit his job. Walked out. And they . . . the VP's bodyguard—held him up. Took the mine presentation. Tried to take the model as well."

He swore, acridly, under his breath. Not in English, but she recognized the tone. "But the wee feller'd never let him have it? Aye?"

"No." She half held back tears, half stifled a laugh. How come you only saw him once, and you know him so well? "He diddled the, the hold-up guy, and he got the model away with him. And going down the range—he had an accident."

She heard the hiss of breath. But he sat quite still, the heavy, thickly creased material of his trouser-leg a dark mass in the corner of her eye.

"Cars—they have steering gear—like a, like a coach." He made a sort of snort. "And the, the steering—broke."

This time he made no sound at all.

"The police said it was driver error. Or bad maintenance."

He gave a short, ferocious snort. "Aye. The polis." The contempt was acid-deep. He cupped a hand and shifted it. "D'ye know who filled *their* fists?"

"I don't think anyone did. Not about that." Far from me to deny all police corruption, Dorian thought. Not with Queensland's past. "But I think—I'm almost sure—it wasn't an accident."

"Aye, but d'ye know?"

"Well, Chris left me a message. I found it after—afterwards. On his—" You're going to explain cell phones and Save files? She caught herself and found her bag, groping for the phone.

"And what bit o' deviltry's that?" He was eyeing it definitely askance.

"It's—oh, Lord." Dorian resigned herself. It has to be sooner or later, and it may as well be soon. "Do they—do you know about electricity?"

"Benjie Franklin's wee lightnin' kites? Aye, but what's that to do wi' this?"

"Uh . . . well, nowadays, we know how to make electricity. Like steam." Gratefully, she fastened on the analogy. "We've figured how to use it, and it drives everything."

His eyes had gone almost round. She reached out to tap the jug. "We heat water. We cook. We," ice, her brain supplemented, they used ice, "we use it to keep things cool." She pulled the refrigerator open, found the milk jug, pressed it against his hand. He let out a sound that was not entirely shock. "And, and—do you know, in, in your time, about the telephone?"

"In Blackston, in the year o' Our Lord eighteen eighty-six? D'ye think the exchange girls carry share prices to an' fro like blackfellas, runnin' round wi' little forked sticks?"

"Oh. Sorry." She tried not to laugh. "Well, this is one of *our* phones." She picked it up. "No exchange. No wires. And a picture too."

As she had for George, she set it on the table and pressed Play.

When the image came up he made one small movement, too quick to call a jerk. Then he sat absolutely still. Only when the image was a minute gone did he shift. And draw breath. And murmur it, just above a whisper.

"Aye."

Crazy, Dorian thought, as her eyes filled. They never met. Yet I don't think Chris will have a better epitaph.

After a minute he said, "What's he mean wi' this—computer game? Palantir?"

"Oh." Let's not try for Gaming 101 either. Not now. "That's what he called the model. It was a joke, a code name, so I'd know what he meant and—other people might not."

"Ah."

251

Another little pause. Then he said abruptly, "So ye think, this—agent—put him away? Chris?"

Dorian tried not to gulp. How'd you get there so fast? The rest of her brain retorted, Because he lived—lives—in Blackston in the goldfield days. He'll have seen worse mayhem than this.

"I can't prove it. I do know the company lied and said Chris was sacked. I know their old manager didn't know about the hold-up." Typical manager, said his snort. "I know someone broke into my flat—my, ah, my room—looking for something, and took his papers. But the model, and his contract, weren't there."

"Aye." His eyes were fastened on her now. He was nodding, and something about his expression was familiar. I've seen him look like this before.

In that pub, she realized. Listening to the miners, with exactly that look. Ire, sympathy, compassion. Determination to do more than talk.

"But I don't *know* what happened, or who ordered it, or what happened to his, his other papers and stuff," let's leave laptops for now, "and I still can't figure what made Chris do his turnabout, and worst of all, I *can't locate the mine!*"

"But ye've the papers? The, the, presentation? There must be a map?"

"There is, but it's all geology. I can't make head nor tail of it!"

"Geology?" The stance tightened, the eyes sharpened. "D'ye have it here?"

"You could read it?"

"What, d'ye think we dance round that press all day singin' 'Mountain Dew'? I've read lease layouts an' reef-maps an' geology reports these last five years." His hand was out. "Give it here."

"Oh, it's downstairs in the safe, I'll just go and get . . ." She was already scrambling up. And computers'll be a crash course too, I hope his brain doesn't combust.

If I come back, and he's still here.

Her feet stopped. He looked up, and their eyes gripped like fists. Then he lifted a hand in earnest and waved her out, adding that twisted, self-derisive grin. "On y'r way, then. I doubt I'm goin' t' melt." The grin changed sharply. "Not yet."

Chapter XII

Dorian scuttled upstairs and shoved open her door on the same counter and TV, generic motel quilts, white and dark bulk on a bed-end. The turn of head, the already familiar irony in that stare answered, You can relax. I'm still here.

Or is relax the right word?

She felt both their faces change and ducked the knowledge yet again. "Here we are," she said unnecessarily, pulling the door shut, setting her laptop on the bench. "I'll just plug it in."

"Plug?" Half amused, half bemused, already accepting that there would be no time to explain. But he was on his feet, hovering over her, bafflement shading into that nearly comprehending curiosity, and that into anticipation of the next marvel she would unfold.

"You have to connect to the power. The electricity." She pulled the lid up. Pressed the power switch. "This . . ."

This is a computer. How can a man to whom cutting-edge tech is a manual telephone exchange have any idea what that means?

Dorian shoved hands through her hair again. "This is—a machine for doing maths. For writing, um, letters and things. For connecting to the Net."

"Net," he said. But it was not a question, it was remembrance. You said that before.

"The—the worldwide—the worldwide telephone network, where computers can exchange information and bring it back, and show it here."

"Computers. The machine. The *machines* talk to each other? It's naught to do wi' ye?"

This is a man who crossed himself and thought you might be Sidhe. He's doing his best, but he's one generation from, maybe, pure peasantry. He could fall into rank superstition any minute and start talking about stealing souls. Mind takeovers. After all, it's not so long since we were making films about that ourselves.

"They're just machines. Without orders, they can't do anything. See, I had to switch it on. And pick a program—tell it what I want." She tapped the icon for her file finder. "It's a keyboard, see? Just like a typewriter."

"A *type*writer!" Suddenly he was right beside her, his beard almost in the keys. "That's a typewriter? Like the wee machine in the bank? That! That's what it can do!" He nearly bounced upright. "Ye drive that with electricity?"

"We do." She had stood up too, her own face was cracking in a grin. Oh, no, he's not a superstitious savage, he's smart and he's open-minded, he hasn't just started to follow, he can guess how it came from what he knows, can imagine the changes, the progress it has to mean. "Let me show you, I'll get up the presentation for the mine."

"Get up? Ah, aye." Jargon, she could hear him thinking, another strange usage to file. But he was staring at the screen now, mesmerized.

"That." He put out a finger, delicately, almost timidly. "That's a—picture? That's—how do they do *that*?"

He's seen paintings, she had time to realize. He'd never have seen color photography. Let alone a 32-shade monitor. The trademark Microsoft green hill and cloud-dappled blue sky suddenly looked like the entry to fairyland.

"It's a—an electric image," she managed, simplifying madly. And he drew a long, long breath, and she thought of the Keats poem they had learnt in school: Cortez staring at the Pacific, on a peak in Darien. "It's photographs, color photographs, they get processed and changed . . ."

"*Color* photographs." He was not stunned, or dazzled either. His own future had opened before him and he was tracing its vistas with sheer delight. "Ye have color photographs!"

"Oh, yes." She wanted to burst out laughing with him. There's a lot of things wrong with our world, but yes, we have miracles too. "But the mine . . ."

He tore his eyes away. "Aye. The mine." But he went on leaning beside her, a tangible presence, the height, the warmth, the sight and sound and scent of him, brought from some impossible distance and yet here, close in more than proximity.

Come on, Dor! she could almost hear Laura snapping. Never mind the touchie-feelie stuff. Pay attention here.

"Yes. Okay." She had copied the presentation on her laptop, just for security. "Here we are."

He bent closer instantly. His stance said he could read the map, had followed it almost as fast as Chris. He made a little attention noise. I see. Reached a cautious finger, touched, then followed something round among the drill-site annotations and elevation lines. The finger came away. He was quiet, still staring. Then, almost at her shoulder, she saw his brows move toward a frown.

"There's words somewhere? The site-report? The geology?"

"Here." She scrolled, bringing another quick breath— surprise, wonder?—to reach the verbal version. He leant in and started to read.

The screen closed mid-paragraph. Reading the motion of his hands she scrolled again. He finished reading and this time it was a definite frown. Then he straightened, stood back and shoved a hand into his beard.

"What is it?" Dorian could contain herself no longer. "Is

something wrong?"

He turned his eyes without moving his head, an uncanny echo of that older man in his parlor. The darkness weighed on her, deepened by the renewed frown.

"An' ye say, ye dinna know where it is?"

"*I* don't know, all those rock-names don't mean anything to me."

"But he told ye. On the, the message. He said, Solitaire Two."

She stared. He stared. When he clearly expected her to leap tall concepts in a single bound, irritation got the better of her. "I don't understand! *What's* Solitaire Two?"

"Ye don't—" He visibly checked himself. You can use the wonders of electricity, that look said, but you're only female, after all. The hard stuff isn't in your sphere. "It's right here." The ironic half-grin came, and he pointed at the floor. "Y'r wee feller must've known the name. It's here. Right on top," the grin was widening now, "o' Solitaire 'One.' "

"Damn it, Jimmy!" It was out before she knew. "What the hell do you mean?"

Then she caught herself. "Okay, okay, I won't swear, and I should've said Seamus, I know—will you just explain?"

She was getting The Look again. Condescension? Disapproval? Disbelief? Then one mouth corner curved a fraction. "Ah," he said, "Jimmy'll do."

"But you said—"

"Aye. I was Seamus wi' the Land League and I'm Seamus when it's Home Rule an' down the Society wi' leaflets an' all." The half-smile came and went and the expression that followed was quite different. "For here," with you, that very specific look said, "Jimmy'll do."

I didn't get that, Dorian thought. It mattered. The look said that. But I didn't get it and I did get that it's not something I can ask. She pulled herself together and infuriation jetted up again. "Then will you explain this, please?"

If, said the amused glance, you don't bite my head off first. But he said, "The Solitaire's the big new reef. Ye do know 'reef'? The gold-bearin' stone?" Her outrage brought an open grin. "T'is the one they found deep minin', the way Dick Cox invented, an' they said'd never work. They've no' long struck lode, an' the crushin' figures've made Peep o' Day look sick . . ." Suddenly he threw his head back and words spurted into a laugh. "See Dickie Cox, when y'r wee Vice President trots up an' says, Hoy, I'm peggin' another one, right on top o' you!"

"Who's Dick Cox, what's Peep o' Day—oh!" Dorian very nearly tore her hair. "What *are* you talking about?"

Now it was his turn to stare. "D'ye not know the Peep o' Day, the biggest mine in Blackston? Or the Solitaire, it's been the talk o' the colonies the last twelve months—"

The sentence broke. For a moment the silence between them was jagged as a cut.

Then he said, very softly, "What year *is* this?"

Dorian gathered herself together. Made her voice as quiet as his.

"It's twenty-twelve," she said.

In the hush, she watched his color change, and the sign in the street came back to her. Blackston One Forty.

For him, it's eighteen eighty-six. For me, it's been a hundred and something years.

It was so quiet she could hear him breathe. Could follow, with an ache in her own chest, the changing look on his face. The not at all joyful comprehension. The successive blows of deduction, and the silent, bludgeoned summation of it all.

A hundred and something years. Here, Dick Cox is dead. Dinny O'Rourke's dead. Patsy—she felt her own breath catch—Patsy Burke is dead, dead and forgotten, it's all gone and forgotten, except—

His eyes had crept to the window. The bludgeoned looked remained, but then his brows crooked again. He put a hand in a trouser pocket and pulled out an old round watch, glanced at the dial. Stared at the dial. Lifted his head back to the window and muttered, "What's come to the shift? I never heard it change?"

The mine shifts, adrenaline translated for Dorian. They must have signaled them, with sirens or something, she had vague remembrances of that in South Australian industrial towns. And of course he'd know when they changed. As surely, as unthinkingly, as a Moslem would know when to listen for the muezzin.

His eyes came round. She did not know what her face said but they suddenly went white-edged as in Landers Street. He took three fast steps and yanked the door open, striding across to the veranda rail.

After a hesitation that seemed year-long, she followed him.

He had both hands clamped on the rail. He was leaning out, staring into the clear sky over Lister Park as if the park did not exist, and his face spoke a nightmare beyond incredulity.

That's east, she thought. And the photographs came back to her, the smog, the dust that would have veiled the sky, that treeless horizon thick with ore-dumps and mullock heaps, palisaded by lofty brick mill chimneys, serrated with mine poppet-heads.

She half-turned instinctively. And as instinctively stopped her hand in its outward reach.

At last he drew his own hands back. Let them fall. His shoulders had sagged with them. He drew a long, long breath.

Then he turned and those eyes were darker than lost memory.

"No wonder ye didn't know," he said. It was soft. The brink of a very different wonderment. His eyes flicked out to the skyline again. "Ye'd see the chimneys, from here. Bonnie Dundee. St. Patrick's. The Worcester. Victoria an' Queen. The Solitaire . . . East Mexican. Peep o' Day." A sudden spasm

259

moved his face. "Aye, even Heuffer's Peep o' Day. T'is gone. T'is all gone. They've pulled it down."

"I'm sorry." Her hands did move then before she thought, touching his shoulder, landing on his arm. "I'm so sorry. I don't—I don't know them, no."

The deepest cut of all. A hundred and some years on, no ordinary person remembers them.

It was another pause that hung forever, and she had no idea how to make it end. Do I say, it mightn't matter? Do I say, Any minute, you could be back there, this could all be gone like a soap-bubble and you'll have the *Miner* and eighteen eighty-six in Blackston, everything like it was?

No. It can never be like it was. Because you've been here. And you'll remember it.

Then pure ice-water ran through her veins. She jerked her head away, from him, the veranda edge, the clean empty sky. He's been here now, how many minutes, how many hours? I remember the streets of his Blackston, another world's lasting reality and that vertiginous terror of being trapped there, oh, God, I wouldn't, I couldn't wish that on anyone, I . . . What am I going to *say?*

A hand touched her shoulder, fleeting as a butterfly. The deep voice with that alien accent said, too quietly, "Come inside."

He pulled the door to behind them, as he had seen her do. She turned between the beds and yet again, they held each other's eyes.

I can't say it. I can't admit it. Even to talk about it, that might make it real.

As if my blasted face didn't say it for me. Because his was transmitting it back, the fear, the inexorable encroachment of reality, the knowledge that the episode hasn't ended yet, this is far longer than it's ever been, and if it doesn't end . . .

He could be here for good.

Then, quite clearly, the look changed to acknowledgment. Acceptance. A wry, characteristic, half-ironic resignation. Before he lifted a shoulder and repeated that long-drawn cadence like a sigh given voice.

"Aye."

"I never thought—I never meant—I don't know why this is *happening*—!" I wish I was a nineteenth-century female, she thought wildly, I could just burst out in buckets of tears and he could pat me and give me a handkerchief and pretend he could make it better, and feel better too.

No. He's never had that sort of pouter-pigeon ego. He sees things—he sees himself—with far too much truth.

She felt him look at her. Look away. Turn toward the window. Push the curtain aimlessly, then finger the material. She swallowed and swallowed again, hunting words, hunting reasons, feeling her efforts strike that insurmountable wall and rebound yet again. Insufficient data. No cause. No explanation. It happens, and we just can't tell why.

And now, what are we going to do?

She moved as aimlessly, to the counter, the computer, the teacup tray. In a minute he'll ask, and I don't have any answers. Why is this happening? What am I doing here? What are we going to do now?

She turned, feeling as if her legs were lead. At the least, I have to face him. Whatever, however little that helps.

He had turned around himself. The hand was back in his beard. He was eyeing her, visibly considering the wisdom of saying something. She squashed feelings as far as they would go and demanded, "What?"

He considered. She waited. He looked under his brows. "I've been thinkin' . . . ."

"Yes?"

"About—*why.*"

I don't have answers, she tried not to cry aloud. I don't even have consolation. I don't have anything!

But, answered the look on his face, maybe I do.

"Do ye—" when it came, it was with outright hesitancy. "Ye're a Catholic, ye said?"

"Yes, I—what's that do with . . ."

"Then do ye still—believe?"

I'm lapsed, she wanted to say, not tallying the time since she last attended Mass, the token observance for her peer group. What's that to you?

But *he* must believe. Or at least, be far closer to a living faith. He crossed himself. He must go to Mass every week, it would be taken for granted back then. So what does he . . . She let her face, her expression ask, as temperately as possible, What do you mean?

"Because if y'r Chris said—a fold in reality. Maybe—that's *why.*"

The puzzlement opened like sun breaking through. He wouldn't say, will of God, divine purpose, Providence, he's lived on the goldfields, he knows how they treat piety. And he doesn't know I'm not an outright atheist myself. But he thinks . . . he thinks that, if there's no logical reason, nothing to make sense of this in science—then it might be—

It might be—God.

Her mind ran back through the theological mazes she last traced, with impatience and inattention, at school. If it's God-given, if it's Providence, then he's meant to be here. That's why he's been yanked out of his own place and time. And however it happened, whatever the price in shock and loss and pain, it's not without purpose. There is a cause, though nothing Chris or Laura ever dreamed.

She looked into his face and he ducked his head and opened

his hands a little, an almost tentative movement, with that self-aware irony reduced to a bare tinge.

"I dinna understand it," he said. "But mebbe—I dinna have to. Mebbe—I just have to be here."

Her throat shut. Her eyes shut and she struggled desperately to stem the tears. You can't say that, so simply, so acceptingly. Not about losing your whole world.

But you did. You're going to accept it. So I can't weep and wail and rub the salt in. I have to match you. If there's a reason, I have to start thinking what it is.

Dorian opened her eyes and swallowed what felt like half a brick and said, battling to keep her voice steady, "Solitaire . . . ?"

He blinked. She saw him work to manage his own feelings. Then he accepted her lead.

"The reef . . . the Blackston reefs're like a horseshoe, wi' the big lodes all to the center o' the toe. The Solitaire's deep. The lode's at a thousand feet. It's under the Police Reserve. Just over there." He gestured east. "An' the Peep o' Day runs right under Landers Street. This one y'r Chris found, it's on the surface." The irony came back, the half-amusement, hurtful this time as watching a crippled man try to walk. "It *is*," again he gestured downward, "right here."

For a long minute Dorian simply stared while the words ran in her head like mice on a wheel. Under the Police Reserve. Just over there. The Peep o' Day goes under Landers Street. This one—Chris's mine—is right here.

But Chris's mine isn't deep. You can work it by open-cut.

She sat down with a thump. He watched her, silently. The irony lingered, but she knew it was not aimed at her.

That's why George jumped when Chris said Solitaire Two. He thought I'd know the reef name and figure where it is. That's why Chris kept doing that odd duck and dodge every time he talked about actually working it, that's why he cursed himself for being so wrapped up in the model and the find and the hoopla, that he blithely made plans for the mine. And then, when he came head-on to the reality, couldn't push it through.

It's not just the water pollution or the cyanide. It's the history. Put in an open-cut, and—

And you have to do it in the town.

Dust, pollution, machine noise and vibration, blasting, probably. She knew something about mine activities from Chris. All those heritage buildings coated with oil-smog and who knows how their foundations would cope, there'd be jobs, there'd be life in the town, oh, yes, there'd be life. But at what price?

And how long, demanded her suddenly sharpened brain, will it take to mine out three square miles of low-grade ore in an open-cut?

What'll be left when you do?

Chris thought you could do it. He had a plan, a first-stage plan. But it wasn't the one Pan-Auric wanted. *It's what the bastards are planning to do.*

And Ralston said Kalgoorlie, and George and Reinschildt talked about the Big Pit.

Her legs lifted her off the bed and she nearly ran to the laptop, grabbing the phone jack, plugging in. She felt him pivot and approach, the presence at her shoulder as she connected and logged on and hit the Web browser icon.

The Net opened. She pulled up a Search dialogue and entered "Kalgoorlie. Big Pit."

The photographs looked no different to any mine-site. It was only when she reached the text that her stomach turned to ice.

The Big Pit, said the company's site, had replaced the old Golden Mile. That labyrinth of separate deep mines and leases had simply been bulldozed away. The Big Pit swallowed them along with the land. It was the biggest open-cut in history, its ultimate width would be over three miles.

But the Golden Mile, Dorian realized, turning back to the layman's map, had been beside, not underneath the town.

Her legs gave out again. She sank down on the nearer bed and stared sightlessly at the laptop screen while the pieces spun one final time.

Maybe Chris would have done it piecemeal. Made small open-cuts, worked around the most important heritage spots. Reinschildt—P-A—was just going to obliterate it all.

"Paid compensation," George's voice said in her ear. "Saved what we can." And I can guess how much that would be, you bastard, no wonder Chris was howling about historical destruction. Four, five, six years prosperity, while you shift the population and make a mock-up of buildings you can't move, and then what? The gold's done. The company leaves, and what's left? A bloody great hole, who knows how many tons of cyanide tailings, and a historical resource that could outlast all the mining booms, that pulled tourists worldwide, gone. Blown away, for good.

The screen was swimming through tears or the red fog of rage. She was pounding a fist on her knee, cursing silently, Hellfire and damnation, now I understand, Chris, I know why you made such a fuss. Whatever tipped the scales, this is what was in the balance-pan.

And they erased you, the way they're going to erase Blackston. They just *got rid of you* . . .

Dimly she knew Jimmy—Seamus? had moved to the laptop. Was bending over, reading what she had read. Scrolling—when did he learn to do that?—up and down the paragraphs. And then cursing, under his breath in that unknown language but with a venom that felt like acid on her skin.

Her eyes cleared. He had propped himself on the counter edge.

Was waiting, silently, for her to look up. To remember him.

When she did, he ducked his head in that little characteristic motion and said quietly, "What d'ye mean to do?"

He doesn't expect me to just sit here and rage or fall apart. He expects me to have a plan. To pick up where Chris left off, and do something about this. To put my money where my mouth is and fight for Blackston. To stand up against a mining megacorp and do whatever's necessary. Whatever it takes. To fight, whether or not I win.

"Ye canna," that deep voice said evenly, "let them cart off the whole town. The *Miner*, the Stock Exchange, the banks, the big houses, aye. But the cemetery." It deepened and almost shook. "There's people—people's graves . . ."

People he knew, Dinny and Dick Cox and Patsy—she felt her own bones flinch. But his voice had already quickened with more than urgency.

"*Bridgie's* down there . . ."

And they'll tear up an old cemetery without a second thought. Her head swam. I don't have a choice. If I don't try, at the very least, I'll never be able to look him in the eye again.

She looked up then. His eyes were fixed on her, dark but no longer impenetrable. I came here, and I'm prepared to stay, to lose them all, that stare said, for whatever I'm supposed to do for you. But you have to give something as well.

"Okay," she said. Her mouth was dry. "Okay. I'll figure something. I—" Think, grateful reason cut in. You already have a plan. Or at least, an itinerary.

George. Then Ben Morar. That'll do.

She got off the bed. Her legs felt as weak as after one of the earlier episodes. "I was going out to the mine," she said. "Chris's old mine, to check their copy of his contract. I can do that. Not tomorrow, but Monday, when the office is open."

"Aye."

266

It held a faint question. What will that do?

"We know their plans now. Where it is. And what might happen. But first of all, I have to know their other plans. About the contract. The model. Because if anything can bring them undone, it's proving dirty work about Chris. The mine—they do environmental protests all the time, and the laws are a lot stricter about mining practices," she could recall things Chris had said, "but really, with a big firm like this . . ."

God will be on the side of the big battalions. In business, as in law. As he had assumed, with the police.

"But if I can get up a criminal charge . . ."

The dark stare had sharpened again, with understanding, with purpose. It was in the different note as he said, "Aye."

She felt unreasonably relieved. Strategy approved. A go-ahead, as important as the one from Dani.

He straightened from the counter. Worked his shoulders. Glanced round with an expression that matched her feelings: We just jumped off the Sydney Post Office Tower. What'll we do, to fill time till we hit the ground?

Then the look altered. "Ah," he said. "Er—"

He's blushing again. What is it this time, heavens, what have I said or done? She tried to look helpful, enquiring, but not prying, and got an openly anguished glance.

"Is there—where is—" Now he was definitely scarlet. "I need—"

Omigod. "Through here," she said, heading for the bathroom door. God, what sort of plumbing would they have in eighteen eighty-six? Not a flush toilet, that's certain. And indoors?

"No, ah, I, I have to—" He was going to seize up altogether, as he had by the park. "It's okay," she gabbled, "just let me show you: in here!"

"A water closet?" The surprise nearly overrode embarrassment. "In*side? Up*stairs?" Kodak, she realized, had just lost out on the wonders of color photography. "But, how, how—?"

"Running water, ah, town water," let's not even try for reticulated town supplies and mains sewerage, "like the Romans, you know, aqueducts—ah, afterwards, you just push this." She indicated the flush, and fled.

The door closed firmly. Dorian shut down her laptop. From behind the panels came the rush of water and a baritone yelp.

"Ye didna say it'd do *that!*"

"I'm sorry, I didn't think, we're so used to it—"

"Aye, well—fit t'shock the wits fro' a body." He caught her eye. For a perilous instant the austerity held. Then it collapsed in a full-chested guffaw.

"A right new chum," he said, a clearly habitual knuckle shoving the cowlick back. "I'll be lookin' for nuggets on the sidewalk next. So if we're not to slay y'r—'megacorp'—" He pronounced it as if it were some exotic breed of dinosaur, "this minute, would ye have any other plans?"

Automatically she checked her watch, and blinked. It said four-twenty PM. Four-twenty, and I never got lunch at all. No wonder I feel like David, fronting Goliath without the sling. Now her stomach rumbled emphatically. Outrunning embarrassment, she asked, "When did you last eat?"

His mouth corners twitched. Drat it, he did hear. Or did he want to say, eighteen eighty-six? But he answered gravely, "Breakfast. Before early shift." She had a fleeting memory of him shaving by candlelight. Then his face changed and he came off the counter with a hand shoved up his forehead. "De'il take it, I told Patsy I'd get the chops tonight—"

He stopped. The silence yawned between them like a pit.

Then he gave his head a little shake. His mouth twisted, and he said wryly, "An' the yields report not written, or tomorrow's leader set. Dinny'll have my ears."

A world lost, everyday connections torn out by the roots.

People left without warning or explanation, a brother-in-law dinnerless, an editor with the day's paper incomplete. Every new thought jabbed her like broken glass. I did this. Whatever brought him here, this is my fault.

"I'm sorry." She heard her voice falter and his eyes switched quickly back to her face. "I never meant—I never wanted—"

"I know that." He spoke almost before she stopped. His own voice had softened again. "We could both do wi' a pick-me-up. Ye can show me what things ye eat," then he put a hand in his other trouser pocket and his face altered ludicrously. "That is—"

Money, she understood. Now he knows the timespan he's almost certain his money won't be current here.

"Come on, that doesn't matter." Inspiration struck. "You'd do the same if I was . . . you'd do the same for me."

"Aye, but t'is different." A woman, she understood, can expect to pass the bill.

"Not nowadays, it isn't. I can pay for myself. I can pay for you as well, nobody'll turn a hair."

She stopped. The look on his face, the stance, setting, solidifying, recalled that weighted recalcitrance with which he had stopped beside the park.

"I'm obliged to ye." Now it was a formidable courtesy. "But I'll do very well."

"You will not, you haven't eaten since whenever-it-was, your blood sugar has to be round your ankles—Jimmy! Damn it!"

"Blood sugar" had piqued his curiosity. She could read that now. Then the chink sealed over. Silently, he shook his head. And stepped back, offering to usher her out.

"Look—!" Oh, hell, I'm too hungry and tired to think, and the stupid man's going to squat there and starve on his bog-trotter obstinacy. "It isn't charity, it's not—" Then inspiration struck again.

"Okay, I won't pay for you. I'll pay you, and you can pay for yourself."

"Eh?"

"You read that map for me. You gave me the thing I absolutely needed most. I'll pay for that. No. Wait, I'll do better. I'll hire you."

He made a little splutter, but the stonewall had not reformed. He was eyeing her with the kind of fascination he might give an exotic snake. "Ye'll *hire* me? What wi'?"

"With money, of course! What, do you think . . . ?" Then history overtook her. *Naturally he thinks you're penniless, no decent woman would have money in his day, she'd rely on her husband, her father, her family.* She found her wallet and peeled it open. "See that? That's a hundred-dollar note. And that's just subsistence cash. I can draw more at the bank, any time."

He was all but goggle-eyed. And that lower lip had softened again. . . . She yanked her eyes back up. She expected him to say, *Dollars? What are you talking about?* What he did say, reviving that scandalized park-side stare, was, "What are ye doin', wi' money like that?"

"It's my . . ." *Travel expenses, hourly charges, Lord, how do I explain that?*

"Y'r allowance? Y'r—father—lets ye walk around wi'—"

"No, it is *not* my allowance!" Bristles rose that Dorian had never known she possessed. "That's my own money. My wages, from the firm!"

"What firm? Are ye," the look was growing more startled by the moment, "d'ye keep the register, in a shop?"

"No, I do not! It's a law firm. My law firm! Lewis and Cotton. I'm a junior partner. A lawyer!"

"A what?" It pulled him up short. Then the stare broke in another open laugh. "Ah, ye never! Pull t'other one, that plays 'Rocky Road to Dublin,' girl!"

Now I know, Dorian raged, why sexism made my mother see red. She clawed for a fitting insult. Remembered her wallet, snatched out her business card.

"Since I don't carry my law degree," she managed to sound icy, "you'll have to make do with this."

He took it with the grin still fading, and the mere style set him back. She pictured the firm logo, the font and layout that said, Professional design. Her name at the center, with L.L.B. behind it. Did they call it that then?

From taken aback he had gone to startled. Perhaps involuntarily impressed. Then his eyes shifted and suddenly he dropped the card as if it had turned red-hot.

"What is it? Did you—"

He had already picked it up. By a corner, as if it were contaminated. The laughter had all vanished. Had become a bleakness that pinched his mouth.

"What is it? Jimmy?"

He held it out and when she reached automatically he dropped it like rubbish into her palm. "I'll believe ye. Ye needn't—" Go on trying to convince me, the tone finished. I don't want to know. He took a step back. The gesture added, If you're going, leave now. Without me.

It's for more than pride, now, that I won't eat with you.

"Jimmy—"

Dorian stopped. I don't know what this is. But clearly, it's not something you can argue round. And even with time, it may not be something that I could coax him to explain.

"I don't—I'm sorry—"

Not just because I don't understand. I'm sorry for whatever transformed you like that. For losing the man I thought I'd started to find.

His eyes came back, bleak as winter peat-water. Met hers, and held.

For a stretched instant the bleakness held too. Then the rigidity left his shoulders, and he let his breath out, a quick *Huff!*

"Ah," he said, and shook his head. "T'is no matter, now. It's no' you, after all. It couldna be, not—" Visibly, he stopped himself. And as visibly, braced for a greater gesture. "Will we go, then, an' eat?"

I don't know what that was. What provoked it, what ended it. But I know when to let well alone.

"Okay." She put away her wallet. "No, wait. I said I'd hire you. I meant what I said."

They locked eyes again. Yes, she thought, holding that stare, still somber, still hinting obduracy. It's a double test. Am I good enough to pay you, if I'm good enough to eat with you?

"I could pay you properly. The going rate's, oh, fifty bucks an hour—"

"Fifty!" If he had no idea of a dollar's worth, the numeral was more than enough. "What in God's good name d'ye want me to *do?*"

What do I *want* you to do?

Her brain should have sprung back with rational justifications, Offer me your knowledge. Be my witness, go with me to Ben Morar, supply protection, if it's just the presence of a man. But some wholly renegade impossible impulse was saying over them, I want you to come over here so I can put my hands on you. So I can feel those muscles I saw. So I can find if that lower lip's as soft as it looks.

Dorian tore her eyes away as if the lids had caught on stickytape. "I don't—!" It came out on a thoroughly unmanaged jerk. Then, blessedly, reason returned. "I want what you know and I mightn't even know you do. Like about the Solitaire. I want you to stick around so I can—I need," Dani's words came back to her, "I need a bodyguard!"

"An escort," she tried to translate, recollecting archive photos, gold-consignments, troopers round a coach. "A witness at the mine, it's out in the bush." His face changed with a look that said he had followed Dani's thought-train. "Somebody with me, just in case—"

When the bemusement wore off, she had expected him to withdraw, to disclaim: I'm just a reporter. I don't do that sort of stuff. But though his face had closed again, it was not rejection. He was measuring her, she realized, the way she did a client. With a coolness, a calculation, that said, Not impossible. Within my competence.

"I don't know if that's the rate for, for this sort of thing. We can adjust it later. Look, just . . ." She counted out four fifty-dollar bills. "I brought this for travel expenses, and I figure an escort's exactly that. I need *some*-one!"

She had not intended to sound desperate, but it worked. His face changed. Then his hand came out. But when she tried to give him the money he pushed it aside and offered her, fingers first and palm vertical, the hand itself.

Oh. It's a bargain. A contract. And it mightn't be signed, but he expects it to be sealed.

His hand was calloused but long-fingered, and despite the roughened fingernails and the stains of what must be printer's ink, well shaped. Hard and warm and firm, a genuine, she realized, meaningful handshake. A contract. Accepted, agreed.

"Okay." She stepped back a pace, trying not to feel thoroughly spent. If I'm wiped out, how must he feel? "Now let's eat. We can find a café, a take-away, for now. Have dinner, tonight—"

"*Dinner?* I canna do that!"

"What?"

"I'm no'—I've no'—" His hands made wild descriptions, of his trousers, the marks on his shirt. "Mucky as a slurry shovel-ler? No' lookin' like this!"

Ohhhh, Dorian thought, at the end of her tolerance. He isn't

273

just a Puritan and independent as a porcupine. I had to get a peacock as well.

"Okay." She held both hands up. Four-twenty, no, four-thirty now, will there be anything still open downtown? "We'll get some clothes. Some, whatever-you-want. I can wait," her stomach disagreed indignantly, "to eat."

We'll have to take the car, she thought, at the stair foot. No time to walk if we want to find a store open. But how many culture shocks can he manage, in one day?

She wavered. He looked back from the parking bay where the next stride had already taken him and gave her that bitten-down grin. "D'ye have one o' these 'cars'?"

"Door," Dorian said, opening it. The seat, she could tell, though odd, explained itself. "Seatbelt." She pulled it forward, demonstrating elasticity. "You fasten it—um." Her own face heated, I am *not* going to do it up from here. "I'll show you in a minute." He was examining the roof, dash, instrument panel, clearly itching to experiment but knowing better than to touch. She slid into the driver's seat, postponing a full-scale tour. "See how it works?" She clicked in her own belt. "Ah, I'm going to start the engine. It'll make a noise."

He laughed at her, out loud. "I'll no' jump out the window like a myall when the train whistle blows."

"Okay, then." I keep underestimating his sophistication. As well as his wits. "Ah, the windows go up and down, but better you let me do that." And let's not, she decided, go into air conditioning. Not yet.

She reversed out. He drew in his breath. She drove forward, slowly. He sat, still but stiff. She turned onto the street, and he gave a backward jerk and yelp and clutched the window edge.

"What is it?" She drew hurriedly into the side-lane. His fingers were white on the upholstery, he looked as if he were stuck on top of a ferris wheel.

"I didna think it could *turn* . . ."

"Huh?" Then time's perspective shifted again and she understood. Trains don't turn this short. Horse-drawn vehicles might, but when they do, there's a horse in front. Not an unrestricted view of the approaching street.

"Sorry." She wondered how often she would repeat that. "I'll drive slowly. Hey, if you put me in a wagon I'd probably jump out."

The patronage earned its rightful withering stare. "T'was just surprise," he informed her with dignity. "I'll no' squeak again." He took a firm grip of the window edge and nodded like Queen Victoria. Drive on.

The only thing remotely resembling a men's shop was the local Target, ensconced behind an imposingly decorated brick front still blazoned, Titley's Emporium. A heritage building, she guessed. And from his appreciative but unstressed inspection, built after his day.

Clothes were another matter. Baggy long shorts evoked sheer bewilderment. Jeans were hotly rejected. "I'm no' *tryin'* to look like I'm on shift!" Fingering the polyester equivalent of dress trousers brought distasteful looks. "T'isna moleskin, aye?" Too hungry for long explanations, Dorian hunted up a pair of fawn polyester/linens that looked the appropriate size, and he condescended to vanish into a fitting room.

Short-sleeved shirts were not an option. Striped polo-necks failed at sight. "T'is a bathin' suit!" T-shirts evoked silent scorn. Eventually he ceded wary approval to another white long-sleeved business shirt. She checked sizes and made her own foray among the underclothes, with a sudden poignant recollection of Chris. *Just grab me some briefs down the supermarket, will you?* But I bet only Y-fronts will pass muster here.

And a razor, she thought, toothbrush, deodorant, shaving cream. What else do men use? Shampoo, he won't go within cooee of mine.

When they reached the checkout he took one look at the assistant's pierced eyebrow and gelled hair and carefully closed his eyes. Well, she thought, he'll learn. Emerging on Landers Street she asked tentatively, "Did you want to see more of the town?" And earned a disbelieving stare.

"More?" He rolled the "r" like a snare-drum. Then he surveyed the crowd like a fulminating John Knox. "Men done up like blacks on a handout day? No' a hat or tie in sight? Women me Ma's age stravagin' about gawpin' an' squealin' like McGinty's goats? An' them—" the wave fixed a cluster of teen-age girls already in their night-plumes: eye make-up, vividly streaked hair, plunging necklines, bared navels, thigh-high mini-skirts. "Them—strumpets—painted like the Whore o' Baby-lon—! See more? Ayyye." This time the extended vowel was pure disgust. He screwed up his face and stalked off toward the car.

Chapter XIII

Hamburger, fast-food outlet, driving at sixty km per hour, electric lights: Dorian ran down her list of culture-shocks as she hung up her damp towel. Indoor plumbing, hot and cold water, shower. Shampoo. Hair dryer? How do long beards dry? Ask later. She put on lip gloss, brushed out her hair. Just as well I don't need mascara. She slid into the electric blue crossover top and plain black evening trousers, settled her shoulders, and opened the bathroom door.

He was contemplating his image, dubiously, in the mirror outside. "Are ye sure," he grumbled, "I dinna need a weskit? And t'is right barbaric to dine wi' no tie. Even a stock . . ." He swung round and went quite still. She did not have to see his face.

Dorian picked up her handbag. Found the room key. Turned, and raised her brows.

"I could bear skirts kilted to y'r knees," he said after a moment. "An' you missin' half y'r hair. An'," a severe quarter-glance below her chin, "a—creation—fit for a music hall. But." An audible breath. "I will no' walk the street with—wi' any woman lookin' like *that.*"

"*This* is what women wear nowadays." Dorian found she had her chin up. "You know that, you saw women down town—"

He shuddered all over. "I saw them." He turned his head away. "I'm cross-eyed tryin' not to see. Decent women, aye, women your—women me Ma's age—wi' their *knees* showin'.

277

Their—I canna *look* at a woman, no' like that!"

He isn't just a Puritan. It hit her like a slap. He's never seen a woman out of long skirts in his life. It used to be scandalous to show an ankle. To see the shape of a woman's thighs, even under cloth. . . . It's more than embarrassing. Worse than obscenity. It hurts.

"Look," she said impulsively, "I'm not doing this to rile you. These are the only evening clothes I brought." I bought them, said a glass-shard of memory, to go out with Chris. "But even if I had long skirts . . . you know, it'll still be—different."

Because other women will still dress like this.

There was another of those fraught pauses she was learning to recognize. Then he sighed and waved a hand. "I suppose," he said gloomily, "I needna look at ye, after all." He picked his way round the bed end. Swinging the door open for her, he added, sotto voce, "Pity, that."

Dorian went out, trying not to blush. But on the threshold he paused, with a little wondering shake of the head. "Walk out the *Miner*'s door for y' midday piece an' . . ." The second head-shake added, Find yourself in another universe.

"The damn *Miner*'s door," she said. "It did the same to me."

"What?"

"I went to walk into the *Miner*'s office—*our Miner*'s office—and I ended up outside yours. In the middle of the night. You," for some reason, her ears felt hot, "were just locking up."

"I was what? Ye were there!"

She felt her breath go out in a sudden astonishing laugh. "I came up on my butt against your front gatepost and I was so—I just sat there like a fool while you walked past. And went off home, I suppose, to bed."

"Ye were *there?* In Landers Street? Outside the *Miner?*" Now it was open consternation. "At midnight? On y'r own?"

"It was horrible, yes. I was so scared . . . I went up the street after you and there were these drunks." His face spoke horror too. "I ran and they chased me, I went almost round the block." She could feel her hair rise and suddenly his hand was under her elbow, he was close beside her, every inch shouting concern. Protectiveness.

"Save us, girl, what happened? How long were ye there?"

"I don't know, it felt like hours. I lost them, then I went back to Landers Street. It was all I could think of. The *Miner*'s office. If I waited there, I thought, I might find you."

As, today, you found me. The inference, her expectation of recognition and hope of rescue hung in the air and his fingers shifted a little against her arm. I'd have known, the touch said. I'd have helped. As you helped me.

"But when I went on the veranda, it changed back."

He drew a long audible breath. Then the silence fell like a plummet into a pause they could both fill.

It changed for you, and you went home. As it might change again. If we went to the *Miner*, if I walked up those steps. Would I walk back into my own time? Would I be home again, and safe?

His hand shifted abruptly, and he stepped away a little. "Off wi' us, then," he said. And the thread of resolve under the casualness glossed firmly: If there is an out, I won't knowingly take it. Whatever I'm here for, if it's my choice, I'll stay.

Beyond hotel bistros and Chinese or Thai takeaways, Blackston offered few restaurants. Dorian chose the White Horse hotel purely because Ralston had mentioned it, and was relieved to find it a modern building, if on an upper corner of Landers Street. By the time they passed a side-alley of poker machines and a main bar raucous with TV sport and reeking of stale beer and cigarette smoke, his face was making her wish they had stayed at the motel. But then they rounded the bar end, and he stopped in his tracks. "What on the—what is *that?*"

"Television." Dorian shuffled concepts desperately. "Colored pictures, moving pictures . . . oh, Lord, I don't know when they started—"

"Movin' pictures? Some feller in California bet he could photograph a gallopin' horse an' sometimes it'd no' touch the ground—but this!"

"I don't know the rest, we need the Net for the history. But they take pictures of things moving now, minutes of it—" she waved at the mass of heaving jerseys and white shorts on-screen—"the whole length of a football game."

"*Football,*" he said, with ineffable disdain. "Could they no' 'photograph' a good hurlin' match?" Then he looked at her and let out his ironic snort. "Ye've no idea what that is, an' you a child o' Kerrymen." She had no time to ask what he meant. He had already sniffed and wrinkled up his nose. "Ye'll no' eat in here?"

"No, there's a bistro, a restaurant, somewhere."

The air-conditioning met with favor—"now, there's a *use* for electricity"—but the utilitarian décor, lack of vista, and menu came in well below par. "Is there no' a mirror in the place? Let alone a chandelier? An',," he investigated the drinks menu with his mouth corners going down, "no whuskey, at all?"

"That'll be," Dorian promised, rising, "at the bar."

There was a minor insurrection over her going too, and a larger one when the only Irish whisky turned out to be Jameson's. "Blackston! An' no' a Bushmill to be seen!" But they sat down at last, he took a long swallow of whisky, a shorter one of water, and leant back, with thanksgiving in his sigh.

And no wonder. For him it must have been the ultimate day from hell. Dorian took a good mouthful of Shiraz herself. Then she remembered the No Smoking sign. When did they invent cigarettes? "Ah—they don't smoke in restaurants nowadays. You might have liked a pipe . . . ?"

"I dinna care for tobacco. Couldna afford it, when I came, an' chose not to, afterward." His eyes dropped to the plastic rose on the table. In the dim lighting, his lashes looked half an inch long. "M'fiddle, now." The pensive look became something approaching loss. "That's what I *would* like. Nothin' like a half-hour wi' the fiddle when ye're troubled in mind."

"You play the violin?" She tried not to sound unflatteringly surprised.

"I play the fiddle. No' that fancy concert-stuff. Tunes an' such. Dance music. Jigs. Reels." He eyed her speculatively. "D'ye dance at all?" The look changed. "But I suppose all that's gone too?"

"I don't think—no, I don't think we dance like that." She tried not to picture his reaction to a strobe machine and an earful of disco beat. "Though we do still waltz." The shard of memory stabbed again: waltzing with Chris. Or trampling, anyhow. He had been a masterful leader, if sometimes unsure which foot he was doing it with.

"An' ye used to waltz wi' him." He said it so softly she thought she had misheard. But there was no mistaking the look in his eyes. Then it vanished. With a shove he sat up straight. "Ah, we're a pair o' wet weekends an' no mistake. Show me here, what is there fit to eat?"

Though disappointed at the absence of "a good roast wi' baked taties and pumpkin. T'is one thing they can grow here," he was willing to try pasta. "Italians, ye get 'em on the field, but they dinna cook." The mention of ice cream brought a distinctly interested gleam. And his first taste of double chocolate-chip created a glazed but euphoric pause. Before the mouthful went down and he breathed, "They do *that* with electric coolin'? I'll forgive 'em the chandeliers."

I wonder, Dorian thought, idling over her coffee, if, whatever upset you on my business card, you've forgiven me?

But if I don't know, Why me, I didn't get to the bottom of, Why you? What are you, what did you do in Blackston, that God, the reality fold, whatever it is, picked on you?

"You work for the *Miner*," she said. "You're a, a compositor?"

"An' reporter, aye."

"That doesn't seem to—explain this. What else do you do?"

He swallowed the last mouthful. When his eyes rose he looked so transparently guileless that she thought with complete certainty, This is it. This time, he's going to lie.

"How do I know?" As she had, he turned his hands out. "Could be, t'is already happened. T'is what I know?"

"The mine site, yes." Words came back. "But you said, Land League. And, the Society. What Society?"

"T'is just a wee workin' man's group." He waved airily. "Nothin' unusual."

The image of that trio in his house shot past her, the tension, the older man's snatch for his hip. "When I walked into your house that day? That was usual?"

"Ah." It was definitely the stonewall now. Bland, but palpable. "Patsy, ye see, Patsy'd never seen ye before. Fair gobsmacked, he was." He manifestly recognized a diversion. "I'm sorry about y'r wee pencils. We dunked 'em in the inkpot, but they still wouldna write." The penitence was over-candid, too. "But Patsy, he wouldna believe in ye." The irony almost revived. "Until he handled those."

And what did he say about me? She declined the bait. "With the black hair, was that Patsy? Okay. And the other one?"

"Michael." A longer pause. "A friend o' mine. I lend him books."

"Ayyye," she said, drawing it out as he did, but with a derisive lift, and startled him to a snippet of laugh. "Look, I'm not the police. And it's not . . ." Not important. Who they are, what they are or were's no matter. In this world, they're long since dead.

He must have followed all too closely. The laughter vanished. He stared before him with a harsh, a more than harsh set to his mouth.

She opened her own mouth and shut it again. I'm beginning to learn, she realized, that he does his own thinking. If you want to persuade him—if you *can* persuade him—the only way is to wait.

With one of those heavy but decisive movements he set aside his plate. "Only fair," he said. "Turnabout, aye." His mouth tightened. "An' it's no' like to matter—now."

Once again Dorian stopped her hand's reach. Shut her mouth. His look turned inward, almost physically moving toward the past. The yet remoter world of his own past.

"In Dungannon," he said, and the silence snapped like ice, "me Pa worked for the old *Catholic Banner.* As compositor. Had 'em put me on, as a boy. When he died in seventy-seven, I'd worked m'own way up. Done three years' indenture, wi' another to run."

He was still looking into that lost, distant world.

"So I could read, d'ye see? Before I was twelve. I read the *Banner* in press. I read the Church pamphlets an' the Wanted posters in the square. When I was fourteen—me Ma'd saved up. She bought me a subscription to the library."

Another prolonged, marshalling pause.

"So I read Grattan, an' O'Connell, an' Parnell, an' stuffed m'self to the ears wi' the rights o' Ireland, an' the wrongs o' tenanting, an' I was red-hot for Home Rule. Never a Fenian, mind ye. I'm no' one for blowin' people up. But I joined the Land League, aye. Went to meetings, helped wi' the boycotts.

Fought evictions, an' spent nights in the hedgerow runnin' from the troops. Not runnin', sometimes." His mouth set hard and he shifted a shoulder suddenly. "That ended, when Pa died."

In a moment Dorian said, "You lost the job?"

"A third-year prentice, tryin' to feed a widow an' five girls? I couldna *keep* the job. I . . ." He stopped, and started again. "Ma's folk're out by Rock, I told you. They took us in. An' then, harvest o' seventy-eight, the taties blighted again."

In a moment he turned his head, that dark, impenetrable, now very near hostile stare.

"Ye'll no' have seen a tatie blight? Like the Great Famine, the forty-five, when half west Erin died? No' so bad in Ulster, we'd the flax an' wheat. An' the McGuigans've thirty acres or so, aye. But they grew taties, not grain."

Great Famine, potato blight, Dorian scrabbled in her meager store of history, wasn't it so bad because that was all the small holdings grew, and all they ate?

She made a small, muted, "Oh." He nodded without looking up.

"An' they had Ma's brother an' his boys, an' . . . I never was much wi' a tatie fork." The mouth corner tweaked. "No' for taties, anyways. So I saw old McKenna at the *Banner,* an' said, Lend me ten pound on interest, I'll emigrate. Australia, there's gold out there."

She remembered Anne and Laura speculating at the Sandbar. We guessed right about the panning dish, if not why.

And I know now, when I first saw him, what he was worried about.

He curled his right hand into a fist, and slowly let it go. "Aye," he said, with a hundredweight of retrospective irony. "Three months at sea an' twelve on the wallaby, an' I hadna made a dust-pile, let be raised a nugget. So I called fossickin' a day."

"And joined the *Miner,*" she supplemented.

"An' joined the *Miner.*" Again his mouth curled. "But there's no Land League, out here."

So you did something else, she knew with pure certainty, you were an activist there and you'd be one here, you joined whatever Society it was, the "wee workin' man's group." In the eighteen-eighties, what would that be? Oh.

"You're a Trade Unionist," she said.

He gave a little jump. Then he carefully let out his breath. "Now, how did ye know *that?*"

"At school. We had a, a Marxist social studies teacher. Well, she voted Labor. I mean, she supported the working class. She taught us Union history. The Tree of Knowledge at Barcaldine, where the Union leaders used to spruik. The big Queensland shearers' strike. The AWU. Australian Workers' Union. The miners' strikes, out at Broken Hill." His eyes were almost round again. "Yes, there were—there will be—strikes out there."

"Strikes," he breathed, as if she had said Eldorado does exist. His eyes said, It happened. Whatever I campaigned for, it came to fruit.

And I'm going to screw up history, she thought in panic, what happens if—when?—he does go back, and it's his own time and he knows what's going to happen? Oh, heavens above. "What did *you* do?" she struck off hastily.

For a long, long minute she could see weights going into the balance, for silence, for truth. Then he said, "On the *Miner*, I started readin' again. Owen, the English workin' feller. O' course, the man Marx. Michael—I'd take books to him. To them. The others on the shift. Down at East Liontown he was, when we met. Then at Blackston. Workin'," for the first time his eyes shifted away from her, "on the Solitaire shaft."

Books. But not just books. Down to the Society, with leaflets. Activists' publications, and . . .

"You printed stuff for them," she said. "At the *Miner.* Wrote

285

things for them." That sound-byte at Baringal Beach recurred. "And Dinny—Dinny wouldn't stand for it."

He was staring at her, very near white-eyed. "How," he breathed, "d'ye know *that?*"

"I saw you," she admitted. "Dinny was in his office, yelling at you. 'Y'll not do it here!' "

She had caught the accent again. He flinched as from the reality. Froze for another long, shifting pause.

Then he let his shoulders down and said, "Dinny's agin Landlords an' Chinamen an' Blacks an' Orangemen, an' he trains us to write for the workin' man. Ye'd think . . . but Unions, no.

"We've had a slather o' Donnybrooks about it," he added, reflectively. " 'I'll keep ye on, y' long-nosed Ulsterman,' he'd yell at me, 'but this red-rag blether I'll not have!' "

"And that was—is—where it stood—stands now? You haven't done anything more?"

He made a gesture she had not seen before, filing a forefinger up and down the side of his nose. "Well," he said. "Well . . ."

You did something else, she extrapolated. Something you think's even morally shadier.

"I saw you," she said. "Down the pub, with some other people. They were talking about a mine . . . people sacked. A shaft not safe."

His hand jumped again. He said, trying for the old composed irony, "Ye've seen a sight more than I know." But for a moment he looked near open shock. Then the expression changed.

"Aye," he said. "They told me that. About the Solitaire. Mishandlin' charges. Careless in the shaft. Jimmy Jones got killed when a pallet o' shoring timbers come undone—fell seven hundred feet. An' people outed for speakin' up. . . . That Wild, Dick Cox gave him the sinkin' contract, he doesna give a curse."

The air went suddenly hollow. His words were echoing as if

286

down a well. She heard herself repeat, "Wild?"

He was holding her eyes, and his own were cold as iron. "Patrick Michael Wild. I reckon," and now it came word by word, deliberately, like pulling the trigger on a gun, "he'd be— have been—y'r great-great-grandfather."

Tit for tat, Dorian's mind said somewhere. This time, he's shaken me.

"But," she heard herself almost whisper, "I'm from South Australia. From Wakefield . . ."

"An' had y'r family nothin' to do with mines?"

"My father's a jeweler! He never—"

"No family stories? No history?"

"Not that I know, I've never heard any." But this was why the business card threw you. Not my degree, or proof of my job. My name. What did he do, that you wouldn't have eaten, let alone worked with me?

As if venturing into an unshored tunnel, Dorian said, "What—was he like?"

"Like?" His own eyes came up. "Ah, he's—he was—an ignorant bull-headed Kerryman, workin' his own contract team round the field an' sure God gave him the Book o' Mines on Sinai. Pray over ye Sundays an' Monday lift the farthing out o' y'r pocket. Or the hat off a lost man's grave."

In Dorian's ears the air seemed to pop. "What?"

"He'd boast of it. The hat some poor devil was wearin' when he died o' the horrors up the road from the Crossin' Pub. They buried him where they found him, an' they'd no name so they hung the hat on a branch, a new cabbage-tree hat. An' Paddy Wild come by a day or two after, an' says he, This one'll no' be feelin' the heat o' the sun, the way I do. So he traded the hat for his own! Wore it a twelve-month after—an' told the story for years!"

It wasn't a tourist pamphlet. It wasn't out of a book or at a

287

museum. I heard it at home. It was his story. *Our* story. That's what *I* have to do with Blackston. That's why me.

He was watching her across the table. It was the same impenetrable, heavy-weighing dark regard. But he did not look vindicated. Even satisfied.

"F'r what it's worth," he said, quietly, "ye dinna look like him."

For what it's worth. What is it worth? When you've just demolished what I thought was my history. When you've just transformed what I know as myself.

"An' ye dinna *act* like him."

That dark, steady stare spelt out the rest: You came to get me in the street. You've hired me. Let me keep my pride. Earn my keep.

T'isna you, after all.

And you made your own decision then, she thought. Not to carry the grudge on. Whatever Paddy Wild did, not to hold it against me.

Thank you, she wanted to say, if her voice had been in control. Not just for absolving me of his sins, or because, having torn away my past, you tried to make some recompense. Thank you for having magnanimity. For achieving forgiveness yourself.

But that doesn't mean Paddy Wild can just be swept away.

"What else," her voice sounded very small, "did—does he do?"

He had picked up her mood change. It came on something like the usual snort.

"Do? Now they've hit the lode he canna do wrong. Dickie Cox's made him manager, he gallivants about town in a cravat an' pony trap, hobbnobbin' with Mills an' Heuffer an' the like, drinkin' an' gamblin' in the Racin' Club, boastin' about the yields. Glory be the Solitaire, an' decent wages an' safety t'hell. . . . Sooner argue wi' a shoat in Limerick mud. Aye, sooner. At least shoats dinna bite."

"Bite?"

His mouth clipped tight and suddenly she saw spilt food, torn papers, broken chairs. His torn shirt, the bruised eye. "You wrote something. And it was more than Dinny then. They came and—your house—"

His eyes shot up and she knew he remembered as well as she. Her hand was out before she knew. She said, "I would have helped."

His face changed. Very softly, he said, "Aye."

I know you would have. I knew then. I knew you understood what it meant to me. I'd already changed how I felt. I would have accepted it.

The table suddenly seemed too narrow, the connection too strong, their eyes were doing more than meet. Dorian caught at the edges of reality: memory's details, a friend's vicarious rage. "That was Wild?"

"That was the polis. A pound in the right pocket." Now the bitterness was uppermost. "Justice. Aye, from the law?"

"The bastard," Dorian heard herself say, deep in her own throat. "If I could get my hands on him . . ."

"Ye'd have his liver an' lights, you an' Bridgie both." It was vivid and quick as lightning over peat-deeps, a flash of memory, a laugh. For a fleeting moment his hand came warm and hard over hers.

"Dinna fret about the house. Ye can fix all that. But . . ." The anger spurted up like steam. "There's men down there riskin' their lives for it, *that's* what I couldna bear. An' no' just Michael. Patsy's workin' there as well." Suddenly he was on his feet, the chair all but toppled, hands clenching into fists. "If they do somethin' crazy 'tween the pair o' them." He spun round and back. "God, an' me not there . . ."

Silenced in public, how can an activist speak? Raised with

terrorist bombings, Dorian could imagine all too well. "Do you think they'll," she could not get above whispering, "will they try—sabotage?"

He gave her another of those white-eyed How-do-you-know stares. Then the frenzy went like a tendon snapping. He slid back in the chair and like George, sank his head in his hands.

"Michael," he said into the tablecloth. "Michael was a Fenian. One o' Davitt's boys. Patsy'd no' be so crazy. But Michael . . ."

A Fenian. *I'm no' one for blowin' people up.* Some kind of extremist. Michael might do it. Attack the mine and destroy innocents with it, massacre the very people he was trying to help.

I have to send him back. Whatever P-A plans or he could do for me, that's his own time and his own place and that has first right.

If that's so, what's he doing here?

Fold in reality, quantum physics, God's providence. Whatever it is, it put him here. And so far—it hasn't taken him back.

I could try it, her brain ratcheted, go down the *Miner,* tonight, this next ten minutes, send him up those steps, let him go.

"Do you want to go down to the *Miner?*" she spoke in a whisper, from suddenly dry lips.

His eyes met hers and held, darker than nightfall, deeper than a mineshaft. Knowledge, and consideration, and then, slowly, the banishment of hope.

As softly, he said, "If I'd been meant to go . . . I reckon, by now, I'd be there."

Waiters passed, the piped music tinkled, some soft-classic pianist. The silence where they sat held like an invisible bubble, an enclave phased out of the world. Then a voice at her shoulder said, "Ah, Dorian? Miss Wild?"

She jerked about. Ralston, hair slicked, in clean short-sleeved shirt and long trousers, was smiling tentatively at her, one hand led captive by a smoothly groomed but barely late-teenage girl.

"I thought it was you." His eyes moved to her companion and registered surprise. "I—ah—sorry . . ." He started to back away and some instinct had her up, ordering, No, don't let him get away yet.

"Sorry, Tom, you're so clean, for a minute I didn't recognize you." In a second he produced a relieved grin. "This is, ah, a friend of mine. Jimmy Keenighan."

He had risen too. Unsmiling, that dark stare very straight and appraising, as he put out his hand.

"Tom Ralston. Tom's a geologist," Dorian babbled ingenuously, "out at the Ben Morar mine."

And if he asks where Jimmy comes from, what do I say?

Ralston never got the chance. "Ben Morar, aye?" It came with enthusiasm. "A gold mine, that'd be? Whereabouts?" Ralston began to explain, urged on by emphatic nods. "A deep mine, ye say? And what'd be y'r yields?"

Ralston's face registered the surprise. "You know about mining? What do you do?"

"I know a wee bit, aye." He sounded infuriatingly bland and he would not look at Dorian. "Always had a fancy to see over one. Would ye be workin' this weekend?"

"Me?" That, Dorian thought, was more than surprise. "I, uh, no, not actually. I, ah—"

They've fired him, she thought. Next poppy down. "But you're still working there, aren't you, Tom?"

"Oh, yes." He had turned hastily. "They've just suspended ops for the, ah, temporarily."

"Is that so?" Jimmy cut her off. A scything glance belied the naivety. *Don't*, it warned her, look shocked. "Ah, well, some other time." Then with heavy-handed gallantry, bowing to the girl none of them had addressed, "We'll no' be keepin' ye, ye'll want to be off, this fine night . . ."

Sheer willpower overrode Ralston's comments, if he had any, swept him and the girl past on a flood of parting generalities. Jimmy shot Dorian a look, and slid back into his seat.

"I can't believe you did that!" She could feel her eyes bugging almost as badly as Ralston's had. "You did a stage Irishman! If you didn't say, Begorra, it was all you missed!"

"Couldna let him start on, Where are ye from, ye strange wee man?" The joviality was quite gone. "An' did ye no' want me to quiz him on the mine, if ye said he was a geologist?"

"Oh! I just wanted to warn you he was at Ben Morar." How did he pick that up, how could he work with me like that, that fast? "But—"

"But, aye." Now he looked wickedly self-satisfied. "But now we know. Somethin' rotten in the state o' Denmark. Shifts've stopped. Lode's tailed off, an' they darena tell the shareholders. Or," the complacency vanished, "somethin' worse."

What could be worse? Dorian began, and stopped. His expression had changed too. He looked expectant, sharply alert. A hunter, ready, waiting to be unleashed.

"What?" she said, and he gave her a surprised stare.

"If they're no' workin', we could go out tomorrow. Have a keek about. Right after Mass."

Right after Mass, aye. I mean, Yes. And where in Blackston, Dorian thought, do I find a Catholic church? As for storming Ben Morar, my God! They emerged on Landers Street and she tried to ignore her stomach's sudden twist. Will I ever walk down here without being afraid?

She identified her car, a familiar if shadowy bulk against the pavement edge. Then the void at her shoulder registered and she swung about.

He had halted a pace or so back, a tall, pale shadow against the pub's receding lights. "I'm thinkin'," he said, when she turned, "I'd best find a bed while I'm up this way. Ye'll be all right," the gesture said, now you're back with your car, "goin' home?"

Dorian leant on the car and let herself shut her eyes. It's been a long day, and I hoped it was over at last.

"Jimmy. It's a race weekend. And the historical thing. There won't be a spare bed in town."

"Ye think, wi' seventy-eight hotels, there'll no' be a foot o' veranda to roll out a swag?"

"Do you *have* a swag?"

Well, no, said the pause. But . . .

"And there aren't." She stopped herself. "There aren't—seventy-eight hotels anymore."

The pause this time was sharp as broken glass.

"There are two beds. It's not—it's quite usual, nowadays, for people to share."

"I couldna." It came out a tone too sharp. He's not just blushing, she thought, he's almost as upset as he was over the skirts. "No, I'll just . . ."

"Look, you've been up I don't know how long and it's late and you must be worn out. You can't run all over town trying to find somewhere to sleep! What if there's nothing? If—"

"I'll be well enough."

It was that quiet obduracy again. Confound him, she thought, as her stomach curled, he can't sleep in the gutter for some stupid scruple. And he said Paddy Wild had a bull head!

"You won't be—you don't know the town! Anything could happen, you could get robbed—mugged—beaten up!"

"T'is still Blackston." He was sounding steadily more polite, and more remote. As if he were drawing away without a muscle having moved. "I'll do well enough."

And can the modern town show him anything the goldfields

didn't do far worse?

"I'll be round to ye after Mass—"

"No!" Sheer panic spurred her wits. "I hired you! You agreed to look after me!"

The abruptness of his halt exclaimed, What?

"We had a contract. We shook on it. You said. You'd come out to Ben Morar. You'd—be here. What if Ralston talks round town, what if someone from the new company's seen me?" She remembered the speed of that reaction to Laura's phone call and felt real fear come into her voice. "What if George, if the manager told them I was asking about the contract, and they come after *me?*"

His hands made a quick involuntary jerk. She guessed the internal tussle that held him rigid. And finally, against the street lights, caught the bend of his head.

"Aye," he said. So quietly it sounded almost hopeless. "I did agree."

This'll be damnably awkward, Dorian thought, wondering why the rest of her should feel something more like elation than relief. What does he wear to bed, and what am I going to wear? I've a nasty feeling a T-shirt just won't cut it for this.

Opening the door, she realized with an adrenaline buzz of shock that she had left her laptop on the counter, plugged in. I'm just lucky it's safe. Then she recalled her e-mail had gone unchecked since morning, and stifled a groan. They know where I am and what I plan. But I've had the cell phone turned off, and what if something's happened down there?

"You, ah, could use the bathroom," she said, flipping on the muted bedside light. "I'll just check my e-mail first."

"*E*-mail? Ye have the post electrified too?"

"Sort of." She nearly had to laugh, despite everything.

It must have eased things for him as well. He came to her

shoulder, watching her boot the laptop, get on the Web, in a silence more like amity than anything since he had got into the car. When she hit her site bookmark, he said, "How d'ye do that?"

"You bookmark . . . oh. This. They call this the mouse. You shift this, the cursor, with it. These are menus: things to do. Put the cursor there, and click. Like using Search."

She demonstrated, typing in her server name. Ran down the results. Opened her mailbox. There was nothing from Anne or Laura, and she sighed in relief. Then with the cursor on Log Out she thought, Do I tell them about this?

About him?

How do I tell them about him?

Her heart sank at thought of the length of explanation, the furore, especially from Laura. Besides, she's bound to be out. It's nine o'clock Saturday night. Anne'll be off-line too. Decisively, she clicked Log Out.

She got off the Web, shut down the laptop, and he drew a long, marveling breath.

"That's better," he said, "than 'ice cream.' " And before she could help it she had looked up in his face and laughed.

"What, then?" It was slightly rueful, mock belligerent, half-unwillingly amused. I know I'm a Johnny Raw. Is it so bad you have to laugh?

"No, it isn't that." She had answered the inference, she realized, not the words. "You just get so much fun out of this stuff. It makes it all seem new."

"It does, aye?" Now he did sound amused. He was very close, she realized suddenly, his height making it seem closer still. Chris never loomed over me. But he's got a good six inches on Chris. The light that drowned in his eyes gave his beard auburn glints. She could smell soap and male flesh-and-blood. And whisky, she realized, a faint peat and alcohol flavor on his breath.

She was suddenly very conscious of the dim light, the closed door, the silent room. Of him.

And he's not going to move back. She knew it suddenly and certainly with that heightened consciousness of a male–female encounter. He's forgotten to be embarrassed. Whisky or something else, he's feeling—easier.

"Dorian." He rolled the "r" a little, as if trying a whisky over his tongue. "How did ye come by a name like that?"

The tone was casual. But the Tyrone accent had softened to that thickened velvet she had heard before.

"Oh . . ." And, she realized, I'm not going to step back myself. "Wilde, Oscar Wilde, he's a famous Irish writer, very witty. He wrote this book called *The Portrait of Dorian Gray*. But he's spelt with an 'e.' My father really wanted a son. So when I came along Mum told him, if he wanted a boy so much, he could have Dorian, but a girl, since he'd made her Wild without an 'e.' "

His lack of sound or movement made her shift her feet. It's a family joke. He probably doesn't think it's funny at all. *I* should move back. He probably thinks I'm shameless and in a minute he'll poker up and scarify *me*.

"I never thought t' know y'r name." His voice had gone lower. Almost, she realized, into soliloquy. "Or who ye were. I thought ye'd just appear, an' disappear . . . an' me no forrarder than O'Driscoll in the story, watchin' the Fair Folk come an' go, wi' him stuck on the side o' the hill. Nothin' more."

The velvet had thickened again. His head was bent, the sidelight from the lamp catching lowered lashes, a mouth corner. The softness, almost in touching range, of that lower lip. Dorian's heart was suddenly up under her breastbone, something had happened to her breath.

"An' then, the day o' the funeral. I looked up, an' there ye were. Like Deirdre o' the Sorrows. After she'd lost Diarmuid . . ."

Something stuck in Dorian's throat.

"An' me thinkin' . . . rememberin' Bridgie. I thought ye'd pull the heart out o' my chest. So sad. So beautiful."

That deep voice lingered over the cadences like a human violin.

"If ye had been Sidhe . . . I think I'd no' have cared, then. I'd ha' paid the Fair Folk's toll, just to touch ye. Have ye real."

The silence whispered like blood in Dorian's ears. All she could think was, Let the spell not break. Not yet.

"An' now . . ."

It was a murmur in his throat. In slow motion she saw his hand come up. Felt the finger slide, lighter than a breath, along the bone of her cheek.

Now it's real.

She had stopped trying not to breathe. Every sense she had was gathered under that sliding, thistle-down touch. Everything else had disappeared into the half-light, the endless pause of tension gathering between them, knotting like the turns of a silken rope.

His finger slipped, so slowly, down beside her mouth. His palm slid out and upward, lingering along her jaw. A feather more pressure and she would feel the rougher skin rasp on hers. But warmth was all she felt, shaping, caressing, tracing another miracle. Then the track of those long fingers, slipping onto her neck. Into her hair.

"It's so soft . . ."

He did whisper, words falling like water into the hush. Then his fingers crooked, gathering strands between them, twitched and half-tightened and he made a sound deep in his throat. "Oh, Jaezus." His other hand came up and they were both buried in her hair, pulling her to him, drawing her face up, "Oh,

Jaeezus," he said as if the floor had given way under him and then he was kissing her.

Quick, clumsy kisses on cheek and mouth and chin, light as a brother's and charged as sparks from amber rubbed on silk, the soft innermost beard hairs barely brushing her skin, her own mouth just tasting the curve of that lower lip.

Dorian's breath went out in a rush that had to fill his mouth and then she stepped past his hands to wrap her arms around and pull him against her as tightly as he would fit.

Not Chris. Her body reported it instantly, piercingly. Not solid and compact and muscled like a footballer. Much taller, narrower, long, spare muscle bands, a leaner, slighter contour to chest and hip. A different shape of mouth on hers. A different way to kiss.

And it doesn't matter a damn, we're here and I never thought he'd be real either, and maybe it's danger and crisis and maybe it's wine or whisky and maybe it's the aftermath, the overload of grief. And maybe it is that encounter after the funeral, when we learnt each other the way ordinary people never do, and we'll never mistake each other again.

He was kissing her in earnest now. She had led to begin but he was a fast learner here as well, his own arms were clamped round her, squeezing her ribs, his hands kneading her back, her shoulder blades, his mouth had closed on hers as delicacy became exploration, not rough, not fierce, but decisive, nearing passionate. As if he were feeling his way, by the warmth of skill and emotion, into the core of music. Not merely the notes, but its life.

And it is music, she thought, feeling the accord build, the dancers' match of flesh and blood she had known with Chris. It is music, it's more than reason's understanding, it's how to forget words and numbers and let the rest of you sing . . .

His gasp did give her a mouthful of breath. Then his head

jerked back. He almost threw himself away from her, stumbling as if he had been hit.

"What . . . !" Dorian staggered a step or two after him before she caught a chair back and held herself up. "What?"

The sound he made could have been split out with an axe. She forgot herself and started forward and he lunged away from her, clear to the further wall.

"Jimmy . . . ?"

"*No!*"

She stopped. I'd sooner he hit me, she thought, in a minute or two. As the tone, as well as the rest, began to hurt.

He had his face in his hands. His fingers had driven into his temples, his wrists shook. Their mutual distress was too much. She took another step, and his head jerked up.

"I didna mean . . ." It was harsh as sand. "I never meant . . ." He buried his face again. It came out very near a groan. "T'was the whiskey. Ah, God forgive me, the whuskey. I should ne'er've touched it. Ne'er done such a thing . . . an' with *you* . . ."

My bhan sidhe, my Deirdre of the Sorrows, who came out of nowhere and near pulled the heart out of my chest. She was moving again before she knew it, her own voice coming out rough. "Jimmy, don't. It wasn't . . ."

It wasn't something loathsome, to deny and repudiate.

It was mutual. Natural. Beautiful.

Something I wanted too.

"Dinna speak to me." He sounded harsher than before. "I'm no' fit for it. I'm no' . . . fit to speak at all. To be in the same . . ." He took his hands down and started moving, his face scraped like stone. And, he did not have to finish, I won't be in the same room with you.

"Don't!" It came out far fiercer than she had thought. "Do you hear me? Stop!"

Fury, hurt, harmony broken, a good dose of frustration atop.

It stopped him in his tracks. He looked over a shoulder, as if expecting to find an ogre.

"I don't care about your bloody morality, or if you think I'm wicked, or you just never kissed a woman before." And outside family affection, I bet you never have. "That wasn't—there was nothing wrong with that!"

His face said without need for words, Not to you. He gave his head a tiny shake and turned away.

"You said you'd stay." Now I do sound like an ogre. Implacable. "You agreed to it."

He turned right round. The look was openly incredulous. You want me to stay, after *that?*

"*We* agreed to it." She let herself glare at him, transmuting the rest into stony rage. "Do you mean to break a bargain—as well?"

"Uh!" It kicked his breath out like a cut from a whip-thong. Then his back set. He gave her glare for glare. You can call me weak, debauched, sinful. You shan't say I broke my word.

This time he let his breath run out, a long, fulminating hiss. Then he stalked past her into the bathroom. There was thunder in the pent, delicately silent closing of the door.

ABOUT THE AUTHOR

Sylvia Kelso lives in North Queensland, Australia, and has been writing or telling stories for as long as she remembers. She has previously published three fantasy novels with Five Star: the well-received *Everran's Bane*, its sequel, *The Moving Water*, which was a finalist for an Australian Aurealis genre fiction award, and *The Red Country*. The follow-up to *The Solitaire Ghost*, *The Time Seam*, will appear in October 2011.

Sylvia Kelso lives in a house with a lot of trees, but no cats or dogs. She makes up for this by playing Celtic music on a penny whistle, and is learning the fiddle as well.